You are trav

A
and

A journey in
boundaries are only that of the imagination.

You are entering The Twilight Zone.

New Line Television unleashes the seminal classic series into a modern incarnation featuring all-new tales from The Twilight Zone. This awesome book features two stories with a sting in the tale that will draw fans into a world of fantasy and suspense like no other!

Into the Light

A teacher sees a glowing light on the faces of people who are about to die, but what can she do when large numbers of staff and pupils begin to emit the glow?

Sunrise

Four students uncover an ancient Aztec relic in the desert, which causes the sun to disappear. Then they discover that only a human sacrifice will bring it back!

More New Line Novels from Black Flame

THE TWILIGHT ZONE#1
MEMPHIS • THE POOL GUY
Jay Russell

THE TWILIGHT ZONE#2
UPGRADE • SENSUOUS CINDY
Pat Cadigan

FREDDY vs JASON
Stephen Hand

THE BUTTERFLY EFFECT
James Swallow

THE TEXAS CHAINSAW MASSACRE
Stephen Hand

The Twilight Zone

INTO THE LIGHT ◆ SUNRISE

Novelization by Paul A Woods

BLACK FLAME

To my beloved children, Victoria, Georgia and Joe.

A Black Flame Publication
www.blackflame.com

First published in 2004 by BL Publishing, Games Workshop Ltd., Willow Road, Nottingham NG7 2WS, UK.

Distributed in the US by Simon & Schuster, 1230 Avenue of the Americas, New York, NY 10020, USA.

10 9 8 7 6 5 4 3 2 1

ISBN 1-84416-151-X

A CIP record for this book is available from the British Library.

Printed in the UK by Bookmarque, Surrey, UK.

INTO THE LIGHT

Based on the Teleplay
by Moira Kirland Dekker

"I have a wonderful secret to tell you. I was climbing a staircase to heaven."

Chris, aged eight, recounting a near-death
experience to Dr Melvin Morse, MD,
on his Into the Light website.

ONE

Stick a pin in a map of the USA. Avoid the extremes of the East or West coasts, and the lowest reaches of the Southern States. Move inward from the rural towns or wide-open spaces. Focus not on the major urban conurbations, but on any one of the numerous small cities or large towns that dot the landscape from sea to shining sea.

Welcome to modern Middle America.

Welcome to one of thousands of places where the next generation of young Americans nurture or waste their dreams.

Welcome to Sunnyvale High School.

Meet Rachel Stark. A young woman whose dream died too soon. But today, Rachel's going to learn that some dreams can be resurrected. For a price...

Welcome to the Twilight Zone.

To look at them all, you would have thought she inhabited a hive of enthusiasm and industriousness. All the fashions of the day, from hoodie-wearing homeboy to Goth girls with their impossibly slicked-down witch-style hairstyles, were represented in her class. Just three short years ago, she'd have regarded their calm and attentive demeanor as a small victory. She scanned the rows of students bent over their desks, scribbling into their blue workbooks. Once it would have seemed like conscientiousness. Today, even in their silence, she sensed indifference—if not outright contempt.

Oh, get a grip, girl. If you can't deal with 'em when they're behaving, whatever made you think you were cut out for this line of work in the first place?

Rachel Stark, twenty-six years old, was a young woman whose dream had died too soon. But today, Rachel was going to learn that some dreams can be resurrected. For a price.

As she raised her eyes from the essay papers she was marking, she saw a familiar figure amble out of the classroom herd toward her own desk. Rachel could never claim to be in high spirits these days, but somehow he managed to make her heart sink a little lower.

Ben Jordan slapped his essay paper down in front of her. In his baggy pants and shapeless Eminem T-shirt, he looked like every PTA board's nightmare. In truth, she knew he wasn't a bad kid. When she'd taken over his English lit class last semester, there had been an inkling of curiosity in him, a willingness to know more that may have denoted intelligence. But that was then.

Now, the pages of his writing paper were pure white and unspoiled. Hell, he'd been so considerate not to deface the watermark that he hadn't even bothered to write his name.

What is it about this place? Is it only me? Or is there something that sucks the enthusiasm out of everyone like some big black hole in space?

She felt the other pair of gloating eyes and the smirking grin before she saw them. Rachel barely had to glance to know that Brian Kelly, the pigskin-shouldered jock voted "most likely to" by every girl in class, was lapping it all up. It always amazed her that Brian should be the center of gravity around which the class rotated—almost literally.

He sat at the middle of a row of individual desks, the demarcation line for a kind of classroom apartheid. To Brian's left sat his trusted lieutenants: meat-faced boys with short haircuts and big physiques. Sportsmen in initialed baseball jackets, marking them down as the fratboys they were so very obviously going to be once they reached college. These were the sons of the professional white middle classes, instilled with the arrogance of those who believe they would automatically succeed in life unless they made a very determined effort not to.

In some of the seats to their furthest left, close to the classroom door, sat their designated girlfriends: the cheerleaders and sometime prom queens, the feline in-crowd whose self-assurance was reinforced by layers of lip gloss and an aura of hairspray. The girls were every bit as vicious as their male counterparts, but with an additional sharpness of tongue—physical violence being something they resorted to only occasionally.

One row back behind Brian, sitting diagonally to his left, was Stacy Johnson, his on-off girlfriend. They sat in close proximity, as if holding court in the class. Brian and Stacy were known to have verbally violent bust-ups and to let fly at each other with dull but obscene invective. The reason for the tension between them, so it seemed, was that Brian was a star player who had never made it to captaincy of the Sunnyvale High football team. Despite protests by his father, a prominent and very vocal member of the board of governors, sometimes Brian's lack of discipline and foul temper on the field could not be excused. His rival for Stacy's affections was, therefore, the team's regular captain—a bulky blond boy who was one of Brian's inner circle, and therefore had to be tolerated.

Despite their on-off relationship, the purpose of Brian and Stacy's close alliance seemed to be to hold dominion. To sound out the unfashionable and the nonconformist. To conduct a purge of anyone who fell short of their standard of dress, disposable income, physical attractiveness and acquisition of status symbols. To wither confidence with ridicule. Or, in the boys' case, to inflict violence after class, where crude verbal insults had failed.

Like some classroom Checkpoint Charlie, Brian sat at dead center, front row, the line that separated the cool (for which read brash, loud and narrowly conformist), from the uncool. To his right were the despised geeks. All nerds and freaks and bedwetters, in his eyes. In short, anyone who failed to make the grade under Brian and Stacy's form of high school fascism.

In Rachel's eyes, it was the class outcasts, those furthest from the jock-and-bimbo inner circle, who were the regular kids. Despite the way the class oafs tried to stigmatize them, they were as mixed a bunch as you could hope to find: bespectacled introverts; skaters and punks; Gothic kids; black kids with braided hair; kids who were absolutely run-of-the-mill normal, but not part of the hallowed inner circle. Many of these kids had been among Rachel's best students, when she started work at Sunnyvale three semesters ago. Since then, many of them had been bullied out of showing any enthusiasm for her subject—or, as she sometimes suspected in her darker moments, had lost respect for Rachel's failing powers as a teacher.

And then there was Ben Jordan. Ben, who sat to Brian's immediate right. Ben, who himself signified the uncoolness factor that Sunnyvale's inner circle despised. Ben, who apparently chose to sit next to the boy who treated him with derision and contempt—either because he refused to back down to him, or else because, in his low self-esteem, he still needed to cling to a deluded belief that he might be accepted one day.

"You've still got a few minutes." She indicated the white-faced plastic clock up on the wall. "Do you want to look it over one more time?" The answer was predetermined. "I didn't study."

She searched Ben's eyes for a moment, but they were too inscrutable, or too blank, to let her know just what his problem was. Mirroring the contempt she felt she was being shown, she distractedly flicked through the book's blank pages. She didn't bother to reprimand Brian for his gloating, grinning-idiot countenance. It was another point scored by popular philistinism. Congratulations, Ben, she choked back her rancor. You've joined the losers' club.

"This test counts for a third of your final grade. I'll have to give you an 'F.'" Like he really cared. Like he saw any point in trying to be teacher's pet when life was such a crock of shit. Ben's studied, sullen indifference gave Ms Stark the message. He may have completed a couple of essays for her when he first joined her class, but he knew now it was all bullshit. One-legged whaling captains and Scottish kings—all bullshit. Getting ragged for kissing up to the only teacher at his grade level who wasn't a fucking dog—bullshit. Mockery from the jocks and the girls in his class—bullshit. Life at school and life at home. Just bullshit.

"It's okay." His voice was light and emotionless. To the rest of the class, he was like some numbed-out stoner who sparked up on the way to class and never left his own little mental cocoon. Except that Ben didn't do drugs.

To Rachel, he was a formerly promising kid who, for reasons she could never fathom, now seemed as burned out as she felt. It was unprofessional, but she hated him just a little for it. And hated herself.

"No. It's not okay." She sighed heavily, blowing off a little steam. Her blue eyes met the brooding dark orbs beneath his shaggy outgrown fringe. It was the type of pensive moment that his classmates had ripped the piss out of Ben for. Treated like a hopeless geek by all the girls in his grade, Ben had the hots for Ms Tight-Ass Stark—at least that's what they'd all said. But if he didn't blush bright red in her presence, or let them break his balls about it, no one could touch him. If he let nothing get to him, ever, then he'd be just fine.

"If you take an extra essay question home for extra credit, I might be able to raise your grade to passing." Damn it, she was *not* going to let him mess up and walk away from his own potential. When he'd first come into her class, she was already feeling a little bruised by experience. She'd had some fine students over the last several semesters, but they were always outnumbered by the bad and the indifferent. Any small gleaming of sensitivity and intelligence had been like a beacon to her, especially over this past year.

"Ben, I really think you should reconsider..." When she heard her own voice, it was always too apologetic, lacking all the fervor she'd first felt when she entered teaching. Besides which, Ben had already turned around and headed to the door. Walking with that clumsy bouncing gait he mistook for a swagger, that the other kids were always ready to mock.

You're such a lightweight, Rachel, she chided herself.

The recess bell chattered out its shrill alarm. From a still-life study, the class were suddenly a bustling picture of life. Pens were downed instantly, as if dotting one "i" or crossing one further "t" was now an unthinkable act. Desks scraped in unison, and their papers hit her desk with the heavy-handedness of a print worker throwing down a batch of *The New York Times*. White, black, sports jock, prom queen, metal dude or dreadlocks, all of them just wanted out. Away from her English class. Back to their real lives.

"Three pages due by Friday, people," she called after them as they vanished, a practiced familiarity hiding her crashing confidence. "Answer the immortal question: 'If they had lived, would Romeo and Juliet have stayed together, or were they Shakspeare's version of Justin and Britney?'" She winced, regretting it almost as quickly as she'd said it. If they ain't interested, she mocked herself wistfully, then dumbing down don't cut no ice.

She was alone in the class now. To some of the more easily intimidated young teachers, it would have been a relief, but Rachel's frustration was of a different kind. Wise-ass comments and the odd dirty joke she could take. Her eyes fell upon the opening lines of the first essay she opened at random: Romeo and Juliet killed themselves cus they were ass hats. Great. If she had to fail Ben Jordan for neglecting to mark his pages with ink, maybe she should consider passing this work of analytical genius with a B+.

She hadn't studied the nuances of the language, from Shakespeare to Donna Tartt, Milton to Brett Easton Ellis, just to let herself be fazed by a few clumsy barbs. But it was the kids' indifference to their own language that she found hard to take—that cold, brutish, unthinking indifference. Indifference, she'd decided, was the real killer.

* * *

Moving down the hallway, students knocked Rachel's briefcase from side to side as if she herself were invisible. It was a fast-flowing stream, so many young lives with so many destinations to get to, whether urgent or frivolous in the eyes of the adult world. No time to stop and stare, she reflected, leave alone to read and think.

"Smile. Your day's officially over." The tanned hand on her shoulder gave the command its gentle authority. Jared gave her a light but powerful squeeze, their familiarity taken for granted by the hurrying students.

"I'm not smiling till next week," she deadpanned, tersely. "Until my days of being a high school teacher are officially over."

"Aww," he teased. "What did the li'l rat bastards do this time?" He was yanking her chain, but she forgave him. Normally, when Jared did this, it offered her a little perspective. It was the one thing that could pull her back out of her depression and into the light. Today though, it just wasn't working.

"They don't do anything," she rounded on him. Today wasn't a day when they could just brush her concerns to one side and head out to burn off stress at the gym together, or grab a cheap bite to eat. "They don't work. They don't listen. They don't fucking care."

Wheww. He could see it was the wrong tactic. The end-of-day exodus flowed rapidly out of the hallway, out into the yard, the car park and beyond. Locker doors clattered open and crashed shut again. Whereas the relationship between Mr Goldman, the popular phys-ed teacher, and Ms Stark, the cranky Eng lit neurotic, was no longer a source of novelty, a few kids still turned their heads and smiled, amused to hear her blow her stack.

It was ever thus. When she'd first got involved with Jared, he was her knight in shining gym shoes. The honeymoon period with Sunnyvale was still a recent memory—but it was very definitely over. She remembered setting the class a homework essay, based on their own choice of poem from *The American Reader of Prose and Poetry*. Maybe, she conceded now, it was a little too over-ambitious at that time. But she'd fed them a little Edgar Allan Poe and Nathaniel Hawthorne, and the dear sweet things hadn't blanched all that much. It even seemed at one point that some of the class were interested in their American literary heritage. If they could take in a little Poe by osmosis, why not hit them with a little modernism and see how they reacted to Walt Whitman and Allen Ginsberg?

It was, it seemed, a bridge too far. It was also the start of Rachel's great revelation: her realization that novelty is all that counts for the American teenager. If some wacko dead poet could be amusing over the space of a couple of lessons, then a serious consideration of his art, and that of his contemporaries, was a matter of crushing boredom in the long run. And the same standard, it seemed, applied to people. Tolerated, even seemingly liked and accepted by some students at first, she'd soon found herself a target of the anti-academic spleen.

When the poetry essays were handed in, it was the first time she'd been hit by the full measure of their indifference. At first, it was a faint novelty in itself to read the contemptuous comments that had been scrawled across the page instead of homework: "Whitman is shit, man." "Ginsberg's Howl? Who cares howl?" The dead poets society this was not. Those two little crits had earned themselves a spell in detention.

But it was after the fourth and fifth, or the tenth and eleventh, abandoned essays that it hit Rachel that she was the target of a backlash. It was something she was unprepared for. Something that earned her little support. Her complaint to Principal Carr had acquainted her with his standard unsympathetic line: if Ms Stark really felt that the class weren't "getting" modern American poetry, then stop wasting their time with it. Take them on the usual disinterested trawl through Shakespeare's *Sonnets*. Anything–just don't confuse your own enthusiasm with something that really matters. As long as the students reach the approved level of literacy to graduate, leave all the artsy-fartsy stuff to the bearded professors. In short, if the kids didn't respond to it, then don't keep feeding it to them.

It had sent her back to the class in a rage. "Okay," she had quietly seethed. "All those who found the set homework subject didn't meet with their approval can sit detention with me tonight. I'd like an essay on 'The Failure of the Modernist Ethic in American Poetry.'" The sullen, disgusted faces told her she'd called their bluff. Brian Kelly and all his friends, Stacy Johnson and her little *Heathers*-style inner circle, could all stay behind. Oh, and then there was Ben Jordan. The formerly enthusiastic Ben, who had disappointed her for the first of many times.

She thought she'd called all their bluffs, and it felt good. Until it came time to sit the detention class after school, and she found the door swinging in her face as the last straggling absentee ran off laughing. She was enraged to find none of them had stayed to write their essays.

Entering the classroom, however, she found one of her miscreant students had written their own poetic dedication in block capitals on the board: "MS RACHEL STARK AINT GOT NO TITS / WHO NEEDS A BRA WHEN IT DON'T FIT? / SHE DON'T EVEN HAVE A FIGGER [sic] / SHE MIGHT HAVE IF HER TITS WERE BIGGER." It was the first time that her students had reduced her to tears.

"Hey, c'mon." Jared's voice brought her back to the here and now. It was time for her to take a reality check. "They're teenagers, remember what that was like? Always knowing better than poor, elderly farts like us in our late twenties? Always thinking you have all the time in the world?"

"That's exactly what I'm saying. It's *their* futures at stake, not mine. Why don't they get that? Why can't they see that someone older may just have a handle on what's important?"

His smooth hands, with weight-machine calluses on the fingers, held her gently at the shoulders. Jared stroked her to the rhythm of her breathing, slowing down as she relaxed and exhaled. This was why she'd grown to need him, as much as want him, when she worked at Sunnyvale. As the school hall emptied out, she could feel less self-conscious about showing some affection back.

Rachel's fair hair and light complexion only served to highlight the fragility she felt lately. Jared's darkness was only a slight tinge to his skin and hair color, a remnant of his Jewish ancestry. But he himself was laidback and kind of weightless, as if he'd drifted effortlessly into his chosen vocation and would never worry his head about anything from that day forth. Sometimes she found this implacable calm, his imperturbable positive outlook, plain maddening. And some days, like today, she needed him to be the way he was.

Ever since they'd first become involved with each other, Jared had noted her tendency toward nervous exhaustion. Noted, sympathized and accepted it. At first, it was something that he could make tender little jokes about, "Hey Teach," he'd rib her. "Try to chill if not every kid in grade makes it to be the new James Joyce." He'd found it endearing and commendable that she should be consumed with her vocation, by the need to communicate with the deafest ears and the most closed-off minds. At first, that was.

Then it hurt to see someone he cared about running herself into the ground. Attempting the impossible. Berating herself for every last shred of incomprehension and indifference in "her kids." Losing sleep if she felt she'd had to mark down their grades too harshly. Tormenting herself if she felt she'd been too lenient, had let the class slide into mediocrity merely because it was easier to accept their disinterest.

It was then that he'd first coined the term "little rat bastards"—almost as a term of endearment. Jared refused to accept Sunnyvale High-Schoolers were a whole lot different to most other Middle-American kids. Sure, some of them—like Brian, who was a good athlete and not half as tough as he put on—needed to have their wings clipped from time to time. Jared knew he'd never be as widely read as Rachel, and it didn't bother him—but he could, at least, draw one literary analogy: "Just keep the tribal leaders in check and the rest of the kids will follow suit. Let the Brian Kellys know who's in charge, and we won't have *The Lord of the Flies*."

He'd come to realize she couldn't do that. As with all the elements of celebrity-infatuated, materialistic bling-bling MTV culture that every teacher came up against, it was a situation not of her making. All the same, she took every last rejection of literary, intellectual or aesthetic values as a personal slight. Kelly and his buddies were not a big problem to begin with. It was only as they came to realize that Rachel took their complacency all too personally that it became a personal issue for them. Rachel had picked herself a battle that she couldn't possibly win.

Jared tried to protect her from herself. To prevent her conscientiousness from turning into a neurosis. "So English literature's just so much dead airtime between recess and the next sports match?" she'd rounded on him. No, that wasn't what he'd meant at all. Rachel's defensiveness told him she knew as much. But she had a point that he just couldn't answer: "What kind of teacher would I be if I looked on my track record as a success? With every class I've taught, the average grades have started spiraling down. There's hardly a single student who pays full attention in class or completes their homework to any kind of acceptable standard anymore. Should I be proud of that?"

But still, it hurt to see her bleed over it so much. In recent weeks, now that her situation had become a full-fledged vocational crisis, Rachel had fixated on the failure of this Jordan kid she used to think was so promising. Poor Rache would never learn—for some people, failure was just a part of their culture. The Jordan boy had a functional brain, two arms, two legs and an asshole just like everybody else. If he'd decided for himself that it didn't matter if he failed, then who was Rachel to take it so personally?

"I know, I know. I'm taking this much too hard," she conceded. "But I was going to make a difference, remember? I was Supergirl with a commendation from teacher training college. I was the one who was going to connect with these kids, make them realize that language and literature are a living, breathing part of their lives. What the hell happened to me, Jared?"

But that was back in the day. Back when Rachel Stark had come straight out of the middle-American town of Springfield, just as pleasantly anonymous as the other Springfields scattered across the US map. Eighteen years old, and enthused by the Word—not the religious fervor that had swept up so many in her community, but left her cold, but literally the Word, written, spoken and recited. Rachel had fallen in love with the English language.

It was a process that had crept up on her, a gradual maturing that led to an introversion she always felt needed to be celebrated, not regretted. It wasn't as if she hadn't had a perfectly normal, loving and outgoing childhood. Far from it. Andrew and Rebecca Stark were fine parents, who had instilled their daughter with that quiet dignity and sense of decency that the American heartland could still be proud of.

Girlhood had been balanced. Barbie dolls and Sunday school. Family holidays up at the Great Lakes. Pajama parties and puppy dogs. And adolescence was even more so. She'd always had a good academic record, and found herself excelling in class. But there was still time to hang out with the girls, even for the occasional boyfriend. Nothing was too serious. Nothing was ever going to get in the way of her future.

Her future. Back then it had seemed indeterminate, and not overly ambitious. But she still felt a golden glow suffusing it, just like the optimist she always used to be. Life could be fun at times, but everything had to be balanced—ordered. Any boyfriend who wanted to get beyond the French kissing stage was quietly and politely jettisoned, with no hard feelings. She had no hang-ups about sex that she was aware of, but the risk of STDs or teenage pregnancy just did not appeal to her sensible nature. Sex could wait—as it did, until she attended teacher-training college, and met her first serious boyfriend. Her first serious, short-lived boyfriend. Good sex, life-affirming sex, would wait until that bittersweet day when Jared first learned how to soothe her pain.

But, back in her early teens, such adult concerns were an abstraction. Something else was happening, something came to color her perception of how she viewed the world when Rachel discovered English literature.

At first, it was a love for what her dad had teasingly called "girlie books." He made them sound like *Playboy* magazine, but she knew he meant specific to her age and gender. But not necessarily to her era. Growing up in the late twentieth century, she'd suddenly found that her sensibilities were more suited to those of her well-educated middle-class counterparts over a hundred years before. The fussing, intricate sentence construction of Jane Austen; the tiny handwritten words that elegantly communicated quaint English sensibilities and prejudices. The overwrought Gothic romantic pastiches of the Bronte sisters, of *Jane Eyre* and *Wuthering Heights*, and the stirring emotions they awoke in a young girl.

It was all standard stuff. It didn't stop there, however. For Rachel found herself, little by little and by small degree, becoming a literary aesthete. She loved to read and re-read the collected works of the celebrated aesthetes themselves, like Henry Miller or Edith Wharton. It was considered precocious for her age, and Rachel soon realized that her affection was not for storytelling, but for the Word itself. The events Miller, for example, described mattered less than the detailed and meticulous manner in which he did so.

From the age of thirteen, Rachel Stark would only ever peep into the kind of books considered appropriate to her age group if she was compiling a critique of them. Superstar biographies were just not for her, and trashy movie or TV novelizations were only of interest when she wanted to parody their style for a school essay.

In latter years, she and Jared had got a big kick out of a rerun episode of *Frasier*. Niles, the stuffed-shirt psychiatrist brother, was advising a patient to visualize some cherished artifact of childhood, and relating it to his own rarefied tastes: "Perhaps a well-thumbed copy of *Middlemarch*... You may have some other examples of your own."

"That's me!" she'd exploded with laughter. "That's me as a little girl!" Jared was immediately in on the joke.

Early on, she'd entertained ideas of becoming a writer. They were soon dismissed. She was not, she decided, suited to a world with a short attention span, and a penchant for building up and then discarding overnight literary sensations. Besides which, the very idea made her fall foul of her own niggling perfectionism. If she was inclined to put every word that she herself wrote under such intense critical scrutiny, then how could she ever give it up to be appraised by an editor?

No, if her future lay in "spreading the Word", then it was as a teacher, an evangelizing pedagogue. Her mom and dad agreed. All her friends agreed. So it was that nervous young Rachel, still wet behind the ears and lacking the kind of life experience assimilated by proxy from the printed page, came in out of the Midwest.

Illinois State University, where she took her degree and completed her postgraduate teacher training, was a little scary at first. On the edge of a big city, its proximity to urban reality might have taken the shine off her dream a little. But Rachel was young, idealistic, and insulated from negative experience. She simply couldn't imagine that a time might come when she would despair of communicating her own enthusiasm to people younger than herself.

Still, she'd needed to find a vehicle to prove to herself that she could open up new educational vistas for the young mind, that she could make a difference. That came with the college's Outreach program, which concentrated on specific neighborhoods in Chicago. At first, it had all seemed a little daunting to Rachel. Kids with literacy problems, well, she thought she could handle them. What kind of an English teacher would she make if she couldn't handle the fundamental building blocks of literacy?

But most of these kids hadn't been selected because they had poor concentration or mild dyslexia. They had family problems. Social adjustment problems.

Problems with the legal system. Problems that Rachel, with her happy, relatively sheltered background, had found it hard to visualize before then. If literacy, and the life lived vicariously between the covers of books, could make any difference at all to these kids, then this was the time to prove it to herself.

Her first major success was the prospect she'd found most daunting. Terry Gantry was a disaffected young urban kid who'd walked out of school. Nothing too unusual about that. The cities were filled with kids who'd become disenfranchised, or who had disenfranchised themselves, from the public school system.

Terry was a little different though. An aggressively introverted personality that gave no quarter to anyone who trespassed upon his space, the boy hadn't just walked out of school. He'd walked out of the home where he'd been subject to violent abuse by his mother's boyfriend, before giving as good as he got with a baseball bat. He walked out of the homeless shelter, where he'd been subject to the lechery of degenerate or deranged older men. Terry had walked out of society, period. He stood on a precipice, from where he would either be allowed to fall or else a safety net might be positioned for him before it was too late. Before his lack of concern for his own well-being led to him becoming a danger to himself. Or his festering alienation led to him becoming a danger to others.

It unnerved Rachel a little to think she'd volunteered to be a component in the tiny machine that tried to save kids like Terry Gantry. When they first met, at a youth hostel where he was encouraged to stay in order to receive free meals, he'd been cold to her. Not threatening. Not aggressive or abusive. Just stand-offish and disinterested. When she said she wanted to help administer to his educational and imaginative needs, Terry just wore a wry smile of disbelief. An offer to obtain any non-pornographic reading materials he required, a deal Rachel imagined would have some of the better-educated urban poor salivating in envy, was regarded as some kind of joke. But Rachel wasn't giving up that easily.

It wasn't always possible to meet with Terry face-to-face. Whether he'd be at the hostel or not when she arrived was pretty much decided on a whim. But still, when he wasn't in attendance, she would leave him books that she'd carefully selected for him. It was immediately apparent from the first day that the boy had a dark, pessimistic view of his life and his prospects. Who could expect otherwise?

But Rachel wasn't going to encourage him to sink any further into nihilism. If he found the all-American can-do school of positivism too patronizing, too ignorant of his life experiences, then she was going to encourage him to read authors who had something to say about humanity's inner darkness, rather than exploiting it. She left him a copy of Poe's *Tales of Mystery and Imagination*—she'd always found him too overwrought and melodramatic for her tastes, but she had to acknowledge him as America's poet of the dark workings of the soul. She indicated the short stories of dark compulsion and obsession she felt he ought to read—"The Imp of the Perverse", "The Telltale Heart", "William Wilson"—and asked for his comments in return, along with any suggestions of further reading matter he'd require.

It seemed a little hopeless at first. The only comments she got back were a scrawled "This guy is WHACK—what the FUCK does he know?" across the Poe anthology. But she'd persevered. Terry's form teacher had spoken of an intelligent, sensitive boy with an ability to shut down when he thought he was under attack from outside forces—or to erupt into sudden, disruptive violence. He was far from illiterate, but he couldn't accept that anyone, or anything, could possibly be of relevance to his sad, disordered life.

The first positive response came after she'd left him a small stack of Graham Greene novels, complete with her guidance notes about why she'd selected each one. Some were returned unread—she could see when he hadn't bothered to even turn back the cover. But others had been brooded upon. And one drew a response.

It was *Brighton Rock*, Greene's novel about a seventeen-year-old kid who led a "razor gang" at the English racetracks. Rachel generally didn't care for books about crime, violence or murder—there were, she felt, so many other facets of being human that needed to be expressed or explored. Criminal behavior was one small aspect that had been blown wildly out of proportion. And besides which—it was something she had no empathy with, and no experience of. It was not something she ever wanted to be forced to think seriously about.

But Greene's themes were universal, stenciled onto a seedy, parochial backdrop. Pinkie, his Catholic juvenile anti-hero, was at least as concerned with the fate of his immortal soul as he was with the older rival he sliced up. For the first time, it prompted a coherent response from Terry: "This kid is doomed, but he ain't dammed. [sic] If a man has to pay for what he's done in this world, is it easier to roll with it if he knows there ain't no one who cares a dam [sic] about him, or if he knows there's a heaven above him and a hell below? I wish I knew."

Just to read those few lines, to know her search for an appropriate text had got the boy searching his own soul, was something she found immeasurably moving. It sparked a genuine dialogue between them. She bought him *The Catcher in the Rye*, another classic of tormented adolescence, and left annotated questions as to how Terry thought the author handled the sixteen-year-old Holden Caulfield's problems. (In truth, the troubled middle-class kid Caulfield's problems palled alongside those of Terry Gantry.)

Then came the big breakthrough. Terry agreed to sit-down discussions with her to debate the content of certain books. She broke the habit of a lifetime and of her profession by bringing along English translations of Dostoyevsky, to get to grips with the big themes of alienation, and what the isolated individual chooses to do with his life. Rachel found the gloomy Russian turgid, and in need of a good editor. But she recognized what Terry's unarticulated concerns were by now, and he ate up *Notes from the Underground* and *Crime and Punishment*.

"If a man knows that there ain't a place for him in this world," he'd written for her in the notes they made at their meetings, "then he stands an equal chance of losing himself as of finding himself if he gets deep into crime."

Their meetings had continued throughout her undergraduate course, along with several other kids she would intermittently work with. But Terry was the first success story. Literature got him to thinking about himself. Not dwelling on his problems, but measuring them against the greater knowledge he was building up of the human condition. For Terry, reading was a living, breathing solution, and less of an aesthetic pleasure, as it was for Rachel.

Terry had ambitions that were eventually unearthed by Rachel and the Outreach project. They were very small–he wanted his own apartment in a building where the cockroaches weren't too ashamed to live, he wanted to earn money in a job that didn't bore him inordinately–but they were real to him. Before he met Rachel, he didn't even consider these modest ambitions a possibility.

So it was that Rachel, working via the Outreach scheme, helped to find him a place to live and to apply for a job working for the city. At nights, he would train in computers, a companionship he found much easier to that of humans, and work for an attainable promotion to the publicity and information department.

Rachel wondered when, or if, the time would come when Terry overcame his alienation enough to settle into a one-to-one relationship. But that was jumping the gun. What mattered far more immediately was that he had found himself a place in the world. That, even with the loneliness he still suffered, he now had the companionship of the great writers and thinkers who boosted his self-knowledge.

As Terry Gantry himself had put it to her, "You really made a difference, Miss Stark."

Jared's faltering response to her self-deprecation spoke of his discomfort. The phrase "burnout" sprang to his mind just as easily as it did hers. But it carried the wrong implications: as if she would never be a useful member of the teaching community again, and the fault was entirely some innate weakness of her own. Besides which—last time he was clumsy enough to say the words, she'd gone stratospheric ape-shit. "You need a break, that's all. You take the job seriously. That's what makes you a great teacher."

"Past tense, please." He didn't know whether she was fessing up to burnout, or whether she was insisting that her forthcoming hiatus was the real deal, the big break from teaching that she'd threatened. Knowing Rachel, it might just be grammatical pedantry—but that would mean she was rekindling a flame of enthusiasm they both knew had been snuffed out.

"Fine. That's what made you a great teacher," he acquiesced. "Deep down, you know you love the little rat bastards." She forced a smile as he placed a modest kiss on her forehead, unwilling to make too much show of their affection in front of kids who, he knew, could be a lot crueler to Rachel than they would ever dare to be with him. "And they love you," he insisted, before taking off for the evening's coaching duties.

That was his way of dealing with things. If a problem seemed intractable, then you lifted the weight with a joke or some groundless optimism. As much as she'd come to hate the frivolous culture that filled her class with rows of bored, uncomprehending faces, she loved Jared for his refusal to take things too seriously. And who knew? He was probably right.

It was in the last few months that everything had become a problem for Rachel. She found it reflected in her relations with Jared's family. Since they'd become close, he'd gradually eased her into every aspect of his life. It meant accompanying him sometimes for his out-of-town visits to see his mother and father, with an occasional quota of sisters, in-laws, aunts and uncles into the bargain.

The family were every bit as liberal and easygoing as Jared himself. He'd inherited their disposition alright. They accepted the fact that she wasn't Jewish without any qualms at all (though she was sure she'd detected a little expectant interest in his mother when Jared introduced her, without any prior ceremony at all, by her first name of Rachel). It simply didn't seem to be an issue. Rachel had once overheard his maternal aunt appraise her conspiratorially as "such a nice girl—such a nice *shiksa.*" But otherwise, such quaint ethnic concerns seemed to be too old-fashioned for them to bother with.

Up until recently, she hadn't detected any reservations at all in the Goldmans about their son's choice of girlfriend. Until that classic family scenario, the overheard conversation at the post-dinner table, gave it away. "Tell me about Rachel," Jared's normally unobtrusive father had whispered to him, believing she still loitered in the kitchen making small-talk with his sister. "She seems a little... 'tightly-wrapped' these days. Is there something that's bothering her?"

It was becoming that obvious. Jared had had to explain that she had a few serious issues relating to her career. That they'd reached a mutual decision it might be best for her to break away from Sunnyvale for a "hiatus"—that was how he regarded it. For her, it was a plain old resignation. Her swan song as a teacher. It didn't matter now many times he told her to the contrary, failing at one modern American high school didn't bode well for transferring to another. It would be like swapping one sense of personal redundancy for another.

And then there were the migraines. The dizzy spells. At least she'd thought of them as migraines—as Jared was quick to remind her, *The American Medical Association Encyclopedia of Medicine* did not regard anyone who didn't experience debilitating head pains as a sufferer. But how else was she to describe what was happening to her? She'd never suffered from anything similar before, but the attacks could be sudden, unannounced, and, fortunately, often disappeared as quickly as they came.

It was the sudden light-headedness, and the flashes of light in her peripheral vision, that convinced her it was migraine. Sometimes, after she lay on the couch nursing herself, she would stand up to look out of the window. That's when she saw lights splinter into a hundred little gleaming fragments out on the suburban skyline. And disappear just as quickly as they'd arrived.

Apart from that, there were no symptoms. Jared had reassured her. "You're sick. Sick of Sunnyvale Fucking High." He'd been forced to concede, by events rather than by Rachel, that leaving was probably going to be good for her. "When you take some time out to worry about no one but yourself, you know those symptoms are going to disappear," he'd told her. "Just leave any little neuroses you might have back at the school, for us poor saps who still work there." It earned him a stinging little punch on the upper arm. But she knew anything Jared said was kindly intended at heart. Just like he was himself.

His infectious light-heartedness was what she often needed to get her through the day. But it didn't stay with her too long. Out in the schoolyard, two boys could just about be discerned running off for the cover of some trees. She could see a beanie hat and a ponytail bobbing off into the distance.

They weren't so desperate to evade identification that they'd taken off completely. Nor did they seem too self-conscious to disguise their mirthless macho laughter, out there in the foliage. In fact, she felt they wanted her to hear their mockery.

And its focus was all too predictable. As she approached the reserved space where her second-hand VW Beetle was parked up every day, she tried not to be wounded by their petty cruelty. Swallowing her rage, she looked down at the flat tire on the driver's side. Slashed in a broken arc by a small but sharp blade, maybe a penknife or small hunting knife.

Oh yeah, they love me alright. They love me soooo much...

TWO

"Yo, Holmes!"

Jose Molina wove an intricate circuit between the sidewalk and two parked cars, skating in and out of the road. With a little more practice and perfection, he could execute a truly rad figure-eight, weaving in and around them. Beat that, Tony Hawk.

It was a cool, breezy summer's day on the streets of Sunnyvale, and the rush he got from burning up the street made Jose feel good to be alive. School was okay, at least when he let it wash over him, but it was truly dope to be hitting the bricks outside.

Picking up some velocity from his wheels, he accelerated on the dorky figure who was cluttering up the sidewalk. "Step aside, ese!"

Jose only recognized who it was in the nanosecond it took to grab the baseball cap from his head. Didn't the dweeb dig that no one wore the peak reversed and tilted down on the back of their head any more?

The cap sailed through the air like a Frisbee, landing perfect dead center in a trashcan. Hey, forget

Hawk—I can give Ben Johnson a run for his money, man!

"Swish!"

"Hey!" The other kid's reactions were several seconds after the event—like those time-delay devices they had on *Jerry Springer* to stop all those stressed-out dudes cursing up the airwaves. As if to play for big laughs, the geek even spun round and took a swing at Jose, hitting clear air like a hundred years or so after he'd shot past.

"Hey, ese! Iron Mike Tyson!"

Jose recognized that Jordan geek from class. He never had a beef with him—Jose Molina's a righteous dude, don't have beef with no one on God's earth—but it was kind of in the culture to mess with kids like that. As far as he could see, Ben Jordan was one slow fool. He'd been a class goodie-boy, but his head was too far up his ass to make the grade either as a dorky grade-whore or as a righteous brother outside on the street.

Jordan was a fool, man, but Jose never had a beef with him. He just saw how all his brothers got into ragging on Ben, and figured he'd go with the flow like always. Besides, Jordan was used to it, he never seemed to care.

Ben's face was a solid mask of passivity. It was the same nonchalant disaffection that he presented to his teachers, to his classmates, to the whole world. But inside, there were fires stoked up in the belly of that benign doofus.

You dirty little motherfucker!

His mind raged, while his face stayed as inscrutable as some teenaged Sphinx.

How'd you like to be on the receiving end of some real rage, asshole? How'd you like to skate straight into the arms of death?

Rachel felt unusually level, for a woman who'd just had the obnoxiousness of the modern American teenager thrust in her face. Maybe it was Jared's balanced optimism, influencing the way she thought about her life. Or maybe it was just the knowledge that none of their spitefulness betrayed any real hate for her. It was just a case of the more bovine members of the herd following their classmates' trail of bullshit.

They sense your weakness, girl, she mocked herself. They smell blood.

Maybe. But even she had to concede she was taking too much of the blame. They slashed your tire because that's what they and their friends do to any teacher who won't punch their lights out. She'd wished Jared was there, to chase after them and make them report to the principal's office. But he hadn't been. She wasn't going to get bent out of shape about it.

It was after the incident with the dirty limerick in class that she'd first run, inadvertently, into his arms. They were already acquainted, to the extent where he'd been known to help out with general prop and spear carrying at the amateur dramatic club. In reciprocation, it wasn't entirely unknown for her to help out with the girls' volleyball and softball teams, if she had the time to spare. And if, more importantly, she knew that Jared was going to be there.

So when he'd caught her crashing out of the classroom in a flood of tears, it seemed at first like a double humiliation. It should have been a relief to meet up with a friendly face. But she'd just wanted to keep her head down and race for the staff car park.

"Hey, Rachel, don't take off... What is it? I mean, have you had some bad news?" They were the first innocuous words of concern he'd ever spoken to her. And it was genuine. When she'd reluctantly walked him back into the class, he'd fallen immediately silent. At first, she thought it was just plain embarrassment. After all, what do you say when a colleague confronts you with puerile locker-room humor about her titties? But the fact that he'd sat her down, dried her eyes with tissue, and then meticulously scrubbed the board clean so that not a single mark, not a trace of chalk dust, remained, bespoke a more tender concern. In the months that followed, when she got to know his family a little, Rachel had become familiar with a few words of Yiddish: her favorite word was one that denoted a human being, a "mensch." Jared, she'd decided very early on, was a fine mensch.

In the day following the insult, he'd shown the rounded extent of his humanity. He'd wrangled out of her the fact that it was Brian's little posse who were most likely responsible. Then, when the class were lining up to be let into Eng lit in the afternoon, he casually walked by and listened to some of the swaggering jock talk. It was Rachel's policy at first not to allude to the incident. No matter how some of the kids sniggered, she was not going to let on that she knew anyone had been writing insults on the board. So Jared followed suit. He hung back and made like he was loitering in the hall on another matter entirely.

It was only when Brian Kelly and his loudmouthed friends were stupid enough to start bragging loudly, to try to dissolve her into an incoherent state again, that Jared had intervened. Once he heard the words, he'd dived into the little crowd and performed some kind of student arrest on the boy. Brian was red-faced and humiliated. His tough-guy status didn't carry much weight with their quietly confident gym teacher. But Jared had picked up on every gloating word, while feigning disinterest.

When he'd frog-marched the Kelly boy up to Principal Carr's office, earning him a month's worth of detention sittings and extra homework, Rachel had been worried that Jared would put himself in trouble. After all, teachers were supposedly permitted only to use force with their students if their own safety, or that of another student, was at stake. But the well-respected Mr Goldman hadn't hurt the boy; he'd merely made him aware of his strength. His soft-spoken straightforwardness elicited the boy's full confession to the principal. It also kept Brian's dad, a school governor and a notorious pain in the ass, off his back for the time being.

No, Rachel had decided, Jared Goldman is a formidable "mensch", and you mess with him to your cost. In fact, she'd formed that opinion before he took action against that bully Brian. On the night before, in fact: the first time he'd made her realize that her breasts were as perfect and as in-proportion as the rest of her body. To the woman he'd quietly desired right up to and way beyond the point when they first made love that night.

It was at times like that that she could sympathize with stupid, self-defeating Ben Jordan, the butt of too many classroom jokes. But she wasn't about to let her stress level rise to match her level of discontentment, so she just trudged on by foot. Past the suburban houses and their picket fences, past the less salubrious alleyways that led to the edge of town, to the bus stop that ran a route to the more affordable block of condos where she resided.

Speaking of Ben, wasn't that the poor sap standing just down by the corner?

He was gazing after the sparks issuing from Jose Molina's skateboard wheels, with the same blank look that drove her so crazy. The skater boy has probably dissed poor Ben, the way they all did, but she wished that just for once he'd engage a little more with life.

His impassive gaze was irritating her, to the extent that she wondered just what he was looking at. But then she saw.

At least, *she* saw.

Jose seemed to be skating into some ethereal light, emanating from his own head and shoulders. It was almost beautiful, vibrating around his head like some pulsating halo. It seemed to fade into the ether as it rose from his golden visage, merging into the crisp clean sunlight of the early summer's evening.

Rachel was momentarily entranced. She looked back at Ben, to see if he registered the same wonderment at what she presumed to be a natural phenomenon. But the boy had reverted to type—skulking off, disinterested and disaffected, at the next corner.

She looked to the clear blue sky for some explanatory atmospheric condition, for the hint of a rainbow.

But, this gentle summer breeze aside, she had seen no regular showers since Easter time. And, as the boy skated out of view, so the golden luminescence traveled with him. Even at a distance, it seemed to pulsate in time to the calm, measured breathing of a physically healthy sixteen to seventeen year-old.

It had broken the day's frustration and monotony, forcing a smile from Rachel's lips. But her fascination was tempered with nervousness. Half in wonder, half in accusation, she queried at the back of her mind whether it was some kind of optical illusion triggered by her nervous state. By stress, or depression, by any of the turbulent feelings she'd had to swallow in her recent teaching career.

It seemed logical.

It also seemed false. As the pulverizing weight of depression seemed entirely absent from her body, so was the lightheadedness and disorientation of high stress. If the sight of Jose Molina, swathed in light, had a delusional origin, then it was concealed from her by her own sense of wonder.

Do skater boys have angel's wings? she found herself asking, her spirits given a jolting boost by her sense of fascination.

No way, Jose, her rational mind answered back.

THREE

She was still pondering the Jose phenomenon when she caught the bus to the edge of town. It was a cramped, uncomfortable service that she rarely used. The narrow seats meant that anyone weighing over one hundred and twenty pounds was crammed thigh to thigh against their neighbor. If your fellow passenger suffered from halitosis or body odor, you would soon know about it.

But still, it beat walking all the way home. Though it may have been no more than four or five sparsely spaced-out stops, it avoided the gauntlet of little gangs that congregated outside the neighborhood of Sunnyvale. These were kids she didn't know, in their hoodies and baggy pants, and they wouldn't grant her the same consideration that everyone bar the most antisocial cases at her school would.

Thinking objectively, she could see that much of her nervousness was based on her perception, rather than the reality. Let them adopt a fake urban homeboy vernacular, and their own casual uniform, and the kids who were only play-acting blended into a menacing whole with the real bad seeds.

Some of them may even be little angels, if you're of a mind to appreciate it, she told herself. She just couldn't shake that ethereal image of Jose Molina from her mind.

Boom! A mobile sound system blurted out. It was loud, but not so clear. In fact its volume control was ratcheted up so close to the max that it was violently distorted. Each drumbeat or sample seemed to strike at the bottom of the spine, each bass chord reverberating in the pit of the stomach.

The shouted lyrics were the usual offensive banalities that put down women and glorified violence—particularly gun violence, the rapper threatening to "put a cap in yo' ass." At least it would have been offensive if she hadn't heard it all before. Now it just seemed boring. With a "bitch" and a "ho" here, a "motherfucker" there, it was striking all the right chords with the suburban white boys who liked to fantasize that they were black LA gang members.

And I wonder why my kids can't get excited about the English language. Seems like the only way to become a teen idol these days is to debase it as thoroughly as you can.

Rachel recognized that, in her mid-twenties, she had truly become an old fart. It was a source of amusement to her. At least, she compensated, I can still think of those "li'l rat bastards" as "my kids."

She cast a carefully nonchalant glance over her shoulder at the kids with the boombox. Sure enough, they were white boys who'd adopted what they saw as the accoutrements of ghetto culture.

One of them had a little goatee beard, just like Jose was trying to grow, to lend the wearer a menacing maturity. They were rocking their shoulders robotically to the brutal rhythm, smiling at nothing.

But she knew they were gaining satisfaction from how uncomfortable they made the older people on the bus feel. Their smugness stemmed from the belief that they were invincible and that their youth was forever. Too babyish, too ignorant, to perceive the skull beneath their skin.

Rachel took a book from her shoulder bag and opened it where her marker lay. It was an obscure literary work entitled *Varieties of Religious Experience* by William James. She had no idea what had drawn her to it. She had no particular spiritual leanings. In fact, even in these god-fearing days she saw no reason to shift her position from that of skeptical agnostic. But the title just drew her in when she saw it indexed, so she'd ordered it from the library.

The rapper spat venom about his big-butted baby mother, and how he had to beat the bitch. If ever I needed a way to illustrate the clash of cultures, this is it, Rachel acknowledged to herself. As the thudding music brutalized young sensibilities, she tried to immerse herself in study of the world's religious mystics. As much as it grated on her nerves, she'd learned how to insulate herself from the modern world's vexations. Particularly those that stemmed from bratty school kids.

Not everyone had that gift, it seemed. Rachel had become increasingly aware of a man sitting almost parallel to her, just one row of seats closer to the boombox boys who were kicking it at the back of the bus.

He was one of those chubby-faced guys who seem to spill out of their formal clothes. He carried a battered leather briefcase and wore a cheap suit, like a municipal worker whose paycheck frequently didn't match the maintenance bills for keeping a car on the road. He looked like he should loosen his tie and undo his upper shirt buttons. Little beads of sweat were glistening on his receding hairline.

"Why don't you turn that down?"

Oh boy.

It sounded as if he'd spent the last few minutes working up the nerve to make that one request. He was trying to sound authoritative, but it just came out strangulated and nervous. Rachel could have told him that he was picking a fight he couldn't possibly win.

The two homeboys who rocked and swayed with the beatbox, surrounded by a coterie of admiring young friends, just grinned. One of them hit the controls till the noise threatened to blow the roof off the bus. The distortion was metallic, the vocals offensive not so much in their content as in their nerve-grating volume.

Great.

Now she could no longer hear herself think. Everyone on the bus, even those filling the front seats, was irritated by the assault on their senses. One middle-aged, overweight man had worked up the balls to say so, and had succeeded only in making matters worse.

Rachel knew it was irrational, but she was feeling mad at the guy. Didn't he know when it was better to leave well alone?

After a moment of stewing in his own steam, he rose indignantly to his feet. Rachel shot him a reproachful glance. He'd already brought about the exact reverse of what he'd intended. What did he think he was going to achieve now?

But when she looked at him closely, it dispelled all such critical thoughts.

The man's sweaty, unprepossessing head was bathed in a golden radiance.

Rachel was taken aback. There was no doubting what she saw. She was closer to him than she'd been with Jose, who'd been fleetingly mobile. Like Jose, it made him stand out from the other people that surrounded him, as if favored by a beneficent universe.

But why this guy, and why now? If Rachel hadn't been driven so crazy by her class, she could tell herself that her golden vision of Jose was influenced by the aesthetic appeal of youth, its sense of freedom and its physical perfection.

No such criteria applied here. But still, as the fat man breathed heavily and turned beet-red in the face, the golden glow enshrouded him as beatifically as if he were a resurrected saint.

"Do something back here, huh? I paid my fare. I've got my rights!"

If he was a saint, thought Rachel, then it was Saint Jude, patron saint of lost causes. Nobody wanted to hear him, burying their noses in their newspapers or pretending to gaze distractedly out of the window. The bus driver determinedly ignored his imploring. Like all of them, the driver had learned to protect his well-being by standing away from situations that hadn't already sucked him in.

Only the fat man couldn't put enough psychological distance between himself and his young tormentors. Only he seemed to think it was worth crucifying himself for.

His face, darting nervously around his fellow passengers to find some moral support, glowed ever brighter within the undulating light that pulsed in and out with his breaths. The golden radiance extended in a shaft from the top of his head to the top of the bus, fading into the grayness of the metal roof. It was so much at odds with their surroundings, with the pettiness and distress of the man himself, that Rachel realized she was the only one who could see it.

No one who perceived what she saw could possibly ignore it.

"Mister, maybe you should calm down."

She found herself proffering unwanted advice. The glow around him seemed to magnify as his breathing became faster and more labored. He rubbed distractedly at his left arm as if disaster was about to strike.

"Get a cop! I want these kids off the bus right now!"

It was less a demand than a plea that somebody should heed him, should take him seriously and come to his aid. And the homeboys at the back loved it, grinning in smug amusement.

Rachel stood and reached one hand toward him. Maybe to quiet him and calm his distress—or maybe to try to touch the glowing luminescence around him that had become unbearably bright.

She never made contact. The discomfort he'd inflicted on himself suddenly knocked him from his feet.

The other passengers were jolted from their complacency, groaning in alarm as the big guy went down with a heavy smack. He'd collapsed in front of Rachel, his eyes screwed up not in unconsciousness but in pain.

She dropped to her knees, prostrate above the still luminous figure. Her hands pushed down on the man's chest, trying to massage his malfunctioning heart back into action.

It was useless. The glow around him was just as bright but had stopped pulsating. If he was still breathing, it was so shallow as to be undetectable.

His eyes opened as the pain seemed to recede, but he was not in recovery. As the fat man stared up toward Rachel, she knew that he was looking past her. His eyes traced the trajectory of the shaft of light that grew from him. As they did, his pain seemed to vanish and the blood-gorged hypertension disappeared from his face.

He wasn't looking at some earthly phenomenon or trick of the light that played on the shape of a fellow passenger.

To Harold Jobson, forty-nine years old, it was an ethereal escape route that led out of our existence and into the essence of the cosmos. Into a greater whole that transcended the pettiness and futility of the scattered pinpricks of consciousness we call human life.

In his former existence, the very concept would have terrified him. In his final moments of pain and crisis, he was only too willing to embrace it.

As his panic and distress faded, so did the luminous halo he was formerly bathed in. In his own eyes the light didn't fade but ascended, until it carried him, pain-free and weightless, with it. Until it was gone altogether, and he was just one sad little cardiac fatality on the floor of a city bus.

FOUR

Respite came in the form of domestic normality. If the working day had been dispiriting then the late afternoon had been a head trip. Less dissipating than the kind experienced by people she knew who'd messed with drugs—but, in its way, just as mind blowing.

As Rachel stirred a pot of chili in their condominium apartment, the mundane task helped her relax and consider the events of the last few hours. The familiar and very welcome sound of rattling keys and a creaking door told her she was not alone. So did the warm embrace and the tender kiss that followed very closely.

"You're late," she told Jared, less of a reprimand than an observation.

"Game went into overtime," he explained.

Just like her, he needed to unwind in the modest, neat home that they shared together. He grabbed a beer from the refrigerator and hung around the kitchen to make small talk. Eyeing her up and down, he couldn't help feel that something was slightly amiss.

"You alright?"

She shrugged. It must have been obvious to him. But then, the day's events were nothing that anyone could dismiss too lightly.

She decided to stick to the bare statement of facts, the rational approach.

"I had to leave the car at school. We can pick it up in the morning. Two of the little bastards slashed my tire."

"Hey, I'm sorry Rach," he piped up. "I'll go speak to Carr in the morning. It's about time he stopped making noises about unity and discipline and started kicking a few asses."

"No, no, it's okay," she brushed it off gently. "Really. It's just an inconvenience." The car was not it. She wanted to tell him about what she'd experienced, but he had to be prepared to listen.

"But I had to take a bus ride home. There was a man on the bus who had a heart attack. I tried CPR but..." she shrugged, "he died."

Jared's demeanor changed. He came over concerned, conscious of his own insensitivity, although there was no way he could have anticipated what she'd seen.

"Hey." He reapproached her, taking her in a warm, protective embrace from behind. "That's awful. That's real terrible."

"It was." She was glad of his concern, but it was as if she was still holding back.

"Have you ever seen anyone die, Jared?"

He nodded. "My grandfather. When I was ten."

Her silent pause told him she wanted to know more.

"It was upsetting." He tried to find the right words. "He was an old man and he wanted us all to be there. He'd been sick for a long time. But it was still shocking. It wasn't so much the illness, it was just that..."

He fumbled for the words to describe the memory. She was attentive, the subject clearly important to her.

"I guess it's that we're not in contact enough with death in modern society. You and I take care of ourselves, we try to eat carefully, we work out and we don't cultivate bad habits.

"And still," he swallowed a small draught from his can of beer, "we're going to die.

"I guess what freaked me out about it when I was a kid is like someone said: we all die alone. We were told Grampa was happy for us to be present, but I didn't see any sign that he even knew. It was like he had his sights fixed on things that were in his mind, memories, whatever. We were superfluous to requirements. Dying is a very personal thing, I think."

It was clearly shaking him, but she had to know more. Even at the risk of sounding heartless, or ridiculous.

"Did anything... weird happen, when he died?"

"Weird? Like how?"

She sighed gently and resolved to tell him the whole story. "Before the man on the bus died, something started happening."

His silent pause urged her to go on.

"I saw this light around his face."

There was nothing more to explain. At least, nothing more she could explain.

"A light? Like a halo or something?"

She sensed he was on the verge of ragging her. His sensitivity would only stretch so far. And after all, the guy on the bus was a stranger to her, it didn't carry the same emotional charge as his grandfather.

"It sounds cheesy, but... Yeah. Like a halo."

She reached for his beer. He handed it to her and grabbed another can from the fridge.

"I can't say I saw Grampa wearing a halo. My family may be of the Chosen People, but I don't think he was ever ordained as an archangel."

She gave him a feeble punch on the arm. It made her feel foolish, but there was no retracting what she said now.

"I know, I know. It's crazy, but it's something I've experienced more than once."

He was wide-eyed and attentive.

"Earlier today, in fact. It was Jose. I saw the light on Jose too."

"Who?" He sounded slightly perturbed.

"Jose Molina. Sophomore. One of my Eng lit kids. He was on his skateboard. I thought it was just the sun in my eyes. I wasn't wearing my shades."

"Yeah," he confirmed her rationalization. "I've heard of that. Sun spots. Gaze a little too long into the light and close your eyes. Imagination comes into play. Those blurry images on the back of your eyelids can become anything–stars in the sky, wild animals."

"Halos of light?"

He shrugged. "Sure. I guess."

"No." She shook her head. "This was something different. Something I could see, something I've only just become aware of."

"So?" He could tell this was heading into uncharted waters.

"So... nothing, I guess."

He was unconvinced, watching her expression intently.

"Hey, lighten up!" She tried to turn the tables back. "Jose was just fine. It wasn't like I saw the light come out of another dead person."

"So that's what you believe happened? In the other instance?"

Checkmate. He'd trapped her in her own logic.

She faced up to her embarrassment. "That's the way it seemed. I was kind of counting on you to laugh and tell me it was all in my head."

Laughter was not forthcoming. He was taking it all a little too seriously.

But then, what else had she really hoped for? She hadn't wanted to be ridiculed or disparaged. But neither did she want to be psychoanalyzed.

"I'm not saying your experience isn't valid, but what you saw is a part of your current state of mind, Rach."

"My 'state of mind,'" she echoed with mild distaste.

"Hey, please," he preemptively corrected her. "No one's saying that you're a flake. But you've just given in your notice on a job you used to love. Unless you decide to put your considerable talents to use at another school, next week you won't even be a teacher anymore.

"Dare I say it? Maybe you're feeling a little guilty."

"Guilty?" She bridled, hardly able to believe what he was saying. "Well, what on earth for? You said it yourself, I've been a conscientious..."

"I know, I know," he interjected, nipping the argument in the bud before it started. "If anything, you've been too conscientious. Think about it. No one can ever seriously suggest that you let those kids down. But I think something inside you might be saying that you let yourself down."

Her indignation was deflated. Not least because it sounded like his argument might carry some truth.

"You've been too hard on yourself, Rachel. I think your mind may be searching for the light, looking for a few chinks to let the optimism come flooding back in.

"And besides," he handled the copy of *Varieties of Religious Experience* that hung halfway out her shoulder bag. "I don't claim to be any expert, but I have read that nervous exhaustion and religious experience tend to go hand in hand."

"Religious experience," she echoed. "I borrow a library book, and it becomes Exhibit A. I'm not about to start talking in tongues and having visions of the Madonna, Jared."

"Hey," he laughed, relieved that their mutual sense of humor was offering a way out of this impasse. "For someone brought up a Methodist I've never known you so much as attend church—excepting weddings and funerals.

"But religion doesn't have to mean church, Rach. I don't have to tell you that. It can mean any human need that isn't fulfilled by the material world."

She acceded quietly. The book she'd been reading told of a plethora of saints, ascetics and seers. From the Hindu Brahmin to Joan of Arc, what many of them had in common was the experience of divine visions in their everyday lives. It would have been humbling to be spoken of in the same breath, if it wasn't just a little bit frightening. Many of these people, including Saint Joan with her angels' voices, would have been classified as mentally ill in today's rational world.

"I guess you're right," she conceded, no longer putting up any resistance. "I've been having a hard time letting go. Those kids will be fine without me. And I'll be more than fine without them. I just had a weird afternoon. That's all."

Jared, with his level-headedness and calmly rational nature, was her rock at times like this. But what was annoying was that the bastard was nearly always right.

Jared drove Rachel to Sunnyvale the next morning, arriving early so that he could change her tire. That annoyance aside, things were much the same as ever. But this time, to her undisguised delight, Rachel found herself engaging with a very small but very attentive audience.

"So why does Mercutio say 'a plague on both your houses?'"

"He wanted everyone dead," piped up Tony McIlhone, a chubby-faced boy with an exploding black bird's nest hairstyle. Tony—goofy but intensely serious Tony—reminded her of Robert Smith, the leader of the Cure, an early alt.rock band that he was surely too young to have known. He was also one of the last stalwarts of her class.

Even though he sometimes kept his enthusiasm covert, he had never lost faith with her. Rachel liked to think that Tony might have been one of the pupils for whom she had "made a difference." Somehow, though, she knew that he'd made more of a difference to her.

Tony was the type of introspective, sensitive kid who always had something to offer in class. Whether a teacher responded to that depended on how astutely their antennae worked. Rachel liked to think that she was properly attuned.

Or maybe, she had thought to herself more than once recently, I'm so in tune with the school's outsiders and misfits that I can't connect with the mainstream of the class. That's why I've become such a lousy teacher. She had to dismiss the idea from her mind just to get through the day—not out of any egotistic compulsion, but because it was belittling toward the kids she felt the most empathy for.

Tony's parents, who were respectable blue-collar, would have liked their son to fit in more with a clique like Brian's. It was all very well for a blue stocking like Ms Stark to encourage his artsy nature—but, like the old cliché went, where was the percentage in that? And besides—since their son had told them about the difficulties the teacher was having with his class, it seemed like she was more concerned with her own problems than with the kids.

That was not the way Tony felt. As he tried to assert his identity and accentuate the difference he felt from other kids with Goth rock and kohl eyeliner, adolescence was a dark place to be. In those circumstances, a few kind words from a teacher were an oasis of light. Ms Stark *had* made a difference to him, though he would never be able to fully tell her how. If he kept his tousled head down these days, to avoid the punches that would otherwise be thrown at it, then he still took pride in all the thought and energy that went into his essays.

He just wished he'd had the balls to speak out a little more in class. To face down Brian Kelly and his posse of morons. To let Ms Stark know he was still with her, and that he wasn't ashamed to show his appreciation to the one teacher who mattered. But it was no use. He hoped she recognized how seriously he took her lessons, how much value he placed in them, but he was tired of being shot at every time he raised his head above the parapet. It must have been like a sea of loneliness for her, stuck up in front of a mass of non-appreciation. But some things, as Tony had already concluded in his young life, just had to be faced on your own.

There was only one other student who dispelled the wave of indifference that washed over the class as soon as Rachel opened *Romeo and Juliet*. Like Tony, she knew Ms Stark was leaving next week, and she wasn't going to be cowed into curbing her enthusiasm today. If they could let her know how much they appreciated her this once, then maybe they could feel better about all the times they'd played along with the class clowns, for whom literature was only ever fit for faggots.

It had given them both a sense of self-worth that wasn't so easily obtainable from their peer group. And of companionship too. She might never have found Tony as a friend if they hadn't been lined up together as Ms Stark's pet geeks. It had cemented something between them. They started to share interests, books and records. They'd even been out together to check out the alt.rock and independent band sections at the mall record shop, and once to the movies to see *28 Days Later* together. It wasn't exactly a date, but she'd made the mistake of mentioning it to her parents and they'd gotten all steamed with excitement about it.

"But Romeo was his friend, right? Why would he want his friend to die?" Rachel sensed that the quiet girl on the adjacent desk to Tony, with the brushed forward fringe and the acne complexion, wanted to answer. All she needed was a prompt to make her overcome her self-consciousness.

"Arlie?" Arlie Bennington came to life.

"Mercutio was dying. He was all alone. He didn't have any friends."

"Bet you know how that feels," sneered Brian Kelly in the front row, his merest whisper never less than a bellow. It was always this way. It was why Arlie and Tony so rarely gave Ms Stark the support of their voices anyway. Why it was easier to keep their heads down and feign disinterest. The "cool kids"—and Tony hated Arlie calling them that, saying they were about as cool as a hot steaming dog turd—had a knack of making you feel stupid no matter what.

Express a little knowledge or understanding—it was worthless. Try to crack a subtle joke—you were pathetic. Worse still, try not to be hurt by them and remain pleasant in the face of their abuse—that was really asking for trouble. It was what made her feel so sympathetic toward Ms Rachel Stark. It made Arlie's blood boil, to think they were losing her favorite teacher down to the same half-witted bullies who could make her life a misery. It was like they'd won.

"Shut up!" She hissed out all the contempt she could summon for Brian, and the handful of others who murmured in appreciation at his witless wisecrack.

"Fuckin' lezzbo, shut your own fuckin' mouth!" Brian wasn't used to being told what to do by a class geek. It rankled. So he resorted to the easiest insults he knew. It fucked 'em up so bad every time, he just loved to do it. It didn't matter whether the little Bennington bitch was a dyke or not, or whether Tony-baloney fucking McIltool was really a queer. The situation was that they were freaks. They were losers. They were so far outside of Brian and Stacy's inner circle that they were on another planet. He could call kids like them faggots or dykes without fear of contradiction—either because they'd be too scared to answer, or else any backtalk to him would just get them laughed out of school.

And besides, if these creepy little nothings didn't fit in, that was as good as being a fag or a lez in his book. Words hurt, he noted with satisfaction. They cut deep. And if some kid didn't like what he was giving them, then they could have a few real bruises to go with the emotional ones.

It amused Brian to know the Bennington bitch and McIlhone had been seen sneaking around the mall together, and were shitface scared that they'd been spotted by Stacy and her girlfriends. He knew it was because of him, and it gave him big props. He could always turn things around on them—anything that made 'em feel good about themselves, he could make it make them feel bad. If pimple-pixie Arlie was seeing Goth-geek Tony, he could still make them feel like a pair of queers. The only question was, were they a pair of bitches or a couple of guys?

"Brian!" Rachel had been encouraged by the interest shown by Tony and Arlie, but the lesson was turning into the same old grinding battle of wills.

She was almost relieved to see Mrs Kropansky, Principal Carr's middle-aged secretary, at the door. Rachel invited her in, no longer caring whether the school administrators saw how much trouble she had controlling the kids. But the thin-faced woman with spectacles on a chain seemed reluctant to cross the threshold.

"Okay, class! Just ease off on each other. I'll be back in a moment. Try not to fret for me."

With the door separating them both from the class, Mrs Kropansky's serious demeanor was unchanged.

"I'm really sorry about the uproar. That Kelly kid is a foul-mouthed oaf. I don't care if his father's on the board of governors or not..."

Kropansky was unchanged. "No complaints on that front, Ms Stark. At least," she regarded the howling bullies on the other side of the glass with mild alarm, "not yet."

"I'm afraid I have grave news I have to tell you. About a pupil in your English class."

Rachel froze. She took a mental roll call of who was present and correct. There was only one absentee who stood out. Suddenly she sensed the nature of what she was about to be told.

"It's Jose, isn't it?"

She didn't know how she knew, but the events of yesterday seemed to point the bad news in his direction.

Mrs Kropansky acknowledged Rachel's prescience with a slight widening of her eyes.

"How... How did it happen?" Somehow, she knew that this wasn't merely an accident, injury or illness. It spoke of the ultimate disaster.

Mrs Kropansky was alarmed at how the teacher seemed aware of the full gravity of the incident. It seemed to her further proof of the young woman's acute neurotic sensitivity. But that was neither here nor there.

"I'm afraid young Jose met with an awful misfortune when surfing the streets." It sounded for one moment like the principal's first lieutenant was trying to be "down with the kids."

"He apparently scaled part of a wall at an angle, then hit the pavement again and misjudged the distance. We're not sure how, but he appeared to bounce off the curb at a busy road junction."

Rachel had to hold herself from going into momentary shock. The thought of the young boy's terrible end was bad enough. The belief that it might have revealed itself to her, and only her, was devastating.

"There was a collision with one of the latest model Chevrolets. I'm afraid there was no hope for poor Jose. But I'm told he never regained consciousness."

The strange ethereal light that traveled full-on with Jose as he rode remained vivid in her mind. It had unnerved her, but at the time it seemed to carry positive connotations. Not just a harbinger of death, surely, but a presence. A life force.

"He passed away this morning. I'm sorry, Ms Stark... Rachel. Are you okay? Do you need me to break the bad news to your class, or . . ."

Her face was stony impassive and her eyes unblinking. It was hard to remain fixed on the here-and-now when the events of yesterday were re-playing over and over.

"No, that's fine, I... I think that I really have to tell them."

There could be no doubting, as she re-entered the classroom, that Ms Stark had a bombshell to drop. In marked contrast to their former unruliness, the class waited in silent anticipation.

It was the first time in months that she'd been able to look into all their faces simultaneously. The first time that she hadn't felt intimidated by the contempt of the bullying few. It was a hell of a way for her to regain her authority. Mrs Kropansky watched outside, from a polite distance, alarmed that the young teacher might somehow disintegrate in front of her pupils.

"I have something terrible I have to tell you."

They were attentive. Every eye fixed on her, with no hint of distraction or boredom. Was this what it took to break through the indifference of the modern teenager? Heartbreak, tragedy and pain?

"I'm really sorry but..."

All of them, even Brian and his lame little jock following, were hanging on her every word. She almost wished that she could have discovered this technique years ago. That each lesson she'd taught could have demanded the attention of the class by playing on their anticipation and anxiety.

"Our friend Jose was hit by a car on his way home from school yesterday."

Total enrapt attention. Unblinking concentration from all of them. If this was what it took to engage a class, you could keep it.

"He died this morning. I'm sorry. I'm so sorry to have to tell you..."

The moment of truth brought no further reaction. The class's sense of anticipation had brought them to the ultimate conclusion before she'd articulated it. But death was just a word. To nearly every kid in the class, it was something entirely new, and they needed to focus inward to understand this new reality.

"We have no reason to believe Jose suffered. He lost consciousness straight away."

It was a hard, crystallized silence. The only way that they could respond. Only the most insensitive fool would have dared to break it.

"Least his parents still have twenty other bambinos at home."

Brian leered, addressing his peers with a cheesy grin that seemed false.

Rachel permitted herself a little mild shock. Even now, at this time, he thought it was right to put himself on display like the obnoxious moron that he was?

He looked along the faces of his high school posse. One fellow jock from the football team gave a nervous, half-hearted smile, as if it was his duty to react to every wise-ass, lame-brained crack that Brian made. But others looked distinctly uncomfortable, averting their gaze from him. None of his girlfriends, present, past or prospective, would let him fracture their steely solemnity.

"That kind of talk is highly inappropriate."

She kept her words measured, her language officious and neutral. She wasn't going to let this overgrown little brat get the better of her.

"Go to Principal Carr's office, Brian."

For once, she knew she had the support of the class. He looked around for approval, for confirmation that his boorishness was somehow cool. He found none.

"I meant now."

He dragged himself sulkily to his feet, making a big play of scraping his chair. Rachel felt she could actually see approval for her action in some of the kids' faces, something they would never normally dare vocalize.

As he scooped his schoolbooks from his desk, all eyes were on him. Including the impenetrable dark eyes of the boy sitting next to him. For one moment, Brian turned his surly, embarrassed gaze back toward him.

Ben Jordan had broken into a little smirk. At his expense.

"What're you lookin' at, tool?"

If Brian hadn't talked himself into trouble already, the geek's nerve in laughing at him would have earned an ass kicking.

But it was enough to hear some of the class break into laughter. The ice was broken. The tension dispelled. They were all getting over their silent boo-hoo-hoo about beanie Molina.

Brian smiled as he headed for the door. Normal service was resumed. Equilibrium restored.

Kelly ruled. Jordan was an ass-feeder.

Rachel declined to get any further involved. The bickering between the two boys was no longer her concern. Though why Ben persisted in sitting close to Brian in class, when it earned him nothing but withering contempt, was beyond her.

Maybe it was a throwback to the days when the new boy thought he could be accepted among the high school's upper league. Before their short-lived tolerance turned to mockery of his clumsiness at sports, his introversion, his lack of success with girls. Before Ben had found himself in the all-important position so necessary to high school life, but which no one ever aspired to: that of the scapegoat.

Many of the class still leered right back at Ben, the way he'd smirked at Brian. In their own way, they were grateful that he was always there to kick when they needed him.

The retinas of Ben's brown eyes grew until his orbs were almost entirely dark. They fixed unblinking on the departing Brian with an intensity that he rarely displayed. No one noticed. No one even noticed when his resentful stare scanned slowly around his other classmates. No one ever noticed.

By the time the recess bell sounded, like a crack of doom that set the teeth on edge, Ben had retreated within himself. It was that same impassive gaze that expressed and gave away nothing.

The bell broke through Rachel's silent reverie.

"Anyone who needs to see the school counselor, there's a sign-up sheet in her office."

Somehow, she knew there would be few takers outside Jose's closest friends. The little sideshow performed by Brian and Ben had seemed to serve some purpose, to let them know that the universe was still as they perceived it. Never did the nasty little ritual of the bully and the scapegoat seem so ordained and functional.

But she couldn't be concerned with their petty games anymore. Heaven knew, she was focused on a bigger picture right now.

The kids had drifted off. There hadn't been the usual frenetic exodus, just a gathering together into little cliques. They needed each other today. Things were just not the same.

There was one straggler who hadn't quit with the rest. She gazed on his doughy, sun-starved face beneath the mass of febrile spiders that comprised his haircut. What did Tony want, exactly?

"His noble soul has climbed to the clouds." He enunciated clearly, like he'd been rehearsing the words in his bedroom mirror or at an amateur dramatic society. "He was too young to leave this earth."

She recognized the elegy from *Romeo and Juliet*, Act Three, Scene One. Was he trying to tell her now, of all the times he could have picked, that she was a good teacher of English lit?

Tony had his own agenda. Like any Goth kid, he was half in love with death. With its poetry and mystery. In love with it, but never really acquainted with it. He took refuge in the morbid romanticism of bands like Christian Death and Cradle of Filth, but he couldn't yet imagine death's sting.

"I didn't want Jose to die."

She understood. She forgave. The boy was clearly excited about getting close to the dread condition he daydreamed about, but didn't want to be accused of ill will.

"No. Of course you didn't."

Tony had a different way of coping with his alienation than a withdrawn loser like Ben. She could imagine him wandering around the oldest plots in the graveyard, excitedly reeling off the poetry of Poe or Baudelaire. It was eccentric and morbid, but, in the psychological protection it offered him, it was a positive thing. But to Tony, death was still just a word.

To all high school kids, death was just a word.

FIVE

Death, for most of us, is not a romantic place to visit. Modern death assaults the senses, not so much with its brutal finality as with the stinging odor of disinfectant. Our ancestors may have listened for the hoof beats of a pale rider on a dark horse. We anticipate the cranking rattle of a hospital gurney.

The most terrifying aspect of modern death, for those looking from the outside, is that it is willfully robbed of its meaning. No mournful requiem or "Te Deum." No statues or woodcarvings of grinning skeletons come to bear away the sickly infant and the octogenarian alike. Just the blip-blip-blip of CAT machines and brain scans. The quiet delirium of morphine that leaves dying souls half-conscious of their decline, as if experiencing the pain by proxy of someone across the other side of the ward.

Those who take the Hippocratic oath are placed on pedestals. They are the secular priests to whom we turn when death's first distant rattle is heard. Modern lips still breathe out exaltation to God, or Christ, or Jehovah, or Allah—but it's a rare human being who wants to run too quickly into their arms, while the doc can hold out any hope at all.

Rachel was all too nervously aware that she was an intruder, a tourist peeking into other people's desperation. The St John of the Cross charity hospital was as foreboding and antiseptic as any other institution of its kind. Its corridors were wide and twisting, echoing with bustling unseen activity always just a few steps away. Painted arrows reinforced the confusing directional signs that pointed to the myriad wards and reception areas.

Its very existence spoke of desperation–many of the patients here had Medicare cover that was inadequate for the kind of long-term treatment, or terminal nursing, that they required. In a few rare instances, admissions had been made to those who had no health insurance at all, though the quality of mercy tended to be more financially prudent these days.

The last vestiges of hope for some patients were displayed in brightly painted walls, or by paintings contributed by elementary school classes. These, Rachel reminded herself, were as merciful a gesture as any other. When the great leveler descends upon us, the dying business tycoon in the luxurious private ward is just as much at its mercy as the impoverished former seamstresses or truck drivers seeing out their days in the local charity hospital.

Rachel had a strong sense of foreboding as she reached the sign reading "INTENSIVE CARE UNIT." It wasn't just that she was intruding where she had no business to be. It was her lack of acquaintanceship with death on a one-to-one level. Her parents were still fit and healthy people in their early fifties. Non-smoking churchgoers who drank a small amount at Christmas each year, they could reasonably expect to see out another two or three decades, as could most of her aunts and uncles and their family friends.

She even had two grandparents who were still alive, her maternal grandfather and maternal grandmother. Of those who had died, Grandpa had suffered a sudden fatal stroke during her graduation year at high school, after years of hypertension and overwork. Her grandmother, bless her, had suffered a lingering progressive illness when breast cancer had jumped the walls after a mastectomy, invading her vital organs.

In neither case had Rachel come closer to their mortality than viewing Grandma's cosmetically prettified face in repose at the chapel of rest. Her medical treatment had been good and thorough, though it ultimately failed to save her, and any suffering the dear sweet lady endured was behind closed doors.

Rachel had stayed, like most of us, unconsciously insulated from death. Now she was actively seeking it out.

She took a deep breath and pushed quietly through the double doors.

The ward was spacious and quiet. Its yellow bar lighting seemed dimmed, diminished by the gray décor so that it gave the room a kind of sepia tint.

Ten sturdy iron bedsteads were set out symmetrically around the ward. Despite the apparent urgent need for them, several beds appeared to be unfilled. A male technician in his thirties paid the tiptoeing intruder no mind. Gazing distractedly out of the window, bored with the everyday occurrence of impending death, he never looked around to check if she was the visiting member of staff he'd assumed her to be.

Rachel drew nearer to the patients, just beyond her field of vision.

She gave a sharp, involuntary intake of breath.

It was as if the metallic gray beds had been transformed into golden sarcophaguses. Their immobile occupants, mostly unconscious, all wired up to monotonously bleeping machines, were enshrouded in a golden light almost blinding in its concentration.

The function and meaning of the hospital were transformed for her in an instant. Her mind had to concentrate hard not to be overwhelmed. This was no center for medical attention, but a hospice for transient souls.

One middle-aged woman slept in a delirium where soporific calm and anxiety met. The partially smiling mouth of her sedated face constantly quivered, as if the final vestiges of her distress remained within the cocoon of diamorphine.

But she glowed radiantly. Her light peaked to a level of divine illumination then fell again with each slow, sedated breath.

"Mrs Eleanor Johnson. Aged fifty-two. Pancreatic Carcinoma."

Rachel looked closer at the sunken face within the halo of light. This lady was younger than her mother. In truth, she didn't look any older but she was drained of her vitality. Drained of the life force that seeped out of her in golden rays. Ready, it seemed, to erupt in one huge glow and quit her little husk of a body.

Rachel felt like she could openly weep, but at the same time wanted to stroke the hand of the dying lady and reassure her that she was not alone. Jared was wrong. These people would *not* die alone. They were part of some ethereal union, dazzling her in their terrible magnificence. As their poor bodies gave up the ghost, these dying souls were generating enough light to illuminate Atlantic City.

As she scanned the semi-circle of sufferers, she squinted through the radiance of Mrs Johnson's near neighbor. "Roy Guralnik. Aged sixty-two. Cardiac Arrest."

Thin-faced and taut-looking, how different he appeared from the heart-attack victim on the bus. And yet how similar their predicament.

She had no idea what the light meant, or whether it indicated that these suffering, departing souls might have an existence beyond their wrecked bodies. But it showed that human life was a force, not some kind of cosmic accident that tied a whole load of water and some internal organs into one bodily package. Whatever their wretched state, the life force they radiated told her their existences all had some universal meaning.

She started at the sound of a voice. A low groan.

In the far corner of the room, seventy-nine year-old Mr Ellis Thomas tried to turn away from his discomfort.

The old man was tired and weak, and no longer conscious that he was tugging helplessly at the wires of his dialysis machine. Cruel, indifferent nature had decreed that the oldest, weakest member of this congregation should be the most conscious of his predicament. But the intense glow that emanated from him told Rachel that his suffering would not be for long. And that the life force he held within him was stronger than the renal failure that was killing him.

"Ms Candice Pelham. Aged nineteen years, nine months. Multiple Organ Failure."

So terribly young. Not much older than her students. Perforated with wires and drip feeds, and a draining tube that siphoned the saliva from her comatose mouth to stop her drowning in her own fluid.

Her medical chart told of an intravenous overdose of crystal methamphetamine. It was the madness of youth that messed with designer drugs, far more powerful than the weed and Mexican mushrooms that the silly potheads at college had used. Meth hadn't just blown her mind, it had destroyed the girl's fragile inner mechanism.

To kids, death is just a word, Rachel reminded herself.

Candy didn't believe she would die while her friends had shot speed and lived. Candy, like most kids, thought she was immortal. Now her pretty little face was deathly pale and wrapped in light. She was united in her condition with people much older, less healthy, than she was. What they all had in common was that none of them had visualized the moment of their death. No one could ever really understand what it was like till they arrived at that point.

Except me, Rachel told herself. A crack has opened in the walls of my consciousness and I'm starting to see it for myself.

Except that there was one gap in the semi-circle of light. One broken body still stranded in a world of blood and gristle, gray wires and tubes.

"Russell Stanton. Aged thirty-two. Cerebral Injury. Persistent Vegetative State."

She couldn't read the scribbled medical notes on his bed well enough to know what caved in the black guy's forehead. It was severe enough to be a small gunshot wound, but it could equally have been some horrible industrial accident.

What was apparent was that Russell would never recover. The faint, intermittent bleeping of the machine that detected brain activity told its tale. But this man, who was dead to the world, was not giving up his life force. There was no glow around his broken head. She could only surmise that grieving relatives, in their anguish, had refused permission to take him off of life support.

At the center of the semi-circle, the light undulated, pulsed and flowed.

"Daniel Corbett. Aged sixty-four. Liver Failure, Sclerosis."

The yellowing old man, who looked as frail as anyone in the room, was conscious of his surroundings. His rheumy eyes darted from the shaft of light that ascended from his own bed, to that of his neighbors. He looked fearful one moment, delirious but elated the next. As his gaze widened, he lifted one bony arm to try to touch his own pool of light, his attention fixed upon it as it led upward beyond the gray ceiling. Rachel now knew that he was dying.

"Hey!"

It was as she'd expected. She may have been on the ward a couple of minutes by now. Or it may have been an hour. She looked back at the technician who was finally paying attention to her.

"You can't be in here."

He waved over distractedly, perceiving her as an unexpected nuisance rather than a threat.

She nodded her assent, but couldn't pull her attention away from old Daniel, whose pained eyes had now met with hers. With a gargantuan effort of will, he tried to raise his head from the indented pillow. It was futile, but he was trying to force his body upward, to travel up into the light that emanated from his bed. The old man had recognized and accepted the reality of his situation. His hospital ward was a departure lounge from this existence.

SIX

In the darkness of the night, the illuminations of the day had still not faded in her mind. Rachel stood alone at the window, taking pensive sips from a glass of wine. She fingered the pages of her library book beneath the lamplight. *Dreams and Premonitions* was apparently a classic work of psychic research, reprinted from 1923 in the new millennium.

She found it hard to concentrate on its contents. "Premonitory dreams"; "Dreams of the dead"; everything that sounded relevant to her situation was related to the nighttime world of the subconscious. But it wasn't something she needed to awaken from. It was something she'd inadvertently awakened to.

"Coming to bed?" Jared called to her from the darkened living room doorway.

"Yeah. Sure." She hesitated. "In a minute."

He knew her mood hadn't lightened. With a minimum of fuss, Jared sat down next to her on the couch. He took the book of proto-New Age wackiness from her hand and closed it. "Are you still thinking about Jose?"

She nodded almost imperceptibly.

"Kinda morbid, isn't it?"

It roused her from her introspection. "I know what I saw." She sighed. "And now I know what it means. I just had no way of knowing. If I had, maybe things would have been different."

He took the glass of wine from her hand and set it on the table. She sensed a lecture on her irrationality was in the air. "Rachel. I love you, so I want you to trust me when I say this: you do not have the power over life and death."

She gave a hollow laugh. Is that what he thinks it's about? That I've developed some kind of paranoid delusions of grandeur? "I know I don't. That is not what I meant."

It had driven a wedge between them. When Jared saw everything in such rational, reductive terms, there was never any room for debate. Not even if, as Rachel sometimes suspected, he didn't have a goddamn clue what he was talking about.

"Baby, you've got to allow for the distinct possibility that this is all in your mind."

"All in my mind." He was getting kind of predictable. "And everything I saw... Everything I witnessed at the hospital, is all in my mind?"

He, too, was getting a little tense. It was time to set some rational parameters for their conversation. "Auto-suggestion, Rachel. You've convinced yourself."

Oh great.

"You've seen these lights, this... optical illusion, whatever, in close proximity with people who later died. It's a very scary experience, Rach, no one's blaming you for the impression it made."

But that was just it. In the first instance, there was nothing scary about it. Jose Molina was skating along looking like Jesus had chosen him for a sunbeam. It didn't intimate death or disaster in any way. She kept her own counsel, letting him continue.

"So straight off the bat you got this association in your mind. You visit a place where you know you're going to meet with dying people, and the experience recurs. Only more so." He placed an arm around her, undermining her rigid resistance.

Screw Jared. What he said made some kind of sense. Like always. "If I knew that was what it was, I could live with it."

Jared could hear her fighting off tears when she spoke. She was genuinely frightened. He pulled her closer and she felt like a little rag doll in his arms, giving neither consent nor resistance to his affection. "It means you did the right thing, quitting your job."

She threw him a quizzical look. Now who wasn't making sense?

"You're exhausted, Rach. You need a rest. I don't know if this thing is physical or it's because your nerves are all shot to hell. But if it doesn't stop in a couple of days, we'll go see someone about it."

"Oh?" She pulled away from him, studying his face intently. Why couldn't he just come out and say what he meant? "Like a psychiatrist?"

Jared sighed. "We'll do whatever needs to be done. C'mon, we got a problem it's better we go to a professional, rather than some John Edward charlatan."

"I wasn't aware 'we' had a problem. Or that I wanted to get attention on some TV psychic show."

Getting her to thaw out now was going to take more than a little reasoning. "I just meant that I don't want the way you feel at the moment exploited by anyone who trades on vulnerable people. Shit, I mean that Edward guy." He warmed to the subject. "He got started on the Sci-Fi Channel and that's where he belongs. You'd never think we were living in the twenty-first century: personal angels and spirit guides, speaking with people who've 'crossed over.'"

"Psychic visions," she interjected. "There are more things in heaven and earth than are dreamt of in your philosophy."

"And they're all one big crock! Don't get me going on that."

"I thought you already were. Like I'm John Edward and you're the great fucking Randi, out to debunk me." It was a stalemate. Whatever the empirical truth of the matter, what she was feeling was real, and she didn't need to be patronized.

They sat apart on the couch, staring directly ahead of themselves. "Listen, Rach." He was the first to proffer the olive branch. "Forget about shrinks and psychics, okay? Let's start with an eye doctor and go from there." As he looked at her through the half-light, she seemed fragile, unsure of herself. "Whatever you're experiencing is valid. I just don't want you losing your sight because you're putting it all down to psychic phenomena instead of seeing a good optometrist."

She relented, held onto him and wearily capitulated. "I don't even care what it means anymore," she insisted as they sank into each other. "I just want it to stop."

Their automatic physical intimacy eclipsed much of her soul-searching and confusion. Images came and went, but they were merely that; visual impressions, not subjugated by the tyranny of rational thought.

Jared kneaded the firm, compact flesh of Rachel's breasts. As he made his predatory ascent up the bed, like a serpent crawling out of her sexual subconscious, he reached for her beckoning upper body. She lay naked. Open and, for now, quite still. Exhausted by wild thoughts and strange events, by doubt and possibilities. She lay passive, but willing for her vital senses to be awakened. To enter the dimension of sensuality and let her rational mind turn itself off.

Her rosy nipples were the first to respond to stimulation. The erogenous zones mocked by stupid schoolboys could elicit a delight they could never take away from her. It was due to Jared, his dexterity and sensitivity. As he worked his way up her body, moistening Rachel's smooth belly with his tongue, he found those other places that had remained inaccessible to everybody except for him.

As he stretched her nipples till they stood erect, she shuddered. The titillating sensation carried down to her genital region, then back up along her spine till it built into a flood of endorphins that reached her head. Into a flood of invisible light.

She stirred, becoming active in an instinctive rather than premeditated way. As Jared rose slowly onto his hinds, he moved his hand to stroke her below.

Rachel took hold of his hand and took charge. She rose up to meet him chest to chest, cheek to cheek. It was Jared's turn to begin to lose himself now. To turn away from all verbal and rational modes of communication, reacting to stimuli alone. To express himself solely in feelings and sounds.

Rachel pulled him further down, resting his back on a pillow among the wrecked bed sheets as she took the dominant position. It was, she knew, what he favored, and she figured maybe he'd earned it. Her own enthusiasm rose slowly and steadily, as she pushed his body down and she towered above him.

The sensation was the right side of extremity. She watched his eyes narrow in intense pleasure. Their meeting in the realm of the senses began to dissolve her fear and anxiety. It was all the more pronounced for what she perceived to be happening to Jared. As he relaxed, letting himself go with the rhythmic flow, she had an impression, almost more of a feeling than a vision, of lights starting to glow around his ecstatic head.

It disorientated her for one moment, but her rhythmic motion never halted. Whereas she'd learned to view the light in fear and trepidation, this time it seemed somehow to belong to the realm they were occupying. For once, the light was only benign. Jared laughed as she threw herself into their erotic tryst with more passion than he thought her troubled mind could currently muster.

He rose, and she sank down upon him. Groaned with pleasure as she worked her way away from her confusion, from his concern. With each small, partial descent, she believed she could see the golden tint suffusing the air around Jared's panting face.

Maybe that was just the illumination of the bedside lamp. Who knew? Who cared? She wasn't going to stop now, just to check the evidence of her own senses. Jared matched her descent onto him with an undulating thrust, and soon they were locked into a mutual rhythm. He rose as she came down, until they became as one organism. Both set free by their nakedness in the warm night air, by the simultaneously hard and welcoming rapport of each other's sexual organs. By the movement that took on a life of its own, dragging them both toward its overheating point zero.

She saw it now. Saw it for sure. A golden white brightness that lit up his ecstatic, almost mindlessly contorted features. It looked right. It felt right.

With an almost clinical exactitude, they worked toward their mutual ecstasy in syncopated double-time. "Oh God..." Jared's head wasn't glowing constantly, but peaked and fell with each deep pre-orgasmic breath. Rachel could only groan. Rational communication was lost to her now, and she felt all the better for it. She felt the great tidal wave building up within her. Jared's excitement was such that he was ready to die at any time. Rachel abandoned herself to the sensation and let it take her completely, in that defining moment of beautiful cosmic madness.

The room was lit as the lights around Jared exploded. As they descended from their emotional and orgasmic peak, she saw the last blinding flash of light emanate from his head. It soon faded, as his breathing relaxed and he fell into the classic male post-coital slumber. Rachel closed her eyes too, but fell into a kaleidoscopic cascade of memories of the last couple of days.

As emanations of golden-white light reached supernova over Sunnyvale High, she saw Jared's unconscious face pass up into one of its luminous shafts and just as quickly disappear. In that one blissful moment, she decided, he'd experienced what the French call "le petit mort"—the little death that follows when a body gives itself completely over to the sexual climax.

She followed him into sleep, but hers was far less restful. It was only as her mind cleared of glowing faces, of school kids, bus passengers and the terminally ill, that she knew she wasn't going to snap back to consciousness in one panicky moment.

When she entered a familiar but softly two-dimensional street, there were no longer any luminous visages or shafts of light. She was safe in the recesses of her subconscious.

"Yo, watch out there, Mizz Stark!"

The sound of a revving engine shot by her ear, as if it was a motorcycle or a souped-up old hotrod.

But it was only Jose on his skateboard. He spun around and backed up to her.

"If yo' the dopest Englis' teacher aroun', Mizz Stark, then I'm the illest skater. Know what I'm sayin?'"

Yes, she knew. In her own middle-aged twenty-six year-old way, she thought she knew. But what did that matter? It was just so nice to see Jose again.

He appreciated the compliment. She never spoke it out loud, but he appreciated what she was thinking. This was her dream, after all.

You're not carrying that light around your head anymore, Jose. You look just like you always did.

He looked puzzled. "Yeah, I'm like I always was! I mean, I'm not gonna start lookin' like some other fool, right?"

They laughed together. But there was an underlying sadness affecting them both. He spoke of it first.

"I gotta skate on, Mizz Esss. See, just 'cos this is your dream an' all don't mean I can stop an' chill. Things is what they is."

The skyline above them kept changing in the amorphous manner of dreams. Whereas it had been the corner of Maple Street, where she last saw him skate away, now they were standing out in the yard of Sunnyvale High. Its glass-paned main building and its outposts, its gym, swimming pool and changing rooms, filled her consciousness. The surrounding streets and neighborhood were eclipsed by its omnipresence. There was nothing more to her world beyond Sunnyvale, it seemed.

Why are you so restless, skater boy? Why don't you stay here with your friends?

Jose looked sad. "I don't know. It's wack. But I ain't trippin'. Gotta go, Mizz Esss."

The horizon opened so that the schoolyard's fences disappeared. It stretched on into the nearby suburbs, and the corporate skyscrapers of the city's center. Jose balanced himself on his board as if he was expecting a great wind to suddenly bear him off.

I'm so sorry, Jose. If I'd known, if I'd understood, I'd never have let you take off and leave us.

"Yeah." He looked sad, gazing down at the wheels on his board that were starting to turn without any encouragement from him. "If I'd known too... But we didn't know, so there's no use cryin'. Just promise me, teacher lady..."

He started to sail off into the great vista beyond Sunnyvale. In a matter of moments, his stature on the horizon grew, rather than declined, as he was sucked rapidly into the city streets.

"Don't let it happen no more. Not to me or my homies."

He was far away, but he never left her field of vision. He skated miles in moments, heading toward some destination out of her view. But she could follow his path, heading toward the ascending shaft of light that awaited him. Toward the end of a rainbow composed of only one color of the spectrum, and the pot of gold at the end that was his own extinction.

SEVEN

Normality can seem like a sickness, after a period of experiencing the visionary faculty.

Rachel reflected on how the religious visionaries of earlier centuries mostly seemed scarred by their experiences. Even a beatific vision of the Holy Madonna, herself swathed in light, could define the life of the visionary to the extent where everything else in it was deemed insignificant.

That was not how she wanted to be, she told herself tersely, as she navigated the bustling corridors of Sunnyvale High School. By today's standards, even in today's supposedly god-fearing world, most of those people would be deemed psychologically unstable.

She was starting to think like Jared. It was a good defense mechanism. Somehow, after the emergent trauma of the last few days, their arguments and a semi-drunken night of surreal dreams had returned everything to normal.

Now, she was starting to view her experiences as nothing more significant than an anomaly. A blip in her general well-being. Probably even symptomatic of nervous exhaustion, just like her maddeningly rational boyfriend said.

As she approached the end of her school teaching career at Sunnyvale High, the lead weight of everyday frustration seemed to lighten. As was the trauma of what she'd recently experienced, she told herself. Everything was getting back on the level.

At the intersection where the corridor met with the entrance to the school's main hall, Rachel turned the corner that led to her classroom. It was there that she became aware.

At first, she didn't want to acknowledge it. But her shoulders began to knot as she tried to ignore the presence of the light.

She didn't even really see it at first. With the banter and clatter of the arriving students behind her, it impinged on the edges of her vision.

On a summer's day like today, the classrooms, with their wide-paned windows, were mainly lit by exterior light. On overcast days, or during the winter, the janitor or the administrative staff would turn on the bar lights that lit the corridor.

Today wasn't such a day. It wasn't unusually bright outside, and the odd cloud even hinted at a rainstorm. But the darkened corridor was not artificially lit.

The sudden awareness of an intense glow behind her, that illuminated everything in her field of vision, made her feel sick to the pit of her stomach.

Only a few short days ago, the idea that a well-lit hallway would fill her with dread would have seemed the worst kind of neurosis. Now, the feeling was inescapable. Her only chance of escaping it lay in confronting it.

This isn't what it seems, she told herself. Thinking of Jared, and his reductive way of thinking, helped to steel her, encouraged her to mock her own fears. But she could not have been prepared for the scale of what she saw.

The hallway and the main corridor were lit up. Pockets of white light tinged with golden rays were everywhere. She choked a little as she beheld the sight that a visionary or seer would have believed divine.

Kids shouting, laughing, walking, running, hurrying, loitering. Everywhere amongst them, bright pockets of light. Only some of them were the carriers. But, as they mingled in association with their schoolmates, they bathed them all in the same luminescence.

When two of the teenagers who bore the light passed each other, or came together, it was unbearable for her to look at them without squinting or flinching. None of the lights arced toward the rooftops, as with the two men she'd recently watched dying before her eyes. But all of them framed their carriers in a heavenly glow.

She could no longer ignore it, or pretend that everything was as normal. A group of pretty girls passed by, two of them framed with the ethereal lights around their heads that reflected onto their friends. In one sense, the scene was calm. None of the kids were aware of anything unusual at all. None of them seemed in pain, or fear, or distress, or anything else that the lights had seemed to warn Rachel of.

But it was too intense to blot it all out. Even with her eyes momentarily screwed shut, the lights were bright enough to intrude on her consciousness.

The kids took little notice of her. To them, she was just cranky Ms Stark. Everyone knew she was about to leave because she couldn't hack being a teacher anyway.

Brian Kelly swaggered by with a couple of his hangers-on. He threw her a look that might have been deemed facetious, but she was too entranced by his glowing demeanor to take offence. Of he and his two buddies, only one of them who wasn't in her Eng lit class didn't wear the glow.

As they passed Tony McIlhone, Brian's swinging arm made a casual swipe at the boy's carefully tousled hair, bringing two fields of light into contact with each other. Tony skillfully dodged the slap, as much from practice as from agility, and threw back some wise-ass quip at the bully.

As the two class enemies stood, mouthing off at each other, they were conjoined by their bright halos as if they were brothers. Whatever lay in wait for these disparate young human beings, her vision told her, their fate would be the same.

Of maybe thirty kids milling up and down the corridor, at least half of them wore the glow. All moving at different paces, the lights accentuated them so that all of their features, each of their movements, were illuminated. It was impossible to look away. It was akin to the most divine vision, or intense drug experience.

But Rachel couldn't look for other explanations anymore. Only she knew what it really meant. The beautiful lights spelled death. Death for all of them.

It was no good hiding behind the veil of reason. Her senses told her what her rational mind wasn't astute enough to comprehend.

At once, all the petty miseries and all the frustrations of recent months at Sunnyvale High evaporated. These are my kids, she told herself. My charges and my responsibility. No one has the same moral obligation to them that I have today.

"My angels in waiting," she whispered aloud. As she opened up her squinting eyes, she found herself studied by one of the few people in the vicinity who didn't wear the light. Mrs Kropansky wore a look of bemused concern instead.

Had she heard Rachel talk to herself?

What difference did it make now? As Kropansky hurried away, there was little doubt that the incident would be reported straight back to Principal Carr.

Rachel told herself it was just as well. Carr would have to hear about what was troubling her sooner rather than later.

"Ms Stark?"

A little voice called to her from within a pulsating field of light.

Arlie Bennington waited for her at the door of the classroom. Her small, pretty features, infused with puppy fat, were framed in a mask of throbbing light.

"Ms Stark... Are you okay?"

She was most certainly not okay. But how to tell the girl what her eyes beheld, what was racing through her mind?

Arlie looked at the tears welling up in her English lit teacher's eyes, and felt a deep sense of sadness.

Rachel Stark had always been kindly disposed toward her. Arlene was a quiet, diligent girl, whose light had often been hid under a bushel. Now it glowed too brightly for Rachel to bear.

Arlie felt for Ms Stark. Like the rest of the class, she hadn't been so tolerant or forgiving of her over the last few months. It was fine when they'd started out. Arlie was inclined to give her all, to a teacher who recognized and encouraged sensitivity and intelligence. But, as the year had wore on, Rachel Stark had given her less individual attention and spent more time locked in a battle to engage the attention of the entire class.

It was like Tony said: "Ms Stark was cool. She came here fired up with poetry and spunk. But she's tried so hard to dumb down lessons for all the assholes that she's forgotten what made her a great teacher in the first place. It's like Nietzsche said, Arlie: 'Wrestle ye not with assholes lest ye become an asshole.'"

Arlie now gazed on Ms Stark and felt guilty. All those classroom jokes about her. All the remarks about munching Prozac once her nerves got frayed. All the dirty little insinuations about her giving head to Ben Jordan, just because she'd been conscientious, or crazy, enough to encourage the zoned-out loser to aspire to something.

Arlie realized, with a sense of hurt and shame, that Ms Stark had been just as encouraging to her. And she'd never once had the backbone to stand up for her when the other kids dissed her, all because she was scared that Brian Kelly would label her a lezzie.

"No, Arlie," Ms Stark whispered. Her tearful eyes were ready to pour, but she couldn't tear her gaze from the girl's face. "I... I need to see the principal."

She turned and fled, as if she was humiliated by the state she was in.

Arlie felt bad. There were often days when she felt that way. A short, studious girl with a bobcut, her classmates could make her feel like the fattest freak in the world if she ate a custard cone in the canteen. On the days when a single prominent pimple appeared on her face, she was of the age and the sensitivity that made her feel too ugly to face the world.

There were not many people in Arlie Bennington's world to help her overcome her feelings of inadequacy, if they cared enough to notice them. Not her mom, not her stepdad, not her elder sister, not her handful of friends.

But Rachel Stark had made her feel, for a while, that she was a special, intelligent young woman. Ms Stark had made a difference. Now, Arlie feared it was too late to say thank you.

EIGHT

Kelvin Carr was permitting himself a third cup of coffee that morning. He watched his caffeine intake, along with his carbohydrate and cholesterol level, but he'd sailed triumphantly through a busy time, and could be forgiven the mild indulgence.

There had been long running battles with the board of governors over the mixed levels of state and private funding for the next semester. Then there was the balance between academic subjects and sports activities. Some of the more fuddy-duddy elements of the board saw it as undermining the school's level of achievement if some pupils were allowed to neglect studies in order to shine out on the football field or the baseball court.

But this was the twenty-first century USA, and Carr had to deal with life as it was. If a very vocal governor, and very useful fundraiser, like Marshall Kelly, wanted his thick-skulled son to get to college on a football scholarship, then adjustments had to be made, a balance had to be struck. Young Brian was no rocket scientist. Out on the field, though, he was helping Sunnyvale edge toward the top of the local high school league. Brian had the attitude of a winner, and Carr saw him graduating with very few problems at all.

Principal Carr's moment of peace was short-lived. He jolted swiftly to attention as his door flew open without ceremony, or even the courtesy of knocking.

It was Rachel Stark. His heart sank a little. She seemed flustered, panicked even.

There had been many meetings with Ms Stark over the last few months, and Carr had hoped he'd attended the last of them. Clearly, even with the imminence of her departure from Sunnyvale (or even her retirement from teaching, he'd heard tell, not that he really cared one way or the other), this was not to be.

"I need to talk to you."

Her red-rimmed eyes implored him. There was an edge of mania to her that went beyond her usual highly-strung demeanor. It bore all the hallmarks of becoming very tiresome very quickly.

Carr glanced over to his secretary, taking her own coffee break on a sofa in the office. She quietly got up to leave.

He waited for Rachel to sit. She was too manic to stay still. Irritated, he rose to his feet, looking at her critically over the top of his spectacles.

"So. What's wrong?"

Rachel found Carr as intimidating as ever. He was only about ten years older than her, but seemed to be from a different culture entirely. He'd regarded her vocational disaffection as merely the onset of personal problems.

It concerned Carr little that her Eng lit class didn't share her affection for musty old books. What were needed were graduates with a good vocational degree of literacy and numeracy, with a smattering of the sciences and, preferably, a proclivity for sports. Sunnyvale High needed to turn out winners, not bookworms.

Nothing in their previous encounters could have prepared him for today, though.

"It's the students. I believe they're all in danger."

She'd wanted his attention, and she'd got it. Even if it came from the crankiest member of staff, there was no way he was going to ignore even a hint of a threat to the school. Attentiveness and alarm registered in his face in equal measure.

"What kind of danger?"

His probing eyes demanded an answer. What he got was a vexation.

"I... I don't know," she admitted.

She was under his scrutiny now, and it wouldn't let up until he could be sure of what she was saying.

"All I know is that if we don't act, then people are going to die."

It smelled of her innate flakiness, but he couldn't let it drop. If there was some kernel of truth to what she was saying, and he ignored her, he might as well go join the employment line now.

He took her by the arm and maneuvered her into a seat. At his desk, he could assert both his authority and the height advantage that was lost if he left her flapping about the room.

"Now Ms Stark... Rachel, you need to tell me, specifically, what the problem is."

He searched her face. She seemed genuinely distressed, but he needed her to focus on their immediate problem.

"Did you overhear someone threaten the school?"

There was no response. Only a reticent searching of her conscience to find the right words. Something was making her hesitate.

"We're on the same side." He reassured her in his best pep talk tones.

"You can tell me the truth, Rachel. Is it a gang thing? Are threats going out between our kids and boys in other neighborhoods?"

Even in such a solidly middle-class area as theirs, the desire to emulate the gangbanger culture was still strong. Carr had insisted that, while Sunnyvale High had no uniform code as such, exaggeratedly baggy, low-slung pants were not appropriate school wear, and anything that hinted at gang colors was pounced on immediately.

"Or drugs? Is there someone selling drugs in the school?" Carr had heard of batches of bad homemade speed that had had fatal effects on local college kids. Expecting it to rock their socks off, its uncontrolled potency had left young people in states of stroke or cardiac arrest.

"No. No."

She shook her head. She needed him to slow down and listen while she tried to explain herself

"It might not even be a person."

Her reluctance to meet his stare suggested she knew just how insane it sounded.

"It could be... a fire."

"A fire?" His incredulity matched her discomfort. "What are you telling me? Is this some kind of health and safety issue?"

"No... I don't know. It could even be an earthquake."

Her words brought Carr up short. He was getting the wrong signals from this.

"I don't understand." He propped his chin forward on his fingers, searching her face. "How could you possibly know about an earthquake?"

She had no answer.

"Ms Stark, we are eight hundred miles from the San Andreas fault line. Why are you regaling me with some doom-and-disaster scenario about an earthquake?"

The distaste he felt for her was barely concealed below the surface. There was something about her rarified air, some ethereal quality that just didn't measure up to what he expected from somebody who lived in the real world.

For her part, Rachel always knew that he regarded her as a flake. She'd been a conscientious teacher, barely having a day off of the job even when it was starting to get her down. She dressed casually but smartly in trouser suits or long skirts, but it was always clear that for Carr, with his pristine suits and tidy nondescript hair, she just didn't make his bogus Ivy League grade.

It was time to level with him.

"I had a warning that Jose Molina was going to die."

She raised a hand to stop him interjecting.

"Not... not a personal warning. Nothing that could be imparted from one person to another. It was a more like a sign. A portent."

His deflation put her perversely at ease. Now at least he'd let her talk.

"I saw a strange light on Jose's face. I saw the same thing again later on a man who was about to die of a heart attack. I believe... I know," she corrected herself, "that it was their life force, their essence, that was about to be given up by their bodies."

Carr shook his head slowly.

"You... saw... a light?"

He struggled to find the right tone to express his derision. But now she'd spoken, it gave her the strength to continue with her message. To hell with Carr's attitude—she was right in front of him, and he had to listen to her.

"I know how it sounds. But I just saw all the kids outside the hall this morning."

She almost said "my kids," but held back.

"The light was all over them; so many of them. And I know they're going to die if we don't save them. It might be a terrorist attack, or..."

The door swinging ajar interrupted her flow. Carr blew a short whistle of relief.

Tony the Goth boy was the benign intruder.

"Are you coming back to class?" He addressed Rachel directly, with an easy familiarity.

She looked determinedly away from Tony, as if she couldn't bear to face him. Carr noted she was playing it to the hilt. He leapt from his desk and ushered the boy firmly out of the door.

"Tell the class I'll be there in a minute."

Rachel could consider her position terminated as of that moment.

The principal regarded her with incredulity and skepticism.

"If you have anything of a specific nature relating to a terrorist threat, Rachel, then I suggest we do our duty and call the federal authorities right now from this office."

What could she say? Specifics were not part of the nature of this nightmare.

"No? Well, I thought not."

She met his accusatory gaze, but couldn't match it. She was bereft, without hope.

"What am I supposed to think? You burst into my office with doomsday warnings of earthquakes and terrorism. Do you feel it's acceptable to sow panic on the basis of one insane idea?"

She had no answer. She felt defeated.

"I can only know what I know." Her voice was drained of its former insistency. "You have to believe me. Or we're letting all those children die."

That was enough. It was below Principal Carr's professional dignity to tolerate this for one moment more.

"Rachel, I've no idea what your problem is, but it's beyond my remit. I'm not a medical man."

He escorted her brusquely from her chair.

"If you're self-medicating in any way, I suggest you stop it now."

She knew he took her for a neurotic. Now, it seemed, she was a substance abuser.

"Or if you've been prescribed medication, then I suggest you ensure it's taken regularly. But either way," he had hold of her arm and was broaching no resistance, "you wanted a rest and clearly you need one."

She was escorted back into the hallway outside his office.

"Go home, Rachel. And don't come back."

She sat alone in the teacher's lounge, without a sympathetic ear. Her sobbing had stopped, but she still held her face in her hands, all too conscious of her red eyes and the streaks of tears.

Rachel didn't look up as he entered the room. She instinctively knew when it was him. Jared had a gentle, considerate gait he adopted when he had to literally tread carefully around her.

She looked up and took a deep breath. Her tear-stained face had regained its composure.

"Who told you?"

"Carr." He sat next to her on the sofa, stroking her hand. "He asked me to check on you."

That was predictable. She was still smarting from her encounter with that officious prick, and needed to know what side of the line Jared was standing on.

"And," he continued with trepidation, "he asked me to make sure you left the school grounds in a timely manner, or he'd have you escorted off."

There. It was said.

He pulled her into his arms, to put distance between the official order he had to comply with and the man that she knew he was.

"I'm not crazy."

She awaited his response. When there was none, she pushed herself out of his arms.

"You do believe me, don't you?"

He felt browbeaten. And more than a little tired of it all.

"Honestly, Rach," he tried to decline giving an opinion. "I don't know what to think anymore."

She bristled at the disloyalty. Her sense of isolation was growing by the moment.

"You're not supposed to think. You're supposed to trust me."

She was on her feet, fired up by indignation.

"And you know something? We were wrong, Jared, wrong! I shouldn't be quitting my job. This thing that's happened to me, this terrible revelation, it's a responsibility. If I'm the only person who's aware of it, who else is there to take a stand?"

He felt despondent. Just last night, he'd believed they'd nipped this obsession in the bud, and Rachel was starting to think rationally again.

"I mean, it's beyond my vocation, it's my destiny. If there's only me standing between the kids and some immense tragedy, then that's how it has to be, that's what I'm gonna do."

He was unsure if there was any way to get through to her anymore. Still, he had to try.

"Rachel... Listen to me. Please listen to me."

She was quiet.

"How are you going to stop something if you don't know what it is?"

There was no answer. No rational answer. But, to her, it was all beyond the realms of rationality by now.

"Or when it's going to happen? Or if it's going to happen?"

"I don't know."

She wanted to cling onto her hope, that the revelation that she, and only she, had experienced, could have some positive outcome. But Jared, with his damned stinking logical mind, was undermining that hope.

"What happened to you only happened to you. It's subjective. It's what you felt and what you saw and what you thought you saw."

So that was it. He thought she was crazy. Plain bat shit crazy, as her old grandpa used to say.

He paused for breath.

"Just go home, okay? I'll see you there later."

He had no more faith than fucking Carr, less belief in her than the surliest kid in class.

"I know you're worried about the kids here, but I'll keep an eye on things. I promise."

She looked on Jared with an emotional numbness. He could obviously no longer believe a word she said. But was she expected to take his promises as read? Because he was rational? Because he was sane?

"Please. Trust me."

But trust was a spent commodity these days, so it seemed.

NINE

Defeat was never more total.

Rachel knew she just had to get the hell out of there. As she approached her car, fumbling for the keys in her purse, she cursed low.

Cursed their blindness. Cursed that tight-assed fool Carr. Cursed Jared and his "reasonable" nature. Cursed the curse itself.

Or maybe I should think of it as "the gift," she mocked herself, cursing again the unwanted ability that had intruded on her life.

Once I get out of this zoo, I can reconsider my options. And I'm going to take my time doing it. As for Jared, he's gonna have to decide whether he can live with a madwoman...

"Ms Stark..."

It was a kid's voice.

Oh, not here, not now!

It was the last thing she needed. She didn't want to be reminded of the heavy sense of responsibility she felt towards them. She didn't want to be mocked by any of her Eng lit class who'd heard their flaky teacher had flipped right over the edge.

And she especially didn't want to look some unsuspecting, doomed student in the face.

"I heard about it. That you've predicted how people are gonna die."

It was Ben Jordan.

She searched his face for a sign of mockery. He seemed on the level, but still...

"Ben, this isn't something I want to discuss with you."

He was persistent, refusing to leave her side as she strode toward her car.

"I was just wondering if it's a lot of people. Like how many are we talking about?"

He was digging too deep. Maybe he wanted to sow favor with his classmates by giving them the latest dirt on mad Ms Stark. But she wasn't playing.

It was good to find her car left unmolested on this last day. She briskly unlocked the door and threw her shoulder bag on the backseat.

Ben was still hovering.

"We are not talking about it at all."

"Why not?"

There was no way the boy was going to let it be.

"Is it because there's a light on my face?"

She was poised to snap back at him, but stopped herself.

It had seemed such an unremarkable thing that she hadn't consciously noticed it. But, despite her irritation at his presence, it had given her a sense of relief.

"No, Ben. There isn't any light."

His youthful, immobile face was as sullen and inscrutable as ever. His eyes as expressionless and impenetrable. But the fact that he was merely himself, not some ethereal shade of a terrifying near future, quieted her nerves.

"But you'd tell me if there was, right? Because I'd want to know."

His concern was merely for himself.

Why should it be otherwise, she asked herself? Some of those goddamn little bastards had made his life as unpleasant as they'd made hers. His self-interest was only natural. But still, there was that aloofness about Ben, that willfully disconnected quality she found unsettling. As if nothing that didn't impact upon him personally could ever really affect him.

"I'd tell you," she reassured him. At least there was one person in this school who wasn't afraid to take her seriously.

"I like you Ms Stark."

She was sure the sentiment was sincere. It was that same sincerity that got his balls broken by the jocks in class—as if there was anything weird about a teenage boy having a mild crush on a female teacher.

"You're all about the truth."

What a strange thing to say.

What a nice thing to say.

But there was still that creepy blankness, even when he was expressing his affection.

"I like you too, Ben."

And it was true. She did. Or rather, she had liked him.

In their early days as schoolmistress and pupil, she saw willing, she saw a relative openness and she saw promise. But Ben had shut all of it down, as surely as he pulled the blinds down on the world at large.

She never really knew what was paining him about his life. Oh, Brian Kelly and his confederation of meatheads were a pain in the ass, for sure. But then, they inflicted the same crap on Arlie and Tony in the same class, and those two had found their own coping mechanisms.

But Ben's response was to shut down. To give up hope in his school career, in his future, in what constituted his own sense of self.

She knew it was childish to take it personally, but he'd also given up hope in her, as a teacher who could have made a difference.

It had bothered her. She'd made discreet enquiries about his home life, but didn't get too far. It was considered untoward for any teacher apart from the heads of his grade or the principal to take too personal an interest.

Besides, Carr had warned her, if there were anything going on that warranted the attention of the school or the social services, then the appropriate authorities would deal with it. Otherwise, someone's family life was off limits.

"What are you gonna do now?"

The kid was more blank than frank, but he was trying to show concern in his own way. That was nice.

"I guess I'll go home."

Rachel sighed at her own understatement.

He nodded in consideration. "That's a very good idea."

Like she had a thousand other options. But he was an immature boy, trying to be helpful toward her the way she'd once tried to help him. And failing just as hopelessly.

They stood awkwardly at the edge of the car park. Waiting for one of them to bring this stilted, faltering conversation to a close.

"Bye, Ms Stark."

Such a simple statement. Yet so imbued with finality.

"Goodbye, Ben," she echoed after a moment's hesitation.

There was nothing more to be said. Avoiding any further eye contact, he turned and ran back to the school with an awkward, shambling gallop.

So that was it. Bye from the pupils of Sunnyvale High School. They couldn't all make the farewell party, but they sent along one of their most despised and alienated schoolmates as their representative.

Bye to three futile years of hard work and aspiration. Bye to her teaching career.

All encapsulated in one simple statement from a messed-up teenager.

But now she was indulging in self-pity, as surely as Ben Jordan himself. There was a life to get on with. Though, in truth, she had no idea where it was taking her from here.

She slid into the driver seat and rattled the ignition key, agitated. For a moment, she just sat and looked at the quiet open road outside the school perimeters.

It didn't work. Trying to put everything that had occurred behind her was akin to pretending it never happened. Oh, it was tempting alright, but it required a kind of self-hypnosis that she wasn't ready for.

Besides which, everything she had experienced still rang with truth. If she bought into their perception of her, to Jared's and Carr's, then she was a deeply disturbed woman spinning out of control. But she didn't feel that way.

In fact, she'd never felt more focused. She wasn't going to hop into the little box they'd built for her marked "Delusional Behavior." Damn it, their explanations for what she'd seen and felt were desperate. They were trying too hard to impose rationality on something that had its own internal logic.

Her interpretation made more sense to her. It was frightening, but it resonated with truth. Intellectually, it still commanded the most convincing explanation. On an emotional level, there was no doubt in her mind at all. But that, she reflected sourly, must be because she was an Unstable Neurotic Female.

A vista of consciousness had opened up to her that wasn't perceptible to anyone else. It was scary, but she absolutely, fundamentally believed it to be true.

And what of its implications?

Everything that had happened was pointing in the direction of disaster or tragedy. And no one, herself included, was doing a damn thing about it.

She could try to pull her mind away from the dread consequences for the kids—for *her* kids—but why should she? It wasn't her who had marginalized her warnings to the point where they were deemed inconsequential.

But still—how much better was it to be self-righteous and proven correct, when you yourself had given up on trying to avert disaster? Was that any better than being cynical and unprepared?

She couldn't stop thinking of her students. Of poor, insecure Arlie and dreamy Tony. Even of brutish, stupid Brian. Of all their classmates, all their young, unspoiled faces, all that promise. Was it really going to be wiped out?

She thought of Ben, one of the few kids she could say with any certainty was going to survive the disaster. She wished she knew how, so that she could tell the others to follow his lead.

Maybe it was his detachment from them that offered the route to escape. As an unpopular kid, he was less likely to be present wherever they were, and maybe less likely to be there when disaster occurred.

Maybe.

But his detachment was more emotional than physical. He still didn't have the sense to put himself apart from Brian and the other bullies in class, as if he had a yearning to be part of the same set that rejected him.

How could emotional detachment save him from whatever fate most of the others would share?

Something about it unsettled her. It was as if her mind were looking for links, connections, for "ley lines," heaven help her, that ran beneath the seemingly unconnected lives of Ben Jordan and his classmates.

"That's a very good idea." His innocuous statement about her returning home played back in her mind.

She was unsettled by him, but there was nothing concrete she could point to.

So was she going to sit there all day, contemplating the steering wheel? Or was there any more positive action that she could take?

Are you kidding? Carr will have me run out of town on a rail.

But there again, what could he do if he found her back on the premises?

Kick my ass back out again, just like he already has. Big deal.

It was settled.

She walked nonchalantly back in through the school gates at the end of a recess period. No attention drawn to just one straggler. And with everyone in class, there was no one around, at least not yet, to notice the return of the errant Ms Stark.

It was madness, but she had to satisfy her need to know, which was so much more than an idle curiosity, somehow. Even if it didn't turn up much, it seemed to be the only course.

Rachel took a deep breath and a turn off the main hallway.

She was among the endless rows of student lockers. It was silent there now. No rushing, no metallic clatter of unlocked doors. Just her and the inscribed names of every student in the school. Many she didn't even know. All of whom, in her desperate, directionless manner, she sought to save from fate.

Working her way up, down and across the alphabetical order, she found the locker she was looking for.

Well, Ben Jordan. Forgive the intrusion but teacher wants to take a peek inside your private world.

She pulled out a small screwdriver from her breast pocket, part of a randomly assembled emergency toolkit from her glove compartment. It wasn't much bigger than one of the smaller electrical tools, but it did its job.

She gritted her teeth and hoped not to attract too much attention. It was just about small enough to sink into the keyhole, working it from left to right in the hope it would give.

Add burglary to the trespass charge, she told herself. Catching herself in the act, it seemed like insanity. How could she have thought the boy's locker would yield up anything that made this little enterprise worthwhile? What was she thinking?

A click and a rattle dispersed the thought.

She'd bust the lock. It popped out of its hole and rattled to a halt on the floor.

Tensing herself, she pulled the locker door open gently to minimize any creaking noise.

It spilled its load immediately. Stuffed full of untidy folders and notebooks, and the boy's private journal, the chaotic mess came crashing to the floor.

Damn.

Scooping up the whole lot, she opened up the first folder at random. In one moment, she was privy to what lay at the heart of one malcontent American high school kid.

TEN

Ben's A4 folder was of the tongue-flap kind. Typical of the boy's sloppy attitude, it had no lever arch prongs, or cord, or anything that would stop the loose-leaf papers from falling out onto the floor.

Rachel tried to keep his chaotic collection together, each of the magazine cuttings or newspaper clippings falling loose due to their irregular sizes. It was as if Ben were harboring a secret passion, a fan portfolio similar to those other kids would dedicate to sports, rock or TV stars.

But even at first glance, she could tell that Ben's obsession was disturbingly different.

The yellowing photos of teenaged boys—mostly younger than him—made her wonder if Brian Kelly wasn't correct in his brutish assessment of his classmate. Perhaps Ben was a "faggot" after all, and was struggling to come to terms with his sexuality.

But the hoarding of photos of unfamiliar faces, the lack of athletic or full body shots, suggested something more than a homoerotic obsession. These high school kids had all made the news at some point, though most of their names and faces had long since been forgotten.

But not by Ben. Most of the faded glossy or newsprint cuttings contained a summation of the news story each boy was grimly attached to. These cuttings had, in turn, been stuck to a piece of colored card with curling edges. Each one carried notes by Ben on each individual kid. It was still kind of shambolic, but it entailed more care than Ben had shown in his schoolwork for some time.

But its content was disturbing. On a more earthly level, it was nearly as unsettling as what Rachel had been experiencing for the last few days. What made fifteen year-old Kipland "Kip" Kinkel stand out from his peers was that, on Thursday the twenty-first May, 1998, he had shot dead his parents before heading off to school. At school, he fired off fifty-one shots, blowing away one seventeen year-old boy in the cafeteria and hitting a sixteen year-old kid in the head who later died next day.

It grabbed Rachel's attention with a jolt. On the long strip of colored board, Ben had marked it all down with a star rating system. Just like he was the high school amateur theatre critic, commenting on individual performances.

Kinkel's "arsenal" won an unqualified four stars. It consisted of a .22 rifle, a nine-millimeter Glock handgun and a .22 semi-automatic Ruger pistol. Ben had pondered in the margins, "More firepower?" in brackets. There was another apparent plus that Ben couldn't make his mind up on. "Kip lives, his enemies die! Way to go!" But, he conjectured in the margins, “Better to live your life in jail–or go out in a blaze of glory?”

Rachel found it all too chilling. This was what a boy who once seemed to have some intellectual potential was devoting his inner life to? As far as she could see, Ben was indulging in a fantasy. But it was a fantasy that was wholly negative, and could only further warp the way that he related to others and the way that his peers saw him. Was this hero-worshiping? Clearly, no one had ever taken the time to check what was going on inside Kip Kinkel’s head. The bigger tragedy to her, it seemed, was that a potentially good kid like Ben was subject to the same indifference.

She flicked through Ben’s dilapidated file. As she’d suspected, the Kinkel boy was far from alone. Ben approached his subject with an anthropologist’s zeal, if not the same insight, trawling back into the pre-millennial years that, for most kids, would be pre-history.

Rachel was a mass of contradictory emotions. She looked on the puppyish faces of Mitchell Johnson, thirteen, a full-faced boy who may have been carrying excess puppy fat, and Andrew Golden, eleven, his pixie-faced, crew-cut little friend. Her melancholia intensified to horror.

They were no more than babies. Surely Ben couldn’t fantasize about being a part of this dysfunctional little pair, however messed up he was in his own head? But something about their sad, squalid story obviously appealed to an appallingly black sense of humor. “SMALL SOLDIERS!!!” he’d written in the space below their pathetic little mug shots.

On Wednesday twenty-fourth March 1998, these small soldiers had dressed themselves up in camouflage. Mitchell had driven his stepfather's van to their place of learning, Westside Middle School in Jonesboro, Arkansas. On the previous day, Mitchell had told some of his classmates, "Tomorrow you will find out if you live or if you die." Tragically, none of them had taken him seriously.

The little boys' arsenal won them a straight four-star approval rating from Ben. They'd grown up in Southern hunting grounds, and they filled the van with all manner of rifles and handguns–including a high-powered 30.06 hunting rifle. They'd drawn their intended victims out of the school into open forestland when Andrew set off the fire alarm. "Slick!!" Ben had written in the margin.

Sick. Rachel shook her head in despair. It seemed to her the most introverted school misfits possessed that morbid degree of sensitivity of which she herself had been accused. But these boys, these high school shooters, were only ever sensitive to the needs of themselves. As for others, they might as well not exist. They were just targets, symbolic receptacles for all the hate and the resentment that the fucked up little boys with the guns felt.

It also seemed that the nation had undergone a series of convulsions in the late twentieth century–a kind of millennial mini-apocalypse that led young adolescent or pre-pubescent boys to explode into violence. She hoped it was a phase that had now passed. She also hoped, against hope that it might pass for Ben—as disturbed as she now realized he was.

After all, why should someone who was now a young man, however alienated, fixate on the misdeeds of his juniors? In some cases, those messed-up kids were probably pre-pubescent.

But the answer already lurked in the back of her mind. It had become a negative cultural icon, the apotheosis of American high school violence. Her memory had already brought it to mind before she thumbed through a big wedge of board-backed clippings stapled haphazardly together.

The first image she saw resonated with the revulsion that everyone in the country had felt when it occurred. Everyone, it seemed, except for the nation's Ben Jordans.

It was a murky "grab" taken from CCTV footage, further downgraded by being downloaded from the Internet. But its content was all too familiar. It showed two young men in beanie hats, teenagers of roughly Ben's age, striding through an apparently deserted school cafeteria with weapons in their hands.

The teenager on the left had his back turned to the CCTV camera, as if overseeing some activity that was off-screen. The boy in the center had strode purposefully, menacingly, down a small flight of stairs on the right, and was patrolling the center of the screen in profile. In his hand was a small automatic or semi-automatic weapon. The timecode at the bottom of the screen read: L 11:57: 20 - 63 AM

04/20/99. The time and date of the Columbine High School massacre, in Littleton, Colorado.

"UBER-HEROES!!!" Ben had written in the space below their picture. "It takes a man to do a man's work!!!"

Rachel's concern had turned to a faint nausea. She recognized the boy in the center as Dylan Klebold, seventeen, and the kid with his back turned as his apparently more dominant friend Eric Harris, who had recently turned eighteen.

Their mutual "achievement" was that they had wasted the lives of twelve of their classmates and one of their teachers. As if to underline the vicious futility of their actions, they ended their killing spree on the morning of twentieth April 1999 by blowing their own brains out.

To Ben, though, this cruel and pointless tragedy was some kind of teenage *Gottedammerung*. Flicking agitatedly through the sheets, it became clear how he regarded their crimes as masterpieces of planning, execution and style. Incredibly, he seemed to believe Eric and Dylan had arrived at the solution to all their personal problems via their vile deeds. American high school, Rachel reflected, is one of the most merciless environments in the world.

Harris and Klebold clearly would have agreed with her. They fretted under the weight of abuse by their counterparts to Brian Kelly, complaining about ridicule and of being made into outcasts. Most disturbingly, they had a vehicle to express their hatred—their "basement tapes." An amateur video they made showed them loading up guns and firing at students in the school hallway. It gave the lie to everyone, herself included, who'd believed if you wrote down or playacted the crime, it took away the impetus to commit it.

"TRUE LIFE ART!!" Ben had scrawled in the margin. It was unlikely he'd ever see the video in total, apart from clips on TV news shows, but his hero-worship knew no bounds. She was more shocked to see him share their Nazi fixation. Heavily annotating a report on why they chose twentieth April to go homicidal, Ben's handwritten scrawl screamed, "Remember twentieth April 1889–birth date of AH SIEG HEIL!!!"

Why don't alienated little know-nothings like Ben ever get the point? The only social misfit that Hitler ever tolerated was Hitler himself. Nazi Germany had been a nation that had put all its jocks, all its Brian Kellys, into jackboots, setting them free to stomp on the faces of its Ben Jordans with impunity.

But to these kids, any expression of anti-social sentiments, of nihilism, was meaningful. Eric Harris had posted a warning message on his website as early as March 1998:

"God, I can't wait until I can kill you people... I'll just go to some downtown area in some big fucking city and blow up and shoot everything I can."

Ben echoed those words like a cry of hallelujah. The scrawled phrase, "I CANT WAIT UNTIL I CAN KILL YOU PEOPLE" appeared with alarming regularity throughout his Columbine scrapbook, in variously colored marker pen.

His enthusiasm was unbounded, unchecked, terrifying. He rated their arsenal at the full four star–on account of their TEC-DC9 semiautomatic rifle and as many as fifty homemade bombs they used to booby trap their school.

In passages relating to the boys' insane plans, Ben excitably acclaimed them as "VISIONARIES!" They had planned to start their attack at 11.00am, as eventually transpired, and to kill upwards of five hundred students. But this was to be only the start.

After the initial massacre, they intended to storm the nearby streets, slaughtering neighbors and the residents of apartment buildings. In the unlikely instance that law enforcement hadn't eradicated them by this point, they intended to hijack a plane and crash it into the center of New York City. The idea had made Ben ecstatic.

"DYLAN BENNETT KLEBOLD, BORN ELEVENTH SEPTEMBER 1981," he wrote, drawing a numerological connection between his nihilist heroes and that grander, but no more terrifying atrocity of two and a half years later. Rachel could detect no disappointment arising from how they only managed to destroy fifteen human beings, including themselves. All she could detect was an alienated empathy; a dangerous, self-deluding empathy.

"If you could see all the anger I've stored over the past four fucking years..." She read Dylan Klebold's self-justifying words, hearing them spoken in Ben's voice. "You made me what I am. You added to the rage... I'm going to kill you all."

His partner in crime's final testament was infamously posted on his website. Ben had framed the text on a single sheet of card, heading it, "THE PROPHECY OF ERIC DAVID HARRIS." The word "prophecy" echoed in her mind. Ben was romanticizing the words of a socially maladjusted kid. He had no real idea of what the term "prophecy" implied, and how heavy it weighed on someone who believed they had the "gift."

"By now, it's over. If you are reading this, my mission is complete. Your children who have ridiculed me, who have chosen not to accept me, who have treated me like I am not worth their time are dead. THEY ARE FUCKING DEAD...

"Surely you will try to blame it on the clothes I wear, the music I listen to, or the way I choose to present myself, but no. Do not hide behind my choices. You need to face the fact that this comes as a result of YOUR CHOICES.

"Parents and teachers, you fucked up. You have taught these kids to not accept what is different. YOU ARE IN THE WRONG. I have taken their lives and my own—but it was your doing. Teachers, parents, LET THIS MASSACRE BE ON YOUR SHOULDERS UNTIL THE DAY YOU DIE."

She found the self-righteousness nauseating. But still, the vague sense that the adult world held some responsibility for Harris and Klebold, that something could have been done to stop them, or even help them, haunted her. It was much too late for them. How much time did she have to save Ben Jordan? Was it too late?

Ben had set Harris's testament in a self-drawn frame, as if they were the words of the Founding Fathers or Lincoln's Gettysburg Address. On close inspection, the detail testified to his confused adolescent mind. Crudely drawn, smiling faces, contrasted by frowns. Death's head skulls. Knives. Guns.

Rachel saw how, on an adjoining card, Ben had attached instructions from some sicko website marked, "Simple Tips for launching strikes." It may have been satire of the crudest kind—or it may have been some fuck-up genuinely encouraging kids to turn homicidal, while hiding behind his First Amendment rights. "Of course you should not do these things or make these devices mentioned here. This is for research and understanding school attacks and tactics," ran the gloating weasel words.

If she was feeling charitable, she might have seen it as someone's unfunny idea of a sick joke. As a part of Ben's personal archive, it literally set alarm bells ringing: "Try to attack an assembly or start a fire to get a fire drill. This concentrates targets into a small area. Try to concentrate on your worst emotional experiences and abuse. If you cannot face your attackers, a firebomb or fire-bottle through a window will simply start you off. It's all on from there."

Then her blood froze. "Taking a hostage, if possible a tiny female, can aid you. Also remember to have a good healthy breakfast. A banana or two just before and even an energy drink such as Red Bull."

The visionary faculty had been held at bay, but now it was going into overdrive. She imagined

Arlie—poor, delicate, shy little Arlie—held at gunpoint or knifepoint by Ben. This was no preternatural vision or prophecy, just a visualization of a damaged young man exploding onto his surrounding environment.

She had to tell someone. This wasn't one of her ethereal visions. How much more real did anyone require that this should become? Her mind seethed with indignation. The constant dismissals, the questioning of her sanity—no one, not the fucking principal or even her own goddamned boyfriend, would accept that her insight, her precognition, had any relationship to the world they lived in.

Well, let them deny this. There was no longer any doubt that the fate of the kids—of *her* kids—was concealed in that strange, twilit zone that she now inhabited, between the everyday and the ethereal.

When she opened the final pages that revealed Ben's private world, a grandiosely inscribed private journal, nothing could remain in doubt for one moment longer. It was headed:

"THE ETERNAL AND EVERLASTING TESTAMENT OF BENJAMIN JAMES JORDAN"

"Whoever opens the pages of this book be warned and be afraid. You are unlocking the TRUTH about what happened that fateful day at Sunnyvale High School. This is my testament to the world and you are privileged to share it. But are you and your children prepared to pay the PRICE for what you have inflicted on me and others like me?"

As she skim read the boy's obsessive rants, she reflected on how it had been all but impossible to get him to hand in an English essay for the last eighteen months. It made her heart sink to realize what he'd been putting his creative energies into.

It was even more disturbing to realize that Ben was writing with an eye toward posterity. He really did seem to believe that by the time anyone was able to peek into his journal, they would be aware of who he was and what he had done. He'd even dignified himself by spelling out his name in full, that peculiar privilege that America bestowed on her most infamous assassins—John Wilkes Booth, Lee Harvey Oswald, James Earl Ray and Mark David Chapman. Or scumbag serial killers like Henry Lee Lucas and John Wayne Gacy.

"This is the blueprint of one of the most momentous events to rock the planet. The moment of TRUTH that was first heard when the alarm bells rang at Columbine. But that was only the BEGINNING. Eric and Dylan were heroic martyrs but they were only my John the Baptists. I am the TRUE MESSIAH OF HATE.

"Be of strong heart, ye who read on. For you will have to face the TRUTH of what you and your children, what your stinking society has done. But while you've been sleeping, some INDEPENDENT GENIUS has taken the matter in hand."

It grieved her to realize that Ben had lifted a quote from George Bernard Shaw, a satiric statement about Jack the Ripper. She'd always suspected that Ben's internal world could be richer and more literary than those of his peers who wrote him off as a loser. Now she could see that, with little or no encouragement, the boy had cultivated something that came close to erudition.

But to what end, what purpose?

His ramshackle frontispiece was prefaced by further words from his hero, Eric Harris. These were no threats of annihilation, but a blood-spattered sci-fi story the boy had handed into his English teacher, three months before his rampage of murder.

The clichéd space opera recalled a hokey sci-fi send-up called *Starship Troopers* Jared had rented from Blockbuster Video. Harris's version told of an attack by space aliens, concentrating on its gory aftermath: "The deathly dark glow of light from above was barely enough to notice the blood and flesh splattered on the large sheets of granite that passed for walls... Arms, legs and heads were tossed about as if a small child turned on a blender with no lid in the middle of the room. Some were burnt off, some torn."

According to the pages made available for public access on the Internet, his Eng lit teacher had awarded him a C+, commenting, "Yours is a unique approach and your writing works in a gruesome way."

Rachel felt that was horribly generous—but then, her perception was tempered by how the boy ultimately regarded life and death as one big video game, full of guns and gore.

What was more disturbing to her was how Ben, a kid who could have developed fine literary sensibilities, had used this crap as a springboard for his personal fantasy-cum-manifesto.

* * *

"It was in the early years of the third millennium that AMERICA was awakened to the pain and turmoil that lived within her. One heroic soldier, one martyr decided to stand up to the RETARDED ass feeders who dominate our society and say NO MORE.

"The battlefield was a place called SUNNYVALE HIGH, but it could have been any other number of schools or offices across the country. IN FACT once the heroic example of the rebel who fought back against the TYRANNY was set, THOUSANDS would follow on. NO MORE would the quiet geniuses suffer in silence. NO MORE would AMERICA'S parents believe that they could drop their little boy or girl at the high school gates and have them turn out into fine little ZOMBIE CITIZENS. As of that fateful and HISTORIC DAY any of the thoughtless MINDLESS little cretins who dared to make their SUPERIORS life a misery would be wiped out. WITHOUT MERCY. From now on, they would PAY AND PAY AND PAY.

"The reason it all began at Sunnyvale was that MIDDLE AMERICAS zombie children picked the wrong goat to pick on. BENJAMIN J JORDAN had been waiting for years for his moment to RISE UP like the KRAKEN out of the sea.

"They poked and prodded him. They INSULTED him and denied his INTELLIGENCE. The jocks called him WUSSY and FAGGOT. The PROM QUEENS and the cheerleaders and every other STUPID little bitch imaginable laughed at him like he was just half a man. Like they wouldn't be down on the floor sucking his damn DICK if he was one of the popular kids with a RICH DADDY and his own fucking sports car.

"It was all good BASIC TRAINING. It put the IRON in his soul and the METAL in his mettle. They could NEVER KNOW just what a favor they were doing him. All the while he was biding his time, waiting his CHANCE.

"At home they trained him up even better. His STOOPID old man never saw the latent genius that lay in his son. He POKED and PRODDED. He RILED and BELITTLED. He called his red-blooded son a FAGGOT all because none of the stupid little bitches would even recognize a GENIUS if they saw one, leave alone give up their STOOPID rich jock boyfriends. His old man said he never had no future but cleaning out the crapper at Burger King.

"Thank you, Dad. If you hadn't been such an ASSHOLE then I might never have shown the WORLD what I could ACHIEVE. I might never have shown my SKILL STRENGTH & COURAGE. I might never have shown MY FEARLESSNESS and felt THEIR FEAR. AND YOURS.

"I might never have set an example and become an AMERICAN HERO."

The ranting first page was interrupted by a section headed "AMERICAN HEROES". Rachel flicked through it impatiently. It was the standard killer-worshipping dross that she'd come to expect from him. She passed over the self-regarding, unperceptive faces of Harris and Klebold that she'd come to despise.

But something made her halt at the other entries. These weren't kids, but grown men. Unattractive, unsure-looking little men, to be sure, but grown adults. Adults with a lifetime of petty resentment festering behind their eyes. Or with that blank, self-insulated look that Ben had perfected in himself.

These "heroes" included a man in his forties named James Huberty–who cracked one day in 1984, and shot dead twenty-one customers at a Californian McDonald's. The text attributed a quote to a message he gave his wife: "I'm going hunting humans."

Ben was ecstatic over this. He repeated the phrase in huge block capitals, highlighting it in every color of marker pen. He also used the phrase as the subheading for his next piece of fantasy masquerading as confession–or was that confession masquerading as fantasy?

"The day when REALITY and TRUTH were brought home to Sunnyvale was like any other. The SOLDIER Ben Jordan skipped classes for he truly had nothing to learn. He'd passed far beyond their infantile level and wanted nothing more to do with their stinking school system."

Rachel winced at his conceit. But she could see now what should have been obvious long ago: Ben was an intelligent kid with learning difficulties. When he found that he couldn't progress beyond a certain stage, his low self-esteem had made him cut off and disassociate. She had a strong feeling of failing him, just as badly as he'd failed himself.

"Outside class he was ACCOSTED by the MORONS who made his life miserable for THREE YEARS. He let them slap him and steal his hat. He let them SPIT ON HIM and call him FAGGOT. He let their leader, JOCKMAN, think he had him all messed up.

"Yeah, BRING IT ON FOOLS. Let them have their fun. It was the last kindness anyone would ever show them. LET THEM ENJOY IT WHILE IT LASTS. If they only knew. But he had BIGGER PLANS to make, BIGGER FISH to fry.

"It was an operation of MILITARY PRECISION and he couldn't be distracted. GOTH BOY passed by on his way to Eng lit and dropped a superior SNEER. Yeah, sneer on, FAT LITTLE MASCARA MONKEY. Your momma's gonna be sneering out the other side of her ASSHOLE when she's scraping your STOOPID frightwig hair off the walls along with your FRIGGIN' BRAINS. HA!"

It may have been filtered through a juvenile mentality, but the hate was all too real. Rachel could feel it coming out of his journal in waves.

"GOTH BOY and PIXIE GIRL are the new teacher's pets in the lit class. They took up the slack when Soldier Jordan directed his CONSIDERABLE TALENTS elsewhere. FUCK 'EM. They too had lessons to learn. They had to learn that GENIUS don't WHORE ITSELF for grades. Goth Boy had to learn that GENIUS can't be marked on an exam paper, it's the will to go one further. Pixie Girl had to learn to appreciate when she was offered FINE WINE, instead of drinking FREAKIN' ROOT BEER."

There they all were, comic-book caricatures of the other students who populated Ben's lonely little world: Brian as the mindless, hated Jockman, Tony as the despised, preening Goth Boy. Was that Arlie as Pixie Girl? And was that resentment that Ben, the boy who put on that his lights were on with no one home, wasn't able to grab a little of Arlie's attention?

Her curiosity as to what archetype would describe herself was soon satisfied.

"Both of 'em kissed ass to MIZZ POETRY HO. They learned all their lines and did all their DUMB-ASS idiot homework but she still knew. GENIUS don't whore itself for grades. POETRY HO was smart. She knew some of what was inside BENJAMIN J JORDAN though she didn't know the whole story. But she was the only REAL PERSON out of the whole damn teaching faculty. The only lady teacher he didn't PUKE to look on and the only teacher PERIOD to show him any KINDNESS. Mizz Poetry Ho was all about TRUTH."

She'd known it, but always thought it was too inconsequential to comment on. Ben Jordan had a schoolboy crush on her. Now it was just too sad. And too alarming.

"She was the one stinking human in this whole FILTHY MAGGOT INSTITUTION who'd escape his revenge. He had to have one LIVING BEING who wasn't scared to tell the TRUTH about what happened.

"Let JOCKMAN and his RETARD BUDDIES splatter like bugs on a windshield. Let the prom queens pray for their momma or a QUICK DEATH. Let Goth Boy BEG for his life and SUCK LEAD DICK.

"The Poetry Ho would KNOW. And Pixie Girl would have to LEARN."

There was something in his ranting that rang true. It may have been a distorted, one-dimensional view of school life, but he was venting his spleen, purging all his seemingly dormant emotions into it.

Rachel flicked through the chaotic text, through Ben's cryptic margin notes and macabre little doodles, searching for a clearer statement of his intent–if, indeed, that was what this was.

She stopped turning the pages. Something relatively mundane, photostat copies of some catalogue pages, arrested her attention. Ben, a young man from a modest background, had been window-shopping for expensive firearms. Her eye hurriedly scanned up and down the pages. They were hunting rifles, and there were several models that he'd asterisked and annotated:

"CZ-550–Czech variation on classic Mauser 98."

"Varmint 550 PO–modern American version of Mauser and Czech equivalents."

"Safari 550 Dangerous Game Rifle–knock a second asshole into an elephant at five hundred yards. Too expensive."

On the next page, one of the entries met with his approval:

"Remington Model 7400–semi-automatic. Powerful. Affordable. Leave this page lying around for the old man to see. He may not know it yet, but this is gonna be his new deer-hunting rifle."

On the next page, Ben had drawn a circle around an ad for Kodiak Super Premium Bonded Core bullets–"for deep penetration."

God bless the Second Amendment.

On a further page, he'd been crossing off a selection of hunting knives. The one that caught his fancy was the American Heritage Eagle Bowie Knife. With a fifteen-inch blade, and the classic curved knifepoint, it seemed to be the right weapon for Ben's fantasy about "hunting humans."

Or maybe it wasn't such a fantasy.

"The day when REALITY and TRUTH came down on Sunnyvale High started with a fire alarm. It wasn't a real fire. But there was real danger.

"BENJAMIN J JORDAN, martyr to the NAKED TRUTH, made sure of that.

"As they all came filing out of their classrooms it was like FREAKIN' NOAH'S ARK, two by two—no, fuck that, they were LEMMINGS running four by four. Then the lead started raining down and they scattered. Four by four eight by eight friggin' sixteen by sixteen.

"THIS is the first moment of TRUTH! CRACK! The first round hits the concrete and they all start squealing.

"BANG! There's some cheerleader hit in the leg and the first one of the prey goes down. There's plenty more where that came from. That's only the first little pebble. There's an AVALANCHE on its way

"Look at 'em all NOW! Not so clever. Not so tough. Not so brave. Not so DAMNED SURE of themselves. Not so freakin' ANYTHING anymore!

"The second round hits and they don't know where to turn. The girl in the ra-ra skirt is still now. HA! Strike up a cheer for THAT!

"There's too many of the STOOPID shits. They're trapped. The school gates are LOCKED and they can only look up to see where the shots are raining down from.

"They're raining down from ABOVE, stoopid! You musta pissed off your one true savior, JESUS KA-RRIST!

"Think again, DUMBASS, cuz you did worse—you offended ME, Ben J Jordan, up here on the ROOF. And in case you ain't recognized it yet, I am now YOUR GOD.

"SPLAT! One empty head blows open like a pink watermelon. Then another, then another. The first of MANY MANY MANY. Good shooting, no, amigo?

"Do you understand NOW? Can you stop squealing and screaming for long enough to recognize the TRUTH? THIS is REALITY. Your popularity, your STOOPID sports games, your smart car, your girlfriend, your boyfriend, your senior prom, your graduation ring, your 'girl and boy most likely to' all count for NOTHING!

"NOTHING. Do you understand now? Do you finally see how everything you are and everything you're so sure of can be blown away by one who has the GENIUS and the WILL to do so?"

Rachel's mind reeled. For all the chaotic flow of his consciousness, the bludgeoning underlining and the constant changes in tense, the mad fantasy was imbued with passion. Ben meant it. The only question that flip-flopped in her mind was whether he had the depraved will to turn his fantasy into reality.

"When all lay in bloody CHAOS, when heads and bodies and arms and legs were a tangle of weeping meat, the AMERICAN HERO came down from his eagles nest to survey the territory he had CONQUERED."

He was back to describing events as if it were a matter of historical record, told from his own egomaniacal point of view.

"There was much BAWLING and SCREAMING and BEGGING FOR MERCY. HA! Don't waste your breath maggots! Only HE WHO HAS THE WILL to destroy has the power to decide who will SURVIVE. Do you think all your STUPID WORDS, all your BULLYING, all your INDIFRENCE matter to me ANYMORE?"

It so obviously did. Rachel was almost ashamed to recognize his hurt and pain. Yeah, indifference, she reflected. Their indifference was always the killer. It was clear that Ben, like her, was simply too sensitive to withstand the minor brutality of an environment like Sunnyvale High. Or any high school, anywhere in the United States. But her sensitivity had manifested itself in an ability to see through a crack in the fabric of reality—into the secrets of life and death that Ben fantasized about having control over. Call it psychic perception, call it madness, even call it "nervous exhaustion," like Jared did. It was still as real as anything ever encountered in her day-to-day life.

Just as Ben's dreams of validation by mass murder were real to him.

"With his Remington 7400 reloaded, the hero JORDAN stalked fearlessly across the yard. He knew that the forces of law and order, the PIGS that the mommies and daddies of Sunnyvale paid taxes for to keep their own PIGGIES safe would soon be upon him. He didn't care. The PIGS had their job to do and he had his DESTINY to fulfill.

"So little TIME to waste. So many INFERIOR beings to wipe out. With his GLOCK pistol cocked in his left hand, BJJ followed the sound of screaming and begging. Whoever was WEAK enough to beg for his mercy was the least deserving of it.

"Oh please, Ben. Let me go home. I wanna see my MOTHER!!!

"BANG! Nice try, Stacy! That's one less member of the Sunnyvale elite who's gonna make fun of the silent kids, the silent GENIUSES, in future.

"He didn't have to aim, just followed the sound of her wailing voice. The DUM-DUM BULLET blasted into her nose and exploded her stoopid BRAINS out the back of her head all over her dumb jock BOYFRIEND.

"HA! Try smoothing that one out with a powder puff, BITCH!

"Please dude! Hey man! You and me never had no beef, right? I never broke your balls with the other guys!!!

"BEGGING for MERCY with pieces of his girlfriend's brain stuck between his teeth. Less DIGNITY than a MAGGOT!

"BANG! BANG! The dum-dums hit the cowering jock in the throat, traveled horizontal down his spine and blew themselves out of his ASS!

"EVERYWHERE there were cowering bleeding STUPID ASS kids. Their CRYING AND PUKING could be heard right up into the heavens. A whole bunch of them prayed for MERCY to a GOD who didn't hear them.

"BJ JORDAN stepped over them and looked down in DISGUST. Their petty little SUFFERING was unimportant. What about the suffering their kind inflicted on others? What about the MURDER OF THE SOUL that's committed every time one of them PERSECUTES someone so far superior to them?

"From the school hall to the outer fence, there were hundreds of dead, dying and bleeding ENEMIES. It was like a scene from the CIVIL WAR. But BJJ knew there was so much more to be done before it could be said that the ENEMY was defeated."

He was exaggerating the likely fatalities in a kind of grandiose frenzy—the way the Columbine boys had when they imagined they could destroy a whole city.

"At the OUTER PERIMETERS the COWARDS ran. Those without the MORAL COURAGE to claim BJJ as their NOBLE ENEMY.

"Say guys, why are you taking off? Why don't you stay and break my balls NOW, huh?

"BANG! BANG! BANG! Whine. Puke. Scream.

"This was a great and HISTORIC day to be sure. The STRONGEST and LEAST VALUED elements of American society, the SILENT SUPERMEN were on the attack. After the heroic MARTYRDOM of BJJ, no SUPERIOR KID would ever SUFFER IN SILENCE again.

"Ben! Ben! Let's work something out here. We never did you any wrong!"

"All HUDDLED TOGETHER, the so-called OUTSIDERS. The SKATER PUNKS and the STONERS and the GOTHS. All those non-conformists who conformed with other non-conformers. All together, all alone.

"You've gotta leave some of us alive! Someone who can tell the world what you've been suffering, give your point of view!

"GOTH BOY—for it was he—could not stop shaking as he spoke. His friends who dressed in every black item from a thrift store trembled behind him. Only PIXIE GIRL had the decency to look ashamed for all the ridicule they'd dumped on him over the last three years.

"Outsiders. HA! What did they know about standing outside?

"WELL TONY, BJJ said to Goth Boy. SINCE YOU PUT IT LIKE THAT, I GUESS I'D BEST GIVE YOU A CHANCE.

"Thank you brother, bless you Ben! As soon as I get out of here, I'll tell the cops not to shoot! I'll tell them you're ready to negotiate, I promise!

"PROMISES AIN'T WORTH SHIT. Why should BJJ have trusted someone who dared to look down on him like he was a FOOL? And he was NOT ready to NEGOTIATE!

"OKAY TONY. BJJ cocked it and unlocked it. I'M GONNA LET YOU RUN TO THE FURTHEST PERIMETER. IF YOU MAKE IT CLEAR, THEN I'M GONNA LET ALL YOUR FRIENDS GO. BUT YOU GOT TWENTY SECONDS—OR I'M GOIN' HUNTIN' HUMANS.

"Goth Boy didn't spare no time to look at his friends before he took off. He panted like someone who hadn't taken exercise in months. BJJ DISDAINED him. He didn't indulge in any pointless sports, but he'd been in training for this GREAT DAY OF RECKONING.

"FOUR. FIVE... EIGHT... TWELVE. It was funny to see Goth Boy's silly hair fly around in the wind.

"FIFTEEN. SEVENTEEN. EIGHTEEN. Goth Boy had just made it. He fumbled around for the hole in the fence where kids used to cut through to take a short cut across the sports field.

"TWENTY. TWENTY-ONE. He'd worked the gap open and was through.

"KA-FUCKING-BOOM!!!

"Whoops Tony, didn't I tell you to be careful where you tread? BJJ's homemade mine was a design masterpiece. It blew Goth Boy plain in half. His guts and his organs blew up into the air and rained down on the heads of his little friends all going BOO-HOO-HOO!"

Rachel shuddered. The boy's fantasy still seemed grotesquely exaggerated, but there had to be elements of truth to it. His scrawled notes in the margin gave a list of ingredients—sugar, glycerin, primer, most of which could apparently be stolen from a chemistry lab. There was no doubt that the Columbine killers had produced their own booby trap bombs, at least some of which were believed to be effective. They'd stalled the SWAT team entering the high school by up to three hours, during which time an injured teacher had died from his wounds.

"All the little outsiders wept and howled for the loss of their friend. BJJ the TRUE OUTSIDER took a TROPHY from the shower of guts that was raining down on them. He picked up Goth Boy's soft gory head by the scalp and rammed the dripping meat of the neck down onto the rifle barrel of his Remington. It squished and squelched.

"As he held it up in the air like a TOTEM the little cowards tried to scatter

"Run, man! He can't shoot us when he's clogged up the barrel with Tony's brains!"

"DIDN'T THEY THINK HE PLANNED FOR JUST SUCH AN EVENT? As they ran every which way across the yard and the field, BJJ took his Glock from his pocket and another glittering prize: a vintage Magnum .45. All he needed to take good aim was a few seconds between each as they fell over themselves or over the other ENEMIES who were already dying. This part of the WAR was a TURKEY SHOOT. With a handgun on the end of each arm, he was *THE TERMINATOR*."

His fantasy was puerile and disgusting. But still, there was something persuasive about its sincerity. If Ben's daydreams of wholesale slaughter were so vivid and so close to his heart, then surely they foretold of the real thing?

Portents. Omens. Rachel found herself back on her alarming hobbyhorse. Ben's inner world was bearing out her worst fears, and she found herself getting sucked into it.

As impossible as it was to conceive of Tony's demise the way that Ben imagined it, she still found herself in his daydream. Tony's tousled head came bouncing down out of the sky, dreamily, surrealistically. His bemused, agonized features, detached from his body, were too pitiful to look upon. But, as Ben retrieved his blameless victim's head, the scalp shone. In his final few seconds of sentience, Tony McIlhone's head glowed as his life force emerged from his flesh. Then it was gone.

Rachel had to tell herself that Ben's warped daydream could never come to pass. But she had no doubt that her vision had told her Tony, and Arlie, and many of their classmates were all going to die.

After pages of lurid gloating over murder, the great American Hero received another challenge to his mission:

"Stop it right there, ese, ain't goin' no further!

"The BEANIE thought that his taco breath spoke for all his minority brothers. For the black kids and the other SPICKS who were too CHICKENSHIT to stand up.

"Me an the brothers all dig where you comin from, see? We all had our share of abuse an prejudice, know what I'm sayin?"

The attempt at replicating Jose's laidback Hispanic drawl was sincere, if maybe unconvincing. Even less convincing was the idea that a streetwise kid like Jose Molina would try to reason with a psycho classmate who had an armory of high-powered firearms.

But then, Jose was already dead. And Ben Jordan needed another imaginary adversary to overcome in his dreams of death and glory.

"The dirty MEX tried to take away from the real importance of what was going on. This wasn't about racial MINORITIES. They already got people wiping their ass 24-7. This was about the real MINORITY, the deserving MINORITY, the persecuted MINORITY."

His self-pity knew no bounds. What was it about these neurotic boy outsiders? Like Harris and Klebold, Ben fantasized that racial minorities were some pampered, privileged sub-grouping of the enemy. In his eyes, no one had ever faced social exclusion or bigotry on the scale that he had "Yo talkin' like you know. Ahm here to tell you you don' know shit!"

In Ben's fantasy, the wiry, athletic Hispanic kid, who had riled him by making a thoughtless joke here, a grab at his hat there, was squaring up to him in the blood-spattered school field. He was the ultimate symbolic adversary.

"Then the AMERICAN showed the MEXICAN the TRUTH. He withdrew the long, curved blade of truth from its sheath..."

Rachel pictured Ben's fifteen-inch hunting knife glinting in the sunlight.

"And let him know that he would never be patronized by him or his LIES."

The blade drew down, under and up in an arc that connected just below Jose's sternum.

"The WETBACKED WELFARE FREELOADER lost all his big brave words, lost his breath. Lost everything when that one heroic blow was struck."

In Rachel's mind's eye, Jose contorted as the long blade drove upwards into his chest.

"Struck a blow for TRUTH. Struck a blow for REVENGE. Struck a blow against the SPICK INVASION and their HIP HOP GHETTO BROTHERS."

The more she focused upon his pain, the more conscious she became that it wasn't real. Jose's crumbling body disintegrated into the grass. This was pure fantasy, composed in a hate-filled fervor when Jose was still alive.

But Jose's death was real. She directed her attention away from the bloody battlefield of Sunnyvale that Ben had created. Behind her, Rachel felt the presence of the light.

She glanced back at a phantom image of Jose, last seen fleetingly in her dream. He smiled at her. "Yo, Mizz Ess." He wore the halo of light, almost blinding in its intensity.

She smiled back. "Good to see you, Jose." But he was already fading, his memory overwhelmed by her immersion in Ben's gruesome wish-dreams.

"Don't let it happen no more," he reminded her. "Not to me or my homies."

ELEVEN

Rachel scooped up the folder of papers and bundled it into her bag. Someone—Principal Carr, the sheriff's office—was going to be forced to consider this. Her petty wrongdoing aside, what she'd uncovered was of far more staggering importance than vandalizing one student's locker. It almost came as a relief when the hand dropped onto her shoulder.

She was startled enough to drop Ben's journal onto the floor. But it was inevitable her unauthorized presence would be spotted. Indeed, she'd almost hoped for it.

Carr was expressionless. His eyes never left hers as she stooped slowly to retrieve the boy's private journal. He took it all in. The ransacked locker. Pilfering a student's personal belongings. Vandalism to school property.

"You leave me no choice." He was broaching no argument. His coldly neutral manner bespoke an unwillingness to communicate.

But this time, Rachel was sure, this time he'd have to listen. "Mr Carr, I know what's going to happen now. I know."

He averted his eyes from her. The gesture was contemptuous, a refusal to engage.

"It's Ben Jordan." She proffered the boy's journal as if in proof. There were no takers. "He's going to hurt the other students. It's all in here."

She presented it as insurmountable evidence. Carr looked on it as the action of a disturbed person.

"Please, you have to take me seriously now. I know what he's planning to do."

He stepped subtly aside, so that he was no longer in her line of sight. He was not the stiff but self-sacrificing figure of Ben's fantasy. Carr was merely petty officialdom at its most obtuse, its most frustrating. The boy's journal, its echoes still reverberating in Rachel's mind, told it differently.

"PUT DOWN YOUR ARMS, BEN JORDAN!!

"When BJJ heard it, it was like the COPS had come already. But no. It was the principal, come to defend the nasty little kingdom that he presided over. But the King had been DETHRONED.

"The AMERICAN HERO already counted teachers among the dead. Lying Agents of MEDIOCRITY, they HAD TO DIE. The sports teacher who'd come running to the aid of his BELOVED JOCKS. DEAD. The science teachers who believed they could try to lead some of the kids away through the labs. DEAD. The only teacher to be spared was POETRY HO who would at least tell history the TRUTH.

"IF YOU SHOW WILLING TO SURRENDER BEFORE THE TACTICAL RESPONSE UNIT ARRIVES, WE CAN WALK OUT OF THIS

TOGETHER. IT'S NOT TOO LATE TO RECONSIDER! PRISON AND REHABILITATION ARE BETTER THAN DEATH, JORDAN. I PROMISE YOU I WILL SPEAK TO THE AUTHORITIES ON YOUR BEHALF.

"More promises. What do you know, all of a sudden he was the MOST IMPORTANT guy around. That's all a body has to do to get noticed in AMERICA TODAY–SHOOT UP A FREAKIN' SCHOOL PLAYGROUND!

"What did the POMPOUS ASSHOLE think he was going to do? Think again and turn around, after all the HAVOC and CARNAGE he'd brought down on their deserving heads? The tight-ass principal didn't understand how there were some things you couldn't avoid. Like a DATE WITH DESTINY. They each had their own to meet.

"The principal was stepping over the bodies to get to him, waving a piece of cloth as a WHITE FLAG. SCREW THAT! WHO DID HE THINK HE WAS?

"Principal Carr should have been grateful to BJJ. He was going to give the SMUG FART his own place in history. Not that he'd ever know about it.

"The PRINCIPAL raised a hand. The AMERICAN HERO shot it off. Surprised as shit, he just stood holding his bloody stump in the air. BANG! One shot from the trusty deer hunter and high school authority got an eyeful of bullet and Goth Boy flesh.

"BANG! The Big Guy was still standing but he had a big hole in the chest to match the one in his eye. BANG! NICE SHOOTING–took the left side of his face clean off. BANG! BANG! Ooh, look, the principal took one in the balls!"

Rachel closed her eyes and found herself outside on the school playing field. She saw Carr making the ultimate sacrifice, crucified on the air by Ben's fusillade of bullets. But, as his reflexes and his body fell to hit the ground, the principal disappeared. His body was nowhere to be seen. Evaporated.

It was the same with the other schoolteachers Ben had gunned down in his daydreams. The rows and rows of dead and maimed bodies he'd visualized, like some huge war or disaster zone, were thinning out. There was no Carr. None of the administrative staff. None of the science teachers. And, thankfully, no Jared.

She realized then that what she perceived was the difference between the way Ben had dreamt it, and the way she knew it was likely to take place. Casual conversation in the teachers' lounge had indicated how they would respond in the eventuality of a Columbine-type incident. As most of the wave of high school shootings seemed to have passed with the new millennium, most of the opinions had been casual, off-the-cuff.

But very few felt there was anything to be gained by sacrificing themselves. "The best bet," opined Jared, with his usual calm logic, "would be to get off the premises and lead law enforcement back to the school, give them some idea of the layout and topography of the place."

Where the shadow fell between Ben's fantasy and the likely reality is that many of the staff would be less likely to risk their lives, hardened by a decade of US high school kids going homicidal. In her projected vision of the event, the teachers' bodies were vanishing because they simply weren't there. Even if they'd failed to get off the premises and locked themselves in the washrooms, nobody was playing hero.

Not even Principal Carr, who Ben had imagined trying to become his nemesis.

It reassured her in one sense, but then re-activated the same gnawing doubt: if no one was going to risk becoming a dead hero, then who was going to save the kids?

"I asked you once to leave. Now I'm afraid I'm going to have to ask the police to escort you from the premises." Carr shot a glance at the busted locker door. "If you leave now of your own accord, we can forget about trespass and criminal damage charges. Otherwise–" Carr shook his head as if it were the most serious thing in the world. He really believed that petty rules were going to deter her from her responsibility.

"No, please, I have to..." She backed off a little, ensuring that the principal wouldn't take the legal risk of manhandling her himself. "I really can't allow you to stop me. You don't understand."

A shrill report split the air. The electric bell rattled their eardrums and set their teeth on edge, so nearby was it. "Oh, perfect." Carr rolled his eyes heavenward. Another irritating feature of an exasperating day.

It electrified Rachel's nerves more than he could know. "Wasn't this scheduled?"

"Of course not." His patience was more than exhausted, it was overdrawn. Up until not much more than an hour ago, Rachel Stark had still been a teacher at Sunnyvale High. Was she so troubled by her delusions that she wasn't aware of day-to-day school business?

"Mr Carr, please," she implored. There was always that formality to their relationship. She couldn't appeal to him in the way the more favored members of staff could, by addressing him as "Kelvin." "You have to listen to me!"

She was soon drowned out. The classroom doors burst open and the students and teachers began to file out. Two by two, bustling wider into four by four, just like Ben had imagined.

Slick. Very slick, she acknowledged the ruse that she believed was unfolding. In her inner vision of Sunnyvale under attack, the schoolyard was not crammed inch by inch with fallen bodies. But the cries and sobs were pitifully louder, the faces of some of the kids recognizable, not just ciphers to appease Ben's bloodlust. Those who were injured suffered terribly, while the dead lay still and silent, until such a time as bereaved families could gain access to their children and weep their hearts out over them. This is how it would be, she told herself.

She felt an impatient yank on her arm. Carr was pulling her away from the thronging students, toward the exit door. "Let's go." The preppy bastard was prepared to risk a lawsuit after all. Anything to remove her from his oh-so-perfect school. She didn't struggle, letting him lead her outside with Ben Jordan's journal tucked into her shoulder bag.

Outside, the clear, crisp daylight came almost as a shock to the senses. It awoke her further to the presence of danger. Carr took her by the shoulder and drew her away from the kids, almost brutally. "I don't know what's going on here," he murmured, his incomprehension feeding his anger, "but if I find out that you're responsible..."

He could glower all he liked. She was in the midst of something much bigger, and he needed to recognize it. "We have to find Ben," she insisted, her fair hair glinting in the benevolent sunlight as she searched the young faces. "Ben Jordan." It was Carr who needed to keep his mind on track, not her.

It was hard not to be overwhelmed by the students. Even on a bright summer's day, so many of them shone with the magnificence of stained glass figures in an old dark cathedral. It wasn't just the dozen or so she'd seen in the hall earlier, or kids she personally knew and cared about, like Tony and Arlie.

It was a golden, ghostly choir of young faces, interspersed throughout the entire assembly of students. Chatting, laughing, chewing, shouting. Silent, distracted, thoughtful, carefree. All of them separate but joined in that universal light. All kissed by the imminent promise of death.

It was difficult to assimilate, to take in all at once. All of them—even Brian and his swaggering brute buddies, Stacy and her smug valley-girl wannabes—

elicited her sympathy, her fear. Enshrouded in light, their blissfully unaware faces looked as if they were already transported from this world. Still they laughed, smiling at their friends, scowling at their rivals. As if this golden summer day would go on forever for them.

Brian and his no-brainer buddy, the football captain he'd managed to forgive for stealing Stacy, looked over in her direction, and smiled. Normally, their grinning faces could ignite a burning resentment within her, as if she instinctively knew she was the target of their mirth. But not today. Their beefy countenances radiated the same blinding light as the kids they'd always bullied. It almost reflected a kind of unknowing innocence.

Rachel never thought she'd feel so much sympathy for a boy like him. Brutish, philistine. Loud-mouthed and bullying. Lionizing the rich and the acquisitive, while looking down on education for its own sake.

No, she really never had much time for Brian Kelly. But it's hard not to feel sympathy for anyone whom you visualize as a victim of extreme violence. When you're forced to imagine their death under the very worst circumstances.

"It was on the BLOODY BATTLEFIELD of Sunnyvale that history was changed forever. When the knuckle-dragging OAFS that used to rule AMERICA were defeated once and for all.

"When BJJ the AMERICAN HERO whipped the ass, stripped the flesh and bleached the bones of their inferior kind in a way they would never FORGET. It took an hour of pursuit, over a thousand bodies of the weeping and the DAMNED, before the SWAGGERING ENEMY, now CRAPPING his pants, was brought down."

Ben seemed to imagine himself as the hero of some Tolkien-esque saga now. His reading, no longer reflected in his schoolwork, existed merely to create a context worlds apart from the modern American life that he despised. That had rejected him, and that he rejected in turn.

Just him and his trusty 7400 against the forces of darkness. Ben Jordan, the last noble American, up against his sworn enemies. And his enemies were everywhere.

"The enemy formerly so full of PISS & WIND.

"It don't have to be like this, dude.

"OH, DIDN'T IT? After an eternity of torment and belittlement, when the hunter became the hunted why did he think anyone should give a GODDAMN about him?

"HOW DOES IT FEEL, JOCKBOY? C'MON, GIMME SOME OF THAT SMART MOUTH! DON'T LET US DOWN, BRIAN–THERE'S ONLY YOU TO DO IT NOW. ALL YOUR BUDDIES ARE DEAD!"

He named him. Through all his layers of violent fantasy, Ben had maintained a kind of distance from his other obsessive grudges. But Brian was different. Brian was his tormentor. For, despite Ben's impassive front, Brian was the bully who stripped him of his last shreds of confidence, and made him cry himself to sleep at nights.

Brian was part of the reason that Ben had withdrawn from the world. He was the inspiration for endless pages of violent fantasy, the last burst of creativity from a boy on the brink of psychological burnout.

But Rachel felt suddenly sorry for Brian. It wasn't hard to visualize him at Ben's mercy. The description was overwrought with melodrama, but it was pure wish-fulfillment.

"The ENEMY had never sweated so much. Had never POOED in his panties so readily or SNIVELLED till snot ran from his nose.

"Oh please, dude, PLEASE!"

It was easier for her to imagine Brian's distress than it was to picture some of the other figures in Ben's fantasy, who, she knew in her heart, were not going to die. But Brian was.

Transported in her reverie to the edges of the playing field, she studied Ben's mania at close hand. The alienated boy, in his red and white checked shirt over a baggy T-shirt, looked far closer to the rural deer hunter than the semi-mythic hero he imagined himself to be. He looked down the sight of his barrel, merciless and calculating, at the boy he'd backed up at point blank range.

Brian, the color drained from his outdoor-tanned face, could only hyperventilate now. Terror had robbed him of his vocabulary, even of the self-serving ability to beg forgiveness.

"When the ENEMY was vanquished, it was with an absolute freakin' FINALITY."

His description made her imagine him pushing the barrel of his rifle into Brian's nose, till the sight almost touched the rim of the boy's nostril. Brian sobbed rapidly and held onto the perimeter fence as if for dear life.

"When BJ Jordan showed how easily and how pleasantly this SCUM could be wiped from the face of the earth, it was an HISTORIC MOMENT..."

With the safety catch off, it only took one firm squeeze on the trigger to disintegrate Brian's face.

"It was a shot that echoed across the nation. NEVER MORE would any sensitive kid have to take shit from an inferior. It was the crowning moment of the Battle of Sunnyvale. From that point on, the rallying cry at high schools across the land would be KILL THEM–MUTILATE THEM–DESTROY THEM!"

The image was so tangible, Rachel could almost smell the cordite burns on what remained of Brian's head. Her imagination had shown her the glow of imminent death around the terrified boy's perspiring head. Fragments of his exploding brain followed the light as it left him, ascending into the air.

She felt all compassion for his pitiful killer start to recede. In "real life," she had hated Brian Kelly a little herself. But, imagining the nature of his death, she realized that, for all his mean, stupid behavior, there was one vicious act he had never even come close to.

He had never held Ben Jordan at gunpoint and denied his pleas to remain alive. But Ben was itching to assume power over Brian's life and death.

"The shots fired–AGAIN AND AGAIN AND AGAIN–until no trace remained of the JOCKMAN's grinning swine face on this planet."

The recurring shots reverberated in Rachel's mind. Ben squeezed off one after the other in pointless, superfluous overkill. The follow-up shots fired chunks of the dead boy's cranium through his sepulchral golden halo, before his life force had fully receded. It wasn't enough to kill Brian once. Like he said, Ben wanted to kill him again and again and again.

"The ENEMY's remains were scattered to the wind when the AMERICAN HERO unleashed one of his doomsday weapons. Within weeks, the power of the Internet would ensure that BBJ's GENIUS was recognized across the whole nation. Every time a bright kid was bullied at his school, he knew he could call on the MARTYR's experience and leadership, preserved on www.highschoolrage.com, and access a whole range of deadly explosives."

Ben's so-called "doomsday" weapon was probably no more than a few basic chemicals mixed with crop fertilizer and primed to blow. But such homemade kits were horribly effective.

Her mind recoiled at the thought, but she imagined Brian alive again—screaming for mercy, and trying to claw his way through the earth to escape. His face pulsated with glowing light, in the frenzied flourish of one about to die. This time, Ben dropped a small makeshift bomb casing down the front of the boy's shirt.

"Move it and I'll blow your fucking head off!"

So Brian co-operated. And Ben moved way back over a hundred feet and fired off a shot at the casing below his shirt. It did blow Brian's head off. It blew away his chest and most of his lower abdomen too. All that was left of him was a bloody pelvic region and his baggy pants.

So many ways for him to kill. So many ways for a kid to die.

"JOCKMAN's moron skull became a trophy to the faithful, preserved from generation to generation of high school kids as a gift from BJJ, who snuck it away from the school grounds during his devastating LAST STAND."

The boy's skull? Ben had already described himself bludgeoning it, shooting it, exploding it till the fragments were broken down into smaller fragments.

What could possibly be left of Brian? How long would eternity have to be, and how many acts of violence would he have to perform, before Ben Jordan could satiate his hatred for Brian Kelly?

His pathological epic suggested one final image of the boy. Brian, with a gunshot wound to both legs, crawled away pitifully, as Ben dived onto him with his hunting knife. She imagined the blade penetrating deep into the pulsing light that covered the frightened boy's face. Its brutal incision sought to cut away the face from his skull, as surely as the light would peel away from him with his dying breath.

She didn't want to imagine anymore. All of Ben's scenarios were sick fantasy—but some of these kids' deaths were going to be real. Something within his warped journal was going to become a prophecy fulfilled. In his sadistic revenge fantasy, time had stopped to give him space to torment and mutilate his victims by a variety of methods, way out of proportion to any hurt, real or imagined, that had been inflicted upon him by them.

In her own inner world, time had stopped too. In the few minutes it had taken her to peruse his disturbed little archive, his inner workings had become clearer to her than she could have wished. It was the zone in which her ethereal forebodings met with the visceral violence of the modern world. It made sense of her fears, but confounded her ideas of what exactly to do about them.

In the external world that we call "real life," the SWAT team would turn up long before Ben had fully carried out his apocalyptic massacre. But, as with the Columbine misfits, he would take enough unsuspecting, undeserving kids with him to make the day go down as a black mark in American history.

But she was adamant that it wouldn't be as a result of her own negligence. Out in the schoolyard, all the kids were present and correct. So many more of them than she might have imagined. Maybe the extent of Ben's crazy dreams was not so exaggerated. Maybe he'd have his high school apocalypse after all.

But the boy himself was nowhere to be seen. She scanned the roof where she expected him to appear, the belligerent young assassin awaiting his moment in the sun.

There was no sign of him. Maybe he'd switched his plan. Maybe he'd confound her expectations.

What was not possible was that disaster wasn't looming. It was too late for her to believe it now. Let Carr look askance at her, like she was one phone call away from the psych ward.

Amidst the cacophony of youthful voices and the chaotic flurry of this seemingly beautiful day, it was a danger that only she could be aware of. The hell with rationality, it was no use.

Then she saw it.

There was still no sign of his awkward, gangling presence. But one brief, metallic glint, reflecting the sunlight, told her he was there. She shielded her forehead with her hand, to block out the sunspots Jared insisted were playing havoc with her vision. Squinting her eyes, she managed to focus on that one tiny detail.

The target sight of a rifle barrel. Barely noticeable, except to one pair of eyes that caught its momentary gleam. Then it withdrew.

She knew that nobody saw but her. The crowd out in the schoolyard was growing. The more kids that were herded out, the more concentrated the volume of human bodies. As she looked at them, the pattern of light that permeated the group separated those who were about to die from those who would live, perhaps with serious injuries.

Teachers milled and thronged. They spoke with each other or took roll calls for their class to ensure everyone was present. Only Rachel knew what a mercy it would be to be absent from the scene.

No one paid her any attention. Those who noticed her were a little embarrassed to even acknowledge it. Rachel Stark's off the staff early, don'tcha know? I hear she's had a complete nervous breakdown. As far as they were aware, she shouldn't have been there, so they studiously ignored her. They didn't see her. They didn't see anything. She had to act.

There were some things you couldn't avoid. Like a date with destiny. Of all Ben's crazed scribblings, she could no longer argue with those particular words.

Carr had relaxed his grip, believing the crazy English teacher situation more under control than the "Smash This Glass In Case Of Fire" situation. It only took a sudden lurch for her to break away. She shot directly toward the doors the kids had just been herded out of.

"Rachel!" Carr hollered after her, more in extreme irritation than alarm. "Mizz Stark!"

But no one gave chase or followed after her. In the empty school hall, she was truly alone. No one would enter until the alarm drill was over. Until it was determined whether this was just some juvenile prank, or whether a fire truly had been detected in part of the school.

Passing breathlessly down the corridors that bustled with life earlier, Rachel knew the main body of the school was deserted. There was only one direction he could have headed in. With a tightness in her stomach and a pounding heart, she opened the doors to the empty hall.

It seemed cavernous in its deserted state. Even her low heels made an echo as they clattered against the polished floor. She trotted from the hall doors toward the podium from where Carr conducted school assembly. Different wall panels contained relics of snapshots of the school's history—from its motto, "Aspire and Achieve," to the football team's most recent sports trophies.

At the glass trophy cabinet, she stopped in her tracks. Maybe it was an optical illusion this time. The light was dim, and her reflection was only partly illuminated.

But she had to look closer. Had to know. As she approached the sliding glass window, her reflection was partially distorted, as if in a clear lake on a stormy day. Her features were so blurred as to make her unrecognizable to herself.

With her nose almost up to the glass, she could just about detect her delicate bone structure and blue eyes. From a distance, they'd been indistinct. Up close, she knew why.

Her facial features shimmered, obscured behind an ethereal light.

She swallowed hard. It was the signifier of certainty. The sign that she was no longer an onlooker, but someone whose fate was intrinsically tied up in events. The guarantee of no escape.

She looked behind her, through the entrance to the main hall and out through the school exit doors. It wasn't too late to run. I still have the option, she told herself. Anything I decide to do as from now is an irrevocable decision. My decision.

Directly in front of her, at the end of the hall, she saw what she'd come looking for. The door was signed, "ROOF ACCESS." It led in one direction, with no other way back. The choice was made. Everything that had happened to her pointed in one direction. To run away from it would be to renege on any sense of vocation, any sense of self-worth she had ever held.

She ascended the stairwell that led to the roof.

TWELVE

As she re-emerged into the vibrant sunshine, her senses were filled again. It was a clear, cloudless day. The horizon beyond the rooftop was blue and endless. The crowd down below was a bustling organic mass, dappled with what appeared to be freak sunspots.

But what the light signified to her was no longer in question. It had only been others, not her, who had doubted it.

She had arrived at the exact moment, what Ben would insist was the Moment of Destiny. His semi-automatic hunting rifle was propped up on the ledge. He made no attempt to conceal it, shifting the sight around to scan his targets below. Waiting for the Moment.

When Rachel had pocketed Ben's journal, loose leafs had tumbled out of it. At first, she didn't consider their contents worthy of any attention. They were primitive drawings, with puerile or obscene captions attached. Vaguely shapeless cartoon figures that made the animators of *South Park* seem like Leonardo by comparison.

As before, it was the violence that underlined their conception that made her look closer. These formless balloon people spoke in captioned blurts that mostly told of their pain or distress: "Ahh, you motherfucker!!!" screamed one, whose face had been turned into a Rorschach inkblot by a crudely drawn handgun. "I want to live!!!" one of the characters' heads pleaded before it was detached from its body. In familiar contrast, the character representing "BJJ, the American Hero" spoke in pompous, portentous bursts punctuated with obscenity.

Rachel had seen enough of the workings of Ben's mind by now. She had no wish to subject herself to any more. But something about one of the cartoons demanded her attention. It was as badly drawn as the others. Ben may have had some crude writing skills that he'd sublimated into his dark fantasies, but he was too disassociated from the outer world to gain the skill and discipline an artist required.

But it wasn't the weakness of the form, or the vicious banality of the content that compelled her to look. It was what one of the pictures appeared to signify. One character, at least, appeared to be female. It wasn't that Ben's crude drawing skills had made her recognizable–it was just that she, like most of his little amorphous people, was drawn naked. Ben clearly didn't have the ability or the inclination to represent clothing. But he'd also distinguished her by drawing on pimpled balloons and a mass of fuzz to illustrate, in jock vernacular, "tits & pussy."

What was more disturbing was that the female character appeared to be hung upside down by a rope, and flecked with black ink scrawl that Rachel assumed represented blood. It reminded her of an instance she'd read about in an education journal.

In the early 1990s, a high school boy in Florida had put together a badly drawn amateur comic book he called *Boiled Angel*, its shapeless characters supposedly based on sadomasochistic poses his sister would strike for him. Like Ben's artwork, their composition suggested the most primitive form of Picasso's cubism, as interpreted by a retarded child. But the content was so disturbingly sadistic that, when a number of co-ed girls were murdered at the state university, the police initially considered the young artist a suspect.

This was of the same tone. It was all the more alarming for the speech bubbles that floated from their mouths: "Ohh, ohh, I love you Pixie Girl!" declared the cartoon figure who caressed her upside-down form, holding a huge knife or a sword in his other hand.

"I love you too, BJJ!" It was the only indication of the other character's identity. Apart from Pixie Girl's gender specific parts, there was nothing else to distinguish the great American Hero from his "enemies." But that didn't matter. All she cared about was whether sick puppy Ben Jordan had any specific plans for one of her students, for one of *her* kids.

Ben turned his head. The sudden awareness of another presence suggested an enemy in his midst.

He was startled, but somehow relieved, to see that it was her. She could even detect a slight smile from within the ethereal light that bathed his face. It dissolved all her fear. Their destinies, she could now see, were intertwined, and it was useless to fight it.

"Hey! Miss Stark..." He seemed so pleased to see her. Almost as if he felt she was automatically on his side. Rachel moved closer, confident that Ben was not going to harm her.

"Hi, Ben." Such a banal greeting. So untouched by the gravity of the situation. But what else could she say? She was no parapsychologist. It was a freak accident of nature that had thrown her perception wide open to his intentions. Now, it was only her who could deal with it.

"You're not here to give me the speech, are you?" Why did he accept her presence so easily? Did he know how inextricably bound together they now were?

"What speech is that, Ben?"

"You know," He permitted himself a little smirk. "The one about how killing people is wrong."

"You're a smart kid. I think you already know that."

His mouth lost its little upturn. She was playing mindfuck with him. No one had called him a "smart kid" for as long as he could remember, not even Ms Stark. She was trying to act like she was on his side, to talk him round to her moral agenda. He wasn't going to fall for that, not even from her. Today was The Day.

"You see, Ben," she moved slowly, not wishing to alarm him and make him trigger-happy, "I know."

She held open her shoulder bag, to show Ben she wasn't trying any damn fool tactic like pulling a handgun on him. From the folder she'd stashed inside, she gently removed his journal. Rachel had scanned the section that the drawings escaped from. It was headed "THE LAST STAND OF BENJAMIN J JORDAN, AMERICAN HERO."

At first, she could find no specific mention of Arlie Bennington. But she'd persevered through the pages of crap, through the self-lionization and bombast, to a point where Ben had started to detail the outcome of his imaginary war.

"As the COPS closed in, they were hampered by the CORPSES of thousands of ENEMIES that formed a great MOUNTAIN OF BLOOD. There was much WAILING & GRINDING OF TEETH. The police were not to blame. They had been BRAINWASHED to believe the lives they tried to protect were OF VALUE. It would take the HISTORIC BATTLE OF SUNNYVALE and the many smaller wars that followed it to make them understand the righteusness [sic] of the SILENT GENIUS. But back at the school it was all BULLETS & BOMBS."

In Ben's fantasy, he had finally flown from the confines of the Sunnyvale High School grounds to a nearby patch of woodland not much more than half a mile away. For self-preservation, he had taken a hostage. It didn't require much imagination for Rachel to work out who he had in mind. "Taking a hostage, if possible a tiny female, can aid you." She recalled those sardonic words of encouragement that he'd highlighted.

"PIXIE GIRL was full of fear. But she wasn't just like the others, the DESERVING VICTIMS." It was the first time he'd used that word, instead of the self-justifying "enemies." In the heat of his excitement, it seemed to her, he no longer needed to make up moral excuses for himself.

Ben's face spoke of disappointment with Rachel, if not total embarrassment. "I know, Ben." she tried to show understanding without appearing judgmental. "I know about the hurt you're feeling. But this isn't some computer game, or a movie."

His face darkened within its supernatural light. She could cut the morality crap right now.

Rachel realized she was going to lose him at any moment. "If you didn't think it was wrong to kill your school friends, you wouldn't need to label them "enemies," or "maggots', or excuse mass murder as some kind of holy war."

That was enough. He was becoming frustrated, his attention switching manically between the assembled throng down below and his interfering schoolteacher. Who told her she could go leafing through his journal? And what was this bunch of crap about "school friends"?

"You hate them as much as I do," he insisted. It was as much an accusation as a plea. Those emotionless eyes fixed on her. Suddenly, she was the one under scrutiny. It wouldn't have felt so uncomfortable if there wasn't so much truth in it. When the job, and her nerves, had begun to get the better of her, she did begin to feel like she hated her students. Particularly Brian, and his philistine hordes.

"You hate all of us." He compounded the offence. "That's why you quit."

"That's not true." And it wasn't. At least not in the way he meant it. It had taken exposure to Ben's hideous journal to truly know what hate was, and to know she didn't share it. No one, she believed now, could ever really know their true feelings about a person until they could visualize them in pain and distress. For most people, basic empathy would erase the petty irritation we mistake for "hate." Rachel knew now that there wasn't a single soul in the school she could claim to hate. Not even Ben, whose dark, festering psyche she had been exposed to. Whose malign intent towards the students she cared most about now followed her around like a conscious waking dream.

His ranting words haunted her. "But she would LEARN. She had been CHOSEN FOR A REASON. Pixie Girl was smart & sensitive enough to realize that she was an HONORED VICTIM."

In her alarm, Rachel visualized Arlie's shy little face. It didn't take much imaginative effort to place herself as a bystander out there in the woods, a witness to Ben's intended kidnapping of Arlie. The insight into his intentions came from his own words. But it was processed by her own faculties, by a perception more closely anchored to reality. She no longer had the patience to see the projected future through his eyes, but could see it even as they spoke through her intolerable visionary faculty.

They smashed through the bracken and fell against the gnarled trunk of a dying eucalyptus tree. Ben Jordan had the butt of his semiautomatic under the crook of his left arm. His small arsenal of weapons was depleted, the rifle being all he had left.

But he had Arlie. He dare not relax the grip he had on her upper arm, twisting and pinching the soft flesh. Her face was dotted with shining tears. Through the golden white radiance that Rachel perceived, Arlie wept glowing dewdrops.

"That... that's the end of the line for us!" Ben panted, as nervous as she was.

But why? Her eyes implored of him without speaking. Why did everything have to go insane? What is this "us?" Why do I have to be here with you?

"PIXIE GIRL would realize soon that her moment of DESTINY was at hand," Ben wrote. "That it was better to DIE alongside a great AMERICAN HERO, with all his LOVE & RESPECT, than to live a life of nothingness among HUMAN MAGGOTS."

Rachel knew Arlie would feel no such thing. The girl sobbed, and the light that signified her approaching destruction pulsed vibrantly with her breath. "Why...? Why don't you give it up, Jordan?"

He winced. As desperate as they both were, it hurt that she called him by his last name. Ben shook his head. "There's no giving it up. There's no going back. What's done is done."

He sounded almost regretful. So why had he gone so murderously crazy in the first place? It had all come without warning when they were out in the yard during the fire alarm drill. The gunfire. The shouts and the wailing. The chaotic stampede. The kids who got out of school by the holes in the perimeter fence. The boy whose foot was blown off by a homemade explosive Jordan planted. Her classmates who died.

Arlie was just too, too sad. And now she was frightened too. When Ben Jordan came down off the school roof, he'd singled out some kids and shot them up close. It was awful. The screams, the blood—and some of them, she was sure, had even died. Stacy, the football team's cheerleader, Brian Kelly and one of his jock friends—they were people who'd never been kind to her, but she could never have imagined them ending like this.

And then there was Tony. It made her so sad, like she wanted to scream and scream until she died. But she didn't want to die. Heaven knew, she wanted to live. If only Tony could have lived, and she could have told him, just once, what she truly thought about him.

The sirens were ringing in both their ears. The helicopters whirred directly overhead. The loudhailers told them that law enforcement wasn't just close behind, it was a mere few hundred feet away.

From Ben Jordan's point of view, it all looked hopeless. Arlie saw his mouth quiver a little and felt he might be as scared as she was. What did he intend for them both? What did he want with her?

"In the final GLORIOUS MOMENTS that made history," Ben had written, "Pixie Girl saw the true worth of BENJAMIN JAMES JORDAN. To die with him at this HISTORIC moment, she realized would be an HONOUR & A PRIVILEGE."

Rachel, the remote onlooker, saw no such thing. She saw an unwilling captive attempting to struggle with Ben as the SWAT team negotiator barked orders from his loudhailer.

"DON'T HURT THE GIRL, BEN! IT'S NOT TOO LATE TO FIND A WAY OUT!"

In his desperation, he dropped the rifle. He twisted Arlie's arm up her back and withdrew his hunting knife from its sheath. She cried out. Her tearful eyes screwed up within that ominous halo.

"TOGETHER at last, in LOVE & IN DEATH, the AMERICAN HERO had finally found his true companion."

"LEAVE THE GIRL, BEN!" The small copse of wild foliage he'd backed them into offered no real camouflage. The cops had ultra-sensitive sights aimed on him, and they saw his every last move.

Reading between the lines of his journal, Rachel had visualized his actions. What she saw, she was convinced would become true. Ben was grimly determined. His mouth fixed into a cruel sneer. Drawing his lips close to Arlie's tiny ear, he drew the sharp edge of his blade across her jugular vein. Rachel saw the golden light of the girl's life force bathe a part of his face.

"In her FINAL MOMENTS, Pixie Girl realized her destiny. BJJ spilled her life-blood to save her from an existence spent with their INFERIORS.

"I love you, Pixie Girl, he told her. In her dying moments, she realized she LOVED him too and told him so. As her BLOOD trickled out of her, they embraced and MADE LOVE for the first and last time, before the ENEMY AGENTS could draw in."

Rachel was sickened. Is this what Arlie would die for? An elaborate sick fantasy about Ben losing his virginity to her, in the moments before they were both killed? It was infinitely depressing to think that the boy couldn't imagine a more positive variation on the theme. To think what love had come to mean to Ben Jordan.

In reality, Rachel knew Ben wouldn't have time to plant his first kiss before a sharpshooter opened fire on him. That they would both hit the underbrush together at the same moment. That Arlie would be traumatized, shaking, losing blood dangerously and rapidly. That Ben would probably be hit in the leg, to avoid shooting the girl they were attempting to save.

"They slashed your tires... Brian and his maggot friends." Ben was goading Rachel, hoping for a response. Wanting her to admit that she burned with hurt and resentment just as much as he did. "Wanna know what they write about you on the boy's room wall?"

No, she didn't want to know anything anymore. She could guess at its crude sexual innuendo, but such things were trivial now. Ben was aching to tell her it read, "Mizz Stark gives head to BlowJob Jordan." Their words were always intended to wound, but just this once they lit a pathetic little spark of pride in him.

But she knew she was losing him now. He was edgy and dangerous. "See them maggots crawl!" he'd written in his journal. His misanthropy was consuming him, and he would not be persuaded that the teeming mass of kids down below amounted to anything more than wriggling worms.

Under the section of his journal sub-headed "AMERICAN HEROES," Ben had included cuttings on Charles Whitman, a respectable-looking young Southerner with an old-fashioned buzzcut. Aged twenty-five in 1966, the photo of the ex-marine suggested he'd be more at home in the previous decade. According to the Internet printout, he'd suffered some kind of psychotic episode that summer, after which he'd murdered his wife and mother. It didn't stop there.

The next morning, his military training served him well when he loaded up with enough weapons, ammunition and supplies to counter the Tet Offensive. Taking a position atop a tower at the University of Texas, he opened fire and didn't stop till armed police managed to blow him away. By that time, sixteen further innocent victims were dead and nearly twice that figure were wounded. Whitman left his own final testament, expressing bewilderment at his compulsions and the hope that medical science may find an answer to what was afflicting him.

But Ben didn't see it that way, of course. His highlighted notes read: "AMERICAN HERO NUMBER ONE: CHARLES WHITMAN–INNOVATOR! Blew a bunch of pesky human vermin off the face of the planet in 1966 when he found himself a guarded position atop a tower at Texas State Uni. All hail Chuck! See them maggots crawl!" Like the sniper Whitman, Ben Jordan had found himself a guarded position above ground level and was ready to start blasting off.

In Rachel's field of vision, his targets glowed. Their faces were indistinct. She couldn't pick out Arlie Bennington, or any other of the specific targets of his malign intent. All she saw was the imminent destruction they faced.

What she hadn't realized until she'd drawn to the close of his journal was how, at the very end of it all, Ben intended to beg for his life. Cutting through the self-delusion, she'd imagined the debased display.

Ben crouched on his knees, trying to stem the flow of blood. Crying. Screaming, "Please, please don't shoot! I'll let you get to the girl! I'm surrendering! Just don't fuckin' shoot me!"

The negotiator and paramedics moving in, with the SWAT marksmen providing cover near by. Arlie, pale and shivering as she turned cold, having lost too much blood already. The light's white radiance shining brighter around her face.

And then, the master plan.

"There was no way in this STINKING WORLD that a great AMERICAN HERO would allow himself to be taken alive. As the ENEMY'S lapdogs drew in, BENJAMIN JAMES JORDAN, aged seventeen, committed the last and most HISTORIC act of his CELEBRATED LIFE. Drawing the enemy in like flies to a spider web, his SCIENTIFIC GENIUS would OBLITERATE them all from this face of this PLANET."

From the crude diagram that took up much of the page, Rachel had seen how he intended to wire himself up with the same explosive that constituted his mines. With a crude detonator, he would be following the example set by Middle Eastern suicide bombers and dragging the US high school massacre into a grim new era.

"It was an APOCALYPSE! With BJJ's act of MARTYRDOM, every one of the PIG AGENTS was incinerated with him. The explosion set off a CHAIN REACTION that hit all the bombs strategically placed around the school, in the streets, in residential buildings. The MAGGOT-INFESTED TOWN OF SUNNYVALE was blown off the map.

"BENJAMIN J JORDAN's body was gone, but his FEARLESS SPIRIT continued its WAR. The same WAR to be continued by his followers–by other HEROS [sic] and MARTYRS, by the secret brotherhood of SILENT GENIUSES."

In reality it would be far more limited, but no less horrible. Rachel imagined the devastating effect on Ben's own body as his explosive pouches were detonated. She pictured the awful impact on the officers standing closest to him. Maybe they would be killed, but most likely they would be cruelly maimed by the boy's attempt at an act of terrorism.

And she could visualize the terrible consequences for Arlie–already in urgent need of medical rescue, if the paramedics who came to her aid were injured or distracted by the explosion, then there would be no hope.

She could see Arlie's body stop shaking on the stretcher that had fallen to the earth. Her small eyes closing as the coldness and all other sensation faded. Her light extending toward the treetops and then fading as life itself faded from her.

Rachel was trapped in a shadow between Ben Jordan's worst imaginings and her own fearful glimpses of mortality. It was, she'd persuaded herself beyond all doubt, more real than anything else she'd ever experienced. And it was so much more urgent.

Still, there was something that didn't adhere to her internal logic. If the vivid death scenes that she'd seen in her mind's eye verified the glowing omens she'd witnessed, then what of Ben? Tony, Arlie, Brian and so many other students—she was convinced they were all in mortal danger.

But Ben? Why had she felt so sure, when the light hadn't surrounded him, that he was about to be spared whatever terrible fate awaited them all?

Maybe the answer lay on the final page of "The Last Stand of Benjamin James Jordan, American Hero."

In an addendum marked "Alternate Ending," Ben had decided that his bloody vendetta might end another way: "As they closed in on him, BJJ stood tall. The PIG AGENTS took his stillness for surrender, but that was their BIGGEST & LAST MISTAKE. As he hit the DETONATOR that set off the first line of mines, the pigs took a massive hit before they entered the forest. Their collective ASSES WERE GRASS. And the CHAIN REACTION set off the other bombs in the school, in the streets and in residential buildings till the whole MAGGOT-INFESTED TOWN OF SUNNYVALE was blown off the map.

"As Pixie Girl lay dying, she looked up ADMIRINGLY into BJJ's eyes. She FINALLY recognized him as the MARTYR & HERO he most certainly was. It was THREE YEARS TO THE DAY since his CRETIN ENEMIES had begun their PERSECUTION of him—the SEVENTH DAY OF THE SEVENTH MONTH. It would be a LANDMARK. From this day forth, he would lead the WAR that other HEROES & MARTYRS would wage against their persecutors across the country."

Rachel had felt colder still as his words connected. The date he'd earmarked for his day of wrath was today—July seventh, a mere three days after Independence.

And their conversation today came into sharp definition. Just as Ben was the only one who'd taken her visions seriously, so he'd taken it to heart. Ben no longer believed he had to die today, because she'd told him he wasn't going to.

Rachel had provided Ben with his Alternate Ending.

"Ben..." She met him face to face, blocking the short space between him and the roof turret where he was resting his gun. "The light is on your face. I can see it."

He paused, silent. His dark eyes searched her own, from deep within the shroud of pulsating light he couldn't see. He knew she wouldn't lie to him. Ben

Jordan, of all people, had become the only man, the only person, in the world who trusted her anymore. And she spoke the truth. Of everything she'd witnessed over the last few days, only he now glowed with such a blinding, sacred radiance. The only thing that equaled it had been her own reflection in the glass, if its distorted image were to be believed.

"You sure?" She gave a gentle nod. Slowly, his inscrutable features lit up into a smile.

Damn, he accepts it. He wants it. It's his destiny.

For Ben, it was as he first imagined it. Now he knew there was truly no way out, but he'd still blast his way into history. Now, the Day of Reckoning was at hand. And Ms Stark was here too–if the Pig Agents didn't take her out, she'd tell the world how it really was.

"You're all about the truth." He held his rifle horizontally in both hands, as if prepared to use the butt in combat. "That's why I'm not gonna kill you."

She stepped forward to intercede, to place herself as an obstacle.

"Stop right there!" His militaristic bark stopped her in her tracks. As far as Ben was concerned, it was beginning. It was on.

"I'm not going to let you kill anyone." She spoke plainly and emphatically, to cover her fear. But Ben was truly transformed. With his homicidal sense of purpose, his rifle, and the light that shone out of him, he resembled the superhuman hero that he dreamt he was.

"How're you gonna stop me? How's anyone gonna stop me?"

She had no answer. Never had death, in the most universal sense, seemed so close at hand or so meaningless.

He swung around and opened fire into the crowd below. Maggots! At last they were aware of his presence. They would always be aware of his presence, even when he was gone.

Lead sprayed across the schoolyard. In that macabre one-second time delay that occurs when violence strikes out of the blue, it took a moment for the kids to realize what was happening. As they screamed and scattered, at least one body seemed to hit the concrete. Rachel couldn't say for sure, but a sickening sense of déjà vu led her to imagine he'd hit one of the school's cheerleaders.

But she wasn't buying into his fantasy. She was here to prevent it becoming reality.

Ben was shocked when Rachel launched what little weight she had against him. She gripped his rifle like her own life depended on it. It almost made him laugh, but the fucking crazy woman just wouldn't let go.

For Rachel, it had come to the endgame. She had nothing else to use against him. No companions, no support, no weapon, no real strength. All she had was her body. Even if he was going to kill her, she was buying Sunnyvale High some time. In the time it took him to beat her to a pulp, or regain his gun and shoot her, at least some of them could make it out of the grounds.

The boy was wide-eyed at how hard she fought. She wouldn't let go of his rifle, every sinew of her fighting to wrest it from her hands. She was giving someone enough time to call the cops on their cellphone.

Angrily, Ben mustered his superior strength and jerked her backward towards him. She lost balance and fell directly into his grip. And kept falling.

Misjudging the force required, Ben had lifted Rachel's feet from the ground, catapulting her body into him as a dead weight. He too lost his footing, falling backward onto the section of the roof he'd chosen as his gun turret.

But there was nothing to stop him falling further.

Rachel took a sharp intake of breath as they both left the roof and entered freefall. She could only stare into the golden glow that enveloped them both as they fell, entwined together. And try to let her mind go blank.

As he plummeted, Ben's mind was racing. This wasn't supposed to happen. This wasn't the historic Battle of Sunnyvale! This wasn't the apocalypse, wasn't the blaze of glory he was meant to go out in... This... this sucked!

In the Sunnyvale High schoolyard, it came as a relief when the bodies hit the ground with a sickening, bone-breaking thud.

It was the reason the shooting had stopped as quickly as it started. The hunting rifle that had wounded one seventeen year-old girl in the leg lay close to the two bodies. At least one of them, possibly both, had to be the shooter. It was understandable that their welfare was secondary to more immediate concerns.

But it wasn't long before Principal Carr identified the heavily bleeding woman as Rachel Stark. Ms Stark's lifeblood was ebbing away from her, spreading out beneath her in a great, dark viscous pool.

The crowd were cleared away from the two bodies, as soon as it was established that urgent medical attention was required.

Carr kept his manner calm and officious as always. Ben Jordan's head was lolling in the manner of someone who'd broken both his neck and his spine. He did his best to attend to the boy, but it seemed hopeless. What had been a faint pulse had now faded completely.

He kept away from Rachel Stark, having already called for paramedics and instructed any trained staff to give first aid. The latter seemed inadequate, to say the least. Rachel appeared semi-conscious, but she, too, was in a very bad way. As she moved her head deliriously around, he felt her eyes bore into him.

Carr had no idea why this poor, unfortunate woman had obsessed about the idea that the school was in danger. Nor did he wish to know. It was all too late now, and that way madness seemed to lie. He could only be quietly grateful to her, and hope that her suffering would not be intolerable.

As her vision began to dim, Rachel had no such trivial concerns. She simply needed to see. She needed to connect with Ben's field of vision, as he quietly convulsed. As the golden white light of his life force danced on his face, his eyes wide with fear. At least he could see it too.

He was compelled to follow the shaft of light that arced out of his body and into infinity. It began to fade, as Principal Carr took off his suit jacket to cover the boy's face.

Rachel had lost control of her physical faculties, but managed to smile as she cast a rolling eye over the other students. There they all were. Weeping. Numb. Shocked. Distraught, and, in at least one case, injured. But alive.

Only moments earlier, many of them had been wearing golden haloes. Now, with the passing of Ben, they had faded into the ether. It was as if it truly had been an illusion, or a photograph dappled with sunlight.

Danger passed, kids. She spoke to herself to keep her spirit up, as the pain grew intense. Everything rosy in the garden again. They would never know. Nor, she told herself, should they ever have to shoulder the burden of knowing. Of seeing.

She felt her hand suddenly jerk as if in a spasm. It was numb, but someone had hold of it, was caressing it.

"Oh God, Rachel..." Jared was breathless, in tears. He'd only just managed to sprint his way back from the sports field, belatedly told of the terrible scene unfolding. But, even if he'd got there earlier, it would only have earned him further distress. He'd been warned that Rachel's internal injuries were likely to be critical, and what he was seeing bore that out.

"It's alright, now." She slurred to him as if very drunk, or going under an anesthetic. "Everyone's alright."

"Help's on the way, baby." He massaged her hand, scared to manhandle her poor, broken body. "Don't leave me now..."

He wanted to tell her she'd done good, but words seemed inadequate. He didn't really understand how, with all her recent bout of madness, she'd managed to save lives. He could only believe that, through her innate goodness, she had.

Rachel was delirious now. Smiling at a darkening storm cloud in the sky that was threatening to break.

Poor, sweet Jared. Too, too rational. He hadn't learned when it was right to be afraid, and what it was pointless to fear.

"It's beautiful," she managed to whisper. He followed her gaze, but all he saw was the dark cloud. The sympathetic atmosphere the heavens had provided for his darkening world.

She was slipping away from him, he knew. "What? What do you see?" he implored of her. He had to know.

Poor baby. Didn't he know by now?

"The lights..." she gently hissed.

They were the last words she spoke before she left him, alone and weeping.

Rachel was fixated on the light she saw above her. It was, as she now recognized, in the nature of all dying people.

Fear faded. Contentment seeped in, as her life force became lighter than her body, and she rose above it.

The light that emanated from her had become an infinite shaft leading into the vastness of the universe. She moved upward, into the light.

As consciousness of all earthly things receded, she was aware of only one human presence. Because Ben had departed so soon before her, and their fates had been so intertwined, she knew that he was ascending too, drifting away on his own separate journey.

His destructive worldly delusions had yet to fall away. He was bewildered, scared, to find himself in the twilight zone beyond this existence. She too, like every other human being, had lived in complete ignorance of what lay beyond.

But she had also learned when it was futile to be afraid. Sucked into her ascending pool of light, she departed with a sense of relief and validation.

Rachel Stark didn't ask to be special. She didn't want to be a hero. But sometimes, fate reaches out a cold shoulder... from The Twilight Zone.

SUNRISE

Based on the Teleplay
by Moira Frederick Rappaport

Story by Katrina Cabrera Ortega

This adaptation would not have been possible without continual reference to *Hueyteotecuhtin: 104 Gods of Central Mexico*, a visual art and literary work in progress. The author is indebted to Lawrence Burton for granting access to his work, and for his advice and assistance.

"Perchance, is your home in the place of the dead?
In the innermost of heaven?
Or is the place of the dead only here on earth?"

Cantares Mexicanos

"America is not a young land: it is old and dirty and evil before the settlers, before the Indians. The evil is there waiting."

William S Burroughs

ONE

Five close friends, looking for a last good time before graduating college and going their separate ways. But their lighthearted search has just turned darker than they ever could have imagined, a darkness found only... in The Twilight Zone.

I remember how the sun blazed down on the Sangre de Cristo Mountains.

It was the start of our third full day there. All of us were there for a little end-of-semester R&R—that is, my college buddies, Noah and Eve, Wes and Amber, and me. That kind of makes it sound like two couples and one hanger-on, but it wasn't that way.

Wes and Amber were an item alright; no one who was around for long could be in any doubt of that. But they were cute. They could be a little too frivolous for my tastes, a little too wowie-mowie. But, along with Evie and Noah, who had a lot more focus, they were probably the nicest people I'd met. As friends, I've never had a bad word to say about any of them.

Wes Mitchell was someone I'd known since my high school days in Albuquerque. When I say known, I guess it was more a case of being vaguely aware of him. He was a metal dude and a cyber head, and I wasn't part of his immediate circle. We knew each other by sight, if not by name. (I mean, I knew him by name back then. Sometimes, I still wonder if Wes can remember my name now—or even his own.)

It was only when we both got to the University of New Mexico that the social dynamic changed. He hooked up with some people from outside the state, who happen also to be friends of mine, and there we have it—after years of sharing the same basic space, Wes and me were finally brought into contact with each other's orbit.

And cyber head had become the operative phrase since Wes graduated from high school. The guy had always seemed kind of easy-going but rooted into his own space. Now he was exploring cyberspace, inner space—basically his own headspace. His hair, which was always kind of long and curled, had got a little longer and wilder, and he was growing a little beard on his chin. It was a progression, an extension of who he'd always been. Just like the way his mind seemed to have expanded without noticeably acquiring much knowledge.

But maybe I'm being way too hard on my brother Wes. After all, the dude's life was an extension of the inner world he lived in. Me? Well, my personal obsessions tended to fixate on things that were far away, in time if not always in space. My inner life was disconnected from the world where I physically resided. Until that summer's day up in the mountains.

Wes was a psychonaut. The space he was exploring was inside himself. Whether there was anything worth discovering in that particular speck of the cosmos is not for me to say. What I have to concede is that his inner world and the organic world, his online cyberworld and the physical outer world, had successfully meshed into one for him. That's an enviable feat to achieve.

And, of course, he'd found himself a soul mate in Ms Amber Hagen. I found it hard not to envy him for that. Even though, if I'm truthful with myself, I could only ever have tolerated Amber's company for as long as it took to grow accustomed to her beauty. Oh, she was an engaging girl—but in the lightest, fluffiest way. Whatever substance Wes and Amber had, it was built on wackiness: on obscure CDs and underground literature; sudden bursts of pot-inspired silliness; computer hacking and astrological moon charts.

It always amazed me how they'd hooked up so close with Noah and Evie. Our brother and sister could not have been more different, in my eyes. First, they were not a couple. At least, when Noah took the time to level with me about it, Eve had told him they could never have a long-term relationship until she'd worked out her priorities, set her personal parameters. It all sounded a little technical to me, but that, I guess, is the take-charge face of the modern woman.

And who can blame her? This generation of women has had a chance to impose their own structure and their own values on their own lives. Even if it's at the expense of male asses like my own that get very occasionally and very sharply kicked.

I'd got to know Eve Bishop and Noah Bailey at around the same time. When I arrived at the state university, I was feeling pretty isolated despite being a local boy. All my small circle of friends from high school had either gone to colleges outside of the state, or to a branch of the state university outside of Albuquerque. It was never that easy for me to make friends. I'm an introvert–a bookish, nervy, caffeine-allergic, un-American introvert. The kind of academic geek who the Europeans must have had in mind when they built their ancient universities, their ivory towers and dreaming spires. The kind who's a misfit in modern America.

It was kind of a warm, homecoming-type feeling to find people who responded to me. To the sense of humor that gets you marked down as a misanthropic wise-ass, if it's aired too frequently and too openly. To an introversion that isn't born of timidity–just from the fact that I don't fucking like most people, and find their values and aspirations completely alien to me.

But Evie and Noah were always cool to me. They always got the joke. They didn't find my total immersion in my subjects anal or creepy, or just write me off along with most of the bespectacled loners in my classes. (See, even I'm doing it now. That's how effectively modern America gets to pigeonhole people.)

Eve impressed me right from the start. She had the bright-eyed, bushy-tailed enthusiasm of the get-ahead chick, without any of the banality or the stupidity that I, in my isolated little heart, had come to associate with the species. She was intelligent, confident, assertive, all these things without any of the shallowness or pushiness that seems to accompany a drive for success. She was a scientist, a biology major, with a suitably rational and pragmatic approach to life.

And Evie had a sense of purpose, and a personal strength—a leadership quality that manifested itself in her physical fitness and her vibrant vitality. She had a kind of tough radiance that I could only admire. Oh, and I guess I ought to mention that, just for a while, I entertained some silly dreams about Evie Bishop. Of all the things I have to confess to here, it's kind of crazy that it still causes me the most pain.

As for me, well my name's Martin. Martin Tierney, for the official record, and I'm an archaeology major. Side order of anthropology to go with that, which some people—like Wes, bless his goatee'd little heart—managed to get confused with my major subject.

My obsession—I think I can call it that without any fear of contradiction, now that you're reading my account—began back in the fifth grade. It was in our American history lessons that we'd first heard tell of the Spanish conquest of Central and South America. It was all part of our overview of the formation of the different Americas that we know today, and it was exciting stuff. But I soon realized I wanted to know more about the conquest.

Not from the point of view of the Conquistadors, the victors from whose perspective history was always written. I wanted to know about the vanquished. The heathen. Those long-forgotten civilizations whose ways were deemed wicked and sacrilegious by the church. At first my teachers put it down to nothing more than childish morbidity. And there was an element of that—my interest, after all, lay in the violent pagan worlds of the Aztec, Incan and Mayan cultures. Their vanished world, and their seemingly barbaric rituals. Was it any wonder my teachers believed my "juvenile infatuation" would pass?

But then, teachers will always pour scorn on anything that's beyond their remit. It didn't take long before I realized there was little they could tell me that I really wanted to know. At first, my interest was fed by depictions of colorful pagan rites and gory human sacrifice in comic books and graphic novels. Sacred virgins and animal gods. Warrior priests and nature spirits. It was lurid, but it was as accurate as anything that I was going to be taught in public school.

It took years before I realized that my teachers literally could not teach me much that was accurate about the ancient cultures of Mesoamerica. State-sponsored pedagogues can only ever communicate the conventional wisdom, and of that there was precious little. It was only as I grew older and conducted my own painstakingly slow research that I realized why: the history of the Nahua culture and religion—for that, I later learned, is what the theology of ancient Mexico was called, rather than recognizable but parochially inaccurate umbrella terms like "Aztec"—was known only to a select few anthropological and archaeological historians. It was a closed-off field, a lost world. It became all the more enticing to me.

I think what I found intoxicating was the sense of vanished power, of decayed majesty. It was the kind of buzz that I imagined other geeky kids getting from science fiction: the sense of a world not so physically far removed from our own, but almost entirely alien. So exotic as to be almost unrecognizable, but connecting with me at some very basic, archetypal level.

My old man told my mother that it was symptomatic of my desire to disappear up my own asshole. Whatever. I found something more substantial, more enticing in the buried world of the past than I would ever find in all of his spreadsheets and profit-loss accounts.

But I'm thinking back to when I was an anthropology major. Events would take a hold. They took a hold of all of us. Up in the mountains, we experienced a resurgence of the Old World, and its ancient beliefs. None of us expected that anything like it would ever happen. I don't think any of us will ever get over it.

But I have to write it down. I guess that, whether I'm sharing this with the archives of the Smithsonian Institute, or whether my words are falling into a void, I need to get it out.

Call it catharsis. Call it a confession. I need to relive this to try to put it all behind me. If I'm ever going to try to get back to my old life, and finish my degree...

But whatever. This is how I remember it. To anyone reading this: please don't judge us too harshly. For a short while, that seemed like an eternity, we were not a part of the modern world. Its rationality, and its moral certainty, all the things that you take for granted, no longer existed for us.

We were trapped in a place where all the lights went out.

TWO

It was precisely 11:44 am. We'd just arrived at the top of the dirt track that led to the cave entrances.

How can I be so anal about knowing the exact time?

Easy. I still have the record of the day's events that was taken on Amber's camcorder. By some unplanned confluence of circumstances, you see, I've ended up as unofficial owner of the tape. I guess no one else wants to keep hold of it.

The sun baked our brows, but we adored it for its benevolence. And then there was that wonderful, timeless terrain. Rocky and granite hard. Desolate but beautiful. It led down into the caverns, and all their subterranean mystery. The others were enjoying the trip, but I felt like I'd really arrived. Truly, I was where both my vocation and my own sweet self told me I wanted to be.

Back then, it was heaven.

I'm right back there now, in fact. That shovel sifting through the earth is playing back to me on the video. Soon as it strikes the ground, another one joins in syncopation. We were really putting our backs into it.

There was our buddy Noah, a whole lot more clean-cut than the bearded guy who led all those animals out of the ark, two-by-two. A righteous dude, in every sense of that overused phrase. He had no problems about letting me influence proceedings on that fine day. The treasure hunt may have been something to which Evie and him had recruited the rest of us, but he still liked to pay lip service to my knowledge as an archaeologist.

It wasn't much more than playing around, to be sure—after all, all the directions we were receiving, all the coordinates we had, were transmitted to us by some kind of satellite system. It was typical, though, that Noah should ask me for advice instead of disregarding me. That he should let me direct the method of the digging, even when the information he already had supposedly pinpointed our target with only a small margin for error.

Noah Bailey had been hospitable to me ever since he turned up on campus. Like I've said, I'm not always the easiest of guys to get to know. It takes the curious nature of someone who is genuinely interested in people, in their own interests and their idiosyncrasies, to make that effort. Either that, or it's someone who's setting someone else up for mockery, to rip the piss out of them—which is the type of person that I, at first, wrongly assumed Noah to be.

He soon proved me wrong. He was an interesting guy. Another science student, majoring in physics, he didn't have that reductive viewpoint that I associate with people who see the universe reflected in a Bunsen burner or a Petri dish. Of course, it might have been something to do with his religious upbringing.

(One of the few times I've managed to make Noah angry was when I called him a "Christian Scientist." Take the words at their face value, and I was dead accurate. View them in a different context, and it was as if I was writing him off as a member of some cranky sect whose views were just as irreconcilable to the physical world as the opposed perspectives of "Christianity" and "Science" are to each other.)

Noah was a sharp-minded guy, and was curious about life, but he rarely pretended that he had all the answers. To get him into that frame of mind, he had to be a little drunk at first, and then the homespun biblical homilies would come spilling out. But mostly, his instinct was just to go with the flow.

He was curious about life, and he wanted to engage with it. He'd make up his mind about things along the way, rather than forming assumptions via a little book learning. (A particular vice of mine, I have to admit.) If it wasn't for Noah, I could never have imagined myself unwinding in the first few weeks on campus by shooting some hoops in the gym, or sinking some bottles of beer in the local fratboy bar.

Noah remains the best friend I've ever had. Nothing, not even my hurt feelings over Evie, will ever change that.

And there was my good friend Wes– the good-looking stoner most likely to get into a girl's pants.

Which, by all accounts, is how he spent a lot of his time when he first arrived at college. They can say what they like about marijuana–it may destroy a person's motivation, but I never saw any evidence that it made Wes want to slow down and keep his dick in his pants.

That's why, I guess, it always amazed me that Noah and Wes became such close friends so quickly. Noah's the type of guy who'll take a few hits from a joint on a Saturday night, and say to hell with propriety, diligence and the sheriff's office for maybe an hour. Wes's way of starting the day, of hitting the bong before logging on, is alien to him. But I guess that's a measure of how five such disparate people had come together as friends. When you have genuine empathy and an interest in each other, then most of a person's quirks are just that and no more. Nothing was worth getting bent out of shape about.

Which was pretty much Wes's whole philosophy of life. I remember how, when Noah first introduced the two of us, he acted like he was meeting me for the first time. Then, when I admitted to Noah that I'd been at high school with the guy, Wes casually confessed, "Sure, I know the dude. Yeah. Know him pretty well." Neither one was the case. But neither, in Wes's way of looking at things, was worth taking the Fifth Amendment for.

As I'd got to know him, it wasn't unusual to find myself invited down to his end of the dorms some weekends. He'd call me to smuggle in a few beers, listen to some of the more trippy techno or nu-metal music, or maybe watch some movies on the communal DVD player. If he invited me to smoke a bowl, I'd either have to make that one singular hit, or else decline. Like I've said, none of us got too exercised by each other's personal habits, as long as they weren't getting in the way of their lives. But, as far as I was concerned, Wes's bong hits were a chemical cosh, and I didn't need to be knocked down on my ass in one fell stroke.

It could amuse me, or embarrass me, when he'd call me along to his room at weekends and forget to tell me he'd invited a girl over at the same time. "Oh, Marty, yeah... This is Katrina... You've both met, right?"

I don't know whether it was me or the girl with the dyed scarlet hair and the pierced nipples who looked more embarrassed. But what the hell, it didn't faze Wes. We just nodded politely to each other as she tried to pull the sheet up tight around the piercings that were fully exposed before I'd walked into the room. I made my excuses and left.

Afterwards, Wes had tried to fathom out just what had fazed me. He seemed to believe I'd invited myself along to meet some girls on the spur of the moment, then freaked out when I found out he'd already made it past third base to several home runs.

"So what it is with you, Marty? Are you, like, gay or somethin'? I mean, it's okay if you are." No, I had to explain to him, I'm not gay. I don't know if I successfully imparted the idea that I liked girls, but was subject to the same inhibitions as anyone else who was singularly unsuccessful with them. That it might take me months to gauge the interest of a woman, and then more time to get myself to the stage where she might be ready to accept a sexual relationship.

Wes could accomplish all that in the earlier stages of a single night. If time passed without any action, he'd figure the girl was a little cranky and didn't care about wasting his time. My agonizing timescale was completely alien to his way of life. Or at least it had been. Maybe it was less so now, now that him and Amber were a serious item.

"The air is thick with tension as the dig begins..."

Hey, that's Amber's voice now. She liked to give these kind of dumb commentaries, like she'd won herself a job on some real cheap-ass cable channel. But boy, was she cute.

"For two days, our intrepid treasure hunters have been trekking through a hellish landscape of towering mountains and bottomless canyons."

Tell it, girl. But we were loving it. The light, the space, the mystery of it all, it was opening our heads right up. I could tell it was doing it for W&A too, without too much chemical assistance. They were using a little pot, maybe, but otherwise the natural landscape was doing for them what only peyote, or Mexican mushrooms, had done before. They were experiencing the kind of ecstatically happy heights that I, with my temperamental aversion to anything that might leave you tripping the universe for eight hours, could share with them.

I guess it might not have been as mind-blowing as the time that, according to everyone who knew him, Wes and Amber had spent a full day screwing under the effects of Mexican yage, or yohimbe bark, or some such botanical head trip. Word had it that Amber experienced head-exploding orgasms several times, but Wes just couldn't make it. Not that he couldn't perform—no, I think our boy always came through on that count. But, for all the energy and passion he was putting into it, he just couldn't make it through that final gateway. On their sexual-psychedelic trip, Wes was traveling hopefully but he could not arrive. I guess there's a lot worse places you can be than head-tripping around, inside Amber Hagen for hours, without ever reaching an orgasm.

"Baking in the pitiless sun, throats parched and raw."

Bang on cue, Wes grips his throat and makes like he's dehydrating. Pure cornball. But they're having fun. Or maybe the first joint Amber and him sparked up this morning has left them a little parched. They were made for each other. Not just because they were a pair of stoners, either. There was something they'd found in each other that seemed like it was going to be permanent. That seemed like it was the kind of thing other people might spend their lives looking for and never find.

It had signaled the end of Wes's promiscuity. As a wise man once said, "Why keep going out for a hamburger when you've got prime steak waiting for you indoors?" Wes knew he'd hit the roof of his potential as a ladies' man the day that Amber and him first got together. There were no more physically alluring women than her on campus—we all recognized that, not just the lucky guy who won her. Neither were any women more suited to his personal style and temperament. Why carry on with your quest when you've already found the Holy Grail? From that day forth, maybe a little over eighteen months ago, Wes stopped shopping for strawberry flavored condoms and secured a regular table for two at the cheap little Mexican restaurant just off-site. It was almost marital bliss.

I don't think Amber comes onscreen till later. It's just nice to hear her babbling voice again. She comes on like a silly, sexy, twenty-three year-old child. The same age as all of us, in fact, in the final year of our university courses. She didn't have a care or a fear in the world. Neither did any of us. But Amber was different. She was a little flaky round the edges, to be sure, but, no disrespect intended to our brother, any woman who chimed really directly with Wes just had to be. It didn't mean she was a damaged set of goods, though. No, I'd be fair enough to say their use of hallucinogens complemented the way they lived their lives, without overtaking it.

It was all on the level with Wes's perception of his PC as an extension of his mind. (Considering that all his time not spent working out or making out was spent in front of the monitor, it was like an extension of his body too.) It was of a part with Amber's lightweight fixation with Native American culture, particularly the whole Castaneda trip about how imbibing some sacred botanicals can make you fly with the wings of an eagle. I say "lightweight" purely because Amber would see that kind of scenario as a beneficially good trip. Me—well, as an anthropologist I know there's a greater significance to old tribal rites than just some kind of psychedelic Disney World.

In the years since my obsession with the Nahua had blossomed, I'd submerged myself in everything that it was possible to discover. I'd traced the rise of the first great Mesoamerican civilization back to southern Veracruz and Tabasco, near Mexico's Gulf Coast. It was posthumously known as the Olmec—after the Olmeca-Xicallana, a people known to inhabit the region during the Post-Classic age of 900 to 1521 AD. But the origins of the Classic age harked back to at least one thousand and four hundred years before that, to a time when the Roman Empire still ruled the known world and the natives of what would much, much later become the USA were living in a land William Burroughs would describe as "old and dirty and evil before the settlers."

As with the Olmec, the name of their first great city would be given the name that we remember it by via the later Mexica people: Teotihuacan, the "Place Where Gods Are Made." The strange, rarefied atmosphere that permitted gods to walk among men always intoxicated me. It wasn't anything like those old movies where the Greek gods played games with the lives of human beings on a chessboard, and sent the most worthy humans to do battle with monsters. This was somehow more earthly, more visceral. The gods that walked among men were represented in Nahua lore by primitive symmetrical carvings and drawings that represented beasts, or flowers, or sometimes even manmade objects. It was a living theology, that took its place among both the living and the dead of this world.

There were times, when I was growing up, when it seemed realer than anything else I knew. It was as if I'd bought into the Mexica tendency to mythologize everything in retrospect, so that it all had mythic significance. My particular favorite was the myth of how a descendant of Quetzalcoatl, the serpent god, had been the last ruler of the ancient city of Tollan. He had sailed away to sea, and promised to return at a time on the Nahua calendar that just happened to coincide with the landing of Hernando Cortez at Veracruz. As to how literally accurate that was, nobody can say. And, of course, it did nothing to avert the conquest. But it set the context for a mythology that merged with history. Where everything had a purpose and a justification, and the living symbolism of Nahua interacted with the physical world that surrounded it.

I'd come to regard myself as something like a modern Mesoamerican; an interpreter of ancient Mexica culture. A rational pagan. It was an affection that earned me scorn from my family. It was seen as symptomatic of my retreat from the hard, thrusting, competitive "real world." But the real world is the physical world, the natural world. And I found the Nahua way of interpreting it, of communing with it, via their very specific rites and ceremonies, to be just as "real" as anything I would ever encounter. It stood firmly apart from the unreality of our media-fed, advertising-saturated communications culture—the kind of thing that my old man would insist, laughably in my opinion, was absolutely "real."

None of this is to denigrate the kind of romantic New Age Paganism so beloved of our dear friends, W&A. Theirs was a kind of marriage between two old soul mates who would never leave each other now. They were too attuned to each other's way of thinking, so tolerant of each other's eccentricities that they'd started to mirror them. They really were beginning to seem like an old married couple, their cozy lifestyle marked by the odd burst of psychedelic flashes.

The Hi-8 picture pans around in a blur. Stick to the voiceover, Amber, you just ain't camerawoman material.

There was Eve. Bubbling, blonde, and brainy to boot. Just as wide-eyed as her best girlfriend, but sharper, more animated. On account of sticking to OJ and coffee, instead of smoking weed for breakfast, I guess. Eve was a bright girl. She was a babe too. One mildly drunken night, I'd even been stupid enough to tell her that's how I felt.

I think it shocked her a little back then. Us academic geeks are supposed to keep company amongst our own kind, right, and not trespass onto territory occupied by the confident, attractive people. It always seemed like it was deemed somehow indecent for a guy like me to have any kind of longings, like it was something I should keep to myself. I'm not saying like I'm *Shrek*, or something. Take a look at the videotape I'm leaving as part of this testimony. You'll see a pretty normal guy. I just don't have the effortless born-to-win attitude of the guys I've been around most of my life, and I guess it shows in me. I guess I should be grateful that people like that can tolerate me, even adopt me as one of their own.

But I realize now that it doesn't entitle me to what they've got. Oh, Evie was kind with me. A little taken back, maybe. "Oh, Marty. . . Honestly, I had no idea you felt that way." It was said with good humor and tolerance, but it had a faint air of condescension like a high school teacher reacting to some sophomore's crush. It was said in a way that informed me I should never want something which I could never have. I never made my feelings to her known again. Truly, I should have realized it wasn't my style. Back then, I had a pretty serious relationship going on with my work. Girls only entered the picture as girl*friends*.

What the hell. It was stupid of me not to realize there was something going on between Evie and Noah. I guess I sensed it in the air, but took a chance in dreaming for a few moments that *I* might be the one. She let me down easy—and Noah was kind too, as I'd always expect of him. Still, there was something in their kindness that made me feel like a backward kid whose feelings they felt they had to protect. It was almost as if there were too many smiles and too many hugs, too much "Hey, bro, how you doin'?" whenever I showed up. That may just be my paranoia. I've tried to train my mind these days not to see signs and connections where there are none, but I suspect that's a part of my nature.

All the same, it became just too obvious that Evie and Noah had become an on-off item, but were too circumspect to be open about it in case it broke my heart or something. That, I think, was the part I found most excruciating.

But hey–I'm not going to get maudlin about women I don't see anymore. Suffice to say, back then I had about the coolest friends a young guy could want.

"And now they are mere moments away from winning this year's GPS Internet Treasure Hunt." Eve is hamming it up too.

Noah, Wes and me were dormed down together at Albuquerque, with Amber and Eve in the campus co-ed quarters. In our different ways, we'd all totally embraced campus life. When our college had set up one of those Global Positioning System scavenger hunts, it was only natural we should all join in.

I only knew a little about how it worked, but Noah was a physics major and he filled me in on the deal. The machine operated in co-ordination with a ring of satellite tracking systems, orbiting the earth. The user segment–which was the device Eve was clowning around with–converted "SV" (that's the "Satellite Viewer" system, if you're a techno-boob too) into position, velocity and time estimates. I'm no gadget freak, but I have to say it was cool. I don't have the full SP on this, but the receiver device carried data frames that were supposedly accurate to a horizontal distance of one hundred meters, a vertical distance of one hundred and fifty-six meters, and a time measurement accuracy of three hundred and forty nanoseconds.

So there we all were. Taking time off from cramming to go treasure hunting in our summer break. Whatever we found was likely to be worthless, but it would have some kind of token benefit attached, maybe a cash prize that you could donate to your student faculty or suchlike. And besides which, it was fun.

"And we're all pumped about it too," says Noah, coming into the frame now. "Except for Marty here who's too busy worrying about his archaeology paper due next week."

Ah, go on. Break my balls for studying.

Amber turns that damn zoom lens in on me, with all the finesse of someone who wants to examine my nostril hair. "You mean my anthropology paper." See, I told you no one ever got it right. Not even Noah, who's not exactly an is-that-my-head-or-is-that-my-hat? type, if you know what I mean. "My archaeology paper isn't due for another two weeks."

It's never comfortable to look at yourself on a screen. Not if you're not a natural performer, like Amber and Evie, anyway. But it's even more excruciating for me to see how earnest I can be. How, even when I was having fun, I didn't seem to loosen up and look like I was.

I just have a serious demeanor. A little geekish, I guess. I really don't feel inclined to apologize for it.

While the others are playing, like little kids digging in the sand, I'm trying to transport myself back in time—say to, oh, the Pleistocene era, nothing too extreme. I'm as buzzed as everyone else, but in my own way. It still looks like it was too cool to be there, sure.

But how much more stimulating, how much more intoxicating, to try to picture yourself in relationship to the geographical formations that stretch as far as the eye can see? That have pre-dated humankind by millions of years, and will still be here when you and your species are long gone?

"Hey, I think I found something!"

That's Noah's voice, offscreen.

The screen whizzes around in a blur again, as Amber focuses on the other guys clambering down into the small hole our brother Noah has dug. Noah and Wes are whooping and hollering, and damn it, I'm excited too.

Even if it's only likely to be some prop stashed away underground by the contest organizers.

"Ladies and gentlemen, we have a winning team... and it is us!" Eve plays to the camera for all she's worth.

But something about it grabs me as soon as Noah releases it from the earth. Encrusted with dirt, whoever had buried it looks like they played for keeps. It's a box, carved out of white stone, with a definite antique quality. Bulky and rectangular, with sharp edges and corners. It seems curious to me that whoever planted it should go to such lengths.

"What'd I tell you people?" Noah beams it out for the camera. "It's all about faith, you gotta believe!"

"Uh-oh, he's headin' for the pulpit." Wes joshes him, sounding like Chong without the Cheech.

"The truth shall set you free, my son..." Noah's laying on the deep-voiced gravitas, like he's some kind of Pentecostal preacher. It's something I could never figure with him. I'm interested in belief systems—I mean, really interested. But they're all specific to their time and place and culture.

And Noah was a scientist. (I should say *is* a scientist—our time's not over yet.) I just don't get how he reconciles his scientific rationality with a religion that grew out of conditions in the Middle East, two thousand years ago or more.

I guess I'm in no position to judge. Call a kid "Noah" and it's an even bet he'll have a bible-backed upbringing.

Anyway, he's the hero of the hour. Everyone is going goggle-eyed over that box. I guess they all expected something a little less imposing. Me, I'm dying to get my hands on it, but etiquette prevails.

Amber comes into the frame at last. Her eyes, below that attractive brunette bob of hair, look bemused. "I thought the prize was a box of CDs."

Her boyfriend laughs. "Dude, those gotta be some golden oldies."

Eve is shaking her head. "No, no..." Precision is her thing. "According to the website, the treasure was only buried a month ago."

I've listened to them for as much as I can stand to. For the first time, I see myself becoming assertive on the screen. "Here... Let me see that." I'm reaching forward. Witless conjecture is one thing. But my enquiring nature has been awakened, something more than idle curiosity. I take the carved rock in my hand. And I'm transported.

The dirt is so ingrained that it takes me a short while to wipe it away from the indentations I can see. Sure enough, they're markings cut into the box. Closer inspection shows strange figures, almost friendly-familiar to me. Angular little animal faces or bodies, mostly in profile. Snakes. Lizards. And a smattering of stars, in the style of some archaic astronomer.

From our modern perspective, it looks crude, kind of cartoonish. But I can recognize it for what it is, and it sends a glow right through me.

The carvings are not illustrations so much as hieroglyphics. They're in the style of Mixteca-Puebla, the glyphic lexicon of the ancient Mesoamerican culture. The only non-verbal mode of communication to bridge the gaps in a nation that covered about one million square miles, with at least twenty-one separate languages and two hundred and sixty different dialects.

"Guys, this is a relic from the ancient Nahua religion!"

Silence. It's an education to watch yourself burbling with enthusiasm, to a group who don't have the first goddamn clue what you're talking about. "Aztec, people... This is ancient Aztec."

Okay, so I muddied the waters a little. Going by the works I've studied, I place the artifact at late-fifteenth-to-early-sixteenth centuries, shortly before the invasion of the Conquistadors—maybe even earlier. By then, the Aztecs were a distant memory, and only some citizens of the great city of Tenochtitlan, which they founded in the twelfth century, could claim Aztec ancestry.

But "Aztec' became a shorthand reference to the ancient Mexica people, after the 1843 publication of *The Conquest of Mexico*, by the historian WH Prescott. So it is for my four non-archaeologist friends.

"Aztec?" Wes is pondering. "You mean like Geronimo?"

Oh Jesus Christ.

"No. No. Not like Geronimo." I watch myself becoming very irritated, very quickly. "He was an Apache. The Aztec, the Mexica civilization and culture were wiped out after Hernando Cortez's conquest of 1521. Their capital, Tenochtitlan, a great city that contained up to two hundred thousand souls, fell to about three hundred conquistadors and ten thousand fellow Mesoamericans. They wanted to see the balance of power changed, but they didn't count on those bastards, the Catholic Church, doing their utmost to grind the indigenous culture into the ground."

I ignore what appears to be a little pique on Noah's face. Not that he's a Catholic, but I figure he's rooting for the same team.

I don't have the heart to tell Wes and Amber how Neil Young, one of their old hippie godfathers, got it wrong in his song "Cortez the Killer": "Hate was just a legend / And war was never known." Murals from the cities of Teotihuacan, Tollan and Tenochtitlan all testified to how honorable it was to be a warrior.

And how, as in every warrior culture, sometimes it was deemed necessary to be ruthless.

But still, the warriors of Tenochtitlan were defeated not by their supposedly peaceful nature, but by weight of numbers, superiority of weapons—Spanish musket guns and swords against the "macahuitl," a flat wooden club lined with obsidian blades—and the introduction of diseases like smallpox, previously unknown to them. Before the Spanish came, Mexico is believed to have held a population of up to twenty-five million. Those who sided with the Conquistadors embraced their own destruction, with disease, more than war, reducing the Mexica population to about one million by 1600.

"They burned every text, every carving, every artifact they could get their hands on. It was so ignorant, man. The Spaniards' own accounts of the time tell of how they piled bonfires high with irreplaceable texts, painted on deer hide or tree bark. Many of the indigenous people are believed to have chosen martyrdom or suicide, rather than forced conversion to the invaders' religion. All we know of the Mexica culture and Nahua religion today is from materials that'd barely fill one big cupboard. And," I underline, getting a little preachy myself, "from anti-'Aztec' propaganda created by the Christian church."

I guess they seem impressed. They're silent anyway.

"In fact, I'm surprised this... whatever it is, survived." I handle the box a little gingerly, unsure whether to open it, and risk damaging it, or to wait until we get back to civilization and place it in expert hands.

But, I hardly need to remind myself, I'm a keen student of the period. Who more expert to examine it than me?

"Why's it buried here?" Eve's question is to the point. The simple truth is, I don't know. But I'll hazard a guess.

"The Mexica never had an 'empire', as such, but they had a wide sphere of influence that we call a 'tribute network'. The ancient city of Teotihuacan's gods are represented in the art of the old Mayan culture; its trade outposts extended as far as Guatemala in the south. Some historians believe the Mexica's 'turquoise road', their northern trade route, may have reached what's now the southwest of the USA. It's more than conceivable that they got to New Mexico."

It's also known that, of the Native American tribes in the southwest, the "Amerind"-speaking Ute and Hopi are descended from the Aztecs. Maybe Wes, for all his confusion isn't such a halfwit after all.

"Or maybe the Conquistadors brought them along later. It's believed the Mexica used to send them off on wild goose chases to look for Cibola, the fabled seven cities of gold, in the north. Trouble was, they used to take noble-born Aztecs along as captives. Maybe," I held up the carved box, "this was buried here as a tribute to the gods by a captive high priest. Matter of fact, this latch," I fingered a metal clasp that had held the box shut tight for centuries, "can only have been a product of the post-Conquistador period. They were using their new masters' skills to try to conceal their old, forbidden religious rites.

"And check this out—these markings..." The astrological symbols on the box include a sun disk, and a band of stars. "This represents Topan, the Nahua heavens. The sun is central to the Nahua religion, each era of human history is divided into five ages of the sun."

Wes is mulling it over. He suddenly pipes up. "So what are you telling us, that this isn't part of the treasure hunt?"

Forget my previous remark. He's a beautiful guy, but he's a fucking moron. Even Amber seems to recognize it at times. She kills the camcorder at this point, bending down to look at the box with the rest of us.

It's probably the last image of my friends that I'll ever see.

THREE

"Screw the treasure hunt. We could wind up in *People Magazine.*" That was Amber's way of looking at it.

"Say dude," Wes said to me, "you're majoring in tomb raiding. How much do you think this would go for on eBay?" I think he was joking, though I'm not sure. Some people have little dreams, I guess.

But me, though, I felt like my heart was lifting into the clouds. I'd found Tlactipac (try saying that exactly like you read it, "Taa-lak-tee-pak.") All Aztec-Nahua words have that basic phonetic quality. It was the place where the lower part of the heavens intersected with the surface of the underworld. It was, according to the Nahua religion, both a part of this world and the center of the universe.

It was also, in that pragmatic way that was peculiar to the Mexica, situated wherever their various adherents decided it was. For Nahua was a set of spiritual beliefs that adapted to the needs of its practitioners—unlike the narrow Christian dogma that replaced it. In the Nahua heavens, known as Topan, their different strata were divided into thirteen levels. It related not so much to any mystical numerology as to everyday practicality. To the ancient Mexica, the number thirteen was the base number of the daytime calendar. Correspondingly, there were said to be thirteen "Day Lords"—the mythical deities who presided over each of the thirteen daylight hours between dawn and dusk. Everything, in its own symbolic way, was totally practical.

The only difference between the workings of Nahua theology and modern-day science is that science has developed methods of empirical testing to gauge cause-and-effect. Science "demonstrates" that the sun rises in the east due to the orbital motion of the earth around it, rather than the symbolic ascension of a sacred eagle into the sky. It's rational, but it's theory-bound. And, to my mind, its truth is no more apparent to the unbiased eye than the Mexica's great symbolic myths.

"Maybe there's something valuable inside," Eve ventured. "Some ancient artifact." I guess she was trying to raise the intellectual tone. As far as I could see, the box, in itself, already was an artifact. No one else seemed to grasp that we'd already found proof of a mighty ancient civilization some eight hundred miles away from its seat of power. That, in itself, was pretty mind-blowing.

"Maybe it contains some rare, priceless jewels or somethin'. Right, Marty?" No, Amber just wasn't getting it. But her attitude bothered me a whole lot less than Noah's usual take-charge approach.

"Only one way to find out . . ." He was prizing the little copper latch that clasped the box shut with a piece of flint he picked up from the cave.

"Hey, be careful there . . ."

"Yeah, if you damage it the price will go down." I suppose Wes imagined he was backing me up.

But it bugged me on a whole number of levels. Only I could guess at the archaeological and historical significance of what we had in our hands. Even then, in retrospect, I see that I only had the merest inkling. And then we had Noah, itching to crack it open like it was a fortune cookie. I have to say it irked me. It was like my knowledge and expertise counted for nothing, like they were some kind of joke.

Noah had snapped the clasp. He lifted the lid slowly, eroding all those years when the two pieces of cut rock had almost fused together as one. I wasn't going to be locked out of this. Jeez, no one else there could even have known what we were looking at!

I was the first to look inside. Once I gleaned what it was, and determined the likely extent of its fragility, I was also the first to place my hand on it. The inside of the box felt organic, nothing was planed off or smoothed down. There had simply been a big incision into the center that allowed it to hold its prize comfortably. The others were all eyes, as they watched me release it from its receptacle.

It was an ancient drinking cup, also fashioned out of stone. Chunky and semi-cylindrical, without the shaped stem that an archaeologist might expect to find on a European goblet of the same period.

With a sheer surface, speckled with dark porous dots, its opening at the top was sealed by parchment hide. Stretched and dyed, it was made from the skin of a furry mammal, perhaps a deer—possibly a rabbit, or a dog. What was surprising is how relatively alive and membranous the hide felt, as if it had been treated with some rare preservation process.

Or maybe this was just an elaborate hoax, after all. How many centuries-old artifacts do you come across that feel like they could have been committed to the ground last week?

"That's it?" Amber found it difficult to conceal her disappointment. "A cup?"

"It's not even gold!" Way to go, dude. Join in with your girlfriend's whining.

I tried to ignore their negativity. In my eyes, we either had a find that was hugely significant, or else someone had hoaxed us with a crock of crap. In any case, I was not going to be brought down by people who weren't qualified to judge.

I held the cup at arm's length, holding it up toward one of the many chinks in the cave that let the sunlight flood in. It was weighty too. "Feels like there's something inside it," I remarked. It produced a clamor of hands.

Eve was the first to touch it. After me, that was. I still felt like I wanted to guard it jealously. But, after all, I hardly had any claim of ownership.

There was a leather string, tied in a small bow, holding the parchment covering against the top of the cup. It was probably from the hide of the same animal.

I held it steady as Eve gently untied the string. Her delicate touch respected our chance find, our discovery, whatever the hell it was we'd stumbled across. Or maybe she was just expecting some big black dung beetle to come tumbling out.

She lifted the parchment off. Despite the relative freshness of everything I'd seen and felt, it was like she was peeling away skin from an organic part of some animal-mineral hybrid. I felt a faint disturbance at that moment—and, if I'm not mistaken, so did the other guys. It was as if it symbolized some kind of union with the human body. With the shape of the cup, and the opening of the parchment, it was almost like the rocky terrain had manifested itself in female form. But I know that's just sub-Freudian crap. I shrugged it off as quickly as it came over me.

As she lifted the protective skin straight off, the contents gave off a faint odor. It's not quite accurate to say it glistened in the light, but I got the impression of some liquid content. Dark. Viscous. Faintly metallic in its smell.

Like blood.

Whatever it was had remained fluid. I'm no biologist, but it didn't make much sense. If I was correct in my reading of the period, then this thing could have been buried here for five hundred years or more. Hell, I don't see how freshly sealed plasma could have kept its liquid consistency for a *week*.

But it was redolent of things that anyone who's ever studied Mesoamerican culture has only imagined. The ancient blood sacrifice that everyone, even the layman, associates with those "bloodthirsty Aztecs." In 1487, during the re-dedication by the High Priest Ahuizotl of Tenochtitlan's Templo Mayor, the greatest temple of the city, it's commonly held that eighty thousand, four hundred victims—or volunteers, given the nature of Nahua ritual—were sacrificed to the old gods over a three-day period. That's the legend, anyway.

For myself, I don't buy it. These days, I don't think any serious student of Mesoamerica would. Think about it: tens of thousands of corpses to dispose of within several days. No modern hygiene methods or crematoria, just crude bonfires.

It's true that the skeletons of Tenochtitlan's dead were put on display upon the skull racks of the temple precinct. Nahua, as a theology informed by nature and by pragmatism, existed hand-in-hand with death. Not as a warning or an admonishment to protect the immortal soul, not as a promise of pie-in-the-sky after mortality and decay—just as a fact of everyday life, to be accepted on its own terms. Its echoes still persist in the quasi-pagan *Dia del Muerte* celebrations today, the joyous death pageant that shows the chink in modern Mexico's Christian armor.

So death and the Mexica got on just fine. And it's true that the invasion of the Conquistadors, who decimated the Mesoamerican nation, also served to suppress the "barbaric' pagan tradition of human sacrifice. But more than eighty thousand corpses, unless burned or buried immediately, would surely have created conditions of disease, pestilence, maybe typhus and cholera.

The Nahua religion, in its mechanistic view of the universe, demanded like-for-like payment. If people took something out of nature, then, to appease the gods and to perpetuate the existence of the Mexica, something had to be given back—principally, their lifeblood. The most credible historians now estimate that up to four thousand "privileged" sacrificial victims met their end at Templo Mayor. That number was achievable. Nahua was a practical theology, and the Mexica were practical people.

And I have no doubt whatsoever that blood sacrifice was a reality.

"Is that blood, dude?" What could I say? Its thick, dark fluid was staring me in the face. I didn't know for sure, but I knew what I believed.

I must have given a small but perceptible nod. "Whoa, get outta here!" It stirred up excitement. Suddenly, we were in the middle of something weird, something novel.

"Go on, dip your finger!" Noah was daring Wes to play stupid games.

"You dip your finger." It didn't seem to have any more significance to them than its gross-out value. It was puerile, child-like.

"I'll do it." It surprised everyone to hear Eve volunteer herself. Probably me most of all. She'd majored in biology, and was the last woman I'd expect to fool around with an unidentified blood sample.

Eve took a deep breath, with all eyes upon her. She lowered her ring finger cautiously. A little hint of "yuck" on her face indicated that it was as wet and sticky as we'd all anticipated it might be. When she withdrew her finger, it was slick with the thickest, darkest crimson, the red stuff that tends to flow from a cut main artery.

She studied its constitution. Sniffed its scent. "It *is* blood." It produced more excitement, with a little token wincing–not least from Evie herself, no longer the objective scientist, it seemed.

"Oh come on, Evie, how?" Noah was incredulous, though he was getting off on how out-of-whack it all was. "I mean, five-hundred year-old blood?"

They both looked at me. As though my reading of the likely historical period just had to be wrong. "Wouldn't it have dried up by now?" Eve asked me accusatorily.

Hell, she was the biologist. "You would think." I was non-committal, having no real answer. "But you tell me: wouldn't you expect it to dry up under non-laboratory conditions after more than a couple of weeks?"

She had no answer either. I still had half a mind to say it was an elaborate hoax that someone was pulling. But, somehow, that seemed too rational. It seems a little crazy maybe, but, by that point, the rational rules of the modern world seemed more distant than usual.

Maybe it was the environment. We'd already spent a couple of days away from civilization, sucked into one of the most beautiful, skyscraping landscapes we were ever likely to see. When I found myself thinking of the ancient Mexica, I was starting to think in the symbolic terms in which they perceived the earth, the mountains and the skies.

Its mytho-history was as real to me as any of the concrete facts I'd been made to memorize at school. I could feel like I'd witnessed the sacking and burning of the great city of Teotihuacan, around 600 AD—even though I had no idea why it had taken place, or even, unlike the later Conquistador invasion of 1521, who the aggressors may have been.

But the cultural origins of Nahua were not yet uprooted and severed. They existed here, now, all around us but invisible in this beautiful, desolate place. It's believed by some anthropological historians that one of the sectors of ancient Mexica society, the Chichimec, were refugees from abandoned tribal sites around the American southwest—particularly those attributed to the Anasazi, or the builders of Chaco.

They had been here, hundreds, maybe thousands, of years previously. I believed I still felt their presence all around. Across the border, it's estimated that over a million Mexicans still speak the ancient Nahuatl tongue without any trace of Spanish at all. Nahua has never truly left the Americas.

In purely symbolic terms, the name "Sangre de Cristo" itself could hardly have been much more evocative—"the blood of Christ." But that had been another blood sacrifice, the one that Noah, and millions of others who shared his faith, had been brought up to believe in. The atonement of God's only son, with his own blood, for the sins of every last one of us, was a myth that Noah's parents and his pastor would deny had anything at all to do with pagan symbolism.

But, as with the Day of the Dead, the last vestiges of the old religion had proven adept at assimilating and adapting. Mesoamerican pagan-Catholicism is its own tradition. Think of the obscure and unofficially canonized Mexican saints, few of which are recognized in Rome. Think of how, in 1519, the pragmatic and adaptable Mexica were prepared to adopt Jesus Christ into the Nahua canon as one of their own gods—before the Christian religion was imposed upon them, bloodily wholesale, two years later. I'd thought of telling Noah how Jesus had become the god of cattle, metal and money, but considered it maybe a moot point...

No such considerations were weighing on Amber and Wes's minds. They were just caught up in what they perceived as the wackiness of it all. "Here," she shoved the camcorder into her man's hands. "Get a shot of me holding it."

She reached out to me for the cup. My immediate instinct told me to keep a hold of it. But she just stood there, with her hand held open, like she expected me to comply. Sure enough, I did. But there was something that made me want to protect our discovery, keep it pure and untrivialized.

"Just be careful with it, okay?" They could tell I was jittery. Maybe that was part of the fun.

Eve, as ever, was levelheaded and considerate. "Let me cover the top, Amber." She held the parchment hide that she'd carefully undone from our artifact. I don't think it was just to humor me, but I appreciated the gesture. Whatever we had was more than a novelty. Assuming that it was authentic, it was imbued with the weight of history. It wasn't asking much, I think, that it be treated with due seriousness.

But to Amber and Wes, it was all still a game. As Eve walked toward her to protect our find, Amber was asinine enough to try to dodge her. Even for her, it was not the cleverest move she'd ever make. However well lit the caves seemed at that point, we were still walking on stony, uneven ground. As she tried to sidestep Eve, she stumbled.

Stumbled, and fell forward, just a couple of steps, before regaining her footing. Stumbled, and let the cup fall from her hands.

It was a moment's horseplay, for which I've long since forgiven her. But she let the weight of centuries drop from her hand. Whatever scientific or historical mystery was preserved in that ancient receptacle, it was spilled, like the seed of Onan, unthinkingly onto the ground.

It thudded to a halt amid a decline in the rocky floor. I thought I heard someone breathe the words, "Oh shit." I had nothing more eloquent to add to that. The blood—what we'd all assumed to be, and now accepted was, blood—trickled freely into the dirt. Amber had thrown away our Holy Grail.

The gravel on the floor combined with the crimson fluid to create a dark-stained dirt. The lifeblood was drained into the ground. It struck me that, in Nahua, caves were seen as symbolic "wombs of the earth." If we were to think in their vivid metaphorical terms, then maybe we were paying homage to our mother, the earth, with the blood of humankind. The thought didn't last long.

In an instant, we were plunged into darkness. It was sudden and total. Complete sensory disorientation.

"Ahh, what the fuck?"

"Hey, I can't see my hand in front of my face, man!"

"No kidding. It's dark."

Deprived of any shape or form, or even some silhouette that I could see, my friends' voices sounded alien, just a little scary. I don't think I spoke. I tried to hold onto my balance, gripping a rock formation that jutted out to the side of me, and look around. My eyes blinked, and blinked some more, but couldn't accustom themselves to the total absence of daylight.

The bright shafts of light that had followed us down the entrance to the cave were shut off. The odd chinks in the cavern walls that had let in a dim glow were invisible. It was as if a power generator had shut down, curtailing the natural light we'd basked in outside the caves.

It seemed impossible. But it was a reality.

It occurred to me then, in my state of mild panic, that it was a misnomer to think of this cavern as a womb. In the mindset of the Nahua, we were in the dark entrance to Mictlan: the underworld.

It was Noah's penlight that let us see each other again.

Panicky and irrational we may have been, but for a few moments there, we'd all lost our bearings. The others looked disconcerted and wide-eyed, and I guess I must have been the same. In the red artificial glow, our faces were brought into sharp definition.

Noah was tight-lipped and intense. Amber and Wes were taut, drained of their natural humor. Eve had pulled on a woolen beanie hat she carried, as if she was feeling a sudden drop in temperature. With her eyes wide and her hair tucked tight inside her hat, the light made her look like the girl from *The Blair Witch Project*.

We conjoined our forces, sharing out the lanterns and flashlights we carried with us in case of an emergency. Slowly, cautiously, we followed and felt our way up to the cavern entrance we'd negotiated with ease only a short while ago. We were like a party of potholers, who'd had to find our way out of an abandoned mineshaft.

Outside, the relief we sought was nowhere to be seen. There was only further darkness. Anything that didn't have a beam of lamplight thrown upon it was a semi-shadow, almost as obscure as in the pitch-blackness of the cave.

In its own inexplicable way, it was breathtaking. We looked to the sky for the sun, but found him daunting in his absence. To all extent and purposes, it was pure night. Up above, the vanishing solar light was not compensated by the moon. It was, I had to remind myself, still daytime in terms of the clock. No sun's rays. No moonlight. Just a huge backdrop of infinite darkness overhead. Even the winking gleam of stars, so many hundreds of thousands of light years away, was absent.

"So what time is it?" It was Noah who spoke first, the rest of us still too shook to find the appropriate words.

Amber checked her watch. "It's not even far past noon. How can it be so dark?"

"It's some kind of eclipse." Eve spoke with level certainty. She was being rational, just like all of us wanted to be.

I had to disabuse her of the notion. "No way. You'd see the sun's halo behind the moon." As it was, neither was remotely visible.

"Then where's the sun?" There was aggression in Noah's voice. I guess it aggravated him that I, the guy with all the answers, couldn't give any of the answers that mattered.

"This is so fuckin' creepy, man!" Wes spoke for us all, but his outburst did us no good. "Like, what the fuck's going on?" He gesticulated, silhouetted in the dull glow of our lamplight. Motioning toward a summer sky that wasn't there any more.

Then a shudder seemed to pass through him. It might have been the panic that he was having a hard time fighting off. But then Evie, who'd already seemed to suffer a chill in the cave, began hugging herself around the shoulders. "Is it me... or is it getting colder?" A definite shiver ran through her, her teeth almost chattering.

There was no response, but no argument. Amber snuggled herself up to a shuddery Wes, relying on their love to keep them warm. There was a rumor I'd heard–and I have to stress it's still only an unconfirmed rumor–that Amber had had an abortion a couple of weeks before we broke to study for our final examinations. I had no idea of knowing whether it was true, but when I first heard it I was a little shocked. I have no doubt that, if there truly was a fetus, then Wes was the unborn's father. In all their touchy-feeliness, I could never have imagined them dumping the child of their love down the garbage chute.

But that was sentimentalism. The truth of it was that W&A both had a whole lot of living and learning to do, and parenthood wasn't yet on the agenda. I was also sympathetic to the idea that a woman's body is her own personal temple, and she should be free to do with it whatever she likes.

And besides, if the unborn child was aborted with both their consents, then it was a sacrifice given up to a higher cause. It had died so that Wes and Amber could truly live. In all my studying of the ancient Mesoamerican cultures, it had become apparent that a living sacrifice, a so-called "blood sacrifice"—though in many ways that's a misnomer, as the blood itself was never the point of the rite—could be a positive thing.

To our modern, rational eyes it appeared too horrific, but there was no doubt that it held the ancient societies together. As they looked to each other for warmth and comfort, I could imagine that Wes and Amber had been bound together, their relationship strengthened, by the sacrifice that they'd made.

Maybe it was the power of autosuggestion, but I think we all started to feel a chill creep into our bones right then. Huddling up together, it was an unspoken assumption that we needed the proximity of each other's body heat to keep warm.

But it didn't feel like the warmth could last. As loath as we were to return to total darkness, this freak climactic change was dragging the temperature down rapidly. On what had been a hot summer's day in New Mexico, we found ourselves in need of shelter from the elements.

The only way seemed to be to return to the caves.

It struck me, as we weighed our limited options, that Mictlan served, in Nahua mythology, as not only the underworld but also one of the several realms of the afterlife. It was not a destination any expiring Mexica would willingly choose.

Not a burning pit of sinners, like the Christian Hell, it was instead a cold, dark purgatory.

FOUR

It was 1:31 pm. I remember the time on Noah's radio as clearly as I remember everything that day. We had set up camp deep inside the cave. It was eerie to see everything once illuminated by the sun's rays now lit by artificial light. Our Coleman lamps and flashlights were arranged in a circle around us. We took shelter and seating where we could, draping ground blankets and rain sheets over the rock formations to try to avoid injuring ourselves.

Noah, Evie, Amber and Wes were locked together in a kind of huddle. With the white light shining on them, part-obscuring their features, they looked like photographic negatives, or ghosts of themselves. With no sane or rational explanation for what we were experiencing, they could only look to each other.

It was then that I confirmed with my own eyes something I'd spotted earlier. Eve, whose cold hand was being stroked by Noah, was wearing a ring on the fourth finger of her left hand. I'd seen flashes of it earlier, but only briefly. Here, in our lamp lit inertia, there was no mistaking it. It was a dark stone of indeterminate origin. I'm not good on these things, and I was looking at it in the white half-light anyway. But ever since I've played back Amber's Hi-8 tape, it's become more and more apparent to me. Was it intentional on her part, to keep the ring out of my field of vision?

I have to stop thinking in these paranoid terms. But there was no doubt that Noah was familiar with it. He gently massaged her hand to keep both of their hands warm. As I studied them both without staring too obviously, I could see that he rubbed the stone's black edges with his fingers. He knew she wore it.

When we embarked on our trip to the mountains, I'd assumed that the Noah-Evie thing had cooled. It had been off as often as it had been on. Now it seemed to me that they were still treating me as a child. Nothing pertaining to their closeness could be said in my presence.

If Noah truly had bought her an engagement ring, then their failure to acknowledge it—hell, Wes and Amber's failure to acknowledge it too, if they were in on this thing—seemed like some kind of attempted hypnosis. If they acted like nothing unusual was happening between them, then I, presumably, would accept it.

It seemed pathetic, and I wondered if that was the way I seemed to them. But, to this day, no one has ever confirmed to me whether Eve Bishop got engaged to marry Noah Bailey. If that's truly what happened, then no remnant of their relationship seems to have survived into the present day.

But shit. Back then we had much bigger things on our mind. I stood apart. In an interior chamber of the cave, the stalactites were icy cold to the touch. My breath was vaporizing in the air. Maybe I would have been better to stay huddled within the group, but I knew that the reassurance they wanted would elude us. And besides, there were other things eating at me.

I couldn't shake the idea that, since we'd entered Mictlan, as I now thought of it, we were playing to a different set of rules. There was nothing that we could be comfortable with. It seemed like a shadow world to me, where our everyday certainties were displaced by a natural world we'd grown too unfamiliar with. By a world that the Mexica, that Nahua, with their blurred lines between myth and history, understood far better than we ever would.

The sun had dropped out of the sky. As far as any of us could see, it might as well have dropped into the middle of the ocean and extinguished itself. But that sounds too mythological, doesn't it?

In the terminology of our rational, scientific age, I guess we had to consider the possibility of a black hole. That a great yawning chasm of anti-matter had opened up in space, and swallowed the epicenter of our solar system. But that, if we abide by the scientific wisdom, would probably mean all the corresponding planets and stars would be swallowed up with it. We wouldn't be stuck in a cave, contemplating our fear of the dark and the unknown. In fact, no living being would be conscious of what had happened at all. We, ourselves, would become anti-matter.

I turned all the ideas over in my mind, more agitated at each passing thought. It wasn't just how inadequate rationality itself now seemed—it was the cold that was starting to gnaw away at me, mocking my attempts to follow each line of logic through to its conclusion, to put my thoughts in order.

Science, I had long believed, was just another form of juju. Why should we accept at face value that something like a black hole exists—freefalling its way through the universe, devouring all solid entities in its path? How is that any different to being asked to believe in the old gods?

If we can believe that a starless black clump of space can draw us into a realm of non-being, why are the old Mesoamerican constructs of the universe supposedly so irrational? How much crazier is it to believe that the serpent god, Quetzalcoatl, and his brother, Tezcatlipoca, created the heavens and the earth? That our world was born from the scaly back of Tlaltecuhtli, the alligator goddess, who they tore in half, while the lower half of her body rose up to become the sky?

The truth is that Nahua, rather than being an "old religion," was an "old science." Its model of the universe was mechanistic, assimilating the Mexica people's needs and their perceptions of nature, rather than imposing an unverifiable dogma from above. On that very darkest of days, their way of perceiving our world seemed no less adequate than the scientific or religious orthodoxies that were of no use to us now.

I still had the box that used to hold the stone cup, which was now lying unseen and discarded in the dark. The astrological symbols, it seemed to me, were a representation of how the Mexica believed the history of the world was divided into five ages—make that "five suns," each different sun defining its own epoch.

The last Nahua epoch, before the Conquistadors invaded, was known as Ollintonatiuh—the moving, or rather "Movement Sun." It was the era or cycle in which, with no authoritative word to the contrary, all of us were still living in that day.

It was also true that the Mexica believed each age of the sun had ended in catastrophe, with the people and animals that lived in that era forced into extinction.

"Once again, the authorities have asked the public to remain calm..."

They finally had Noah's X-FM satellite radio tuned into a news station we could pick up through the mountains. It crackled and hummed. They hung on its every word. Amber clung to Wes, and now Evie hung onto Noah's arm too. They craved reassurance from each other, just as they needed to hear that this insane situation was under control in the outside world.

Maybe they were right. Their thoughts, like their temperaments, were outward directed. They were good people, cool, beautiful people, all of them. None of them were venal or materialistic, but they all had that extrovert, reach-for-the-sky optimism that people tell me modern America is all about. They were going to go far in our world, all of them.

But me, I was alone in the dark. It wasn't just my body, but my mind was in a cave too. I was telling myself it was just my natural introversion, but I knew it was something more. Only I recognized our situation for what it was. I knew that we were in Mictlan.

"The US Government Administration's scientific advisers have stated that they can so far offer no definitive explanation as to why the sun appears to have disappeared from the sky..."

"Appears to?" Eve spat out the words in disgust. "What do they think this is, some kind of grand illusion? Like David Blaine just made his next million by making the sun go out?" They snorted in derision, the steam pouring from their breath. Humor was a line of defense, but I could hear the line weakening. Noah hit the dial.

"...sporadic outbreaks of panic, caused by the freak climactic conditions. Reporters in Chicago, Brooklyn, the Bronx and San Francisco have told of rioting, as the cities were plunged into conditions of premature nightfall and many companies have sent employees home to conserve heat and power. Several department stores and electronics warehouses have been raided by looters, taking advantage of the small number of staff. Police commissioners and their spokesman have declared that zero tolerance will be shown to anyone taking advantage of the current situation, and that a curfew may have to be declared."

"Hey..." Wes had been trying to roll a joint to keep his fingers warm, but they were getting too frostbitten to retain their sense of feeling. "Don't go postal on us, people!"

He still thought the situation had comedy potential. Noah wasn't so sure. "How the hell they gonna impose a curfew?" No one responded, but they could hear the deadly seriousness that crept into his voice. "I mean, a curfew is generally during the hours of darkness, right? What are they gonna do, shoot anyone who comes out on the streets before the sun comes back again?"

They were silent. My friends all knew this was much bigger than some freakish inconvenience that dropped out of the blue. What they didn't have was the mental framework for understanding it.

"Meanwhile, in central Florida, temperatures have plummeted from a record one hundred and ten degrees in the shade to six degrees below zero Fahrenheit. The shock climactic change has taken many residents unawares, and we're receiving reports of increasing fatalities among the state's senior citizen population. One elderly couple, believed to be vacationing from New York City, were found dead in the street after darkness fell and they were unable to return to the safety of their hotel. With many similar incidents, there are as yet no official forensic reports, but it's believed that the shock of the sudden freezing conditions..."

"Hey, heavy shit." Wes's downbeat tones belied his choice of words. "My grandma always vacations in Miami, you know. She's not there now. But I hope she's alright."

"I hope everyone's alright." Amber cut in. Her simple words spoke for everybody.

Eve reached for the dial again, in irritation. "Somebody somewhere's got to have a handle on what's going on. We can't just wait here and listen to news stories, we need to *know* something!"

I agreed with her, but I kept my own counsel. We were a long way from the world we knew. The only connection we now had with it was what the news media deemed fit for our ears. But that's how America deals with sudden disaster. If a hurricane tears up an Okie town, or an earthquake hits California, if there's a power blackout, or even if terrorists stage an attack on a major city, it's always the same advice: stay home; tune in; keep watching/listening to this station. To quote my parents' record collection, in the words of that old song: the revolution will not be televised—but stay tuned for rolling news coverage of the end of the world.

"Warm weather climates have been especially hard hit, as surface temperatures continue to drop at an alarming rate." It was a male newscaster's voice this time. The same brisk efficiency and fake intimacy as the woman on the other station. Almost interchangeable, apart from the timbre of their voices. Keeping the nation informed, but telling us nothing that could possibly help the situation.

Their adopted distance from the bad news they brought us, every varying degree of disaster dished out in the same clinical manner, spoke of our distance from the natural world. Can you imagine, if their world were gripped by sudden climactic disaster, that the Mexica would have announced it in such neutral tones? The Nahua way was to engage with events—human beings were not apart from the environment they inhabited, or the gods who presided over it. They were all playing on the same stage.

"Public service announcements are being given out across the Midwest. In Wisconsin and Minnesota, the public are being warned to stock up with essential supplies and foodstuffs and remain at home for as long as the freak conditions last. In central Milwaukee, a fire at a public housing project has been blamed on lack of heat and light. Local sources indicate that the extra power required to keep essential industries running has had to be diverted away from domestic use. It's believed that the victims of the fire, which is still raging out of control, may have been trying to heat or light up their apartments with a highly flammable liquid, such as kerosene..."

The full gravity of it all was filtering through to us. The darkness, and our isolation, compounded it. It was as if, for us, the unseen, unknown great disaster had already happened. In our cold, dark little corner of the underworld, we had a greater sense of the kind of desolation the rest of the world would soon be plunged into.

"This is kinda scary," said Amber, sounding suddenly fragile, like a little kid. It was a superfluous remark. We all knew how we felt about it. What was not yet clear to anyone was exactly what it was.

There was a crackling from the radio that might have been static, or the rustling of incoming computer printouts on air. "We have just received a number of reports relating to regions adjacent to the

Arctic Circle." There was a rustling and an intake of breath. For all the reporter's sense of urgency, it was still easy to envy him his air-conditioned office, and the emergency generators that were doubtless pumping light and heat into it.

"In Alaska, Northern Canada and Greenland, temperatures have already been recorded at a record low of minus ninety degrees Fahrenheit for this time of the year."

"What? Shit, no..." As one of the scientists among us, Eve's alarm could be taken seriously. Wes and Amber looked at her cautiously, as though afraid to ask just what it meant.

"Communications have been hit in these regions, and reports vary as to the state of the local populations..."

"Jeez. I could hazard a guess."

It was Wes who decided to brave the truth. "Minus ninety... That is like, way below fucking freezing, right? I mean, it's *total* freezing point?"

Eve shook her head slowly. "No. Absolute zero is minus four hundred and fifty-nine degrees Fahrenheit. But minus ninety is much too low to sustain human life if it persists throughout the seasons."

I'd been observing from outside. There had been a constant babble from within the group, as if the sound of their voices was the only reassurance they could offer each other. Now there was silence. They watched the vapor rise out of each deep breath as the air grew colder and thinner. The implications were too much to take on board, too serious to ignore.

"Earlier reports from Moscow that the armed forces have been called upon to quell civil unrest have proven difficult to verify. All communication from the Kremlin has currently ceased..." The radio sounded another death knell. "In the past hour, Russian state TV suggested that the Ukraine had been declared a disaster zone, and that troops had been mobilized to deal with the rapidly climbing mortality rates."

"All they can do is bury their dead," Noah reflected aloud. "That's the only way they can 'deal' with it."

"Similar scenes in Finland, and parts of Scandinavia. Requests for international aid from the Swedish and Norwegian governments have had to be temporarily declined, as each country tries to contain the disaster occurring within its own borders. Scientists and environmentalists are locked in urgent debate about the root cause of the crisis. So far, conjecture about the world suddenly entering another Ice Age due to the so-called 'greenhouse effect' has been dismissed."

"Global warming," Evie barely whispered. "Now there's a joke that's not funny anymore."

There was a loud blurt of static. The newscaster's voice was lost, though it kept threatening to break back in like an electronic ghost of itself. Noah turned the dial again, listening intently as it wound its way around another few degrees. Finally, he stopped on a female voice that sounded identical to the first newsreader we'd heard.

"The President has called an emergency news conference at the White House, for 2:00 pm Eastern

Standard Time. We repeat: a state of national emergency has been declared throughout the USA, due to the grave situation in Alaska, across the north and Midwest, and much of the eastern seaboard. All citizens are advised to stay home, and to try to conserve heat and energy. Martial law is expected to come into force later today in most states. The military and National Guard will be engaged in protecting vital industries and power supplies. Citizens are advised to stay off of the streets until such a time as the state of emergency no longer exists. The National Guard have issued a warning that anyone believed to be engaged in looting will meet with an armed response..."

Amber lunged at the radio, hitting the power button. She couldn't bear to hear another word. In our isolation, bad news from the outside world was deepening into despair. She released her cellular phone from the deep pockets of her pants and started hitting buttons.

"I'm gonna call home," she murmured. "Make sure my folks are okay." Amber hailed from Austin, TX. Like most of us, she was used to sun-kissed home territory. No part of the Southern States or the southwest had been declared a disaster area, as far as we could tell. And yet, the knowledge that her mom and dad were trapped in a dark world that was rapidly losing all its warmth, just as we were, was enough to bring her to the edge of panic.

"Good luck." Eve had adopted a tone of fatalism. "It's not gonna be easy getting a signal."

Amber impatiently punched the call button and waited. The way she cocked her ear told us the outside world was now dead to us. She shook the phone, as if the fault could be adjusted by jogging some displaced component, then tried the numbers again in rapid succession. It brought the same lack of response.

In her frustration, she pitched her cellular into one of the cave's crevices. We heard it smash, its fragments submerged beneath the all-enveloping darkness.

"This can't be happening." Amber shook, as much in fear and shock as from the cold. She grabbed a blanket and brought it tight around her shoulders. Still, she shivered. Wes reached for her hand. She didn't offer hers in return, too preoccupied with trying to keep her thin, heaving torso steady.

"I mean, this is crazy, right?" Wes was looking to the others for validation. "The sun just doesn't disappear. If it did, it'd be like the end of the world or something." If he was trying to reassure Amber, he might have picked his words a little more carefully.

"Listen, listen," Eve tried to break through, the voice of reason. "They must have every scientist in the world studying this thing. Someone, somewhere, is bound to figure it out!"

"I think maybe I already have."

All their eyes were suddenly on me. I guess they believed that I, archaeologist supergeek, had crawled off into my own hole to tremble and cry for Mommy. But I'd been doing some hard thinking, outside the constraining envelope of rationality.

They wisely gave me the space I needed to explain myself.

"Absolute zero. That's..."

"Minus four hundred and fifty-nine degrees Fahrenheit," Eve reiterated, soullessly.

"Right. Minus four hundred and fifty-nine. Now, correct me if I'm wrong, but that's the temperature at which all living matter stops moving. Am I right?" Her silence acceded.

"All the dynamics of life stop. No organic functions. No movement of energy. Nothing. A dead planet. It would, by any meaningful definition, be the end of the world."

"That's the theory," she interjected, seeming pissed-off at me. "But what difference is that going to make to us? To anyone, anywhere in the world? All of us would be dead long, long before it got down to that level."

Amber choked and put her hand over her mouth. She was either stifling an involuntary sob, or the urge to vomit.

"We've rediscovered the ancient Mexica, the Nahua world, inside these caves—the Aztec way, if you will." Their silence was as much bemusement as it was attentiveness. What the hell, it gave me the leeway I needed. "And it seems to me their way of looking at the world was prophetic. Ollintonatiuh was the fifth age of the Aztecs, the last era, the age of the 'Movement Sun.' It's also the era we're living in now."

"Which counts for what, dude? I don't want to have to be the one to say it, but this is not the time to repeat a lecture from your anthropology classes." Bravo. It was Noah who expressed his irritation first. But at least he was civilized about it. And at least they were still listening.

"Don't you see? Each of the Aztec epochs, each era, had an end that was final and cataclysmic. Once the age of the Movement Sun finishes, then the sun stops working. Once the sun stops functioning, then life on earth becomes unsustainable. Absolute. Fucking. Zero."

They heard me loud and clear. They didn't like what they heard, but they couldn't ignore the connections I'd made. "Okay, Marty, time out. That's the off-kilter approach we know and love you for, but where's this shit getting us? Huh?" Noah was insistent. "I mean, what use is this *X-Files* craziness now? What does it tell us about the trouble we're in, the trouble that the whole damn world's in?"

There was no sense in my holding back. "It tells me that we did it."

It sounded as insane for me to hear it from my own lips as it must have sounded to them. But I was deadly serious. We were in a predicament that was unprecedented in world history. All our rules and certainties, our science and rationalism, didn't count for anything anymore. I could only understand where we were now by means of an older science, a pre-scientific science.

"We... did it... The five of us?"

"I'm here to tell you that's a crock, man!" Wes shared Noah's distaste for my logic, and was more demonstrative about it. "What the fuck are we supposed to have done?"

I wouldn't be fazed. I spoke as calmly as they were indignant. "This cave. Finding the Aztec sacrificial cup alerted me that it was a part of the ancient world, of the Nahua world. Caves are dangerous places in Nahua. They're boundary points, places at the edges of the sacred realms."

"So?" Amber, formerly so attentive and polite, was becoming hostile too.

"So in the Nahua world, myth and history are one and the same. They intertwine. The Nahua universe is an ordered realm. Each cause has an effect. When the Conquistadors brought the Nahua High Priest to these mountains, a clandestine sacrifice was carried out. It was the type of ritual that was banned under the Spaniards. It was the offering of yolia to the Gods of the Sun."

"Which was what, exactly, dude?"

"Which was the life force. To be specific, it was the human heart. It would be removed from the sacrificial subject as quickly as possible."

Amber looked queasy. I'd never known her be especially squeamish, but I guess that the gruesome image, on top of the trauma she was already experiencing, was too much.

"Which accounts for the blood?"

"Absolutely. But it's a misnomer when we say 'blood sacrifice': it's only the by-product of the ritual, it's not the real deal. The blood was preserved—eternally, it seems—as a relic of the sacrifice to Topan, the Nahua heavens. Then we arrive.

We chance upon an enclave of the ancient world. We dig up a religious tribute that was supposed to be buried for perpetuity. We take the remains of a sacrificial tribute to Topan, and we negate it. When we spill the blood inside a cave, we turn it into a secondary tribute to Mictlan, the Nahua underworld.

"*We* turned off the sun."

To say they were speechless seems an understatement. I guess I stunned them into silence. Wes gave a little nervous chuckle, blowing cold steam out of his face. No one else seemed to know what to say. It was Amber, finally, who spoke for the group.

"That is so whacked..."

Screw them. I knew what I believed, what I still believe, to be true. If they had any sounder interpretations, they could let me have them. Suffice to say, none were offered.

I took the blanket out of my backpack, and threw it over both shoulders. After working myself up to make a speech, deflation was letting the cold in. Soon, I too started to give an involuntary shiver.

"Hey, you think I want to believe that? That we're all responsible for the biggest disaster ever to threaten the planet? Don't think I'm off on some little ego-trip, I'm calling the shots as I see 'em." I was starting to rant, I know. But the time for calm seemed long since past.

"If you see science as the answer, go on, give me a scientific explanation. Stephen Hawking says there are 'wormholes' in time and space that lead from one part of the universe to another and people believe it as an article of faith, 'cuz that's 'science' and not 'magic.'"

"Marty..." Eve spoke gently, wearily to me. "I know you're sincere in what you're saying. But don't you think you're blinkered to other possibilities? I mean, basic coincidence."

"No, no. Let me tell you about coincidence," I cut her off. "I don't wanna get too Jungian on you, but in Nahua there was no such thing as coincidence. Each cause had an effect. If they saw everything in symbolic terms, it was because symbols worked for them. I mean, the Mexica army would never fight at night for fear of offending the Night Lords who watched over 'em. Sounds silly, right? Until we're plunged into eternal night here, and you start to realize they were only behaving cautiously in their dealings with the natural world."

"Whoa, whoa." Wes spoke quietly, like he was conserving all his energy to compensate for falling body heat. "I'm not hearing you anymore, Marty. What I suggest is, we all pack our stuff and get our asses back to Taos."

"That's a thirty-mile hike in the dark," protested Noah.

"So? We got lanterns."

"Lanterns or not, we go scrambling down this mountain, someone's gonna break their neck." Eve, in her doggedly rational way, was right. Whoever had a solution, then someone else had a counter-solution. We were being frozen into inertia.

Amber shivered uncontrollably under her blanket. "Least it would help me forget about the cold." It was all she could do to try to stop her teeth cracking together as she spoke.

But the cold, like the darkness, was not about to recede. "Better get used to it," I told her, maybe a little cruelly. "It's going to get a whole lot colder." Eve gave me a solemn glance. She knew exactly what we were in for.

"How much colder?" asked Noah.

"You don't want to know," shot back Eve.

"Yeah. Yeah I do. I need to know. We all got a right to know." Every pair of eyes was on Eve. Me, I knew where we were heading anyway.

"Without the sun's rays," she explained patiently, "within a couple of weeks the temperature's going to be something like one hundred and fifty degrees below zero."

"Wait up." As he'd done with me, when he didn't like the answers he was given, Wes got defensive. "Are you saying we're all gonna freeze to death in two weeks?" As if it was somehow Eve's fault. But then, as I reminded myself, it was the fault of all of us.

"No. Not exactly." Her answer was equivocal, but it provided no relief. "You heard the radio reports, same as all of us. Human life won't endure such extreme temperatures. Countries around the Arctic Circle have hit minus ninety already and are demarcated disaster zones. By the time we hit one hundred and fifty degrees below, all life on earth will be dying."

There was no answer he could give. The fear of death that's innate in us all is made more tolerable by a belief in religious myth, whether the Christian heaven or the five designated afterlife regions of the

Nahua. But even someone with no religious faith could be reassured by a sense of continuity: that the world, our relatives and our friends, would be able to go on without us; if we grew old, had grown-up children and grandchildren, then their continued health and happiness mattered a whole lot more than our own deteriorating state. They were our lifeline to the future.

But what of the great communal death? Of the passing of everything and everyone you ever knew, or loved, or understood, or valued, or took for granted? What possible consolation could there be anymore?

"This is the end of our age," I commented. No one contradicted me.

But Noah wouldn't be defeated. "There's gotta be some way to stay alive. Some other way to keep warm."

And there was, of course. It must have been close to a couple of hundred millennia since mankind had first learned to produce fire from dry wood—a historical timeline that made the Archaic Period of Mesoamerican history, which produced the Aztecs a mere two thousand years ago, seem recent. But humanity's eternal spark, both literal and spiritual, could not be rekindled in a world with declining oxygen.

"Forget it," I told him. "If the cold doesn't get us, then the thinning air will."

Amber began to panic. "So either we freeze to death, or we suffocate?"

What could I say? With hindsight, it may seem like emotional sadism. But I wanted them to know. I wanted them to understand that my reading of the situation wasn't just based on superstitious hocus-pocus.

Wes started to pace. His breath came out of him in hurried, vaporous bursts. "Two choices, man! Those are our two fucking choices?" The lethargy that intense cold normally produces was kept at bay, for the moment at least. But his hysteria wasn't doing him, or any of us, any good.

In less than two hours, we had passed through the last golden days of our youth into a dark purgatory, a Mictlan, where we awaited our own extinction. But the transformation was so complete that we could barely remember how we had felt such a short time ago.

A wave of fear and desperation passed through us all. The stark austerity of the lamplight, the icy cold that cut like a knife, all conspired to rob us of any residual comfort. We were condemned. Each of us could only look into the others' young faces and see their friends' imminent death, as well as their own.

I had to speak. I had the feeling that if I didn't try to express how I saw our situation now, then the moment would pass forever. "Listen up. I know what you all think of my interest in Nahua, in the Mexica religion, and I really don't care. But you have to listen to me just this once."

I had their attention. Despair had erased all other options, and they were prepared to give me just a little bit of their minds. "There's a physical and a symbolic reality to all of this that go hand in hand.

If we're to have any chance at all, we gotta recognize both of them."

FIVE

For a brief moment, I'm sure they hoped to find salvation in what I had to say. But I wasn't looking for false hope. I wanted them to understand things as I did. Then, and only then, could we face the most difficult choices any of us would ever make.

"Marty, if you know something, you'd better tell us." Eve was becoming impatient. Maybe she felt I was yanking their collective chain. That they were even prepared to give me a second chance testified, I guess, to their sense of hopelessness

"It's the pictographs." I expected a collective sigh or groan. But no—they were still prepared to listen, to grant me the benefit of the doubt. "I've been studying them." Indeed I had. Intently.

Closer inspection of their faded antiquity showed me the significance of the crudely carved figures. The snake was no common or garden adder or constrictor, but Quetzalcoatl, the serpent god, one of the most significant figures in the Nahua canon. And, despite anything you may have picked up from pulp fiction or dumb horror movies, also one of the most benevolent.

For Quetzalcoatl was one of two sons of the most fundamental power in the Nahua universe, Ometeotl—a "sacred fundamental principle," rather than another human or animal deity. Alongside his brother, Tezcatlipoca, he demonstrated the moral duality of the Nahua universe: how, unlike in the Judeo-Christian tradition, all the tones and shades of human behavior were represented.

One of the smaller animal figures carved into the box was, I'd assumed, some kind of bobcat. Closer examination revealed it to be a man's face clothed in the striped fur of the tiger: Tezcatlipoca. He and his serpent brother were light and dark—or, like Apollo and Dionysus in Greek mythology, order and chaos. Quetzalcoatl, despite his fearsome appearance, was concerned with construction and creation. Tezcatlipoca, on the other hand, represented selfishness and destructiveness, a tempter god, a "Trickster" in the terminology of Native North Americans.

Which isn't to say that Tezcatlipoca was a Satan figure. He and his brother were the twin opposites of human nature. The Mexica laws existed to punish wrongdoing in the earthly realm; the gods were merely there to represent humankind in all its strengths and frailties. And even a light-bringer such as Quetzalcoatl was respectful of the violent laws of the universe.

The long, slightly curved blade that appeared between the two brothers' images was the symbol of Tezcatlipoca—his sword made from obsidian, or volcanic glass. Both brothers, both "good" and "bad" in banal Christian terms, demanded the necessity of the ultimate violent sacrifice.

Hovering over them was the Sun. The hint of a human face appeared within the writhing mass of rays that extended from the orb. And again—the fearsome obsidian blade. There was no doubt in my mind as to what the purpose of the bloodletting ritual had been. Humankind, nature, the gods—all had to pay ultimate tribute to the Sun.

I explained all of this to my four brothers and sisters. They listened but said nothing. Understandably, it wasn't what they wanted to hear.

"So, Marty." It was Amber who broke the long, pained silence. "Is there something that we have to do?"

Had no one understood me at all? I couldn't hide behind concepts and explanations anymore. They wanted to hear it straight, so they ought to be ready for it.

"We have to perform a human sacrifice."

There. It was said. The response, or rather the lack of response, was as I'd anticipated. But no one overruled me. No one told me that I was crazy, or dangerous. No one said that I'd lost my mind, or that what I was saying was out of whack.

I understood the importance of blood sacrifice to the human race. In the Mesoamerican studies I'd undertaken since I was a boy, I had watched, in my mind's eye, as the Mayan dynasties offered up their fellow human beings atop of their pyramids. As, in the translated vernacular, they would "roll down the pyramid steps," after a devotional act of decapitation or the excision of the human heart. I'd agreed with the anthropologist Walter Burkert when he wrote that *Homo Necans*, "man the killer," was a more appropriate name to describe the development of our species than *Homo Sapiens*, "man the wise." Killing did not negate the wisdom of the human race. To the contrary: it had been crucial in its development.

I'd studied how human sacrifice had been the engine that drove early Mesoamerican civilizations—their early art, architecture, and even astronomy directly related to man's sacrificial relationship with the old gods. The innate cruelty was at first incomprehensible to me. Why should a great people like the Incas of early Argentina and Chile engage in something as hideous as burying children alive? What gave the Maya such a hunger for the spilling of blood that human sacrifice was the main theme of their culture's art? That obtaining human sacrifices was their main purpose for waging warfare?

But I also knew that the Maya's decapitated human sacrifices, "the chosen ones," were said to attain similar powers to the *Tius*, the mountain gods to whom they were dedicated. The child sacrifices at the Inca capital of Cuzco, during their six-monthly solstice festivals, were the most revered of children—*capacochas*, those who died, Christ-like, to atone for their society's sins against the gods. That the late Inca goddess, Tanta Carhua, was a deified child sacrifice herself, who had died in tribute to Veracocha, the Inca god of the Sun, the god of Thunder, and the Moon. Unlike the unilateral atonement of the Christ, these great and terrible deeds were believed, were observed, to have an effect. Such was their perceived efficacy in ensuring fresh water and crop growth that the privileged child sacrifices became an item of trade throughout the Andean outposts of Inca civilization.

Even in the modern day, it's believed that some southern Chilean shamans, or *machi*, have been known to practice human sacrifice to avert earthquakes or volcanic eruptions. In modern Bolivia, one prominent archaeologist has claimed the tradition of cutting the throats of teenaged virgin girls to ensure mineral yields from the mines still persists, in secret. As does the Inca tradition of sacrificing innocents to buy protection for the cocaine trade from the gods.

I had seen, in my mind's eye, the many sacred horrors of the Mesoamerican civilizations—from the most squalid latter-day child sacrifice to the grandiose mass slayings performed by the mighty Aztec state. None were ever performed in a state of cynicism or even mild disbelief.

It was Noah who broke ranks first. He moved away from the group to speak to me up close. His muscular, lightly trembling arm hugged me around the shoulder like the close buddy I considered him to be.

"Martin. You know, I appreciate what you're saying. I mean, we're in a terrible, horrible situation that none of us could ever have imagined. But we can't give into it." He turned and looked me straight in the face. We were standing far from the lamplight, so I felt his eyes burning into me more readily than I could see them. "Some kinda madness may have overtaken the world. But that don't mean things will get better if we go crazy too. If the world goes insane, it might be some kind of comfort to be crazy, but we can't, you know. We can't."

I understood. If what I was saying was so far beyond the moral sense he had of himself, then so be it. I couldn't persuade anyone to go so far against his nature. But I was convinced that I saw the reality clearer than any of them. I wasn't trying to overcome Noah's personal morality–it was my moral duty to make everyone aware of what our options were.

"That's madder than a fucking sack full of rattlesnakes, man." One by one they joined us. There was no hint of levity in Wes's voice. He, too, was just calling it like he saw it. "I mean, everything's gonna be cool again if we just drop one of us over a cliff and say prayers to the big Aztec Boogey Man, right?" He laughed bitterly. "If that's all the hope we have then we are totally eff-you-see-kayed, brother." He toyed with the reefer he'd rolled earlier, placed behind his ear for safekeeping.

"Why don't you spark it up?"

"Say what?" It must have sounded strange coming from me, now, at this time and this place. I was never a big pothead, so why, Wes was asking himself, should I be encouraging him to get fucked up now, of all times?

"Why do you smoke, Wes? Because it opens your mind to all kind of psychic impressions that are floating around out there in the ether. Am I right?"

He shrugged, continually shaking as if his body accepted it would never get any warmer. "I smoke to get high, bro. Not to get high-falutin.'"

Amber had joined us now. "It opens my third eye. It makes me aware of stuff that I might not understand, otherwise." It was as if she needed to shift the weight of what was bearing down on us, just for one moment. To remember the lightweight, trippy little world she'd taken for granted, before darkness fell at noon.

"Right. And that's when you become aware of all the things that science can't even begin to understand. That sense of meaning, of underlying patterns and associations that we all have but won't admit to. The kind of thing some people go looking for in astrology charts or tarot cards."

Amber was nodding enthusiastically now. I caught a whiff of pungency in the air. With unseen sleight of hand, Wes had lit the joint and taken a couple of deep hits before passing it to Amber. For a moment at least, I had their rapt attention.

"The absolute awareness we all have of being looked at. I'm not talking paranoia here. I'm talking about how, if I go and walk down a level here to the next incline, into pitch darkness, and you're watching me from a distance, I *know* that your eyes are upon me."

They both nodded enthusiastically. "So how does science explain that? Simple answer: it can't. Most people acknowledge the phenomenon, and some scientists try to shrug it off with vague talk about a 'sixth sense'—undermining the same rational stance they cling to like a life raft. The fact is that certain unseen forces play a direct cause-and-effect role in our lives."

Noah didn't like me sounding off again. He was starting to look upon me with what I regarded as suspicion. He and Evie, the moralist and the rationalist, disdainfully shook their heads when Amber offered them a puff of the joint. I could see they wouldn't consider this the time or the place. But I wanted to show them that the normal rules of behavior didn't apply, just didn't work anymore.

Breaking my normally abstemious habit, I accepted a deep hit from the joint, then another. It was heady stuff. Almost instantly, I felt a tingling glow spread out to the end of my cold fingertips.

"It's the same with Nahua. I'm not saying the Mexica had everything slam-dunk accurate, and that the sky actually was made from an alligator's belly. But these were symbols that worked for them. They treated them with due seriousness and it paid off. Why do you think they maintained those rituals for so many hundreds of years?"

"Because they were an ignorant, primitive people who had no real idea of the workings of the universe?" Noah poured cold water over any spark of empathy I tried to light.

"That's not in the spirit of multiculturalism, if you don't mind my saying, bro." I needed him to be quiet, so I could articulate my thoughts. If I had to play the PC card, so be it. It struck a chord with Amber, who'd majored in Native American Studies. She was buzzing along on my words. "And besides," I fired off a little barb, "how does the spirit of scientific enquiry apply to someone who thinks an executed man rose from the dead to save us all from Hell?" I was tempted to say Mictlan, instead of Hell, but I was pissing him off enough.

"So, uh, how did the Aztecs make things happen? I mean, their sacrificial rites and all." I had Wes hooked.

"Consider the God Xipe Totec." (That's *Shheeep* Totec, to the uninitiated.) "We might call him a fertility god, as the Mexica used to pay tribute to him to ensure the ripening of the maize plant. But every year, at the festival of Xipe Totec, he would be incarnated in earthly form by the holy men and high priests."

"So how was that, Marty, that they were reincarnated?"

"Incarnated. Picture this... You're a Nahua high priest, right? You're a regal figure and an all-round righteous dude." I think I saw the slight upturn of a smile on his face. Wes was escaping our discomfort and fear by projecting his mind somewhere else. "You got beads and decorative jewelry all around your shoulders. You got a kingly mane of black hair that you wear like a big hat."

He was transported. I described to him how, during the fertility festival, the flesh of human sacrifices would be collected for the priests. The holy men would wear full bodysuits of human flesh—stripped from the chest, or the breasts, right down to the lower abdomen just above the pubis.

"Whaaa? That's just whack. He slipped on some other dude's skin like it was a T-shirt or something? Was this, like, the bodies of executed prisoners?"

"It may have been. Or it may have been from the bodies of willing sacrifices. What people fail to recognize is that it wasn't a punishment to be a human sacrifice in the Nahua religion. It was a privilege." I described how Wes, as a high priest, would have impersonated Xipe Totec by being wrapped tight in the epidermis, muscles and veins of a sacrificial subject. This would go on for a scarcely credible twenty days. Though the Mexica were adept at preservation processes for all forms of animal hide, the corpse-coat was still going to get pretty rank over that time.

Wes closed his eyes. I painted a verbal picture of him as a human being in a state of grand metamorphosis. Like a rare butterfly emerging from the shell of a larva, he would be reborn, triumphant, as a greater man than he was before.

"At the climax of the ceremony, you, as the high priest, would be unwrapped from the dead meat. Out you step, a healthy man escaping a decaying body. The Mexica saw it as symbolic of the maize husk desiccating before it gives up the fully formed yellow cob inside. That ceremony happened year after year after year. Why would they have gone to those lengths, for all that time, if the ritual didn't work for them? Are we so close-minded that we don't credit them with observing crop failure if the rite wasn't performed successfully?"

"What, like, skin am I wearing?" Wes cut off my flow. He was in a heavy-lidded reverie, while Amber was wide-eyed and staring, the red veins in her eyes bulging out.

"What are you wearing?"

"Yeah. I mean, do I have the skin of some big bad dude, or what?"

"Well, I guess. You could have the body of some Mex criminal. But it's just as likely that it'd be the body of a warrior—dying as a human sacrifice or as a war hero, it all bestowed similar status."

"Yeah. Yeah. I can see that." In my own mildly stoned state, so could I. But Wes was disassociating from the cave, from everything around us. "Like a second big pair of biceps to stretch over my own. Buff me up, right?"

"Yeah, I suppose..."

"Or a pair of pecs, big pair of pecs. Hanging over my shoulders like some pigskin football. I'm a big, mean motherfucker."

This wasn't where we needed to go. I tried to pull his mind back on track. "Or you could have a woman's body. The rites weren't sexually exclusive. You could end up with a traditional hourglass figure—trim waist and a big pair of boobs."

"Oh shit. Oh shit!" He laughed, but he knew he shouldn't. His mind was somewhere between a freezing cave in New Mexico and the ancient Mexica world. Between rationality and ritual. Between amusement and all-out hysteria. "And how do I get my pair of lady tits? Does she, like, have them cut off?"

I pictured the vivid scene myself. "No. No, the bodysuit comes complete from the wearer. They'd make a sharp incision with the sacrificial knife, cut down through the fatty tissue to the bone, then continue the cut at the same depth all the way down the body. Then it's very delicately peeled off in one piece, leaving the vital organs and the skeleton."

"Will you fucking quit this?!"

Amber's shrill insistence brought us back to our cold, hard reality. I'd freaked her out. Or, at least, I'd added one more unpalatable image to those that were already plaguing her mind. She hurriedly passed the end of the joint to Wes, who snapped out of his reverie. Eyes wide open, he seemed suddenly alarmed, stamping the smoldering butt underfoot.

"This is no good, Marty. We don't need any more madness." Noah spoke calmly, but emphatically. Wes was suddenly stricken by agitation. He kept moving from one foot to the other, more conscious of the cold than he had been before. Noah was right. Psychic projection had done him no good at all.

"I'm just trying to show you what I know—what all the evidence points to. It's here," I insisted, beating my knuckles against the pictograph on the stone receptacle. "The blood sacrifice to the sun, pouring the blood into the sacred cup, burying it in this cave after Cortez arrived with his Conquistadors. Just like everything the Mexica ever did, it served a purpose. It had an effect. It was reality." I wasn't trying to mentally damage anyone. I wanted to save us.

Wes was virtually hugging one of our Coleman lamps. Almost burning himself, his body shaking in a cold spasm, he needed to hog as much heat as he could. "Yeah, c'mon Marty. Stop fucking with our heads, man."

"Look at me, Wes!" I wasn't going to take this constant disparagement anymore. I held the key to all of this—no one else. "You see me laughing? You see me smiling? You think I'm ragging you somehow?" No. No one did. At that moment, I realized that no one doubted my sincerity. But that, it seemed, was the big problem.

"That cup of blood we spilled... It kept the sun up in the sky for the past five hundred years."

Noah was fired up in an instant. "Will you stop and take a listen to yourself? Do you know how insane you sound?" He was getting in my face. He felt threatened, I know. I was also painfully aware that Noah could whip my ass, should he choose to do so. But this was no personal competition.

"We destroyed a sacred tribute that was made by the ancients. We took a sacrifice to the Sun, and turned it into a tribute to the underworld. We have to rectify that. For the world to continue to live, we have to sacrifice one of our lives. Nature only yields up what you give back to her. The Mexica understood that." I think my friends understood too. But they didn't accept it.

"If you have to sacrifice a virgin, you can count me out." Amber tried to make light of it, to preserve her sanity. What was sane or insane was no longer an issue to me.

"Can't we just cut our fingers and bleed into the cup?" Eve suggested a half-hearted compromise. But at least she saw that something—a ceremony or ritual—would have to take place. It was the first time any of them had acknowledged that what I said pertained to reality. "I mean, who's gonna know the difference?"

"No." I shook my head fervently. "It's not about the blood! That was just the by-product, a souvenir of what happened way back. And those to whom we're paying tribute would know. Nature would know. The gods would know."

I remonstrated eye-to-eye with Eve. She clearly thought I was nuts. What worried her far more, I think, was that she felt she was going nuts too.

"It's about the life force. It's about yolia." I cupped my hand gently over the curve of her breast, so that my distended fingers could just feel the rhythm of her beating heart. Eve didn't move, scarcely breathed.

It elicited dumb, hysterical laughter from behind us. "Okay, I've had it now! C'mon, Marty... tell 'em! Let 'em all in on the secret!" Wes, too, was moving closer to his personal breaking point. He howled in forced mirth at some private joke. "What's wrong with you guys?" He motioned toward our buddies and comrades. "Can't you see when the dude's laughing at you? Go on, fucking tell 'em, Marty! Tell 'em how you just wanna take your mind off how your nuts are frozen numb with the cold!"

I was scared too. Every eye, every mind was on me. But they were becoming hostile to my interpretations. All the truth I had to offer was unpalatable truth. I had the feeling that, if I pushed the wrong buttons, I might become the victim of my friends' fear and incomprehension. A pointless sacrifice, dashed upon the rocks, whose shed blood would benefit no one.

It was time to show the extent of my seriousness. I reached slowly into the carved box, dipping my hand until it was swallowed past the wrist. The second artifact had remained concealed within the receptacle. The more I'd considered our situation, the more relevant it became to me.

"Oh my god, Marty–" Amber was the first to speak, her voice high-pitched and fragile, barely audible, like a little girl.

"Joke's over, dude." Wes spoke solemnly, trying to bolster his words with a touch of menace. "This is not funny anymore."

The long, stone sacrificial dagger gripped tight in my right hand would have been a major archaeological find, at any other time. The carved wooden handle featured a rendition of a mythic Jaguar Knight, in jade. The blade was decorated with a small mosaic made up of eyes and teeth. They represented Itzli–the Nahua God of sacrificial knives. As always, there was a working deity attached to every part of the everyday world. And human sacrifice, to the ancient Mexica, was a part of that world.

The others read my stance as potentially aggressive. It wasn't meant that way. But I had to show this wasn't a game, wasn't a joke, and never had been. It grew more deadly serious with each passing moment that the old gods remained offended.

Only Eve felt confident enough to confront me head-on, to appeal to my reasonable nature. "Marty, please. You're talking about murder." Her eyes implored me. "About killing one of your friends."

She made me ashamed. "I know, I know." I couldn't meet her gaze. "But it's not murder. Not really. I know how crazy it sounds, but–"

"Fucking crazy is right!" Noah hollered at me. If I'd encountered his doubt and suspicion before, now I had his outright hostility. "You think you're gonna save the world with this fucking dumb-ass paganism?" He could barely find the words to fit his contempt. I felt that, if I hadn't been holding that antique weapon, which was not dulled or blunted by time, he'd have rushed me.

"We have entered into a contract with the old gods. We didn't know it, and we didn't want it... but it's too bad and too late." I wasn't backing down. "When the gods created the human era, Ollintonatiuh, the age of the fifth sun, Nahua tells us they created everything our new species could possibly want. But the Sun hung stillborn in the sky. There was no light and no heat, just like today. So the gods committed suicide–they gave themselves in sacrifice, so that the Sun gave life to our world. The gods were reincarnated, but the Mexica had to repay them for their sacrifice many times over. And now..." I would no longer accept any challenge to the sincerity of my supposed madness, "so do we."

When he realized I wasn't about to go on the attack, Noah calmed a little. But for me, there was no respite. "Yeah, well, before we start carving each other up on the word of this lunatic," he wrung every drop of mockery from the word as he motioned toward me, "how about we try something a little less drastic?"

It sounded sensible. Oh-so-rational. But the time for rationality was long passed. Even Amber recognized that. "Like what?" Never was a question so damning in its simplicity.

"Like having a little faith for a change!" Noah's voice resonated, pumping out steam like an industrial chimney, but he didn't hector or shout. "You know, faith can move mountains." Faith can also be a great crutch for people in times of doubt—as we were seeing now, in our good friend Noah. But faith is also its own reward, and it rarely provides the faithful with anything other than faith itself.

I wasn't about to let Noah turn our predicament into an evangelical meeting. "So what do you want us to do? Sit around and wait for a miracle?" I'll admit I was openly contemptuous. But then, I was only reflecting Noah's contempt toward my own belief.

And belief is a different thing from faith. Belief demands that you act upon whatever you believe in, that you participate in your own destiny. Faith allows you to preach humble pieties while the sky falls in. Or the sun goes out.

"No. I don't want us to sit around. But everything happens for a reason. Part of a divine plan."

"God works in mysterious ways."

"Yeah. Yeah, something like that."

"We have some common ground, you and me, Noah. Your faith, and my belief. Both of them seem crazy to the rational mind." I wasn't out to win any contest. I just wanted to extend a hand to the man I considered a brother. To the funny and kindhearted guy who'd befriended me in my first semester. "But my belief, what I've come to believe now, can be put to the test. The Mexica ordered their world by it. They believed that their own faith was like a science, based on observable cause-and-effect. I know it sounds insane to you, but I gotta tell you that it's all that we have left."

I think my love and respect defused Noah a little. But he wasn't buying. He shook stray hairs from his fringe out of his eyes, and continued shaking his head at me. "It's blasphemy. What you're talking about, it's pagan blasphemy. It's false idols, and worshipping serpents, and bloody murder."

"I never said it was rational," I conceded. "I said its relationship to our world was observable. Christianity is about having faith that you'll inherit the Kingdom of Heaven when you die. That's fine, if it's what you believe. But having faith and sitting put at this very moment means that we'll all die—not just one of us."

"What you're talking about is on the same level as black magic, it's like voodoo."

"It relates to our world, Noah. In all the early Ages of the Sun described by Nahua, the different species that inhabited the world became extinct at the end of each period. That's not mere superstition, that's folklore as science. In the second eon, the Age of the

Wind Sun, the only people to survive their great floods did so by clinging onto the branches of trees and de-evolving into monkeys. It shows an awareness of evolution that some Christians, even today, are still trying to deny."

"My faith is not a science." He spoke gently, but sounded wounded. Whoever instilled God into Noah Bailey could consider it a job well done. "It's a comfort, and it's a framework. It's a good set of rules to live by. It says: Thou Shall Not Commit Murder."

Oh please, not moral absolutes, not now. We had no time left for that. "Nahua described the living universe. It didn't proscribe human behavior."

"And the divine plan is nothing to do with us killing each other."

"That's fine, 'cuz I don't wanna die. You don't wanna die. None of us wanna fucking die!" Wes's bewilderment and frustration were all too apparent. He didn't give a damn about our theological argument. Why should he? "So let's stop hanging around talking about dying, and make sure that we carry on living."

He folded an arm around Amber, who was shivering uncontrollably. "Right." Eve backed Wes up, staring accusatorily at Noah and me. "Nobody is going to kill anyone. And we're not gonna sit around praying for divine intervention, either. This is not going to be an ego-match between two little boys. We have some serious shit to take care of."

The way she started bustling around, it made both of us feel shame. We lived in the era of the take-charge woman, and it was at times like these that you saw just how practical the female of the species could be. "First things first: we stop trying to create a whole load of hot air with our mouths, and get a fire going."

Amber got caught up in the rush to actually physically do something, rather than arguing the toss. "We passed plenty of wood on the way up here. It may be cold out, but it's dry, so it's gonna burn." Bless them and their girl-scout instincts. They made me feel useless, like a spare prick.

"Well then, let's get moving and start collecting some. We'll all feel better once our teeth stop chattering." It was a pep talk, a boost to morale, but that was all it was. I appreciated Evie for what she was trying to do: keep us alert and active; take our minds off our predicament; increase our body temperature with physical activity; wake us up, to fight the temptation to lapse into sleep as the cold intensified. "We've got blankets, bottled water, enough canned food for a couple of days." Her optimism seemed indomitable. Enough food for a couple of days. But in a couple of days...

Eve had her eye fixated on all those little things that would make our immediate situation more tolerable. It was laudable. For my part, I couldn't concentrate on what seemed trivial; at this stage, it seemed to me like a different form of madness. But then, as everyone seemed to think I was crazy, my opinion didn't carry a great deal of weight.

"If we survived college, we can survive this, right?" Evie's can-do approach was just what Amber needed to hear.

"Damn straight, girlfriend! For all we know, once we've got our shit together and bedded down, the sun will be right back where it belongs in the morning."

Her good news was lighting up Wes's face too. "That would be so tight." To our two dear, sweet stoner friends, it was a hope against hope, a real candle in the darkness. Evie was their Santa Claus and Easter Bunny all rolled into one.

Noah was ready to do something positive too. He'd taken a verbal ass-kicking from Eve, same as I had, and he was still pissed at me, but he wasn't going to use his bruised feelings as a get-out clause. As the three of them set off back to the mountain range outside the caves, guided by torches, blankets tied tightly around their shoulders like outsize sweaters or Mexican ponchos, I was the only one to stand uselessly apart.

But I was where I was. Let everyone else dream of a bright new tomorrow, if that's what they needed to get through to the very next moment. I was still stranded in Mictlan.

I raised my eyes to the flickering silhouette that was Eve's shadow, grown monstrously distorted in the lamplight. I expected maybe hostility, resentment at what she saw as my insane preoccupation. Instead, I recognized the same sensitive temperament I'd noted back when she turned me down, ever so gently, for a date, while insisting we had to stay friends.

Evie Bishop gave a big, deflating sigh. With no one around that she had to be big for, she let the confidence drain out of her like a punctured helium balloon. It was as if all her positive energy was a front, and, in the absence of our friends, she could allow herself a state of emotional exhaustion.

Eve gazed at me distractedly, looking neither at me nor through me. She sagged, her back propped against the lumpy contours of the wall for support. The blanket fell from her shoulders. It was as if she didn't even have the motivation left to stoop and pick it up.

I did. I retrieved her blanket from the ground, draping it around the delicate shoulders that seemed too cold for her to even shiver. "That was a very fine speech," I told her, with no hard feelings.

"Yeah." She managed to crack the ghost of a smile back at me. "Wouldn't it be beautiful if I could believe it?"

SIX

It seemed like forever. With only two lamps left in the cave, it was as if our world was truly shutting down on us. Night was eternal now. And the cold... well, the cold was our constant companion. It constantly worried, cajoled and bothered us. I could steel myself to forget its omnipresence, but it would get under my skin. Insinuate itself into my respiration. Burrow itself into the very core of my being.

Eve was no better. She spoke little, conserving her breath. We were sat close, tight, but we never touched. Maybe she needed to maintain her distance from me, still suspecting me of fantasizing about being her lover. Maybe, but I attribute nobler motives to Evie Bishop. She had sought to inspire our friends, the people who shared our predicament. But here, in the dark, she was as frightened as any of us. I knew she didn't want me to see the difficulty she had in controlling herself. In fending off the shakes. In ignoring the continual urge to urinate, so as not to keep returning to an unlit rock enclosure. I saw through her. She cared enough not to want to add to the sum of my own fears.

"What time is it?" When she spoke, it was as if I'd sat through a short lifetime of solitude without hearing another human voice. In truth, it could only have been a matter of a half-hour—maybe even only twenty minutes. When life is reduced to its bare essence, stripped of all comfort and distraction, every moment is eternal.

"Clock says 5:59." I didn't bother to differentiate between am and pm. Neither would have been meaningful anymore. On a summer's evening, 5:59 suggests the fullness of life. The abundance of light and warmth that lasts up to the late setting of the sun. In the morning, 5:59 is the time when many of us start to emerge from our sleep. The last minutes of darkness before the slowly encroaching dawn. Before sunrise. We no longer lived in either of those times or places.

I only had to turn my head and focus my eyes a little in order to catch the glowing clock face on the radio. Eve could have done so with as little effort. That she refused told me she was getting scared. Scared to note the passing of time. Frightened to see how our perception of it had slowed so intolerably. Terrified to acknowledge how time's passing only seemed to intensify our predicament.

Her curiosity related to the absence of our friends. They had gone scrabbling their way back up to the lower ledge what seemed like many hours ago. It was only our discomfort, and the slow passing of time, that made it seem that way. It seemed as if everything had come to a premature stop already, and the slowing of time meant that they might never return. It was an illusion, I know.

Outside, if we keened our senses, there were distant noises that told us the world was still there. Strange, unidentifiable shrieks and howls. The cry of nocturnal birds, prematurely awakened. The distressed call of a cold coyote, somewhere way off in the desolate distance. The disorientation of animals who had never known temperatures to drop below freezing point, who were suddenly deprived of the environment that sustained them.

It may have taken just as many hours before we heard them returning. Or it may only have been a few minutes. Whatever. I'd told myself to stop watching the clock. We first heard the cautious crunching of climbing boots, finding their way down the dirt path that led to the cave's tunnel. At first, it seemed like only one pair of feet, till the out-of-sync rhythm told us that our friends were returning. Eve hugged herself at the shoulders and sat wide-eyed, attentive. I knew her apprehension was because she had sent them forth with a message of hope.

"All I know is, I never seen the sky that way. It's fucking creepy. Who ripped the stars out of the sky, bro?" There was a difference in the way Wes spoke that I find hard to articulate in this journal. His voice was imbued with its customary wonder, but stripped of all its joyfulness. It was as if our desperate circumstances had truly dawned on him outside, in the mountains of eternal night.

"It's like, wherever the sun has gone, the stars have gone too, right?" Amber sounded on the verge of tears, if her composure hadn't already given way.

"So whoever knows the reason why we can't see the stars, they can tell us when the sun's coming back. Right?" It was almost an accusation. As if it was all of us, the people with the big ideas and the big mouths, who should give up the explanation that would remedy her distress.

Noah was the first shadowy figure whose half-lit form re-entered the enclosure we now lived in. He emptied his burlap sack of a pile of dry combustibles, then began to replace the lamps and torches in the semi-circle that surrounded us. When we saw his face in the half-light again, it was set in a look of grim concern that I imagined reflected my own. Return to base. Back to square one. No progress. Nothing changed.

"It's damn crazy." His hurried breathing may have been exertion, or a little panic setting in. "There's no kind of eclipse, or natural phenomenon, or whatever that can block the starlight out of the sky. It was just like half a moon, hanging up there alone, orphaned in all that blackness."

There was awe in Noah's words, leavened with a bewildered despair. When darkness had fallen that day, his rationality had told him that the heavens would be in their place at nighttime, as a prelude to the inevitable, welcome return of the sun in the morning. But the heavens were now almost devoid of light, a pure black void, with only the silver glint of a crescent moon to compensate.

"You know..." I focused my mind and my words, trying, like Eve, not to dissolve into a mass of trembling limbs and chattering teeth as the chill air assaulted my inert body. "There's a Nahua myth: the 'Tzitzimitls,' the Twilight Monsters. Each star, it was said, is a spidery creature that will descend from the heavens on silken threads, on the day that the world ends. Then they'll devour the souls of the living."

My words met with silence. Rather than disconnect me from the group, their icy response drew me back into the fray. I was sure I gauged an exchange of dark looks between Noah and Wes. Whatever had demanded their attention out in the open air, I felt sure it hadn't distracted them from discussing me and my madness.

"It sounds crazy, right?" I wasn't trying to sell them an agenda anymore. I had tried, and failed. My beloved friends had even managed to undermine my belief in the ancient Nahua way of thought. But I wasn't going to be ignored. "But tell me this: how many scientific, rational explanations can you come up with for what you've just seen?"

"Will you SHUT THE FUCK UP?!" I'd addressed all of them, collectively, but it was Noah who exploded. His rage cut the air like a carving knife through ice. Suddenly, I felt my heart pump. Despair can tranquilize a body, weighed down with its grinding inevitability. Our icy netherworld was alive with motion again.

"I just can't tell you, Marty, how pissed I am with you using this situation as a platform for your stupid fucking obsessions!" He was getting up close, in my face. It was a physical challenge, one I hadn't anticipated. I stood and backed up, stumbling a little over the sand and rocks.

"Can't you see what is real, Marty? Real people, real suffering? Real fucking trouble?" He had me backed up against the wall of the cave. I was vexed, uncomfortable, not knowing which way this was going to go.

"I know, it's real to me too. I just wanted to, I just—" It's strange how the sudden proximity of physical danger, from something as mundane as an angry friend, can smash through your senses in a way that slow, inevitable annihilation just can't. He had me lost for words. Hell, I was truly scared this time.

"You just wanted to what? Have us all look to you as our group leader? Give you big props for being the only one of us assholes who truly knows what's going on? Tell me, Marty, 'cos I'm getting mighty sore trying to work it out for myself." Even in the magnitude of our predicament, it seemed to me we couldn't put aside our petty human rivalries and jealousies. To our brother Noah, it seemed that the only reasonable option was for him and Eve to take up their usual take-charge position. But they had no answers and no solutions, and it was eating at him so bad.

"Okay, you've made you point now! Back off!" The words of remonstration, when they came, were not from me. Evie was on her feet, shaken from her despondency. Her face was almost as close to me as Noah's, the vaporous carbon dioxide exhalations from her mouth and nose blowing upward into mine.

She stretched a gentle, protective arm between us. It brushed against my manhandled form, but it was

Noah she clung to. I could never get anywhere near to the physical closeness that was still between them. Her feminine grip tightened, and he was encouraged, rather than pulled, away from me.

Noah stepped back. He looked at me with a kind of agonized despair, his eyes gravitating toward the cold ground. He motioned with his hand, as if to push me away from him. Maybe I was exaggerating his regard for me, but I felt it signified shame at the way he'd exploded rather than any animosity toward myself.

"We've all got our ways of trying to cope." Evie stayed hanging on his arm. She walked him back to the uneven rock formations where we were whiling away our time. Whiling away what remained of eternity. "Your belief—your faith—is your coping mechanism. It's a wonderful thing, and no one's going to argue with you." She raised a hand, as if to fend off Noah objecting to her rationalization. But he didn't have the inclination to fight his spiritual corner, just as I was losing heart in mine.

"Marty's the same way. His is just a little more esoteric, a little more eccentric." As ever, in the war of comparative theologies, it was considered a heresy for anything to be placed on an equal level with Christianity.

Noah slumped, exhausted. We were reaching the stage where any energy exerted was much too much. It detracted from our need to stay huddled around the fire hole in a group position, radiating as much warmth as we could amongst ourselves. Our need to reserve energy and stay awake according to the diktat of our body clocks, rather than let ourselves fall into premature slumber and a drop in body temperature.

I knew his grievance wasn't with me so much as with our predicament. Let me rephrase that—with the whole world's predicament. And I guessed that what Evie was saying was essentially correct. My interest in Nahua and the old gods *was* my coping mechanism. One of its major differences from Noah's was that it wasn't something I carried around as a personal dogma all the time. It just seemed to me my knowledge and my interest had collided with reality when we hit these mountains. When we inadvertently found ourselves in the last enclave of the ancient Mexica.

Beyond that, I had to ask myself whether it was becoming an article of faith. I was fascinated by the old Nahua ways. I have to be honest enough to admit I was starting to admire them. But did that mean I had a literal belief? It vexed me. Right then and there, in that black pit, in that terrible moment, it wasn't a question I could answer.

That the ancient Mesoamericans had myths and rituals that described everything that was happening to us, that had cause, and effect, and possible remedy, was something I found so impressive as to be overwhelming. But how much of that was from a basic human need to understand—or to pretend to understand—and transcend our circumstances? To escape the horror that lies behind all belief, all faith, all dogma: that everything is merely a human construct, at the root of which is a meaninglessness and a futility to our existence that is too terrible to comprehend. So terrible and so horrific, that it becomes a dire necessity for us to build belief systems that disguise this terrible truth, to bury all our gnawing doubts.

Had I really been so willing to put my trust in an ancient superstition, to the extent where I would contemplate killing one of my best friends, or maybe myself? It seemed impossible to me now. The admonitions of the group, their despair that my bloodstained pagan path should be the only route offered to them, had made me too self-conscious to trust myself. The only defense I have is that, in seeking a way to understand and to overcome our terrible circumstances, I was being truly human.

"It's nuts, isn't it?" It was Amber speaking. Bless her, her way of expressing herself always sounded like a flair for understatement. "The Creator, or Mother Gaia, or someone has turned out all the lights in the sky. And here we all are at each other's throats." It was simply put. Well put. Its simple sentiment was enough to make Noah and me momentarily ashamed. Him, for his macho-man crap. Me, for the unspoken assertion that I'd consider sacrificing my friends.

"I mean, why can't we just hang together until this things passes?" Those words may seem reasonable enough now. But we were trying to survive in a black pit of despair. In an icy slough of despondency. "I mean, all our shit's gone a little crazy, but surely, surely we can..."

She was shaking. It was hard to tell whether the force that rattled us to our bones was pure cold or total fear. Wes draped an arm, wearing his blanket like a cape, to provide an extra layer of cover for Amber. "I don't know, baby. What's happened, and what we're seeing now. It feels like something permanent may have taken place. Like we somehow gotta adjust–"

"Something permanent." Eve echoed the words. The reality of it was too devastating to contemplate. And here we were, facing it head-on, with no distractions that could possibly make us look the other way. "Sub-zero temperatures and falling. No light or heat from the sky. If Darwin were a bookmaker, I don't know what odds he'd give us on the 'adapt and survive' strategy." Eve's words were cruelly accurate. Like the freezing darkness itself, they spared none of us, least of all her. In a sense, we'd already adapted. When we set out to the mountains from our campsite that morning, none of us had any real sense of what it was to face our own mortality.

"No. I don't believe it." Noah spoke softly. It seemed to me that he'd never challenge Evie with the verbal aggressiveness he'd shown me. Still, her eyes widened at the challenge to her all-too-rational pessimism. "Things have to change. Things always change. This won't last forever. I can't let myself disbelieve that life will go on. That's my 'coping mechanism.'"

The icy silence spoke for itself. The fire crackled with dead bracken, too hot to approach at its epicenter but throwing out insufficient heat to stop us shivering. That things would continue to change, no one was in any doubt. But these particular changes had their own downward trajectory. In the centuries and millennia gone by, changes in the earth's environmental conditions had occurred that had lasted for eons. Our new age of darkness could easily outlast every person on the planet who was still alive.

"I know how I'm gonna cope." Wes wheezed aggressively into the flames, his uncombed hair catching sparks from ignited twigs. His fingers worked furiously at his rolling papers, too fast and too shaky to avoid spilling a little of his potent weed on the ground.

"Oh Wes, please... I mean now?" Eve's dismay was no more than the tired admonishment a worn-out parent might give to a naughty child. Neither Noah nor me had anything to say on the matter. I guess we just felt everyone had to go to hell in his own way.

"Like you know of a better time, Evie? You're already telling me I got no chance of surviving this thing anyway." He had a point. As Wes's fumbling hands lit up, he took a long, pungent hit and offered the joint to Amber. For maybe the first time since they'd been together, she declined. The memory of her last high, and where my anecdotes about Nahua ritual had taken her, was too close at hand, too real.

"Not till we get out of this place, baby." She always addressed Wes with the same laidback affection with which he spoke to her. Now it was tinged with sadness. "Till we get some light and laughter back in our lives." Amber had made a sensible bargain with herself, not to smoke marijuana again as long as we were trapped in this dark underworld.

"That's fine, girl. Real fine. All the more for me." He said it like he was wounded by her refusal. He took another deep hit and exhaled a jet stream of pale smoke. Like some miniature comet that trailed around the cave, its tail dissolved into the same icy vapor that hung all around us.

Noah and I both watched Wes closely. Normally, his habits bothered us not a bit. Now there was something deeply inappropriate about what he was doing.

"If this is the only way I'm getting my head outta this damn hole, then that's what I'm gonna do." It was a hollow boast—as if temporary disorientation would make any difference to his situation at all. But Wes made a big play of it, puffing out smoke like it was the key to the kingdom.

"Take it easy there, bro." Noah urged caution without reprimanding him. It was very noticeable that Wes's hands, which shook with cold before, were moving spasmodically like the wings of a dying bird.

"I am taking it easy. I'm taking it easy like there's no tomorrow. 'Cuz from where we're all standing maybe there isn't any." Wes's red-rimmed eyes stared wild and manic, with not a hint of his usual stoned relaxation. His chest rose and fell, not just as he inhaled and exhaled smoke or the biting air, but with his rising heart and pulse rates. Wes was smoking himself into a state of panic.

Amber looked anxiously at her man. He was pulling back on the secondary blanket that he'd draped over her, till it left her semi-exposed. Suddenly, it was his needs that were all-important. The sudden influx of cannabis into his bloodstream was radically lowering his blood pressure. With it, he was destroying his body's resistance to the cold.

"Hey! Wes! No more chill pill! Lay down next to the fire and get yourself re-heated." Eve's attitude was no-nonsense. But it seemed she was a little too late. Even from the distance at which I stood, I could hear a dull thud-thud-thud that was either the rhythm of Wes's boots pounding manically against the floor or the palpitations of his heart.

He was losing control now. He pulled both blankets from Amber's shoulders and hugged them to himself. It did little good. His torso and his legs shook as uncontrollably as his hands. The end of the joint now hung like a burning ember from Wes's lips. It was held there like an act of defiance. Until Noah's hand made a sudden sweep that knocked it from his mouth.

At first, I thought Noah had punched out our brother Wes. The palm of his hand was open, not clenched in a fist, but it made a swing that coincided with Wes hitting the deck. I wasn't alone in forming that impression.

"Noah, you asshole!" Amber's reaction was swift and shrill. Wes's legs had collapsed beneath him, taking him down in a clumsy heap. He yelped in pain from the small stalagmites that grew out of the floor and must have almost punctured his back. He began to shake more violently, till he started to convulse. Rolling himself into a fetal ball on the hard rock floor, it looked to me as if he was going into an epileptic fit.

"What the fuck?" Noah's annoyance was turning into alarm. "Has anything like this ever happened before?"

It took Amber a few panicked moments before she realized he was addressing her. "No. I mean, I don't know. He's got a little too freaked out, but not, not like—" It was pointless to hassle her. She was getting almost as panic-stricken as Wes himself.

I saw a more practical strategy. "Evie! Get the stove lit!" It was my turn to give orders now. As Wes shivered and writhed in the fetal position, I turned my back on the others and reached down to him. He extended a shaking palm as if I were the helping hand that was going to pull him out of his crisis. It wasn't what I had in mind. Grabbing the fabric he clung to as if it were a security blanket, I pulled hard till I wrenched it out of his unsteady grip.

"Hey, take a reality check, Marty! We don't need to make matters worse!" I didn't have time to explain myself to Noah. Sometimes action is required, not futile debate. Wes rolled over on the floor, his nose facedown in the dust. His legs folded almost in two, buckling backward at the knees as he tried to contort himself into the shape of something smaller, ever smaller.

I flung both blankets back at Amber, who was shaking violently herself. "Here. Take 'em!" She didn't refuse. I knelt and gripped Wes by his undulating shoulders. There was no resistance. He held onto me, as if my touch would deliver him from the physical and psychological trap he'd laid for himself. He tried to clamber into a kneeling position, but I wanted him malleable.

"Noah! Help me get his legs!" He wouldn't refuse me now. He may not have seen exactly what I had in mind, but I had the will to follow through. As he took Wes by his quaking knee joints, I motioned to him that he should follow my lead. I exerted every muscle and pushed. Across the ground. Noah followed suit. Wes groaned as he was sent rolling toward the fire pit. Until he was just about able to halt himself, his smoldering T-shirt spattered with instantly burning holes.

"Wesley! Oh no!" Amber's alarm was understandable, but it was unnecessary. Noah raised a gentle hand to hold her off. He could see what I had in mind now. Me, I was tending to Wes.

"Just hold yourself there." My weight was enough to pin him down, something I could never do when he was healthy. "Don't worry if it burns. It won't burn long enough to do you any lasting damage." Smoldering sparks were already threatening to ignite his hair. They soon crackled and faded into his scalp. "Get warm. Just get fucking warm."

He understood. His hyperventilation was starting to slow a little, breathing in acrid gulps of heat rather than stinging blasts of cold air. Momentary odors of burning arose from his scorched clothes, expiring as soon as they rose into the air. Nothing could be hot enough to create an unquenchable fire anymore.

Eve understood too. She brought the bowl of drinking water I'd suggested she heat on the stove. As Wes rose unsteadily onto his hands and knees, whining to himself, I held the bowl directly beneath his face. He recoiled from the scalding steam, but I wouldn't let him go. I pushed his face forward, his eyes closing in self-defense as the quick bursts of hot vapor filled his pores. They were only warm for an instant, before they too rose to join the freezing vapor that ascended to the cave roof.

It was working. Wes breathed deeply, but not as rapidly. The closer he got to receiving first degree burns, the less panicked he became. "Nice move." If I didn't feel frozen to my very soul, my heart might have warmed to Eve's compliment. She knew now that, in the moments when all seemed lost, I had the balls to act. They all knew.

"All that effort. All that energy." Noah's voice rasped in the freezing air. "Just for one person." We clung fast to our blankets. The meager amounts of heat we'd been able to grab for ourselves were being soaked up by Wes. Amber knelt and massaged his shoulder as he pulled himself back together. Even for him, the respite would be short-lived. Amber would have to throw the blanket over him as soon as there was no danger of catching it on fire. As soon as the embers were dying and the fire needed to be replenished, which would be very soon.

"I'm sorry, guys. I'm really fuckin' sorry." I feel we might have given him a more compassionate response, if we weren't all becoming so intently focused on our own discomfort. If we weren't hugging our blankets to our own bodies, seeking a form of escape that wasn't forthcoming.

"Yeah. Just get yourself back together, bro." Noah spoke, icily. "But if you pull any shit like that again, I swear to God I'll fucking kill you."

Eve hugged herself at the shoulders. Her face searched around the half-light, watching the trails of icy vapor rapidly ascending with our every breath. "It's getting much colder, isn't it?" I asked her.

Her answer wasn't direct, but it wasn't evasive. "The earth's comprised of a whole bunch of elements that retain heat. Without the sun's rays, or its radiation, that store of energy is gonna be depleted. Unless we go boring through these rocks, through the basalt and nickel, right through to the earth's molten core. Pretty soon, that's going to be the only part of the earth that retains any heat."

"So how long?" I put the unpalatable question that no one else wanted to ask.

"Nobody knows how long." She was sharp, a little defensive. "There's no way of measuring it. This has never happened before."

Wes was apart from us now. He stayed prostrate, with only a quivering Amber giving him her undivided attention. We were all locking down into our own little private hells. All our energies had to be spent on guarding against the freezing cold, on not letting it overwhelm our senses.

Noah hit the radio dial. Anything, it seemed, was better than concentrating on the here and now. "Citizens are warned to stay indoors and to do their best to keep safe and warm. The National Guard has issued a statement warning that it will not tolerate—repeat, not tolerate..." The announcer sounded as chilled to the bone as we were. I figured that his station's offices had to be functioning on emergency heating, or it would have been impossible for any of the talking heads to work. But the earth was getting colder. The retentive heat that Evie had spoken of had given way to something different: to the radiation of cold air by all the icy rock and freezing earth that this planet contains.

"New York City has been officially declared a disaster area. Reports have been coming in over the last few hours of a series of fires at the city's places of worship. Reports state that the Old St Patrick's Cathedral in Manhattan has burned to the ground, with severe loss of life. It is not known at this point whether it was an act of arson or an accident arising from an attempt to provide heating for the congregation."

All of them, everyone in the world outside was just as frightened as we were. All of them congregating in their desperate, huddled numbers to plead for mercy from their respective gods. Noah lowered the volume. These endless snatches of doom and panic only reinforced what we already felt. There were no snippets of good news to be had.

"This has got to end soon, right? I mean, this can't go on forever." Amber sought our collective reassurance. It amazed me, after all we had been through. After the terrible news that came to us uninvited on the airwaves. But then, experience has taught me that the human capacity for self-delusion is infinite.

"Nothing this crazy can be sustained. I mean, you said it Evie–nothing like this has ever happened before."

She was on the cusp of hysteria, arguing with herself. Had she not heard what Eve had said? But, because her optimistic nature wouldn't let her visualize the logical end, the bitter conclusion, Amber refused to accept it as a reality. "Sure, Amber. That's right." Eve smiled indulgently on her friend. "This can't go on forever. Nature will have to redress the balance." She had difficulty forming the words. It took a great deal of concentration, of sheer physical effort, to complete coherent sentences by now. Eve had decided it was better to reassure Amber with fairytales than to waste her breath on more words of foreboding.

"'Cos when this is all over, when the sun comes shining through, I'm gonna invite you all back to my mom's house in Austin. My sister and me, we're gonna have ourselves a party that lasts for days. You're all invited, everyone I know is invited." She hugged Wes. Both of their trembling bodies were locked together, feeding off of each other's body heat. Her words were making Evie despair. But Amber didn't see that. She was locked into her own reality, into a world that was far away from the darkness we now resided in.

"That'll be so cool, baby. That'll be dope." Wes had regained the power to speak. His glazed eyes joined Amber in her waking dream. His discomfort was almost overcome by intoxication. He was truly stoned. He had gone through hell, through a living nightmare and medical danger to get there, but it was the only place where he wanted to be.

"And we can have a barbecue burning in the backyard that'll feed everyone in the neighborhood for days. Everyone can drop by, like all of our friends, and all my mom's friends, and it'll be like the two generations coming together. Everyone can get happy. Everyone." Amber can't have known how painful it was to listen to her pipedream. Or maybe she was too far disassociated from our immediate reality to care anymore.

"And you, my little baby," she hugged Wes, their bodies shivering in syncopated unison, "can put away the weed till we have something to celebrate. 'Cos when the sun comes up again, everyone's gonna be higher and happier than they've ever been before." Wes wore a crazed, forced smile. He tried to laugh along with Amber's beatific vision of what life would be like when we all got home. It came out like a strangulated sob.

Maybe the rest of us were losing control in other, less noticeable ways. Noah, my mortal enemy just a short while ago, had turned inward, passive. Looking so much more haggard than the healthy twenty-three year-old man he'd been just one day before, he shook constantly. Unlike Wes, he seemed to have adjusted to the temperature, his respiration matching his new body rhythm.

But still, he was drained. At that moment, there wasn't one last scrap of residual energy to be dredged up from Noah Bailey's nervous system. I know. For my perception of the state Noah was in was grounded entirely in the way that I felt. We were in this together. We were heading the same way.

"Brother." He extended his trembling hand to me. "No hard feelings, right?" I accepted. Why should there be any hard feelings? What, now, could make any difference to the ultimate outcome? Why should I resent my brother Noah, for expressing the natural fear and resentment that were running through his head, through all of our heads, at every gnawing, intolerable moment?

He seemed relieved for me to take his hand. We hugged each other by the shoulders, combining our falling body heat. I was touched to be accepted back into the fold. But I also felt his despair. And I knew that he felt mine. I knew he could accept me again because my crazy ideas, my insane assertiveness, were on the retreat. Maybe I'm too cynical with hindsight, but it seems that Noah forgave me because I was no longer adding to his torment by making him think the unthinkable. Because I no longer claimed greater knowledge of this shadow realm than he had. Because I would no longer try to persuade him to go against his own moral instincts. Because I was now as defeated as he surely was.

Eve quit nursing Wes and Amber. She joined us. "I guess all we can do now is wait." It was as solemn, and as useless an admission as I'm ever likely to hear anyone make. All we could do was wait. Wait. The word was pregnant with misery. Wait for the inevitable. Wait for nature to take its course. Wait for the end.

"Yeah. I guess that's all there is left to it." I searched her face. She averted her gaze. This stoicism in the face of total defeat didn't come easy to Eve. She didn't have Noah's inbuilt faith, his personal rock, to cling to in the face of despair. I knew that she had the will to try anything, no matter what the personal risk or cost, to get out of that dark place. She would have tried anything she believed to be rational. But what I'd proposed was so far beyond the pale, it seemed it would just be a plunge into further darkness.

The three of us embraced each other in a group hug. What would seem to me like embarrassing, TV-influenced behavior at any other time became an imperative means of sharing our pain. Our despair. None of us could bear to look the other in the face, to avoid recognizing the fear we already felt deep within ourselves.

In our last hours huddled in the darkness, all vitality, all initiative, all optimism, seemed to be just a cruel joke. A thought crossed my mind, about the fate of people who froze to death when their bodies capitulated to a peaceful, terminal coma. I felt a painful twinge of envy. For the first time, I despaired completely of this existence and envied the dead.

SEVEN

In the deep dead of night, we huddled together to try to take refuge from the cold. I felt endlessly grateful for my friends accepting me back into the fold. If they had rejected me, there would have been no comfort anywhere in this darkened world.

We were huddled together around the pit of the cave. Trying to warm ourselves on the mass of dried bracken and tree bark we'd doused in propane from one of the lamps. The lamp was now extinguished for good. Our world grew darker, and all warmth seemed a distant memory, a forlorn hope. We were too cold to sleep, too tired to converse.

Each one of us was turning inward, to meet our private fears. Eve was sorrowful, her tired, beautiful face a symbol of humankind stripped of its hope. Her former optimism now seemed like false hope, but no one dreamt of blaming her. Hell, if they could accept *me* back, the guy who contemplated bloodshed in the name of the old gods, then who'd say a word against her? Hope wasn't a crime. It was just futile.

Wes stared darkly into space. He wasn't high anymore, and his pensiveness was not some stoned reverie. To be totally straight, in such dire circumstances, must have weighed heavily on him and Amber. But the baggie of weed they carried with them would only inspire panic now.

Amber's hands were no steadier. But it wasn't a drug thing, it was the abrasive, biting coldness that bit into her bones. It bit hard on us all. But Amber didn't seem to have an inner refuge where she could take herself. Where the freezing air and the palpable despair seemed to be the province of someone else.

Amber fussed and fidgeted, cutting a hole in her sleeping blanket to pull over her head. Her frostbitten fingers shook all the time, barely able to control the penknife in her hand. Her full, sensual lips quivered. They seemed to be turning blue.

Maybe, I conjectured, maybe her response was the best defense. I'd read stories of Arctic exploratory expeditions when sick party members had given in peacefully to the cold. Acceptance sometimes seemed the quickest path to death from hypothermia. Maybe Amber's discomfort would stop her giving in so easily

But for how long? And to what ultimate purpose?

Noah's despair matched my own. We weren't wasting words on each other anymore, but mutual respect had been restored. I'd backed down in the face of my friends' moral revulsion. Now there was no horror; no chastisement. And no hope.

As Noah held a pocket edition of the Holy Bible to his breast, he didn't waste his breath on sermons. The good book was his solace, and his alone. If anyone required its consolation, they had only to ask him. But Noah was sorrowful; his young eyes suddenly lined and shadowed. His faith was a last crumb of comfort, in the face of our inevitable fate. It could no longer raise his spirits, but it promised him deliverance. It promised him salvation. It promised him the strength of his faith would seat him at the right hand of Jesus. But it was all in the hereafter. It was all a promise of pie in the sky. It offered us no hope for here, now, in the material world. I saw no hope in Noah's face.

And me? I too felt bereft of hope. My mind had gone spinning into a whirl of mythic fantasy, just a few hours before. Now, it seemed to me that it was a symptom of what was coming down upon us. Noah had his theological fantasy for comfort—I had mine. But now it seemed like insanity, even to myself. For just a short time, it had offered an imaginary avenue of escape.

To engage with the Nahua Gods had seemed like a chance to change what was occurring in the physical universe. Was that a delusion? Psychosis? Paranoid schizophrenia, or some such catch-all psychiatric term?

It hardly seemed to matter now. For the shortest time, I'd imagined I could halt the paralysis we all felt, avert the endgame now playing out so miserably. If I'd been deluded, then I had good reason to be.

The radio tuner faded in and out of different FM wavelengths. For most of the time, the voices turned into a wailing electronic distortion, with hardly a single word discernible. It seemed useless, pointless, to submit ourselves to the cacophony. But better that than just the silent, freezing, devouring air. Better that than the drained sound of our own voices.

As a distantly familiar female voice drifted back in on waves of static, Wes moved his hunched shoulders from beneath his blanket. He reached for the radio, his shaking arm seeking to cut off the aural intruder. But Amber reached out her own quivering hand to him. For all her emotional fragility, she had the forbearance to tolerate further communiqués from the doomed world outside.

"It's been thirteen hours now since the sun seemed to disappear from the skies across the world." It sounded like she might be the same female newscaster we'd heard earlier in the day. Why didn't she go home? Why didn't she spend the final days with her loved ones? Maybe, I wondered pointlessly, maybe she doesn't have a close relationship, and maybe she'd prefer to see it all out with her people down at the station. Or maybe her newscaster colleagues hadn't shown for work, not wanting to leave their own loved ones alone to face the eternal night. Or maybe it was some other woman altogether, and my mind was just finding pointless details to obsess over, rather than facing what seemed to be the inevitable.

"The global death toll continues to rise. Our Central Asian correspondent reports that the major cities of the Indian subcontinent have descended into chaos. In New Delhi, Bombay, Calcutta, Islamabad, Karachi, Lahore; tens of thousands, perhaps hundreds of thousands of people are believed to have already succumbed to sub-freezing temperatures."

The newsreader's voice sounded resigned and weary. Just yesterday, this would have been the biggest news story in world history: in one of the hottest, most densely populated regions of the world, people were dying wholesale of the cold. Now it seemed barely worth remarking upon. It was just another wearying detail of our universal mortality. People were more immediately concerned with their own pitiful chances, or those of their families. Or just trying to lock their mind against the freezing chill air that bit right through to their bone marrow.

"Further reports suggest the wider population has descended into hysteria. Suggestions that some families are sacrificing their own children to the Hindu idol Kali have met no firm denial." Wes seemed to sniffle a little. Amber reached out to him, holding one shaking hand against his chest. I recalled how Wes and Amber had long planned to hit the hippie trail to India. To make the journey through rural towns and mountain regions, and wind up on a beach in Goa, or on a mountaintop in Nepal, to spend some days of spaced-out bliss.

Wes wept right then, I felt, at the sudden demolition of all their dreams. It wasn't just that they were never going to get to India now. It was that that particular dream didn't exist anymore. Their haven of anti-Western spirituality, their imagined Mecca of peace and love, was a horror. But the Hindu faith first rejected materialism not because stoners like dear Amber and Wes thought it was cool to do so, but because, like all great religions, it adapted to the needs of its time and its region.

The Hindu gods encouraged the lower castes to reject the material world, accept poverty and early death, because it matched their life expectations. It was the same as early Christianity preaching meekness and acceptance to its followers–they were a persecuted group of people who'd been made pariahs in the Roman world: what other angle could there be but "the meek shall inherit the earth"?

Noah narrowed his glaring eyes in horror at the news. It wasn't the betrayal of a hippie dream for him, as it was for Amber and Wes. I know that he heard echoes of my own pagan solution, in the rumors of sacrificing children. And so did I. What beautiful, naïve Amber and Wes could never accept was the innate horror in the universe. Their mindsets were still attuned to a utopian version of Noah's Christianity–there was "good," and there was "evil," and ne'er the twain shall meet.

But the universe, along with the more profound pagan religions, was never like that. For every dark deed, there was a bearer of light to balance it. Good and evil co-existed in equal quantities, often within the same person–or the same deity. The Kali-Yuga, the six-armed Hindu Goddess, was the bringer of both life and death. New Agers and neo-pagans may have looked on her beatific smile as all-benevolent, but Kali also carried a sword, and, in some descriptions, a basket of human skulls under her arm.

Her existence in the Hindu pantheon told of how their wise men, their Brahmin, accepted that death and violence were an integral part of the human condition. That the lives of individuals were as nothing, provided that the existence of the world continued.

How logical, then, for the lower-caste cult of Kali worshippers, who still persisted in the modern world, to turn to her in this time of ultimate crisis. How terrible, and how very understandable, that they should steel themselves to take the lives of their most beloved, or their youngest. That they should sever the top of a child's skull, just as their ancestors had done, to earn the favor or the mercy of Kali.

Their great tragedy was that the sun had not fallen out of the sky because of an offense to the Kali-Yuga. For all the doubt I'd experienced in the last few hours, I knew. I still knew.

Wes stared unblinking into the middle distance. The only faculty that remained to him was his sense of dread. All else was shut down. He barely reacted as Amber draped the blanket she'd cut into a poncho over his head.

"Reports suggest that explosions registered in and around the Hyderabad region of India may have been the result of military aggression by Pakistan. Suggestions that nuclear warheads have been launched by India's Muslim neighbor, whose leaders went on record today as blaming the Indian government for the current crisis, remain unconfirmed. In Beijing, the Chinese government warned that it would not tolerate a nuclear exchange on its borders and would retaliate accordingly. Further reports that China's vast rural population has been virtually decimated in the space of a single day were neither confirmed nor denied by the Foreign Ministry."

So it was on, then. The Apocalypse. The final days, that Noah's bible had told him would be announced by the coming of four great and terrible riders in the sky. Announced with all the crazed fervor of a mundane weather report. Simply accepted as a depressing fact by five young people too preoccupied with our own misery, by our own discomfort, to kick and scream and rail against the dying of our world. In that cave, our little worlds were ending not with a bang but with a collective whimper.

"Earlier appeals today to the United Nations to make Africa the center of international crisis relief were firmly rejected by world leaders. While accepting that the overnight temperature drop and the obliteration of entire crops in the region will mean likely death for the majority of the populations of Central, Eastern and Southern Africa, and certain death for all those already infected with the AIDS virus, leaders of the European Union nations pointed to their own crises at home."

Noah's brow unfurrowed. For a few moments, there was a bigger picture to focus on than our own suffering. He'd spoken before of going to one of the stricken African nations, of Uganda or Rwanda, to be a part of what he called the "universal healing process." It was a nice sentiment. I can reject Noah's spiritual beliefs without mocking his need to extend a helping hand. But somehow, for all his good will, he'd never got around to it. Like most of our buddies, I guess, he'd been too much of a party guy.

To hear him speak sometime, you'd think he headed straight out of the "Bible Belt" to Albuquerque. But you'd be wrong. Noah Bailey was the son of a good Anglican Protestant family up in Idaho. Their creed was no more fundamental than most, and a good deal more liberal than many. But Noah had been fed God with his mother's milk. He'd often laughed to me about this inherent need to do good that he felt. "Don't lose patience with me, bro," he'd slurred on one drunken, good-natured night when he'd got into his God kick. "I just got the Lord in my larynx." He wasn't pious about it, and, truth be told, he'd never found a focus for his do-goodly godliness.

Now he never would. Now, I believed he could see how totally, ruthlessly pragmatic the laws of the universe could be. Once, he would have kicked up some shit about the Euro-weenies denying aid to Mother Africa. But now, I believe he saw there was nothing else they could be expected to do. In the last reckoning, everybody will do what they have to, to protect their own interests. Many will go much further than they could ever have imagined possible.

"Gunfire has been reported in the streets of Brussels and Strasbourg, close to depositories for food aid to the Third World. It is believed that armed gangs are fighting battles for control of surplus food supplies. An EU spokeswoman has stressed that the current crises are due to sudden climactic change, and have not precipitated any serious domestic food shortages. She stressed that government-recommended retailers and supply centers have enough supplies for at least two weeks."

Noah gave a bitter laugh. "Hear that?" He spoke low to me, his voice whistling in the internal wind. "The Third World's gone to hell, but the West has got it licked. We can last for, ohh, two weeks." Food supplies or not, it still seemed wildly optimistic to both of us.

"Meanwhile, the European Union has been criticized for failing to put its own emergency relief operations into action. Most of Northern Europe has now been declared an international disaster area, along with Scandinavia, the British Isles and Ireland."

It was my turn to get lost in memories. Ireland was the mother country—at least as far as my parents were concerned. My recollection of it, as a small boy, is of strange people talking in funny voices; the green landscape; and rain, everywhere, damp and cold. It had been a short blip in a life mostly spent right here, in the benign sunshine of New Mexico.

I'd lived a parochial existence, but I didn't regret one moment of it. It seemed to me now that my aversion to cold climates was a foretaste of what was to come. Of the time when I, and the rest of the planet, entered the freezing purgatory of Mictlan.

I munched from a bag of trail mix. It was tasteless, masticated over and over in my mouth before I could swallow it. I passed the bag to Eve, who followed suit. The joyless chewing ritual was a semblance of life, a mark of the fact that we all wanted to survive, no matter what. The radio merged into static bursts again. It was as if the tuning dial was finding its own chaotic way around the airwaves. No one made a move to re-tune it or shut it down. It was inevitable that the selector would roll its way back to disaster.

"Government authorities in most states have been engaged in clearing the bodies of homeless persons and street people from the nation's cities, in an effort to avert outbreaks of disease." It was a male newsreader again. Bringing trouble back home, where it all started. "Operations have been stymied by widescale rioting and looting along with the freak climactic conditions. An announcement by the Attorney General earlier this evening placed all States of the Union under martial law, to be coordinated by local military and law enforcement officials until such a time as the crisis ceases."

Just for one moment, I thought Noah was going to cast his pocket bible into the bonfire pit. Instead, he threw in the last of our pathetic little batch of firewood and closed his eyes. Steadying his hands, he clasped the book and locked himself into silent prayer. I appreciated the gesture. But, as I was aware of its total uselessness, I appreciated his silence more.

"The Army and regional divisions of the National Guard have already been stationed to protect emergency food supplies. Due to anticipated crop failures that are expected to follow the crisis, Congress has called an emergency debate on how to avoid a national food shortage over the coming weeks. Suggestions that the government's protectionist measures, designed to make America self-sufficient in farm and crop produce, have caused the crisis were denied by the Department of Agriculture. As a departmental spokesperson indicated, all the United States' international trade partners are now engulfed in similar crises."

It was a small consolation, but we were protected from the insanity of the outside world. In our cave, we were focused upon the tiny universal details that afflicted all of humankind. Extinction now seemed imminent, but it would not be at the hand of our fellow man.

"It's finally happening. It's all going fucking crazy out there." Noah's words were more a breath than a whisper. I sympathized. But then, I sympathized with the looters and rioters too. The time for rationality had long since passed. Why accept the word of someone who promises to protect life and limb, when they threaten to blow you away if you go scrounging around for food? With every public announcement that was made, it became clearer that the madness of the moment was infecting the government too. They made official edicts, they followed procedures, they made promises and issued warnings. None of it amounted to a damned thing. It was so far beyond the limits of the politicians' experience, of their imagination, of everything they'd ever conceived of, that to have faith in government seemed crazier by far than Noah's policy of hoping and praying for a divine miracle. Or my own belief in the symbolic significance of the Nahua gods.

"In Iowa, the overnight damage to wheat field crops and related farming industries has already caused a state of emergency. Retailers and trading points throughout the state have reportedly 'run dry' due to a rush of panic buying. Aligned to this is an unprecedented wave of looting in rural areas, with civil defense units called in to protect food retail outlets and emergency supply stores. Iowa has now become the eighth state to be declared an official 'disaster zone' by the federal government."

Eve wept. Each involuntary sob hurt her chest, as she was forced to gulp down more freezing air. There was nothing anyone could say to her. She was an intelligent, enthusiastic chick who was just thrilled to get out of the cattle-belt region of the Midwest that she hailed from. But I knew she'd always return there, brandishing an honors degree and some too-handsome, too-successful fiancé. However far she'd come from her origins, whatever the future had held in store, Evie would always love her mom and dad. Love her two brothers and her sister. Love people. Love life.

But life had taken her on a strange detour. And me? Well, I hadn't been close to my people in years. Not since the old man divorced Mom for a Hispanic girl a few months younger than me. He knew I'd gone to the state university, but showed little interest in my academic choices. I mean, degrees in archaeology and anthropology doth not a successful real estate salesman make, right?

My elder brother, Bobby, was more sympathetic, but he kind of felt like I was from a different planet. He got through college on a football scholarship, he dated prom queens; he got a job as a broker for an investment bank on Wall Street; he broke off his first marriage engagement when he found someone who was a little more glamorous. You can see how he'd gel with someone who wants to turn his back on modern America and study ancient cultures.

I thought of Mom, who was never that interested in my choices either. But at least she wasn't disparaging. She rarely said anything very much at all. I hoped she'd be bunkered down somewhere with the other ladies from her bridge club, or her book discussion group. Hell, I even hoped she was with some guy. It was better than facing this alone. And if I'd been there, it would have been like facing it together, all alone. Just the two of us locked into our mutual incomprehension of each other.

But then, if my friends and me had all been at our homes, my mind kept insisting, none of this would have happened.

"We here at KXTNC Radio wish to extend our hopes and wishes and our heartfelt prayers to our listeners as this crisis unfolds." Sounded like she was the station's main anchorwoman; one of those well-modulated white-bread voices. She did a good job of keeping her tones level, speaking in a way she obviously believed was reassuring. I don't know who she believed she was fooling. Deep down, she must have been crapping herself with fear just like the rest of us.

"We promise to remain on the air and provide you with any information we can to help you through these uncertain times. In a few moments, we will be repeating an address to the nation by the President of the United States, first broadcast on this station at 8 pm. Great Eastern Time."

The Head Honcho himself. It was hard to know what he could add to the slew of apocalyptic tidbits we'd endured all day. But still—in our cold little corner of Hell, the lost faces of my friends seemed to grow attentive. Even Wes seemed to prick up his ears a little. Maybe hearing from the guy at the helm would provide them with some kind of reassurance.

"My fellow Americans.

"It is my solemn responsibility in this time of crisis to speak with you directly. This great nation of ours has suffered a devastating misfortune over the last twenty-four hours. It has arrived without announcement, without warning, and without ceremony. It appears to be, as many people are saying, an Act of God."

If only your speechwriter knew the half of it, Mr President. I hadn't seen Noah, Evie, or Amber and Wes so attentive in hours. It was like they were searching for scraps of hope in the presidential address that were coded, that they would have to decipher.

"The people of the United States have endured disasters at home before. Whether it be a natural catastrophe, such as the earthquakes that briefly devastated both northern and southern California—or whether it be the fruits of manmade wickedness, such as the treacherous attacks upon our nation on 9/11, a date that has gone down in the annals of infamy.

"The one constant factor has always been this: America has endured. The people of the United States value their freedom, and the great benefits that being part of a mighty nation such as ours brings. But Americans are also a hardy people, a people who, historically, have always had the strength and the endurance to finally triumph over adversity."

"So say something, dude," Wes whined, his voice becoming higher-pitched each time the air became colder, more difficult to breathe. "I mean, we know we're all Americans."

"Shit..." Noah's senses had woken up. It reawakened him to the gnawing cold that made him twitch his facial muscles in pain. "How high you think they've got the emergency heating turned up in the Oval Office?"

"And so it is that, in this hour of need, this literal time of darkness, the people of the United States are being tested once again. This is a time of fear and uncertainty. But also a time of wonder. Wonder at the mysterious workings of our world. Of the heavens. And of God Himself."

"But what's *He* going to do to help us?" Amber's plaintive cry was that of a little girl. Like the rest of our friends, Amber Hagen, our beautiful space cadet, put too much faith in the rational world. And in the Judeo-Christian world.

"Just as you, the American people, can be assured that God is on your side, so you can be sure that every member of the United States government is working fulltime to bring us through this crisis. Your representatives and your armed forces, your scientists and your civil servants, will not let you down in your hour of need."

"Just don't lift a Hershey bar if the National Guard are on duty, dude."

"This crisis, and the inexplicable conditions we find ourselves in, will soon pass. Of this I have no doubt. But until then, it is incumbent upon you, the citizenry, to give your government and your military the absolute cooperation we require to make America a safe and powerful place again."

"I think his key word there was 'inexplicable,'" I whispered to Noah. "They have less idea of how to handle this than they do about how to send an astronaut to Mars without his skeleton imploding."

"In the present time, be assured that all our efforts will be directed toward restoring you and your families' lives back to their former level of safety and security. And that all our prayers are with you.

"God bless America."

I guess "stunned silence" is the appropriate phrase to describe our response. Not because of what we'd heard, but because of everything that remained unsaid, all the countless questions that remained unanswered.

"That's it?" Noah was disbelieving. Not even he needed homilies about how God was on our side now.

"What else were you expecting?" He had no answer. But that was the whole thing–nobody had any answers. Nobody except me, that is–or so my ego or my conscience kept telling me.

"Radio KXTNC's announcers will now be taking a short break from the airwaves." At last, the staff had decided to go back to their civilian lives. Whether they would return to their jobs hardly seemed worth the conjecture. "We leave our listeners with a selection of devotional music and hymns." Then, finally, the one faltering note in the announcer's warm, homogenized tones: "God love you, and God bless you all." That one innocuous little statement sent a chill through our group. She sounded on the verge of losing it, of bursting into tears.

Then it was just the tape. The familiar wheezing church organ started to pump away. I recognized the hymn that I'd detested from the time they played it at my grandma's funeral.

"Rock of ages, cleft for me / Let me hide myself in thee..."

In its mournful tones, it wasn't a song of validation or hope. Just a plea for solace in the face of despair. It could only underline our sense of helplessness. We were in the great rock caverns of the Sangre de Cristo mountains, but they offered no place for us to hide. The funereal tones wafted away on a wave of static, almost as soon as they'd arrived. I didn't know whether our FM tuning device had drifted, or whether KXTNC was off the air for good.

Noah crouched forward on his knee, staring ahead of himself. Nodding slowly. "So this is the end?" He shot a nervous laugh into the air, at hearing himself speak the words. "All over. Nothing left to say." No one contradicted him. No one answered. No one even knew whether he meant the end of public service announcements on air. Or just the end. Period.

The silence was a cold blanket over us all. The air was filled with a radio static that no one wanted to turn off, in case the outside world should break in again. We were barely able to meet each other's glances. There really was nothing left to say. Amber shakily poured herself a steaming cup of coffee from a flask. Once it was full, she barely touched it, simply warming her hands around the cup or letting the steam float up into her face, until it too was overwhelmed by the icy cave vapor.

Then, in a heartbeat, she became manic. "This is all my fault, isn't it?" No one answered, not wanting to confront the question. Nor did any of us deny her charge. "If I hadn't spilled the blood, in the cave, it's like Marty says, I messed up their sacrificial rite."

I wasn't about to contradict explanations I'd already made. But neither did anyone else argue against me, from their own rational or moral point of view. Amber was about to become hysterical. But only Eve seemed to sympathize with her friend. She reached over and extended her hand. Something not even Wes, lost in his own unfamiliarly sober thoughts, felt compelled to do.

Amber gradually calmed as Evie patted and stroked her. Women are so much better at expressing emotion, without any concrete reasons for doing so. Reassured by Eve's compassion, Amber took a deep breath and regained control of herself. She rose to her feet, moving away for a little solitude. Tiptoeing gingerly around the interior chambers and sharp inclines, she found herself among the rock formations and descending stalactites where I'd done most of my thinking. I could only guess at the confusion in her mind.

There was a sudden blurt of white noise. Electrostatic peaked and fell. Human voices twisted their way out of the aural cacophony, like evidence of ghosts or alien beings captured on audiotape. The American communications industry was not dead, at least.

It was another female voice. But this time she was an interviewer. Not everyone had deserted the broadcast networks for the homes that would become their tombs.

"And is it correct, Professor Benway, as some scientific commentators have been saying, that life on earth will not be able to sustain itself for more than a few weeks?"

"Two weeks." The answer was aggressively precise.

"Are you saying that all of us, the human race, are literally facing extinction after...?"

"Not after. Within. Two weeks. If we look at the average rate of decrease for global temperatures, then there will be no place on earth at the end of that period which supports temperatures higher than a maximum one hundred degrees below zero Fahrenheit. There is simply no chance that any form of life will be sustained."

The scientist's tones were clipped, matter-of-fact, sparing nobody's feelings. It sounded like he bore a grudge against his fellow scientists because they couldn't avert our collective doom. Or maybe he was just deeply, deeply pissed at himself.

The lady interviewer fought hard to choose the right words. Objectivity counted for nothing now. We were all in this, every last living creature on the planet. "So is it fair to say that..." She swallowed. Hesitated. "That temperatures around the world will reach the point of absolute zero."

"Ah, the fabled absolute zero." The professor had obviously been asked about this many times over the past twenty-four hours, and seemed to oddly relish it. "That's something different altogether. It's an empirically tested temperature, four hundred and fifty-nine below, at which matter ceases movement. That refers to everything, not just sentient life forms—all atomic, sub-atomic and molecular structures, all cellular life."

"So there will come a point—" The interviewer was obviously finding it difficult to continue.

"There will come a point very soon when all life on planet Earth will cease to exist. But that's highly theoretical. By the time it happens, none of us will be here to observe it."

Eve's face was set in stone as she listened to him clinically describe our destruction. It was the selfsame description she'd used, but wrapped up in a protective shell of bravado. As each point was brutally hammered home, her expression hardened until a small vein stood out on her forehead. Her face petrified. Maybe it was the biting cold, but a small trail of tears also seeped from the corners of both of her eyes.

EIGHT

The time was 6:48 am. Our fourth day in the Sangre de Cristo mountains. Or should that be fourth night? Either way, it was entirely possible it would be our last.

I don't know whether I'd slept, or just passed into some semi-catatonic state. I pegged my return to consciousness as the moment when I became conscious of everyone else. I'd found my attention to the here-and-now receding as the temperature slipped lower. Everyone else seemed to be experiencing the same thing, to some degree. The cold was supremely fucking with our heads.

We were still huddled around the fire. I think I'd slept for a while, or at least gone into a state of dissociation, in that position. Nobody wanted to leave the fire. Nobody wanted to leave the protection of the group's combined body heat. We were sitting so close together that there was nobody who wasn't touching somebody else. I was shoulder-to-shoulder with Noah and Evie.

But still the cold bit through to our bones.

The radio had stayed on all night. The static crackled in a way that had become so familiar that it was almost a language to us. There were no further words—of encouragement, or desperation—to be heard on the radio, and we accepted the noise as a substitute for silence. Still, no one objected as Amber bent over to turn the radio off. It was only an incoherent blurt, but the possibility remained that a human voice could waft back onto the airwaves to read the obituary of humankind.

Wes grabbed weakly at Amber's arm. He held it still only for as long as it took him to read her watch. "It's still early, right?" Even now, he was seeking some kind of reassurance. "I mean, maybe it'll come up."

I shook my head. "Sunrise was supposed to be twenty-six minutes ago." I was just as scared as he was, but I had no time for false hopes. None of us were grasping at desperate straws anymore. All we had left was a fatalistic weight that hung grimly over us. I once read a quote, I think it may have been by the Russian writer Chekhov, that said, "One must go forward, without hope and without despair." It was only now that I realized the fallacy of that remark. Living without any hope at all can only breed despair.

"My grandparents were gonna move to Florida to get away from the cold. How's that for a joke?" Wes made the wise choice. He capitulated. All we had now was gallows humor. The comedy of imminent annihilation.

"My brother's getting married next month." It was my turn. What the hell, if you can't beat 'em, die with 'em. "It was going to be a real big wedding. My brother's an investment broker, and her people are big in property. Can you imagine what social strata the guests orbit around in? Hell," I permitted myself a grim laugh, "I'm almost relieved I won't have to go."

"We're not gonna see them again, are we?" Amber wasn't playing. For her, the belated realization was too immense, too crushing, to fight it with feeble jokes. "My mom, my sister... for all I know, they could be dead already." Her melancholia was infectious. Wes reached for her, whispered into her ear. It was an almost embarrassingly intimate moment, but such details were inconsequential to us now.

"Baby." His voice shook with anguish, with the impact of what he was forcing himself to say. "They're finished. We're finished. It's all over... No, no," he tried to brush away the tears rolling from her eyes. His every attempt at making her accept our fate only succeeded in distressing them both even more. "It's really over."

"No. It doesn't have to be."

Evie's insistence was as strident as it was unexpected. It shocked us all, me included. "I won't accept it. It doesn't have to be over. Not if what Marty says is true." She must have been steeling herself for this moment. Truly, her resolve was a fierce beast to look square in the eye. Eve Bishop had made a decision, and for her there was to be no going back.

"We want to live, right?" She searched all our faces, daring us to answer to the contrary. Daring us to slip back into the gloomy fatalism that seemed like our only recourse. "We want to save our families? Want to see our parents again?" Eve could hardly expect a response in the negative. "We want to save the world?" She was trying to ignite the vital bursts of optimism that had seemed so painfully futile. But no one was going to deny her. No one would deny her will to live, or our desire that life itself should go on.

"Then one of us has to die."

Evie, in hardening her heart to cruel necessity, had made me want to live again.

NINE

We were truly five now. Five locked together by circumstances of our unwitting making. Five as an organic unit. Five individual organisms that, no matter how we squirmed and writhed, could not escape the destiny we'd inadvertently chosen.

Everything I saw now was from the perspective of the Nahua universe. Even our number appeared to me to have hidden significance. On one level, it signified our doom: the cycles of Mesoamerican mythic history always ran in clusters of five. Our age of the moving sun, Ollintonatiuh, was the fifth sun cycle of Nahua. It boded ill. The fifth cycle surely meant the end of everything, once it had come to its natural conclusion.

Five was the number in Mexica numerology that completed the circuit. It was always noted that no more than four cups of Octli, the booze made from cactus sap, should be imbibed: the fifth cup would make the drinker truly drunk, and, so it was said, vulnerable to the supernatural forces of the Nahua universe.

But Nahua always permitted the option of changing circumstances. By symbolic actions, vital adjustments could be made. If we found the strength and the courage to do so, such an opportunity existed for us now. If we adjusted the number of our group, then we would no longer be five: the number most vulnerable to the psychic assault of sacred forces.

If we could only steel ourselves, only put our petty fears aside, we could reduce ourselves to four. Four, in Mexica numerology, was the number associated with the Sun, and solar heat. If five had ended the fifth cycle of the Sun, then the possibility existed that four could restore it to the sky.

This may sound insane. So be it. By this point, I no longer cared. I saw a world swathed in darkness, full of frightened people whom sanity and rationalism had failed. Our only hope lay in the irrational. In the physical and mythic world. In the Nahua universe.

I carried the essentials of the ceremony from the interior chamber of the cave. I felt enervated, adrenal, motivated largely by fear. It was daunting, but it raised me several levels above the crushing pessimism I'd been laboring under.

My brethren remained seated around the fire, stomping their frozen feet to keep their circulation moving. They were all as scared as I was. Strangely, none of them seemed to note my own trepidation and fear. Apart from Evie, it was as if they believed I was acting out some long-cherished fantasy.

"This is insane, man." Wes's fear was most palpable of all. "Totally and completely." As I placed them atop a slanting rock ledge, he couldn't take his eyes from the Nahua tribute box or the sacrificial dagger. I refused to react. This was our reality. Wes could denounce it, or refuse to accept it. But he couldn't change it.

As unnerved as he seemed by my glacial façade, Amber was no less disturbed by her best friend. "You're not really thinking about... doing this, are you?" She was begging Eve for reassurance again. She'd find none. Evie may have been scared, but she also had the courage to accept universal laws that, only two days ago, she had not even been cognizant of.

"It may be the only chance we have." Her voice was measured, neutral. She'd made a decision not to give way to anyone's fears, including her own, or to her own moral qualms. Eve was not letting herself be touched by empathy or pity. She watched as I carefully set the implements out on the rock. The connotations were clear to them all: mad Marty was setting out a sacrificial altar.

In reality, unless one of us were able to find the courage to offer him or herself up to the Sun gods, it would have been impossible to subdue an unwilling subject on that rocky surface.

"So where... How do we start, Marty?" It was as reasonable a question as I'd heard since the sun fell from the sky.

"I'm setting the sacred implements up to face 'Acatl'—east," I explained to Eve. "It's the direction of origination, of birth. And it's the place where the sun used to rise in the sky each morning. Where it was born.

"The Nahua universe," I continued to explain, "was orientated toward 'Calli'—the west. Where 'Cuauhtemoc,' 'eagle falling' or sunset, would take place every night, and the sun would begin its descent into the underworld. It signified the fatalism of the ancient Mexica, their acceptance of death, of our transient existence. Calli is the direction that the entire world is facing now, if you get my drift."

I tried to look into their intent faces. The lamps lighting them from below had the weird effect of black and white expressionistic lighting in some college play. "So how do we change it, Martin?" Eve spoke for them all. "What is it we have to do?" They were less interested in the Nahua universe than in what they had to do to appease it. I can't blame them.

"Well, I guess... First we have to decide who the chosen one is."

It detonated an emotional bomb. Noah jumped to his feet. "You mean choose a *victim*, don't you? Why can't you say what you mean, Marty?" It was raw anger and revulsion, maybe leavened with some hate. My dear buddy, my good friend Noah was starting to hate me. It was as if they felt that I'd maneuvered them into this situation, rather than the extreme circumstances. Rather than our offense against the old gods.

"Hey, you can fucking count me out too!" Wes had found his backbone in Noah. Swept along by the tide of events, he'd seemed incapable of making a stand on his own. "Nobody, but nobody, is making a victim out of me."

"Please, guys. We need to stop this victimhood crap." I may have pleaded politely, but I wasn't backing down. Not now. Not with everything in our world at stake, and everything to lose. "No one's looking for victims! We need to be heroes. And whoever of us plays the central role will be the greatest hero of all. Nahua has an afterlife, a special heaven called Tonatiuhcan, that's reserved for warriors and human sacrifices."

Wes's hatred was starting to burn into me too. He'd tripped on New Age spirituality and alternative religions, sure, but faced with such a visceral, living theology he was proving himself unworthy. "They were the most revered human beings of all. Offering oneself up for sacrifice, it wasn't just on a level with being a war hero—it was the same thing. People who died mundane, unremarkable deaths went to Mictlan—to the underworld, to the cold dark caves. That's where we are now. That's where the rest of the world is too."

It didn't diminish his suspicion. That I was able to articulate my beliefs made it all the worse. It was as if the laws of science, of human behavior and morality, had all been destroyed by Martin Tierney, the pagan heretic.

"We're all in this together, Wes," Eve appealed to him. In the very last ditch, in the hours after twilight's last gleaming, she was becoming my rock.

"Not me," Wes shook his head. "Not this time. No fuckin' way." It was then I realized his problem wasn't with me. Not with my beliefs, or with the way I'd imposed them. His problem was with himself. Behind it all, poor Wes was too much of a coward to make it.

But Noah still thought I was some kind of crazy autocrat. "So what's the procedure here?" He was confrontational, trying to psych me out. He didn't trust me running this bizarre sideshow. Didn't trust how my perception of events had overtaken them. Didn't trust their lives in my hands. "A secret ballot? Show of hands? What?" He scanned me, and Evie too, up and down, with equal suspicion. "Sorry, but this happens to be my first human sacrifice, y'know..." His words dripped with acid.

Eve felt intimidated. "How did the Mexica make their decision?" Her question was little more than a breath, a whisper. She felt the stigma of being associated with my ideas. Felt the fear of following them through to their logical conclusion. And the greater fear of doing nothing.

"It was an honor." I was defensive. It was only my beliefs that were under attack, but I didn't know how long it would stay that way. "It was never a punishment. The perfect sacrificial subjects would have been young people from the highest echelons of society. They would have been granted the privilege of living as the god they paid tribute to for one year—like Quetzalcoatl, the serpent god, or Tezcatlipoca, the twin creators of the earth and the heavens."

"And then?"

"And then they died an honorable death."

Noah grimaced. Shook his head. "Sure. No sweat for the Aztecs. They didn't have to choose one of their best friends." He extended his arm, waving toward us all in an arc motion. "Someone they went to school with." He looked on Wes and Amber, both scared stupid, with a desperate compassion. "Roomed with." He looked hard at me. It was an accusation. Right then, I felt his wounded sense of betrayal. Maybe he'd never believe me now, but I ached because of it. I just couldn't allow myself to be swayed by it, is all.

"What are you telling me, Noah? That this isn't going to be easy?" He had no answer. I guess he wasn't expecting a rational response. "Do you think this is gonna be any easier for me than it is for you? I'm prepared to make the ultimate sacrifice if I have to, and it scares me to the bottom of my soul."

"So why are we even talking about it?" Amber's outburst was a plea, an accusation, a cry of outrage. "All this talk about who we have to kill, and what we have to do." She deflated quickly. Descended into despair. "I thought we were all brothers and sisters, right? We love each other."

Nobody could challenge her sentiment. If we dared to follow the deed through, it would be for love that our brother or sister died. "I mean, Marty says that the Aztec world has five ages of the sun. If the age of the moving sun has already ended, how are we gonna know if we can bring it back?"

Nahua time was cyclical. As their calendar years were never numbered above fifty-two, or an absolute maximum of one hundred and four, it was taken for granted that time would eternally recur. Ollintonatiuh, the fifth Sun Age, may have ended, but the Mexica saw the past as a living, organic thing that had an ongoing relationship with the present.

But I couldn't have explained that to Amber. Not then. Not in the state of anxiety that blinded her as much as the darkness we now dwelled in. "Or what if it doesn't work? What if it's all just a crock of superstitious nonsense?"

Our dear sweet Amber—who caressed crystals to maintain her spiritual equilibrium, who arranged the furniture in her rooming house according to the edicts of Feng Shui, who picked and chose from Hindu and Buddhist scripture to decide who, or what, she'd like to be reincarnated as—now wanted to fight on the side of rationality.

"And besides, even if this works, and we're able to put the sun back in the sky—how do we live with ourselves afterward?"

That was something that no one could answer. Not even the gods. But Eve took it as a challenge. "If we don't do something soon, we'll never know. We won't be around to measure if we had any effect."

Her manner was cold. It had to be, to inure herself against the horror of our situation, and the greater horror we would have to embrace in order for it to end. Noah was appalled. "So that's how it is, huh, Evie? An empirically-tested scientific experiment? Can't make an omelet without breaking a few eggs? No pain, no gain."

"Yes." Her voice had a hard, stony urgency. It stopped Noah in full-flow. "Yes. What else do you expect me to say?"

Wes turned away from us all. His rising sense of panic wouldn't allow him to concentrate. He thrashed around the uneven lower strata of the cave floor. He wanted out. He wanted to be away from the darkness of Mictlan, and the heavy choices that had been foisted upon us. But there was nowhere to turn. "I don't wanna die."

"No one wants to die, Wes. We just have to do what fate has selected us to do." I thought it might reassure him. As scared as I was, I was ready to embrace what I knew to be inevitable. The only reassurance I needed was that I was morally understood. But Wes didn't see things that way.

"I don't care. You're talking about being sacrificed like it's some kind of fucking privilege, but I'm not down with it. I don't wanna fuckin' die!" Some may say his viewpoint was rational. But rationality was done with. It was over. It left us no room for maneuver.

"I'll tell you one thing." Noah pointed an accusing finger at Evie and me. "If we go through with this, we'll have a black stain on our souls forever. Nothing can ever atone for it, it's the ultimate sin."

"You really believe that?" I wanted to confront him, to cut to the very core of our conflict.

"Sure I believe it. I believe it with all my heart. You think I should take all this terrible pagan shit seriously, but leave Christ out of the equation?"

It was what he *had* to do. Judeo-Christianity was all about proscription—"Thou shall not..."—but Nahua was about description: it described the universe and its symbolic laws; it described how to interact with them and exert an influence. But there was still some common ground I could reach for, the Christian iconography so influenced by pre-Christian belief systems.

"Remember who made the ultimate blood sacrifice, Noah. Remember whose flesh and blood is symbolically devoured by the Catholic faithful. Think of the Roman soldier's lance impaling Jesus on the cross, and the blood that flowed into a goblet. According to legend, his blood sanctified the cup and it became the Holy Grail."

Noah breathed quickly, unable to inhale much of the painfully cold air before exhaling again. I know he saw the validity of what I was saying, but he was angry that I should devalue his faith by comparison.

"It's like Jung said: the mythic archetypes are always there, in every culture. Now we know how real they are. The Mexica had to bury the evidence of their blood sacrifice away from the Spaniards, the Christians. But can you say that what we found was less potent than the Holy Grail? Why should a blood sacrifice to the Nahua gods have any less power than the blood of Christ?"

He looked as if he could kill me for those words. Evie came to my rescue. "Remember, Noah: God sacrificed His only son to atone for the world's sins. We have to follow His example to save it." She put it into terms he could understand. But it was still imposing Christian morality onto a chaotic pre-Christian universe. The real universe. The one that we were trapped in, and had to contend with.

But I would meet him halfway. "One life to save billions. Put it into those terms, and it's a sacrifice worth making. Am I right?"

"Not if it's your damn life being sacrificed!" More basic, more visceral, than Noah's moral objection was Wes's absolute need to cling onto life. Eve gently met his eyes. Her flinty demeanor softened. "Wes, you know, one out of five is pretty good odds. If we select by a process of chance, it's better than what the world is giving you right now."

Evie had become the best proselytizer for the Nahua religion I could imagine. By a cold, logical process of elimination, she'd decided that a barbaric pagan ritual offered everyone the best choice of survival. So she was running with it. She was beating the drum for blood sacrifice with more fervor than anyone since the sixteenth century.

Even Amber seemed partially convinced. "Maybe they're right, baby?" Those beautiful, dark bewildered eyes pleaded with Wes. "If it's only one in five, then it's less of a chance that it's gonna be either of us" The flaw in her logic was obvious. As there were two of them, there was twice the possibility our sacred victim would be chosen from that one couple. Wes saw it straight away. But there was a submissive despair in him that made him capitulate. His concern, as all of us could see, had been solely for himself.

Now he was ashamed. "Those odds are bad enough," he softly acknowledged to her. "It's a son of a bitch, though. If we're all gonna freeze to death, I guess it's better than that." The ultimate flaw, I guess, from a rational point of view, was that everyone weighed up their chances in the light of the ritual's likely effectiveness. Fervent belief was required more than ever now. For my own part, I never doubted or wavered.

Noah bolted. He grabbed the sacrificial knife from its facing-east position. Suddenly manic, he made his ultimate protest. "Okay..." His voice rasped, hoarsened by the freezing air and its depleting oxygen content. "So we're all so anxious to kill someone."

As he grabbed my arm, I thought he'd slice the palm of my hand open with the long stone blade. I was so steeled for bloodshed, I'd become still and impassive. Instead, he slammed the handle into my hand and made me grip it tight. Noah stood back, facing me as I held the knife at a downward angle. "Let's see you do it, Marty. Let's see you kill me!"

This wasn't the way it was done. This wasn't the way at all. "Don't be so stupid, Noah."

"Stupid?" He was advancing on me now, his eyes blazing with anger. I backed off. I wasn't about to try to defend myself with a sacred artifact. I've always known Noah could whip my ass, and that wasn't the issue in question. "I'm telling you to turn your words into deeds, how stupid is that? What's the matter, Marty? Can't do it if you're looking me in the eye? Maybe if I turn my back."

He turned slowly around on me, offering up his shoulder blades, knotted by the cold, for me to plunge in the sharp stone blade.

"Noah, stop!" Eve tried to give moral support. Neither of us was calling for random violence. The helplessness of our situation, the horror of the only way out that I knew, had pushed our Christian brother to his breaking point.

He rounded on her. "So what about you, Eve? Here's your big chance. Sacrifice a friend and write him off to a statistical probability ratio. Sound good to you, Amber?" She was far too fragile to deal with him in this state. We had all, by now, reached the ends of our tether.

And Noah laid on the menace, as if he was equally pissed with all of us. He stalked around, pivoting toward Wes. "C'mon now. You want to live, right? That all you care about, Wes. That a brother should die to save your own cowardly hide?"

"Back off!" It was going to get ugly very soon. Wes didn't have my distance, my ability to stay aloof. And Noah's targets were scattered all over. He couldn't decide if he hated me more for suggesting the sacrifice, or Wes for being too scared to submit to it.

"Well, is it Wes?" Noah lost it. He grabbed Wes by the collars of his zipper jacket and slammed him backwards, against the cave wall. I expected immediate retaliation, but it was a long time coming. Wes was either too shocked, or too hurt by the impact of rock on his vertebrae, to respond. His breathing became more rapid, hoarser, in the manner I'd already heard in Noah—in the way that we could hear happening to all of us, if we focused attention on ourselves.

"Damn it, Noah. Leave him alone." I swear, if Amber could have done so, she'd have taken up Noah's offer to let her kill him right there and then. She stepped in, putting more space between him and her boyfriend. Noah turned and pushed her away. Amber lost her footing, went stumbling to the floor on her outstretched hands. To see our kind, genial friend act like a thug was as shocking to me as my pagan beliefs must have been to him.

He advanced mercilessly on Wes, pinning him to the wall. "Don't just stand there, man? You wanna save your skin? Then all you gotta do is– "

Noah broke off in mid-sentence. He was proffering his chest, protruding his pectorals through the short-sleeve shirt that he froze in beneath his hoodie. Daring Wes to smash through his breastplate with the knife I still resiliently held.

His bravado broke down. Suddenly, he didn't have the energy to form another word. Each breath became increasingly audible, more labored, coming upon him in rasping shudders. He grabbed at his chest like some stupid meth-head suffering cardiac arrest.

But my brother Noah always took care of his body, just as he mollycoddled his mind with the Bible. His eyes grew wider, partly in fear, partly with the effort of sucking in the cold, sharp, hostile air.

We were all alarmed. Screw the fact that he'd wanted to kill us all just moments previously–or, as he'd claimed, wanted us to kill him. His actions were just as bizarre as what was overtaking him now.

Nothing was right anymore. Nothing could be as it was.

Noah sank to his knees, gripping a boulder for support. He tried to keep himself aloft, to support the kind of chronic respiration that I'd only ever heard in a child asthmatic or a dying emphysemic smoker. "Can't... Can't..."

Eve cradled him in her arms. I felt an inappropriate pang of jealousy. "Shhh. Don't try to talk. Conserve your breath." Wes had experienced similar problems, but kept himself still, while Noah had rampaged around like a mad bull.

"It's the air–it's getting thinner, isn't it?" Amber's simple observation struck home. The nagging cold we'd grown almost used to was hitting new lows. Very soon, the air wouldn't be breathable at all. It forced a hurried reappraisal. Whereas, before, the fact that time was running out had formed the backdrop to our life-and-death arguments, now it was irrelevant. Now there was no time left at all.

Noah raised his eyes to meet Evie's. Defeated. Desperate. Apologetic. Frightened. Noah was loved. We all shared the concern that he should refrain from working himself into a frenzy, to keep his respiration at a normal level. But, if the gods should sanction it, we knew now we were ready to sacrifice his life. To sacrifice any one of us, just for a chance that this should all end.

Eve stalked determinedly away, her vague outline only perceptible through the dying embers of the fire. She threw more dry wood into its mouth and stoked it a little. Reappearing out of the darkness, she stared us all down with a grim earnestness.

"If we're gonna do this thing, we're gonna do it right." She held out five twigs retrieved from the firewood. Snapping one in half, she threw one end away and replaced the other with the four longer twigs.

"It's a lottery. If the fate of the world can rest on a spilled cup, then ours is down to who draws the short stick."

TEN

By the time Noah was able to breathe with some semblance of normality, the rest of us were finding it increasingly difficult. I guess he was still having problems. But then, as not one of us could any longer inhale without pain or exhale without wheezing, it had kind of brought the average down.

Huddled all together in the semi-darkness, for the last time, I got the sense that we were not part of a dying world, but of a dead world. In our desolate cave, conditions would soon be too inhospitable for us to endure. No one deluded their self that the world outside was survivable any longer. If the gods bestowed grace upon us, we would not be rescuing our world, but resurrecting it.

Wes shook uncontrollably. I didn't know whether it was due to the shriveling, debilitating deep freeze, or his own fear of what was coming. I doubt that he did either.

The sacrificial dagger and cup were positioned toward Acatl. Propped on a rock shelf, they were ready to do their work. In the darkness, it was the final truth. We were finally faced with what I'd depleted my energies in arguing for. It was the most daunting prospect I would ever face. For a moment, I wondered if it would be better if we were all dead anyway. I had to dismiss the thought from my mind. The frozen rock and the unforgiving earth were ready to take us at any time. But it was always better for the species to survive. I had to believe that. The sufferings of individuals were as nothing. Continuing existence was everything.

Eve had taken control. She was to be our ultimate mistress of ceremonies. It didn't excuse me the responsibility I held for what was about to happen. But it dispersed part of my load. Eve had my full moral support—though, truth to tell, she was too feisty a woman to need it.

She also had the support of Amber. Our dear, sweet, trusting, beautiful friend understood that difficult decisions had to be made. Her fragile faith was preserved by the young woman that she trusted most in the world, now presiding over those selfsame decisions. But Eve let go of Amber's hand, which was gently squeezing her own, when the moment of truth came. Now, we were all alone and no longer beholden to each other.

Eve held out her fist, containing five twigs of seemingly equal length. "Okay, who's gonna be first?" She tried to rally us like a female gym teacher at high school. There were no takers. No one wanted to rush into the void. Noah looked away. This time, he couldn't persuade himself that we wouldn't actually go through with it.

"Somebody has got to choose." She searched her dissolute friends for the heroes I'd spoken of, and found only scared kids. "Have we not made up our minds to do this?" They'd made up their minds only in as much as they'd been cajoled, indoctrinated and bullied by Eve. But mostly by me.

"Marty?" It was inevitable. Every pair of eyes burned into me. I didn't need to look to see them. Let's see now who has the courage of his convictions. The strength of his belief. I wondered whether I really was prepared to die for Huitzlopochtli, the Nahua God of the Sun. It seemed such a quaint idea somehow. But still so numbingly appalling. If I were to draw the short stick, I would have to follow my conviction through. I'd have to make sure my friends prepared to kill me in the correct way, and that my body received the appropriate ritual mutilations.

I sucked in a breath of chill air. My hand shot forward to meet my destiny. It wouldn't stop shaking. I could barely hold it still enough to select a single stick, rather than grabbing all five from Evie's hand.

I felt its length by rolling it around in the palm of my hand, moments before I let my eyes see it. I've only experienced that kind of relief twice in my existence, both within the same twenty-four-hour period. The second time, it would be with a deep profundity that eclipsed even this, the moment when my life was spared.

But I sincerely hope never to have an experience of such intensity again. I know my mind could not bear it anymore.

As I held the long twig up to show them, I couldn't expect my friends to share my relief. What might mean salvation for me could be certain destruction for someone else. I think a tear was running from my eye as I opened it. But then it may have watered due to the intense cold.

I cast my twig into the fire. "Who's next?" Eve's voice was a searching accusation. Despite my relief, I started to panic as to how we could actually go through with this. Each facile little drawing of sticks brought us closer to what would have been unthinkable mere days before, even to me.

Wes's breathing was labored and heavy. Its vaporous trail brushed my ear as he raised the courage to lean forward. Just as I must have shook like some malfunctioning toy puppet, so Wes moved in deep-focus slow motion.

He never got the chance. Noah broke in, barging between us with a rude decisiveness. He snatched violently from Eve's hand. His chest started to rasp again as he hyperventilated. Slumped back between us, he was expressionless. He held his stick aloft. It was roughly the same gnarled shape and size as my own. For Noah, part of the agony was over. For Wes, his chances of survival had just been reduced by a further twenty-five percent.

It blew his resolve. He was panicking, looking around to see who would go before him—then looking back to ensure they didn't actually take a long stick and reduce his chances further still. His eyes implored to Amber. Clearly, he didn't believe he could dive in alone, and was asking her to take the plunge with him.

It was the biggest decision any of us would make in our lives—hell, maybe the biggest decision anyone in this world would ever make—and we were reaching it by the most primitive means imaginable.

But Amber didn't want to make her own choice. She looked down at the remaining twigs protruding from Eve's fist, her eyes flickered around the rest of us, then darted toward some hidden spot in the cave, as if looking for guidance in the darkness—all in a nanosecond. Her agitation became infectious. I'm sure we were all hoping somehow that chance would exclude her, though the options had diminished and someone, surely, had to pay the price.

It produced an antsy impatience in her man. It translated into courage as Wes hissed, letting out some of his pressure-cooker tension. In the same breath he grabbed decisively for Eve's hand. His fingers uncurled around one of the thin pieces of wood. Then, just as quickly, they drew back, as if his ass couldn't back up what his guts told him to do. But he made a second grab. Ensnared the twig in the palm of his hand and closed his eyes, before his conscious mind could remind him of how chicken-shit he was feeling.

We all watched as Wes drew back with his fist clenched tight. He was a portrait of still tension. If it wasn't for the freezing air that turned his breath to a gaseous mane around his head, he could have been a clay model. But then his reflexes uncoiled as slowly as his breathing. His tricep loosened and his fingers began to unfurl. It was a move that could never be retracted, and he was steeling himself to face it.

He'd drawn a long stick.

His eyes closed back up again. This time in relief instead of agony. I swear he'd have burst out laughing, if he wasn't conscious of what had to happen next.

Eve gently returned Amber's gaze. It was like Wes had granted her a little courage with his own impulsive bravery. But she'd endangered herself by waiting, and she knew it. Odds were reduced to a straight fifty-fifty live-or-die, no one to blame but herself.

Eve seemed more self-possessed than any of us, though she was facing the same odds. She gave Amber a little encouraging smile. Amber tried to return it, but her pretty face was too forlorn, her long hair sinking into her stooped shoulders. But still, she went for it.

We didn't have to look too closely to know how it'd gone. If she was fragile before, now she was a broken doll. Her downcast head and quivering lips almost elicited pity.

Almost.

I'll never know whether Eve, my fastest convert to the ways of the old gods, had rigged the draw. After all, the long sticks and the short stick were all dealt by her hand, and she seemed less scared than any of us—that is, except me.

"Oh God," Amber broke right down and wept, her slender shoulders heaving. "Oh my God..."

But even if Amber had been dealt a bad hand, there was a symmetry to this. She was an innocent who'd made a big mistake. A little stoner airhead who'd never given any deep thought to the way the universe worked—just putting her faith in horoscopes and crystals, and crap like that. But it was her thoughtlessness that paid tribute to Mictlan, to the icy cold and dark that was enveloping us, that was swallowing up the whole world.

Her vaporous sobs implored to us all. Her distress made its appeal to our emotional side, to our feminine side. But now we were returned to the essence of the natural world, to the time of the warrior. Compassion was an irrelevance. Personal feelings were negated. The natural balance of the universe had been overturned, and we all had a role to play in restoring it.

Amber tried to control her sobs, each gasp eating up too much of our thinning air. "You guys aren't really gonna go through with this, are you?"

She looked from Wes, to Eve, to Noah, to me. None of us gave a response. I was feeling buoyed up by our unity, by their recognition that we were now bound by ancient rules that only I had recognized.

"You can't. You just can't!"

None of us moved forward, but no one backed off. With a few short, imperceptible motions, we had reassembled as a tight concentric circle around her. No one seemed ready to act yet, but the circle would not be broken.

"You're not gonna let them kill me, right?" she pleaded with her boyfriend, desperate words punctuating our collective silence. "I mean, you love me, right, Wes?"

Wes was impassive. He no longer seemed like her panicked, mess-up soul mate. He must have still felt for her, but he knew now, like the rest of us, that he was just a cog in the ancient mechanism that ordered the universe. Or maybe he was just relieved that it was her, instead of him.

"Eve. I'm your best friend... Who you gonna dish to if I'm not around?" Her words were pathetic. But, just for a moment, I thought we would see Eve crack. There was a glint in her eye that might have been moistness, but I was willing her to stay composed. What was about to happen was a kind of justice.

"Somebody say something!"

She looked from face to face, but found us equally inscrutable. She had less air to breathe, and less room to maneuver. Without noticeably advancing, the circle had grown tighter.

"Please, please..." she begged of us, more hopeless with each labored breath. "At least let me write a note to my mom. Let me say goodbye to her. Can I at least do that?"

No one answered, but no one denied her pleading. It seemed that the moment of truth was approaching but no one—maybe not even me—was about to rise to it. She took our silence as consent, looking for an out, for any slender little straw to clasp at.

"I've, I've got paper in my pack," she stammered, trembling from her head to her toes. "I'll just, I'll just go and—" She made a decisive move to break away from our congregation.

But the circle would not be broken.

That painful *smack*, when it came, woke us all back up to the reality of our situation. It was the crack of rock on bone, made more sickening by the wet slap of her splitting scalp.

Amber was down on her knees, fighting to stay sentient. Dark blood stained the bottom of her curling hairline. Her dazed eyes rotated as her legs gave way and she slumped, still semi-conscious, to the floor.

Noah stepped forward. The bloodstain on the rock in his hand was almost a different color, bright crimson against the porous gray. Noah, our God-fearing brother, had become Cain.

ELEVEN

The reality of it was shocking. I could no longer connect what we had to do with the sight of our fallen friend. Amber kept trying to raise herself from the cold stone floor by pushing upwards on her hands. It was useless. Her dazed face, lit grotesquely by the lamplight, begged our assistance. Her eyelids drooped down, flickering heavily as the moist blood from her scalp ran into her eyes. Her attempts to speak were pitiful gurgles. Drool flowed from her once beautiful mouth.

None of us could raise a finger to help her. It was something we'd have paid any price not to have borne witness to. But it was also the point of no return. My words of belief had brought us to this point. Amber was still living, but seriously injured. The only way forward, the only way to ensure we had not needlessly wrecked her life, was to perform the sacred rite.

Her rolling eyes looked up from the floor to Evie. They found no compassionate mirror of the pathetic sight she had become. She looked to me. As Eve must have done, I felt the deepest, most profound horror. But I couldn't afford the luxury of pity. It would destroy me as certainly as we had to destroy Amber. Wes squinted his eyes into the middle distance. He could not accommodate the vision of what he'd allowed to happen to his baby.

"So what are you guys waiting for? Are you gonna help me out here or what?" We had denied rescue to Amber. We had no such option when it came to assisting Noah. I looked upon my friend, my brother. He was driven upward into bloodlust–not sadistic, not sexual, but by the urgent need to complete the deed only he'd had the balls to commence.

I couldn't let him down. If he was now psychologically a thousand miles from the moral and spiritual certainty he used to feel, then it was because of my indoctrination. I owed Noah Bailey, in a way that far exceeded any humane obligation I might once have felt toward Amber Hagen.

Movement made me fully conscious. I felt the cold again. It was a sign that shock hadn't left me too numb to act. I felt my way toward the rock ledge where I'd placed the stone dagger and cup. Taking up the sacrificial knife, I placed it to my lips and kissed it gently. It was a show of devotion that could have been substituted by a priest with a crucifix.

"Uuuuuhnoooo... uuuuhnooo..." She was coming round. It was truly pitiful, but she couldn't be allowed to disrupt what had to happen. "Wezzz, pleazze, don't let them." Wes shut his eyes and turned towards the darkness, covering his ears. Maybe he could see what truly needed to happen. Or maybe he just couldn't face it.

Noah was on top of Amber. He was having trouble trying to grip her in an arm lock. As dissipated as her strength was, she pushed and scratched and flailed at him with her feeble fists. It reminded us of how she was a fit, healthy young woman who had only been injured, not fully incapacitated. We could not rely on fate or providence to complete the deed that had to be accomplished by ourselves. And we could not rely on anyone else to direct the proceedings but me. I was now a high priest of Tenochtitlan.

"Eve, help me!" Amber's resistance had pushed Noah toward a level of brutality he would never have contemplated. Evie was alarmed by his request. Her eyes darted from one darkened corner of the cave to another. She wanted to sink into the shadows, to cease to have anything to do with the sacred atrocity that had to unfold. To cease to exist.

"Grab her legs!" I wasn't tolerating any resistance. We were all in this together now. Eve returned my gaze in alarm. I had no pity. Not for her, not for the whining airhead who writhed below Noah and me as we pinned her arms back. I was in charge now. Eve could quit barking orders and start acting on 'em.

She did as she was told. That was good. We were fulfilling our obligations. But still the circle wasn't complete. "Wes, get over here and help your girlfriend!" Don't ask me why I had to put it in those terms. I guess I genuinely felt his presence would make things easier for her. But there was something else, an observance of the sacred protocol to be followed.

"Pleazze, pleazze, don't kill meee!" Her whining was pitiful, but it was becoming more than a little annoying. How did she expect me to coordinate what had to happen if she kept bleating for a life that was already lost?

"Wes, get your ass over here and grab her leg! We need to be four, it has to be four!" That he drifted back over, zombie-like, was an acceptance that I had taken charge. Only Noah had the strength and the fortitude to accept what had to happen without flinching. Evie and Wes would now comply because they had to. Because there was no other path to take.

Amber writhed as each of us gripped her shaking body. "We have to reduce our number from five, the number of the end of days, to four, the sign of the sun. Don't you see that?" Of course they didn't. But my pagan logic now reigned supreme. There was no one else in this freezing pit of darkness who recognized the laws of our universe.

"Take her to the pit! Drag her over to the pit!" Despite how hard she fought and twisted, it was surprisingly easy to raise her limb by limb. It was going to be much harder to subdue her before she died. We had no sacrificial altar to speak of, but I had to consecrate part of the ground in the name of the Sun Gods. She had to be facing Acatl.

"Oh pleazze, pleazze..."

I pulled her arm around so that the others followed my lead in pointing her head eastward. I touched her forehead with the handle of the stone knife.

"Amber, our sister, I am blessing you in the name of your divine father, Huitzilopochtli." (Read "weet-zeel-oh-poch-tlee", the most powerful of the Sun Gods.) "I ask you to recognize the honor and the privilege that are bestowed upon you, in allowing you to pay earthly tribute to the mighty Father of the Sun." I spoke my own improvised, bastardized version of the Nahua rite, desperate that my brothers and sisters should understand what was taking place.

She wasn't hearing me. All her remaining energy was devoted to her futile kicks and screams.

"Man, I just can't. I just can't go through with this." Wes was despondent, defeated. His whimpered protest carried no real element of defiance. He'd let go of Amber's weakly convulsing leg, unable to fulfill his obligation.

"You will go through with this. You have a part to play, bro. We cannot allow her to die like this." For one moment, for one brief flickering nanosecond, they thought I'd lost heart. It would have been a mighty relief to Wes and Evie right then. Noah looked angry and perplexed, but followed my lead in gripping her arm tauter, tighter, until she yelped with the pain. Amber momentarily stopped pleading, concentrating instead on trying to catch her sobbing breath. She fought hard to retain the little cold air that she was able to inhale.

"A Nahua sacrifice does not die kicking and screaming. It's traditional for them to leave the earthly plain before the sacrifice is made. The high priest got them high on octli, the cactus moonshine, and ololiuhqui—morning glory."

"You mean, like, acid? Mushrooms?" Wes got my drift. When it came to psychedelic drugs, I knew I could rely on him. But nothing I said could impinge on Amber's consciousness now. She moaned low and wept, oblivious of my agenda. "We can't do that, Marty." It was not a moral objection. "I mean we totally don't have any."

"You got a mickey of something?" I wasn't waiting for a reply. He'd backed off of holding Amber still, so I had a more crucial task for him. The vapor around her right thigh suggested she'd urinated in terror.

"Yeah. Yeah, we got some malt liquor. I mean, we never drank 'cuz it got so fucking cold."

"So go get it!" They would have to follow my lead now. I gripped her tighter by the wrist, irrespective of any pain I was causing her. I looked in Noah and Eve's eyes and dared them not to follow suit. We all knelt and pinned her down, stretched her out, as far as she could go, her back tilted upwards on the uneven ground.

Wes reported dutifully back with a long tube of malt liquor. "Open it." The pull ring popped and we heard the fizz of beer bubbles in the darkness. The cave's temperature must have kept it colder than any liquor store icebox. "Feed it to her. Go on, make her drink!" Wes tried to cup his hand tenderly behind Amber's head, to prop her up rather than pour it straight down her gullet. She threw her head from side to side, trying not to let him touch her. He realized then that she would never be tender to his touch again. "Make her drink!"

Wes forced his pinkie into her mouth to try to keep it open. He yelped as her canine tooth bit down hard. It did the trick for him. Whimpering to himself, he pushed her head down flat, then poured the amber beer straight into her throat. She swallowed at least one mouthful before her head jerked forward and spat the second straight in his face.

"Here, gimme that! Take hold of her arm. Let go of her and I'm making you the sacrifice!" Wes took me seriously. They all knew to take me seriously now. As Wes, no longer her laidback lover man, held her down at the shoulder, I jerked Amber's head back by her lustrous hair, pinning her down by a fistful clasped at the roots.

"Drink, Amber. Don't make it difficult for yourself."

She gurgled as I poured a good draught of it straight into her mouth. Passing the half-empty can back to Wes, I switched over quickly and pinched her nose. If her survival instinct wanted her to keep breathing, she'd have to swallow the malt liquor quickly. She coughed and spluttered as it went down, some of it taking the wrong route into her windpipe. The next time she'd know to drink it all down like a good girl. As she took the rest of the tube down in reluctant gulps, her concentration, and the sudden ingestion of alcohol, made her resistance less fierce. But she'd still fight back.

"Wes, how much weed do you have?" It was a straight question, but everything seemed to be dumbfounding him.

"I dunno. I guess just under an ounce of purple haze. I couldn't take a hit now, not here." No one was asking the stoner idiot to join in a pot party.

"Bring it all here with your bong, your lighter, everything!" He understood now. Even poor Amber, writhing beneath us, understood. Eve and Noah were stalwart. They did their duty with a steel resolve. Evie's love of her friend, her feminine empathy, had all given way to her new conviction. And Noah—if I was a high priest, then he was my novice, my initiate.

"Here. Take it." Wes offered me the pipe with the long glass bowl, his baggie of grass, everything.

"No. You take it. Unless you want to be the one to perform the ceremony?" He acceded. Below me, Amber renewed her struggle again. Hers and Wes's personal vice, something that had been a lifelong pleasure, was about to be turned against her.

"Put it close up to her face. Make sure you got her mouth and nose covered."

Wes came through. He pushed the oval mouth of the bowl tight over her own, so that the glass pinched hard on her skin. Amber screwed up her eyes from the pain. I had to harden my heart as I started to feel pity. With nowhere to run to, she seemed to be trying to hold her breath to stop the smoke being pumped into her. She didn't want to return to the world of dreams she'd loved so much. This time, she knew she wasn't coming back.

Wes knew the procedure. He packed the feeding bowl tight with purple and green weed and held his lighter flame on full as it started burning. As the smoke rose up the pipe shaft in huge hits, he prized two fingers between the top of the bowl and Amber's face, pinching her nostrils tight.

Amber moaned, but in rushed the smoke. After three big hits of it, the feeder was almost empty. Amber's eyes were wide open. Not in pain but in an effort to focus. The blood capillaries in her eyeballs expanded, as the hallucinogenic rush took hold.

"We're all out of this one, Marty. Do I?"

"Just keep lighting it. Keep hitting it up till it's all gone."

"She'll be out of her mind, dude. It's too much for one."

"Yeah. I know. Just keep doing it." Wes realized it was the only positive thing he could do for her now. One bowl followed and then another. He was able to relax his grip as Amber's resistance died a little. Her eyes rolled, veering from a mellow sleepiness to sudden staring alarm. From wanting to drift off into her dreams to the haunting reminder that she was here, in this cave, in the temple dedicated to her destruction.

Wes fired up one, two, three more bowls, till there was little more left of his stash. Amber was beyond the realms of her most trippy experiences by now. We no longer had to keep hold of her arms and legs. She tossed this way and that, but it was a slow, dreamy motion.

Every small movement, every little thought, carried her mind in a different direction. Her face was pale, and I could feel her pulse racing, having been force-fed more potent marijuana than it was possible for a person to assimilate. When I knelt close to her on the floor, I could hear her palpitating heart. Yolia. The life force.

When her gaze tripped off into the distance, chasing dream-images into shadows that were empty, I hoped she really had departed the rational realm. That she'd entered the metaphysical reality of the gods, and recognized the divinity of what would be her final act in this world.

"Take the climbing rope and cut it into four. Bind each limb so that it's facing a different point of the compass. Make sure her head remains facing east. And make it loose. There's no need to inflict pain."

I was sincere in what I said. This was to be a sacred devotion, not a charnel house slaughter. My initiates followed my every word. I took the sacred dagger and kissed it once again, reversing it so that I could touch Amber's head with the handle.

"Our sister, the Daughter of the Sun, we dedicate this sacred action to you and the gods who have chosen you to incarnate them. Both you, and this sacred weapon, shall be our tribute to the divine. The sun shall rise again for you, Amber."

Her disorientation was such that she no longer knew whether the ceremony was as terrifying as she felt it was or as sacred as I told her it was. Or whether it was all just some cosmic joke. She mouthed something but she couldn't speak. She couldn't weep, or protest, or laugh, so her amorphous facial expressions suggested hints of all three.

The moment was upon us. "Take her arms and legs. Pull her tight." Eve and Noah were panting with trepidation, with exertion. They did their duty. Amber began to moan. "Take her other arm, Wes, hold her down tight!" He seemed like he might burst into tears. I wouldn't relent. Maybe I was bullying him into the unthinkable. Maybe, but we all had our role to play. He took hold of her arm.

"Now tear through her T-shirt. Rip all the fabric off. Take off her bra." Wes gazed at me in alarm. So did Evie. This was going to be so much harder for them than even they had imagined. And as for me... I can only guess what their thoughts were of me at that point.

"Go on, do it! It has a purpose, Wes, just fucking do it!" Sobbing audibly, Wes pulled back Amber's blanket poncho. He took her T-shirt with the Chinese Yin-Yang symbol by the scruff of the neck, and tore downwards. "No, no, don't..." She managed to form her final words. I swear Evie was weeping now too, but she didn't desert her post.

Wes took the shoulder strap of Amber's bra and pulled it gently down. It revealed one milky white breast and uncovered part of the other one's nipple. It was no good. We couldn't afford to be halfhearted. I reached down and grabbed the second shoulder strap myself. I pulled the elastic taut and slashed with the sharp edge of the dagger. It cut loose immediately, leaving a long, thin scratch across the top of Amber's left breast. She yelped and shook a little.

I wrenched her underwear away and let it drop. Away from the sacred implements of our makeshift altar. She was beautiful. Wes had been a very lucky guy. Now the gods would be lucky.

"Huitzilopochtli." I addressed our master, the Sun.

Wes wept profusely, but never dared desert our sacrificial circle. Amber's breasts had a pallor that was never exposed to sunlight. They were not of voluptuous size, but they were womanish, nurturing. In the all-consuming cold, her nipples stood erect, as if with anticipation.

"Do it, Marty! Will you just do it?" My standing on ceremony was too much for Eve. Her nerves had cracked.

The crack of Amber's breastbone split the air. I drove the long, stone blade deep into the sternum between her two breasts. It cracked again as I rammed the handle home hard with the underside of my hand. This time the bone smashed. Its percussive splintering was a necessary tribute to the gods, a part of the ceremony.

Blood flowed freely all over Amber's undulating torso. Moans of disbelief and anguish from our friends muffled the sound of her breaking bones. They couldn't drown out her cry. It was the most piercing sound I have heard in my entire existence. I had believed, had hoped, that her mind was already with the Nahua Gods. That it might be immune from the trivial detail of bodily pain. But her scream will stay with me forever.

"We dedicate the Yolia of Amber, servant of the Sun, to her divine master!" The moans of my friends intensified as I drove my hand deep into the wound. Through the moist broken flesh and imploded bone. Deep down, to the left of the splintered sternum, deep into the membranous sac below her left breast. Until I could feel her heart beating in my hand.

"Behold the Yolia! Behold the power that lights the sun!" Wes fell away to vomit as I pulled his girlfriend's heart from the chest cavity. All of us were splashed with her blood, as I cut the aorta and the pulmonary arteries loose from the vessel that they powered.

It was a clean cut, the organ still pumping in my blood-drenched hand. While the heart still lived, I had to make the sacred tribute. I dashed across the cave, into the dark tunnel that led into the eternal night. "Huitzilopochtli!" I held the soggy organ aloft, waving it in the direction of Acatl, where the Sun used to rise in the east.

The sacrifice was successful. I had performed as I should. As I returned to the cave, the horrified looks from Eve and Noah told me I was drenched from head to foot in blood. But then, so were they. I held the sacred stone cup aloft, and let the divine organ slip down into it.

"It's the heart." I explained to a horrified Evie. "That's the purpose of the sacrifice. We don't have to hide what we've done from the Conquistadors." I held the cup to my lips and kissed it. Breathless, exhausted, I sank to my knees to pay final tribute to our divine sacrifice. To our beautiful friend.

Amber lay entirely still now. Now that the sacred deed was done, her beautiful body was defaced by a gaping wound and a tangle of slashed veins and arteries. But she had played her part well, however unwilling. For all the violence done to her, she now seemed at peace. Her eyes, so wide with terror and disbelief during the ceremony, had fallen closed. She no longer had to watch as I pulled the living, beating heart from her chest.

TWELVE

At 2:14 am, the cave remained in natural darkness. Working under the lamplight, I kept warm with each mound of earth that I shoveled up. The hole was deep enough now. My bloodstained hands held the sacred box with due reverence. Its clasp was broken, but the weight of earth that would bear down upon it again would be enough to keep it away from prying eyes.

I replaced the box in the earth, and dedicated it to our master the Sun. The sacred tributes contained were the sacred dagger of Itzli, and the heart of our divine sacrifice, Amber Hagen—deep within a holy cup which would, I had no doubt, preserve its youthfulness and pure spirit for many centuries to come.

But we were still in night. We were also deep into nighttime, and I had the faith and optimism to believe that this endless cold night may eventually pass. In that respect, I may have been the only one.

As a group, we were drained. Just about an hour ago, I'd felt validated. I was the high priest who was saving the world. And I still fully, fundamentally, believed in that. But now that divine, insane, necessary deed had been performed, my role was over. I was back to being a geeky, insecure college student. And I felt burnt out. Exhausted. I'd kept bursting into tears when I was cleaning up the detritus of our sacrificial deed. I guess I didn't present too convincing a picture of confidence to the others. But they would see.

Evie was a shell of herself. I swear, if she'd still believed at that moment that life on earth had been extinguished forever, it wouldn't have mattered to her. She sat near the dying embers of the fire pit. No one had returned into the night to gather more firewood. No one was trying to relight the scraps that remained. The temperature was as low as it had been at any time since we'd holed up there. Yet Eve was no longer shivering. To look at her, you might have believed that she'd shut down. Gone into a state of psychotic withdrawal. Her chemise and her fleeced zipper jacket were streaked all over with blood. Just like my own clothes. But I was making a conscious effort to stay active, keep my mind engaged with the situation. Eve seemed like she'd given up on everything.

Noah was almost as withdrawn. But he was contemplative. There were signs of life in him. He tapped gently at the icy façade of a frozen puddle with the heel of his training shoe. It was a distracted, repetitive motion. I thought he was trying to see himself in the ice. To squint through the darkness that still pervaded us. But the ice cracked, and he reached slowly down. Patted a bloody paw down into the icy water. Rubbed together the two hands that were almost as caked with blood as my own. And started to scrub them clean. Like that Roman governor two thousand years ago, our brother Noah was trying to wash his hands of the deed.

And then there was Wes.

His mind couldn't accept it at all. He was jealously guarding Amber's Hi-8 camcorder and playback monitor. It was now all he had left of her, and he wasn't letting go. He had the tape that would wind up in my own possession. Playing it from end to end. Over and over.

"Greetings, PBS lovers!" The faint, metallic echo of her voice came round again. "Glad you could join us for what promises to be the trip of a lifetime!" Behind the camera, there was a flash of her fingers passing a joint back to Wes. He took a deep hit and stood back in the line-up with the rest of us.

"Okay, so who have we got here? We have Evie Bishop!" Eve waved at the camera in a cheesy send-up of all those cheap home video TV shows. "The biologist with the mostest. Voted girl most likely to develop a safe alternative to collagen implants. Oh, and to run for president one day!

"Moving further down the line, we have Noah Bailey. Not only is this lovely young physicist as buff as he looks, ladies, but he's a moral dude with rectitude!" Noah hammed it up, crossing his arms to pump his biceps, and flashing the camera a quick profile shot.

"But if it's brains not brawn you're after, girls, take a look at our contestant number three, if you will...

Mr Martin Tierney!" I looked as stupid as things like that always make me feel. "Marty is an expert in archaeology, and any other 'ology' beginning with an 'A.' During the course of our expedition, our very own Indiana Jones will be telling us how the modern world is going wrong. Alright!"

I don't know if it was only me who felt a twinge of nausea at hearing it again. Maybe Wes was too locked into his own grief and denial to care what she was saying.

"Oh, and who is this fine specimen of masculinity on the end here? Why, it's Wesley Mitchell, the boy who put the 'mating' into information technology!" Wes was cracking open a mid-morning tube of malt liquor as Amber spoke, pouring a few mouthfuls of it into paper cups for us to pass along. The four of us locked arms and raised our toast to the camera.

"Well, cheers, baby!" Amber returned our toast. "That's beautiful." She got a little mushy for a moment. "Friends now and forever, huh? But hold on a second, guys, because here comes..." She'd locked the camera onto auto, her voice becoming distant as she raced into shot. "Ms Amber Hagen, the bane of the Native American studies faculty!" She bustled playfully into shot. Full of life and good humor. Full of love. She made a big play of standing on tiptoe as she smooched up to lock lips with Wes.

Wes killed the playback. Only so much was bearable until it became an intolerable reminder of her absence. Of his lover and our heroic, self-sacrificing friend. He sank back into near-catatonia, staring over at the unlit side of the cave. Where Amber's zipped-up sleeping bag rested in the shadows, filled with her eternally sleeping body.

THIRTEEN

By the time I finished tamping down the last mound of dirt, I was emptied out. Drained of everything. All my fear. All the horror of what my conscience had told me I'd had to do. All physical discomfort. All emotional connection with my past life.

I threw my shovel to the ground, and sank down against the wall. Eve and Noah matched my weariness. They sat silently together. Eyes gazing upon the burned-out fire no one had bothered to replenish. Still emitting vapor trails from their respiration, but strangely resilient to the cold air that seemed natural to us by now. Their psychological make-up and physical sensitivity both altered, irrevocably.

If they still had any expectation that our deed may have rescued us from our fate, then it was not detectable. Evie and Noah may have been stronger people now, but something inside them had died. Or perhaps slept. For they gave the appearance of two somnambulists—neither properly conscious, nor in a restful sleep. Eyes wide open and staring. Refusing to close, but seeing nothing.

Maybe they saw me the same way. I wasn't able to communicate with them either. All need to explain myself had vanished, with the passing of the deed itself. All I had left was a little irrational hope. A sliver of optimism for our world's future—a single grain of hope against hope that there may even be a future.

But they seemed bereft. Maybe they considered themselves in the presence of a murderer. A deluded fool who allowed his dark fantasies to infect an already desperate situation. As far as I was concerned, the delusion was theirs. But I could see the basis of their fears. Maybe they feared that they were now murderers. That they had been sucked into a deed they could neither comprehend nor justify to themselves. In which case, I was truly alone.

Wes was inconsolable and unreachable. He'd refused to help me bury Amber's body. Feeling her as a dead weight would have been an intolerable burden on his mind. Too real, too solid. Too visceral a reminder of the flesh-and-blood human being he'd loved, only a few short hours before. Of the precious, beautiful girl he could never replace. The girl he had sacrificed to a force he neither knew nor understood.

"I just stood there, I stood there and let 'em kill you." He sobbed quietly, inconsolably, to a memory he could barely face. He hadn't been able to watch as Noah and me lowered the bloodied sleeping bag into the hole we'd dug. Hadn't been able to say goodbye. Was no longer able to watch images of her face flicker by on the Hi-8 monitor. Could no longer reconcile himself to the memory of his betrayed partner. To the woman he had held down in preparation for her blood sacrifice. To the woman whose lips would never breathe the words, "I forgive you," to him.

I wondered if Wes would kill me, if he were given the chance. I couldn't dismiss the possibility. But it didn't seem as if he had the spirit for revenge. He'd seen me kill, in a manner that was alien and abominable to him. He'd accepted it on the basis that it might mean we'd all continue to live. It might mean that he would continue to live.

He was a spent force now. I'd led him into the unthinkable on the basis that all would be well again. What a sick joke it must have seemed right then. How obscene the idea must have seemed to them all. After the brutal exertion of will that allowed them to do what needed to be done, there had been only a slide into despair. Into the same hopelessness that they knew before, with the added weight of guilt.

If anyone were going to kill me, it would be Noah. In the silver half-light, I found his accusatory gaze fixed on me. It was expressionless, emotionless. It gave nothing away. But Noah had made a trade-off and felt cheated. He'd abandoned his spiritual certainty and his moral framework. Seen from the vantage point of his religious beliefs, he was now of the damned.

It had struck home when I asked him to say a few words over Amber's body, to be met only by a look of disgust. What business do you have in the Kingdom of God? I could almost hear him asking. Wasn't it you that made us all relinquish it in the first place?

But it wasn't like that. I'd tried to make them understand: different theologies have different purposes. I'd never had any objection to Noah needing Christianity as a moral framework, and as reassurance. My concern was that it failed to meet our needs. It bore no relation to the pragmatic physical universe.

But I guessed Noah and Evie now felt our blood sacrifice bore no relation to anything. Except to maybe the realization of my fantasies. I'd robbed Noah of the Kingdom of Heaven, left him with only a howling dark void. If he and Evie were not conspiring to kill me, it was only because they believed all of our deaths were still at hand.

When it came, it seemed so unfamiliar that it almost inspired panic. After peering into the semi-darkness for so long, the changes creeping into my peripheral vision seemed illusory at first.

The arcs of light crossed and merged. They seeped in through the roof of the cave, rather than emanating from our circle of lamps and torches. It wasn't just the squinting reaction of my eyes to the flood of light, but a sudden lightheadedness that made me feel it was unreal.

Shafts of sunlight were entering the cave. They poured down the entrance, from the mountain range outside. They entered as particles of light, gradually but observably returning a golden glint that our senses had forgotten. The cavern was illuminated. The tiny world we'd retreated to was bathed in rays.

It woke Wes from his torpor. His head, like a listless hangdog on his shoulders, became aware of the patch of light glowing in his lap. Slowly, his eyes came to life. Following the path of a beam of natural light, he looked to the ceiling, And wept. Silent, copious tears.

The luminous clock on the radio said 6:32 am. As we were reaching the end of the summer, in calendar terms, the sun was rising later. In this case, it had risen a couple of days later. I opened my eyes fully to the light without the instinct to flinch. My body temperature felt normal. Neither shattered by a sub-zero drop, nor overwhelmed by the now unfamiliar heat.

"I don't believe it... I just don't believe it!" Noah was on his feet, suddenly animated. Everyone raised their eyes to the pieces of golden sky filtering through the cavernous tunnel. Energy and motivation returned to our group. We were alive. Truly alive.

"Oh, it worked, Marty, it worked!" I didn't mind the saltwater taste of Evie's tears entering my mouth as she embraced me. I'd waited too long, and assumed I'd never know her kiss. That it should herald our return to the world, to vital existence, was the ultimate validation for me.

Noah didn't want to celebrate alone. He prized us apart and gave us both a big salutary bear hug. We were alive. We would continue to live. Our world would continue to live. Our relief was so total that it spilled over into hysteria. We cried, and laughed, and hugged, and told ourselves we would love each other forever.

Evie pushed gently away from us. There was one other figure among us who remained alone and apart. Wes kneeled, silently sobbing, above a slight indentation in the earth. It indicated Amber's last resting place in this world. Eve reached her strong, kindly hand down to stroke his hair. He wheezed aloud through his happy, distraught sobs, but it wasn't to her. "We did it" He caressed the unmarked grave as he spoke. "You did it, baby."

Eve took his happy-sad head in her arms like that of a little boy. She let him sob into the breast of his baby's best friend. We were bloodied but validated. All of us had had the courage to face the challenge set by the ancient Nahua world. Every last one of us had risen to it, however damaged we were by the experience.

"What you say we take it outside then, bro?" Noah looked on me with warmth for the first time since the sun went down. And that was another age, another eon. Now we were ready to embrace the new one.

Our group reassembled. Evie gently pulled Wes to his feet. Ours was the friendship that had endured. Through doubt and fear and despair. And death. Now we were four, we were no less strong. It would be difficult to face life without Amber—for everyone, not just for Wes. But she would always be with us. An absent friend, whose presence would never be far from the periphery of our consciousness.

Now we had a big old world to reacquaint ourselves with. We made our way up the cavern tunnel as one, with Eve making one last-second fallback to grab Noah's radio. As we ascended the cave tunnel to the lower-level mountain ridge outside, life came flooding back into us, as we entered back into it.

As we reached the cavern's entrance, we were already suffused with a glow. But nothing, not our hopes and prayers, fears and dreams, could have prepared us for the glowing radiance of that beautiful day.

"Would you look at that?" Noah was the first to make it to the ridge. He shielded his eyes from that blazing benevolent fireball in the eastern sky, and gazed around the panorama. The natural world, with all its giant rock formations, its lowland forests and lakes, the towering mountains and bottomless canyons that our dear friend Amber had spoken of, was overwhelming.

As we basked in the sun's rays that bathed our skin, we could feel an uncomfortable pride in restoring nature's balance. "It's beautiful, isn't it?" No one was arguing with me. "Can you imagine all the places that lost their light and heat, that descended into the underworld just like we did, waking up to this morning?"

"I bet they're celebrating all over the world." Evie's face was flushed with the joy of being alive. For all the shadows that had been cast, light still prevailed. The ancient Mexica had been right: light and dark in all things. In all life, and all human beings.

"Yeah. They've all been through their darkness. Now everyone's got a second chance. Let's hope we never forget what it really means to have the blessing of nature." Images of the dawn after the darkness proliferated in my mind. How many had perished? How many places had been environmentally affected? How many lives had been lost or damaged by human stupidity, by the tendency toward panic and hysteria?

My friends seemed unwilling to give headspace to all the heavy implications. What we had been through was, after all, as devastating as anything on Earth. Like the rest of the world's population, we had won the right to begin our lives again with a clean slate.

Eve turned on the X-FM radio. Instead of letting the automatic tuner dance its way around the dial, she turned it manually, notch by notch. This time, she was eager for news of the outside world. After a few minutes of bleeping and whirring, she hit a station.

"Well Frank, I don't need to tell you, this is one especially fine morning that surpasses all our expectations!" The radio crackled and popped with distortion.

"It sure is, Linda! I never thought sunshine in early July would seem like such a remote possibility!" The two talking heads had hit their own personal sunshine buttons. It was totally unlike the usual oleaginous crap you hear on a news station. They laughed along with each other. We laughed along with them.

"Get a load of those two old dudes! They sound wasted!" Wes, dear Wes, was coming back out of his shell. He had a life to live again. And he was right: it did sound like breakfast time was cocktail hour for the anchorwoman and her newsreader. And why the hell not?

Their sunny tones enhanced our pleasure at being back in the world. Eve retuned the dial a little to clarify their voices "So without further ado, on this beautifully bright morning—on this beautiful, bright, historic morning—let's hand over to Frank for the news headlines."

"Thank you, Linda." Today was going to be a universal day of mutual and self-congratulation. As numbed and exhausted as I was, I felt I had the right to be more self-congratulatory than most. Cancel that: all of our group had the right to feel a special, heroic status. All of us, present and departed.

"Global panic has given way to international jubilation. The sun has reappeared in the heavens today!" Light had reappeared in our lives. There was no doubt about it. The relieved, exhausted smiles on the faces of my friends told me that we all knew we'd played our part. "After scenes of unrest and crisis dotting the USA..."—things were truly back to normal now, the focus wasn't on "the world" but on home sweet home—"order is currently being restored as we speak."

"Order down the end of an automatic sight, dude." Wes was regaining his sense of humor rapidly.

"Yeah, well, maybe this station's a subsidiary of Fox News or something. Let's listen up." For once, I was happy to let them gloss over the unpalatable details that didn't fit the station's news profile.

"The White House has issued a statement explaining that the president is currently in close contact with heads of state across the world, assessing the levels of damage that many nations have already endured. It is fully expected that, once any short-term crises have been brought to an end within our domestic borders, the United States will play a leading role in coordinating international efforts to bring the world back to stability."

The sudden smack on the cheek I received was less uninhibited than before. But it was no less affectionate. Right then, we were all Evie's brothers. Her spirits were high and her mood was contemplative mellow. It had little to do with the propaganda being pumped out by the radio, but everything to do with the sense that life would go on. That our homeland was still here. That the world was still here.

"The president is expected to make an official speech later today, thanking the American people for their fortitude, and giving thanks for the support and expertise lent by the government's scientific task-force."

What? No thanks to the Almighty? I found myself asking. It seemed to be stretching credibility to claim this one for the US scientific community. After all, we knew what had put the sun back in the sky. But then, I told myself, only we knew. It was only natural that the authorities should try to look for rational causes of the crisis. But for me, it was straining credulity.

"Scientists at the Keck Observatory in Hawaii believe that the unprecedented solar blackout was the result of the earth passing through an extremely rare low-temperature sector of its plasma field. "

It was Noah who reacted first. He darkened. "So what's he talking about?" The question was addressed to me. "The plasma field?" Noah was the scientist. Why should I be able to tell him what the term signified? As it transpired, he knew full well.

"The existence of such a phenomenon has long been theorized. The earth's plasma field, as seen through the eye of the TRACE satellite camera, resembles a kind of gaseous comet enclosing what astronomers and scientists call the earth's magnetosphere." Noah shut down the radio.

His demeanor was intense, accusatory. "I knew it. I fuckin' knew it! What we did was madness." It was as if the rational world had emerged from the shadows and heaped a sack of guilt down upon him.

Now that I'd performed the ultimate sacrifice, taken the ultimate risk, he wanted to beat me around the head with science. "No!" I had to defend my perception of the truth. Everything depended on it. Everything. "Don't you see? Science is just another religious orthodoxy. You're letting 'em mess with your mind! They have no idea of what happened, they just have to rationalize it all!"

I looked to Eve for support. I found none. Her mind was churning with the terrible possibility. "We did what we had to do because *we* made the Sun disappear. And *we* brought it back!"

I found my backup where I least expected it. "Marty's right, man!" Wes was insistent, emphatic. "None of us wanted to do it, but we did what had to be done. You can see that Evie, huh?" Wes, who had made the most daunting sacrifice out of the four of us, would not be persuaded that it was all in vain. Like me, he needed to believe. Eve said nothing. She seemed unable to speak. Despite the golden radiance of the sunlight, her face grew pale. Gray.

"Oh no Oh no... " Noah groaned and shook his head. There was a recent memory flashing his eyes that wouldn't leave him now. I made a grab for the power button of the radio.

"If they got you so convinced, let them justify it to all of us! I need to be told how the hell a 'plasma field' could do that." Noah gripped my hand tight. He forbade me to go any further.

"I don't need to be fucking told. I've studied the earth's plasma field."

"Well if you've studied it make us all understand! I need to know. I don't need to be conned by scientific bullshit." I recognize now that I was becoming hysterical. But science doesn't have a monopoly on the truth. Science can be just as blinkered as organized religion.

"The magnetic field of the earth extends by about ten times its radius toward the direction of the sun. There's a shock front called the magnetopause that's formed by the solar wind." He reeled it off heavily, tonelessly. Threateningly. Our God-fearing brother knew all this as much by heart as I did the tenets of the Nahua religion.

"So how does that make the Sun fall out of the sky? Huh? You better explain to me, 'cuz otherwise this just sounds like one more fairytale!" He reached the palm of his hand toward my face, warning me that one of us had better shut my mouth.

"Plasma is a mass of atomic particles. There's a whole load of plasma created by the pressure of gravity at the center of the Sun. It's been observed that sometimes it carries out to the earth's magnetosphere during a magnetic storm."

Eve was crying. This time, it wasn't tears of exhaustion, of relief, or joy. It was just pure, wailing, snot-nosed despair. Her own status as a science major had reasserted itself. All that mattered to them now was rationality. She was lost to me. And part of her was now lost to herself.

"There's conjecture that a heavy influx of ionized, energized plasma into the earth's magnetic field could block out the sun's rays. Some scientists believe it may have caused the climactic change that occurred at the time the dinosaurs became extinct."

No, no, no! He wasn't going to blind me with science. Why in hell was a fully paid-up member of the God Squad talking about dinosaurs anyway? Didn't his religion tell him the earth was created about five thousand years ago?

"No one's ever been able to put the hypothesis to the test. Up until now." It was an accusation. In its cold logic, it inferred that I had murdered Amber Hagen, and made accessories out of my friends.

I reached for a long shrub growing out of the mountainside, lowering myself to sit on the ledge before my legs gave way. "But how can you know? How is science anything but just another belief system?"

"I only know what I can see with my own eyes." Noah was solemn, unforgiving. As unforgiving of himself as he was of me. For having listened to what he now believed was my insane rationalization of insanity itself. "I've seen satellite images of the Earth's magnetosphere and its plasma field. I've never seen any Aztec sun god. All I saw was you..."

It downed me. Took all the fervor out of my own argument. Left my downward face trying not to weep into the hands that shielded it. Trying not to dissolve into traumatized guilt the way my friends were all around me.

"We only did what we had to do. That's right, isn't it Eve?" Poor Wes could not be abandoned, left adrift in that way. He couldn't let himself think that what occurred was some kind of obscene cosmic joke. But neither Eve nor I could help him. It was all I could do to keep myself together.

"Didn't we?" He too began to weep. Eve's face was haunted. She was unable to speak. To this day, I have never exchanged any further words with Eve Bishop. Maybe the only reason Noah didn't kill me that day was because his terrible rationality had reduced him to wracking sobs. Or maybe he couldn't bear to transgress the laws of his God anymore.

And me? My mind was a vortex of fervent belief and doubt; of certainty at my own moral courage, and a haunting, gnawing fear. All their faces, our physical predicament, Amber's last moments, all flashed through my memory.

But what I believed had happened was confused. Random fragments of the Nahua belief system clashed with disconnected scraps of memory. All my esoteric knowledge, all my rationale, was divorced from itself.

An inappropriate word from the ancient Nahuatl language came into my mind. "Ahmocualli": literally, "not good." Or, to take it to its logical conclusion, "evil."

FOURTEEN

Since the time we reached level ground again, I've had little contact with my four friends. Rumor tells that Noah got himself involved in the "healing process" after all. The last anyone heard, he was in central Africa working for a Christian aid charity. In these strange days, it takes a brave man to do that.

I've heard tell that continental Africa may not recover, in our lifetime, from that one forty-eight hour period of ecological havoc. Its people have suffered crop failures on a scale never envisaged even during the worst periods of the last century. Its mortality rates have continued to rise until few people even have a chance of reaching middle age. The people blame the governments. The tribal elites blame other tribes. And everybody in Africa blames the Western world.

It's a selfless human being who will enter such a tinderbox. Only a devout soul like Noah could seek it out as a way of atonement. To share the living conditions of those suffering people may be a way of expiating guilt. Or of losing himself. No one knows if he will ever return, or whether he ever intends to.

Wes sought to lose himself in the opposite direction. He's the only member of our group I've encountered in the ensuing weeks. I wished I hadn't. With his baby gone forever, and the memory of their psychedelic experiences together, Wes threw himself into chemical abuse as far as he could go. But things are a whole lot different now.

The botanicals that used to give Wes and Amber their natural highs, their weed and their mushrooms, are a rare commodity now. During the forty-eight hours of Mictlan, most of the world's illicit crops—whether growing wild, in greenhouses, or in a box in someone's closet—were wiped out. Anyone who wants to get high on them had better be prepared to spend much cash for little return.

But drugs are a perennial human need, and where nature has failed then ruthless people rush in to fill the void. Psychedelic trips have been replaced by ever more powerful forms of speed: smoked or injected. Natural opiates are supplanted by a whole glut of synthetic painkillers and sedatives, bewildering in their variety and their dangers.

When I last saw Wes, I found him via some of his drug buddies who hang out in this less-than-salubrious old bar. I wanted to check on his welfare, to try to make my peace. It was a mistake. When I set eyes on him, he wasn't looking well, but he looked like he was itching to get well real soon. By any means possible. His face had sunken a little, and his wired eyes looked like they were about to pop out on stalks. But what truly blew his mind was seeing me again.

He never reprimanded me, or told me to go away. Matter of fact, he never said anything at all. The rush of memories and nightmares long suppressed were almost visible in his face. I'd brought it all back in an instant. If he was up before I'd walked in, then he'd need to get way, way down to escape it all now. I made my excuses and left.

I've not seen Evie from that day to this. I put out word on the grapevine that I'd love to hear from her, that I'm concerned to know that she's doing good. It elicits less than zero. Some while back, I heard that she was in therapy. Probably pacified by one of the post-Prozac generation of serotonin boosters.

It seemed a wholly rational response to an irrational situation. But friends can be guarded. Protective of mutual friends who don't want to be talked about, or jealously protective of their own private knowledge. I've since heard suggestions, swiftly retracted, that "therapy" could be read as a euphemism for hospitalization. That more effective treatment and medication has had to be administered in the event of her complete mental breakdown.

It's only a rumor. I have no way of knowing whether it's any truer than any of the half-truths and delusions I've been fed. Evie won't speak with me. If she feels the distant echo of our deed getting louder, coming closer, then I have to concur. I feel it too. I know it's coming.

In the weeks following our return to civilization, all the authorities were occupied by rescuing the States from chaos. Our statements about our friend's disappearance elicited little response. Amber's family, her mom and her sister, were naturally beside themselves with worry. But, as order was restored, and law enforcement started working again in the way that it used to, I heard that an investigation got underway. It's no more than I would expect.

They haven't contacted me yet. They will. Maybe when they've started scouring the Sangre de Cristo mountains for traces of our dear lost Amber, to check on details of my statement. Or maybe they're already there. Maybe they'll only come for me when they find her final resting place, close to where we buried her amputated heart as a gift to an ancient Mesoamerican deity. Then, and only then, will I tell them what truly happened.

And what did happen? What do I actually believe occurred?

I don't know. I know only uncertainty. Like the rest of my dear friends, my heart and mind are forever burdened. But I believe that, for a short time, I was touched by the old gods. I don't believe I will ever fully return from the place where I was then.

There is no escape from the shadows of doubt. I will never again emerge into the day.

But for Eve Bishop and her friends a bitter chill remains. Haunted by uncertainty, they can find no peace of mind, no escape from the shadows of doubt, trapped in an endless night only in... The Twilight Zone.

ABOUT THE AUTHOR

Paul A Woods is a writer, researcher and editor, working in publishing, television and magazine journalism. His specialities are the macabre, crime, cult cinema, and the extremes of modern and popular culture. Author credits include *Weirdsville USA: The Obsessive Universe of David Lynch*, *King Pulp: The Wild World of Quentin Tarantino* and *Ed Gein – Psycho!* TV credits include *Clive Barker's A-Z of Horror*, *Journey into Evil* on the case of murderers Leonard Lake and Charles Ng and a documentary on the life of cult author Colin Wilson. He lives in North London.

Also from Black Flame
Twilight Zone #1

MEMPHIS • THE POOL GUY

by Jay Russell

"Lethal injection," Doctor Rosoff said. "It's the law in this state."

"No," Ritchie cried. "You've got the wrong guy."

"It is the most humane way," she explained. "The subject feels no pain at all. Well, hardly any pain. We can't really be certain, can we? Still, no one has ever complained afterward. Heh heh."

She laughed. The dark-haired doctors all laughed.

They advanced on him in formation.

Ritchie threw his hands over his eyes.

And screamed.

The sound vanished up into the air. Ritchie opened his eyes.

He was standing beside the swimming pool at the Hunts' mansion in Brentwood. The pool water was crystal clean, glistening in the bright noonday sun. Lying on an extravagant chaise lounge on the wooden deck was Mrs Hunt. She lay on her stomach soaking up the rays, her top undone and the bulk of her marvelous rear exposed to all and sundry thanks to one of Thog's miraculous thongs. Ritchie couldn't take his eyes off her tight, bronzed ass. Then he heard a sound like a leaking bicycle tire coming from behind him.

"Psssst."

He looked across the pool, and saw Cheto the gardener nodding at him, a lascivious leer plastered across his face. Cheto made an extremely obscene gesture with his hands then followed it with an action using his fingers and tongue, which Ritchie had never seen before and couldn't exactly interpret.

But he got the general idea.

"All done now, Mrs Hunt," Ritchie said.

She ignored him. He took a few steps closer, until he stood at the foot of the chaise lounge.

"Mrs Hunt? I'm all finished here."

She opened her eyes with a grunt of annoyance. She propped herself up on one arm, turning sideways to look at the pool guy. Her top dropped away, leaving her breasts exposed to him. She didn't seem to notice.

"Mitch, is it?"

"Ritchie," he said eyes glued to her tits. "My name is Ritchie."

"Whatever," she said. "What is it that you want now?"

He knew exactly what he wanted. From across the pool he could hear Cheto yelling: "Go for it, bro. Do her! Take that bitch, Pool Guy!"

Mrs Hunt either didn't hear him or couldn't be bothered.

"I'm all done with the pool," is all that Ritchie said.

"Do you want a round of applause?" she jeered.

"I'm supposed to get paid today. Mr Hunt promised. Cash, he told me."

"What about the rat?" Mrs Hunt asked.

"The rat?"

She rolled her eyes in exasperation. "Did you get rid of the rat?" She asked.

"I didn't see no rat," Ritchie told her.

Mrs Hunt looked at Ritchie, glanced at the pool and looked back at Ritchie.

"What do you call that then?" she asked. She casually waved her hand in the direction of the big swimming pool. Ritchie turned to look.

Lying on its back, kicking its legs in the air, was the biggest rat Ritchie had ever seen in his life. It was the size of a German shepherd, with whiskers as long as Ritchie's arm and black eyes as big around as softballs. The rat was swimming in a tidy, tight circle, spitting mouthfuls of water in regular bursts, like a park fountain as it did the backstroke.

"Oh," Ritchie said. "That rat."

"Yes," Mrs Hunt said. "That rat. Were you just going to leave it there? Is that what my husband is paying you for?"

"Okay. I'm on it," Ritchie told her. She rolled back over and closed her eyes again.

Ritchie watched the rat do the back float around the pool. He tried calling to it first: "Here, boy. Come on, Mr Rat. I got some nice cheese here. Eeek-eeek."

But the rat wasn't falling for that old trick. He wasn't born just yesterday.

Ritchie found his skimmer lying on the deck by the side of the pool. He extended the pole to its full length and tried to use the net at the end to snare one of the rat's jerking legs. But every time he managed to hook a paw, the rat just rolled over in the water, sliding itself free.

Then the rat started laughing at him.

Ritchie got mad. Who did this rat think he was laughing at him? No bastard rat was going to make a monkey out of Ritchie Almares!

"You're going to be sorry, you dirty rat," he warned.

The rat merely spat out an extra high fountain of pool water and went on about his happy business.

Then Cheto was suddenly standing next to him.

"Hey, Pool Guy," Cheto said. "That's some fine piece of rat, huh? That rat got eyes for you, bro, I can tell. You ever score any rat pussy?"

"Say what?" Ritchie asked.

"Hell, yeah! Them rats are hot. And they just asking for it, bro. Dressing like that, showing off their little rat booty. They want it, bro, you know they do. So go ahead and give that rat what it needs."

"How am I going to get rid of this thing?" Ritchie said.

"Aww, don't be that way," Cheto groaned.

"I'm not going to get paid if I don't get rid of it. Leonard's going to kill me."

"Use this then," Cheto said with a sigh. And he handed Ritchie a gun.

A big, black gun. Ritchie had seen it before, he was sure. But where?

"Shoot him in the cojones, man!" Cheto urged.

"Yeah. Okay," Ritchie said.

He turned back toward the pool, but the rat was gone. So was Cheto. And Mrs Hunt. Ritchie still held the gun in his hand.

An awful screeching racket came from behind him. Ritchie turned around and saw the rat standing on his hind legs, wearing a black Speedo bathing suit. The rat advanced on Ritchie.

Ritchie held up the gun, pulled the trigger.

His shot went way wide. He wasn't used to the recoil and the gun jerked out of his hand.

The rat looked really mad now. It looked...

Its eyes. The rat had those tiny, black eyes that bore into Ritchie.

The better to see you with, Ritchie heard in the back of his head.

The rat's red nose began to twitch. It snorted out a line of lime green rodent snot.

The better to smell you with.

Ritchie felt a raw and primal fear generated from deep within. He tried to back away, but found he was glued to the ground, his legs turned to pillars of stone.

The rat opened its mouth, revealing a spiky array of tiny sharp teeth.

The rat leapt and Ritchie screamed.

And he found himself in a white room. There was a bank of video monitors in front of him and a large mixing desk dotted with buttons and switches and joysticks. A big plasma screen covered one wall, and two humming black boxes sat along a third. The fourth wall was blank. Ritchie somehow expected a window to be there, but it was just a blank wall.

Ritchie knew he was in the control room of VirtuaCorp. And he felt very afraid.

On the desk in front of him was a lone CD jewel box case. The label on it read: *R ALMARES: ACTUAL.*

Ritchie picked it up, examined both sides. There was nothing else but that label and a single, silvery disk within. He didn't want to look at what was on that disk. He knew he didn't want to watch it.

He removed the disk, opened the tray on the console and placed it inside. He pressed the button and the tray whirred closed. The drive began to spin.

The "Play" button on the console lit up and Ritchie found he had no choice but to press the blinking green button. One screen on the bank of monitors lit up and Ritchie watched the scene unfold.

Ritchie is standing poolside at the Hunt place. He is wearing his usual Pool Guy uniform: dirty black shorts, a torn T-shirt and a raggedy old pair of flip-flops. The pool is a filthy mess and the job is taking Ritchie twice as long as it should do. The Hunts must have had one whiz-bang of a pool party the night before and there is garbage strewn everywhere. Cigarette butts and roaches float on the scummy surface of the water and Ritchie has already had to fish two dirty condoms out of the filter. Broken bits of glass litter the wooden deck and Ritchie has already stepped on a shard of a broken champagne bottle.

Ritchie hates these rich bastards with a white-hot passion. He hates having to work for them, to clean up after their parties. He hates being party only to the detritus of their wonderful lives, never getting any closer to the world of Dom Perignon than the splinters of broken bottle he has to pull out of his big toe.

Ritchie hates being a pool guy. He hates his life.

He gets out his skimmer and extends the pole as far as it goes. He starts to fish the floating garbage out of the deep end of the pool, scooping up a net full of cigarette butts, when the skimmer catches on something floating in the water. It is the stem of a broken wine glass and the jagged edge is very sharp. It cuts right through the netting and all the shit that Ritchie has so carefully skimmed out of the water plops back in and floats away.

Perfect, he says to himself, just what I needed.

He hauls the skimmer back in and examines it. It is useless. Tossing it aside, he walks back over to his pick-up truck to get the smaller one. He will have to wade into the pool to use it if he is going to be able to reach all the junk in the water. He hates that.

As he rummages through the shoddy tools and equipment in the back of his truck, Ritchie hears the front door of the Hunt mansion open. He peers around the side of the pick-up and sees Mrs Hunt emerge from the house. She is a hot little piece of ass and many is the night that Ritchie has laid in bed imagining the thousand and one uses he could put her to. Today she is wearing a tight micro-mini skirt that runs right up to Krakatoa—and wouldn't Ritchie love to see that erupt—and a narrow-cut silk jacket over a form hugging white blouse. Her long blonde hair shimmers in the California sunshine, framing her round, soft cheeks and a pair of pert crimson lips. She sees Ritchie looking at her and offers him a polite smile of recognition and a little wave of her hand.

He nods back at her and thinks genuinely nasty thoughts as she gets into her red Mercedes rag top and backs out down the driveway.

What do you have to do to get a woman like that, he wonders? But he already knows the answer; it's no secret in this town: You got to be one rich bastard.

Ritchie gets his skimmer and wades into the pool to clean out the scum of the Hunts' fabulous lives.

He steps on another piece of glass on the bottom of the pool and screams out a stream of vile curses in response. The too heavily chlorinated water—and whose fault is that?—feels like acid in the cut.

Ritchie hobbles out of the pool and sees to his injury. He is sitting down on the soft chaise lounge by the side of the pool when a shadow passes over him.

Mr Jerry Hunt looks down at the pool guy.

"You all right there, Mitch?" he asks.

The son of a bitch simply cannot get Ritchie's name right and it drives him crazy. Three times a week Ritchie cleans the bastard's pool and he can't even remember his name. Ritchie can't bring himself to look up at his employer.

"Ritchie," he says through clenched teeth. "It's Ritchie. And I cut myself on some glass in the pool. There's busted glass all over the place."

"Ritchie. Of course. Yeah, we had us quite a blowout last night," Hunt says. "Things got a little wild." And he sniggers. Hunt always sniggers. Never laughs or chuckles or guffaws. Just sniggers. Ritchie hated it.

"Got to be careful with glass," Ritchie says. He can't seem to slide the shard out of the sole of his right foot. It hurts like hell.

"Well, you know how these things go," Hunt says. Another snigger. "Par-tay, par-tay."

Ritchie doesn't have the faintest idea how "these things" go, or why Hunt pronounces "party" like he's one of the boys from the hood. Ritchie has never been any closer to a Brentwood mansion pool party than cleaning up the mess the next morning. Given the rancid circumstances of his life, he is thoroughly unlikely to ever get any closer.

"Uh-huh," he says.

"You should get that looked at," Mr Hunt tells him. He points at Ritchie's bleeding foot.

Ritchie finally looks up at Hunt then, to show his contempt, but he jumps back slightly.

"Shit!" Ritchie yells.

Hunt is holding a gun in his hand. He sniggers yet again.

"Oh, sorry there, Mi... Ritchie. Didn't mean to give you a start."

"For, Christ's sake, what are you doing with that?"

Hunt held up the big, black gun admiringly. He ran a hand down the long, smooth barrel in an almost masturbatory way.

"This is just an old friend of mine. Actually, we came out for a little hunt."

"What the hell are you hunting out here?" Ritchie asks.

"Rats," Hunt whispers. "Brentwood's overrun with them at the moment. The city council's going to pay dear for not dealing with it, don't you worry. Till then it's every man for himself and the rats against all. Have you seen any today? There was a big one that came out at the party last night. Damn near ruined the whole soiree. Ladies screaming... and not for the right reasons."

Another dirty snigger.

"No, I ain't seen no rats, Mr Hunt," Ritchie says. "Not any to shoot, at least."

The remark goes right over Hunt's head. He only ever half-listens to anything the likes of a pool guy says. Ritchie tries out a snigger of his own.

"Well, give us a holler if you see one," Hunt tells him, tapping his pistol again. "I'm going to go check out over by the dumpster. That's where we saw it last night. Then I'm heading out to the studio. Listen, make double sure you close that gate behind you today after you drive out. You forgot last time. Okay, Mitch?"

Motherfucker, Ritchie wanted to yell. He did not forget to close the gate. He's always doubly careful about details like that on the job. But he just nods and Mr Hunt starts to wander off. Then Ritchie remembers.

"Hey!" he calls out. "Hey, Mr Hunt!"

Jerry Hunt turned around, his one thick eyebrow raised, gun still in hand.

"We're supposed to settle up today, remember? You promised you'd have some cash for me this morning. You owe me for that extra week, too."

Hunt slapped a hand to his forehead in exaggerated, comical fashion. A dopey smirk took over his lips and another little snigger escapes.

"Oh, hell, Mitch, I entirely forgot about it. You're dead right, but the thing is that I haven't got any cash on me at all. I can write you a check—"

"No, no!" Ritchie yells. "Listen, I got to have cash and I need it today, Mr Hunt. I got rent due and a roommate who's a pain in the ass, you know? You promised you'd have cash for me today and I really got to have it. I'm depending on it."

"I do apologize, Mitch—"

"Ritchie! My goddamn name is Ritchie!"

"Sorry, sorry." Another snigger. "*Ritchie*. You're right, I promised you cash. But I simply don't have anything on me at this moment. Do you understand that? I'm not a big cash guy. Now, if you just give me your address, I will have an envelope with the cash couriered over to you later this afternoon after my meeting at the studio. Now, you can't beat that for an offer can you?"

Ritchie is still shaking his head. He *can* beat that. Cash now. In his hand. Clients have made promises to him before and they never deliver on them. No one ever remembers what they say to the pool guy. Out of sight, out of mind.